To new friendships, including those I've made over the course of this series. This one goes out especially to Crystal Lacy, beta reader, friend and all-around cheerleader. I'm lucky to know you!

ARCTIC HEAT

———

ANNABETH ALBERT

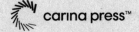

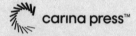

carina press™

ISBN-13: 978-1-335-00809-1

Recycling programs
for this product may
not exist in your area.

Arctic Heat

www.CarinaPress.com

Printed in U.S.A.

ARCTIC HEAT

Chapter One

Come for the snow. Stay for the ranger porn. Owen couldn't help his smile as he surveyed the large Department of Natural Resources meeting room. He was really here in Alaska, doing this after it being little more than a daydream for so long. Happy shivers raced up his spine. His fellow volunteers were mainly fresh-faced college kids and retirees, but he lingered over the uniformed rangers near the front, trying not to stare but probably doing a miserable job of that. Because *wow.* These guys made drab green and khaki downright sexy with their broad shoulders and generous muscles and rugged jawlines.

The orientation was for new winter state park volunteers like Owen, who would spend the season living in remote locations to assist rangers and other paid employees. Experienced rangers would be educating them on everything from avalanche risk to generator operation and state land use regulations. Some returning volunteers and rangers were there for the CPR and first-aid certification refreshers, chummy people who obviously already knew each other and laughed and joked as they helped themselves to the coffee station set up at the side of the room.

He was scoping out the people he might be assigned to work with, and one particular man who stood by himself kept catching his attention—a uniformed ranger who had a few years on him, probably putting him at forty-something, just shy of "silver fox" and firmly in "yes, please" territory with his strapping build and iconic good looks. The DNR ads for the volunteer positions would undoubtedly get triple the response if they slapped this guy's picture on the materials. Hell, if winter in Alaska wasn't already on Owen's bucket list, one glimpse of those steely blue eyes might have done the trick.

He was hoping to be assigned to work with some cool people, since he'd be in close contact with only a handful of people on a regular basis, and he knew from experience how important team chemistry could be. He'd take anyone easy to get along with, but man… Talk about chemistry. Ranger Blue Eyes took the frisson of anticipation thrumming in Owen's gut and transformed it into something warmer and more intimate. And damn wasn't it nice to feel that sort of attraction again, after all the nagging worries that it might be gone for good.

Owen wasn't particularly vain, but he was damn observant, and he'd caught those eyes looking his direction more than once. Sure, part of it was undoubtedly that Owen had misjudged and overdressed in a nice button-down and dress pants and stuck out in the room filled with khaki, flannel, and denim. And maybe some of it was that he was one of only a couple of Asian people in the room. Maybe the guy was simply curious, but Owen had transformed *curious* into *interested* more than a few times.

And because Owen was nothing if not a man of action,

he took his tea, orientation packet, and notepad closer to the guy, trying to come up with a good opening on the fly. However, before he could speak, a broad-faced woman with dark hair clapped her hands at the front of the room.

"All right, let's go ahead and find seats. We'll be getting started in a few minutes, so get your coffee now!"

His ranger prey immediately took a chair, and there it was, Owen's chance to spend the next few hours basking in hot ranger vibes. He was in perfect position to slide into the chair next to his dream guy and offer him his best smile and—*fuck*—slosh hot tea. That part had not been planned at all, and judging by the man's glare, the intrusion was hardly welcome.

"Oops. Sorry! Are you okay?" Owen passed him a napkin, resisting the temptation to dab at the guy's damp uniform pants himself.

"I'm fine." The ranger continued to frown as he soaked up the tea, which had splashed both his pants and the desk arm of the chair. "It'll dry."

"I'm not usually so clumsy. I'm Owen. Owen Han." Carefully arranging his stuff first, he stuck out a hand. "I'm new here."

"I figured." He took Owen's hand, which was as warm and firm as Owen had hoped. And the tiny smile that tugged at his mouth was almost intoxicating in its endearingness. "And I'm Quill Ramsey. Not new."

"Figured." Owen tried another smile, this one hopefully not too flirty but still inviting more conversation. "Nice name. Not sure I've heard that one before."

"Eccentric mother." The way Quill said *eccentric* suggested relations between him and his mother were strained. "Apparently she circled all her favorites in the book, then picked at random."

"That's kind of cool, actually. I'm named after the high school teacher who made my parents work together on a class project. Moms, right?"

"Yeah." Quill's tone didn't exactly encourage more talking, but Owen was nothing if not friendly. And persistent. His sister the therapist called it aggressively extroverted, and she wasn't entirely wrong.

"So, are you helping with the presentations or here to get recertified in the first-aid stuff?"

"Both." Quill's mouth quirked in something close to a grimace. Owen dug his voice—low and deep, Western without the twang. The he way he spoke like there was a tax on each word made Owen feel like he'd earned a gift when Quill continued. "Didn't realize I'd let my CPR lapse—we had support staff changeover in our field office, but still, I should have known. And yeah, since I'm here, Hattie talked me into leading the discussion about avalanche risk awareness." He gestured in the direction of the woman at the front of the room before his eyes swept over Owen again. "Not that all of you will need that lecture. You interning here in the home office? Heard they were getting a few folks in finance and business relations."

Owen had to bite back a groan. He really should have gone more outdoorsy with his wardrobe choice instead of "need to make a good first impression." He well knew he looked young, but he was beyond tired with reading as a college-aged twink instead of professional adult. And maybe he had been in finance once upon a time, but he was bidding that life good riddance. "Not a business intern. I'm thirty-six. I'm scheduled to winter in Chugach State Park."

"That so?" Quill blinked, and Owen kind of liked knowing that he'd caught him off guard. Good. Maybe he could surprise him in other ways too.

The ranger's mouth moved like he wanted to add more, but Hattie clapped her hands again and called their attention to the podium. As she began her welcome, which was accompanied by cheerful PowerPoint slides, Owen couldn't resist another glance over at Quill. His assumptions might be irritating, but he was everything Owen had always imagined an Alaskan ranger would be. Damn. He really needed to find out where he was stationed stat, because Owen would like nothing better than to be snowed in with those biceps and those intense eyes. Talk about a dream winter.

Thank God the too-chatty newbie wasn't going to be Quill's responsibility. Someone else would have to keep him alive until spring, because this guy was a popsicle waiting to happen. It wasn't just his wardrobe choices that were more suited to the accounting department— his carefully styled dark hair and hipster glasses said he was the sort of high maintenance that never meshed well with the hard, often grueling work of winter parks management. At least he had the sort of build that might be able to keep up—surprisingly muscular arms and shoulders on a lean body. It had actually been his build that Quill had noticed first, his uncanny resemblance to a certain state champion butterfly swimmer who Quill had obsessed over a million lifetimes ago.

But that was then, and here and now Quill couldn't get distracted. He was here as a favor to Hattie, not to get caught up in any fresh eye candy. Besides, if the guy's build had pulled one memory loose, his voice and relentlessly friendly demeanor had hearkened back to another, reminding Quill a little too much of JP, who'd had that similar never-met-a-stranger thing going on that Quill had never fully understood. He'd never figured out why some people enjoyed filling a perfectly good silence with inane questions. He'd had colleagues for twenty years without ever needing to have a deep chat or fill in personal details. He liked working with competent individuals, appreciated hard work and a positive attitude, but mainly he enjoyed his autonomy, liked the days that passed without ever needing to make small talk or figure out the sort of social niceties that had never come naturally to him. God, he hoped they didn't assign him a talker for the winter. That was the last thing he needed.

Also not natural? Sitting through long meetings. God, he felt like he was back in college again, sitting through a lecture he didn't need, fighting the urge to find something else to occupy his attention. The margins of his agenda called to him, the siren song of white space needing filling, but he wasn't twenty anymore and he wasn't going to let his colleagues catch him doodling. He could make it through some boring introductions and reminders that he'd long since memorized. So he kept his pen firmly capped and tried not to let his attention wander too much to the newbie, who was leaning forward, attention fully on Hattie, occasionally jotting a note in the small red leather notebook with a bullet-shaped silver pen. His good taste in accessories spoke to a certain level of income and comfort that Quill didn't usually see from the seasonal volunteers.

Owen had a way of biting his lip when he wrote that directly challenged Quill's resolve to let in zero distractions. The guy's eagerness really was strangely compelling, and Quill had to resort to making subtle hash marks with his department-branded pen to keep from staring. He was beyond relieved when Hattie declared a break after she and a ranger from Kenai finally finished a presentation on department regulations and policies.

Quill made his way to the front of the room because he might be antisocial, but he wasn't *that* much of an asshole friend. "You're doing great," he told Hattie as she clicked around on a laptop, setting up the next topic. "All settled in? How's Val?"

"Val's okay. Still fighting morning sickness, but we're on track for a March delivery. Having a house again is such a novelty. I think I'm driving her nuts with all my plans for the nursery."

"Good for you." Quill tried to mean it. It wasn't Hattie's fault that her on-again-off-again girlfriend had shocked them all with a proposal and a serious case of baby fever. Now Hattie had a desk job, a baby on the way, and for the first time in fifteen years, Quill had to face a winter without his best friend, his right-hand person. She understood Quill like few others, gave him the space he needed while still being a positive, helpful presence in his life. And instead of giving their office another ranger to replace her, budget cuts meant that the department in all its wisdom was bringing in a winter caretaker volunteer for the Hatcher Pass area that was Quill's primary jurisdiction.

"It'll all work out." Hattie squeezed his arm. "For you too. Change is good for all of us."

Quill had to snort because if there was one thing he

hated, it was change. Give him the same brand of boots, the same turf to patrol, the same menu, and the same friends, and he was a happy ranger. The change from Hattie to someone new had had his back stiff for weeks now, tense with worries over who they might assign him and how they might get along—or not.

But he tried to keep his voice upbeat for Hattie's sake. "Says you. So, which of these is our person? Or people? Did they give us a couple?"

"Ah. About that." Hattie shuffled a stack of papers next to her laptop, looking away. "Your caretaker's been delayed. We're trying to reach her by phone, find out what the problem is. She's a recent college grad and seemed super promising. But one way or another we'll have something worked out for you by tomorrow at the latest."

"Fine." His back went from tense to rigid. Fuck. More uncertainty. There was plenty else Quill wanted to say, chiefly that he didn't want to winter with someone who'd skipped the training. And that a recent college grad was undoubtedly too green to start with. But this was Hattie and she was trying her best with her new position, and budget cuts and unreliable people weren't her fault.

"You're up next. Try not to scare them too much with winter weather risks. Smile."

"Hey. I'm not that scary." Presentations were a part of the ranger job, but he'd typically let Hattie handle a lot of the tourist education duties because yeah, it wasn't his favorite thing. And he supposed he did tend to come off as a bit dour, covering his nerves at talking to a crowd with warnings and reminders.

"Yeah, you kind of are." She shook her head, but her

voice was laced with affection. Turning her attention to the crowd milling about the room, she directed people back to their seats, then introduced Quill in the sort of glowing terms he'd let only her get away with.

His stomach did the weird quiver it always did before public speaking, something he tried hard to ignore. He wasn't the shy kid who hated being called on anymore, and despite his unease, he was prepared with picture slides of different dangers. Twenty winters in, he knew his stuff, and he tried to remind himself of that as he got started.

Stupid tips about eye contact and imagining the audience in comical situations had never worked for him, so he focused on the back of the room as he explained the risks unique to Alaskan winters. However, his attention kept drifting to Owen Han and his earnest expression and shiny pen moving across his page of notes. Surprisingly, something about his concentration settled Quill, made his voice surer and stronger, made him feel like he was speaking directly to Owen instead of the room at large.

Of course Owen, like a good chunk of the audience, was ill prepared for what lay ahead. Even people with a lot of snow experience in places like Minnesota had trouble grasping what an ever-present danger avalanches were.

Quill took his time with lots of pictures and patient explanations, trying to keep in mind what Hattie had said about not scaring people, but he needed them to understand the often harsh realities. It was a rare winter when he didn't see at least one fatality, usually from a human-triggered avalanche, and he was determined to do his best to make sure that none of the volunteers ended up a grim statistic. The more he spoke, the more comfortable he became, but he was still relieved when he reached the end of his slides.

The audience had some good questions, including one from Owen about avalanche beacons. Despite the whole resemblance to JP thing, Quill liked his voice, which had more than a hint of California to it—casual vowels and easy confidence. Too much confidence really, assuming that technology like the beacons were foolproof.

Quill explained their limitations, but he wasn't terribly surprised when Owen caught up with him again in the line for lunch.

"So why tell backcountry visitors to get beacons if they often fail to make a difference?" Owen asked, notebook out, which really was rather adorable. And smart, taking this training seriously. Made Quill respect him that little bit more.

"Well, they *can* save lives, but everyone in your group needs one, not just a few designated persons, and you need to practice with them. Most people skimp on the number of beacons or they never practice, so when disaster strikes, they're not prepared. Beacons don't substitute for preparedness. And some people use them as an excuse to get overconfident or take risks, and that's also problematic."

"So practice is key." Owen jotted down notes in a crisp, precise handwriting.

"Also, not to get too gruesome on you, but a certain percentage of victims will die from hitting trees and rocks on the way down. The beacons only work if you survive the ride."

"Ah." Owen's skin paled as he considered this fact.

"Makes sense, I guess. And you did a great job, laying out all the dangers."

"Thanks." Quill's neck heated as he wasn't sure what to make of the praise. Lunch was a simple buffet of sandwich fixings, chips, and cookies, but the line in front of them was slow as people took forever deciding. He supposed it was only polite to try to keep the conversation going. "Have you been around snow much yourself?"

"Well, I grew up in the Bay area, so not much snow there. But I worked at a Lake Tahoe ski resort a couple of winters in college. Summers too. And I've been on other ski trips. I like snow," Owen said with the sort of authority of someone who'd never had to deal with months on end of the stuff.

"That's good." Quill wasn't going to be the one to burst his bubble, but volunteers like Owen had a tendency to not make it through their first real winter. Loving snow wasn't the same as being able to cope with the dark, frigid days that defined an Alaskan winter. But he'd promised Hattie he wouldn't scare the volunteers, so he simply added lightly, "Being able to ski will definitely be a plus for you."

"I hope so." Owen gave him another of those near-blinding earnest smiles. And such was Quill's luck that the guy had deep, movie star–worthy dimples, which had always been kryptonite for him, even more than public speaking was. They made heat bloom low in Quill's gut, made the rest of the line seem to fade away. The dimples were probably part of why Quill had initially placed him as being younger, but up this close he could also see subtle smile lines around his eyes that said he was indeed on the wrong side of his twenties.

This close also meant that he could smell the guy's crisp aftershave—a clean, modern scent that probably cost more than Quill's boots, but hell if it didn't combine with those dimples to utterly disarm him.

"The line moved." Owen's smile this time was more crafty, like he'd figured Quill out and intended to exploit that knowledge.

"Thanks." Quill grabbed a plate and the nearest two slices of wheat bread. Owen might be nice and hot as hell, but he was also dangerously distracting. And Quill knew better than most how deadly even a few moments of misplaced attention could be. The smartest course of action would be avoidance and to thank his lucky stars that he wouldn't be snowed in with those dimples.

At least Hattie's person wasn't likely to pose the same sort of temptation that Owen did. His gut churned again. He really did need all this uncertainty settled. And if he felt some regret over moving away from Owen as he took his food over to sit near Hattie, he stomped it down. He had a job to do, one that didn't leave room for much else, and that was simply how it was.

Chapter Two

Ranger watching didn't lose its appeal for Owen even as he ate his lunch. He made friends with a nice retired couple, both volunteers who would be based out of Settlers Cove where they'd be living in a small log cabin for their second straight winter. The husband was working on a mystery novel, and Owen enjoyed the conversation even as his attention kept getting dragged away to hot ranger watch. Not wanting to make a pest of himself, he'd let Quill make a beeline for his friend, the female ranger who seemed to be running the day's agenda. But even from across the room, Owen found himself glancing Quill's way more than was prudent.

It wasn't that Quill was flashy, the kind of hot man who knew he was hot and who exuded that sort of swagger. If anything he was stoic. Reserved even. Like someone from an old Western, more concerned with doing a job well than how he looked doing it. His confidence seemed to come from a lot of earned experience—he'd certainly known his stuff during his part of the presentation, and that competent, zero-bullshit persona was incredibly attractive. Owen would much rather unravel a man like that than be blinded by the charms of a more outgoing sort. *Been there, done that, didn't even get a T-shirt.*

Something about the past few years had turned him off pretension, made him value genuineness because time really was too short to deal with fake people and their fake problems. And it wasn't like Quill was the only good-looking man in the room—there were plenty of other spots for Owen's eyes to roam, but somehow he kept getting pulled back to Quill. He liked the intent way Quill listened to his friend, leaning forward, giving her his full attention for some lengthy story that had him laughing at the end. He had a great laugh, deep and resonant without being overbearing—more of that *realness* Owen craved.

As lunch wound down, they started preparing for the afternoon's first-aid classes. Quill's friend Hattie came around with a DNR hat with pieces of paper in it.

"We're dividing into groups of three or four for the hands-on portion of the first-aid training," she explained.

Owen would totally be lying if he didn't admit to making a wish before he selected a number. He was one of the last people to draw, and around him, people were already moving into groups.

"Four," he said as he opened the piece of paper.

"Okay, you're with Quill—he's the ranger over by the door—and Nancy, who will be wintering at the Chilkat Preserve this year."

"Sounds good." Apparently, some wishes did come true, and he had to work hard not to beam at Hattie before she moved on to the couple next to him. Not wanting to appear too eager, he took his time making his way over to where Quill and a tall, thin woman with long curly red hair stood.

Soft spoken, Nancy had a reticent demeanor, and Owen spent some time trying to bring her out of her shell as they waited for the first-aid instructor to start. She reminded Owen of one of his sisters in her shyness, and making her comfortable took priority over more flirting with Quill. She was a fellow first-timer but had spent the summer volunteering in Yellowstone, part of a plan to take a year off between college and graduate school.

"Smart. I went straight through, and I was so burnt by the end," Owen admitted. God, he hated remembering school, the constant worries that he wasn't good enough, wasn't measuring up.

"What's your degree in?" Quill surprised him by interjecting the question. Was he simply being polite or was he as curious about Owen as Owen was about him?

Please let him be curious.

"Finance. I was an investment banker for a decade or so."

"Ah." Quill nodded like he'd expected similar, and part of Owen chafed at proving him right and wanted to explain that he could have gone for something more outdoorsy but had let expectations push him down other paths. But before he could launch into an explanation, the first-aid class began.

The first part of the class focused on assessing a situation. After a brief overview of triage principles, the instructor passed out papers to each group with scenarios for them to work on brainstorming approaches.

"Thanks." Owen accepted their group's pages from the instructor, a short older man with a lengthy résumé as both an EMT and a ranger. Readying his pen for note taking, he glanced over the sheet before turning his attention to Quill and Nancy. "So, they've given us three scenarios to break down. I figure we should go in order. Now, the first is pretty straightforward. A skier has taken a fall and been brought to the ranger station by two members of their skiing party. We need to assess the injury and determine a course of action. Ideas?"

Quill gave him a slow blink, head tilting to one side. "You used to being in charge?"

Fuck. Of course, Ranger Umpteen Years of Experience would expect to be the de facto leader. "Sorry. Holdover from college and grad school—I was always the one running group projects. You want the paper? Or maybe Nancy would like it?"

It wasn't simply that he'd been the social one able to mitigate group politics and infighting, but he'd always been the one who cared the most, the one who ended up in charge because he couldn't stand the idea of mediocrity. But this wasn't a classroom, and he needed to remind his inner nineteen-year-old that he wasn't going to impress anyone by being a model student.

"I'm good." Nancy gave a fast shake of her head.

"Me too." Quill leaned back in his chair, smile tugging at his mouth, clearly amused. Which was better than pissed. "You go ahead and take point. Save us the writing. What should we do first?"

On the spot, Owen had a sudden and unfamiliar attack of nerves. He really didn't want to screw up with Quill right there waiting to correct him.

"Obviously, visible injuries should be assessed, but I'd also be super concerned about the possibility of a head injury, and I think I'd probably start there, seeing how lucid the skier was, looking at the risk factors for concussion or other head injury."

"Not a bad idea." Quill gave him a little nod. "Anything else?"

"Hypothermia," Nancy contributed.

"Great." Owen jotted that one down as the three of them talked through the rest of the scenario. He kept their group on track, moving on to the other questions, leadership coming as naturally to him as ever, even if he was a little more self-conscious about that thanks to Quill. Because maybe he did care about making a good impression, even as he tried to remind himself that no one was grading this portion of the training.

After the exercise, the instructor moved on to how to handle the specifics of various injuries, using the items in the emergency kits they'd have access to. The next group activity involved pretending to ready an accident victim for transport.

"So one of us has to be the injured person." He did a fast read of the next handout after the papers came around.

"I'm… I'm not big on being touched." Nancy licked her lips and looked away.

"No problem." Owen was about to volunteer himself when Quill gave a firm nod.

"Guess I can be the guinea pig. You guys be the first responders on the scene. Go easy on me?"

"I'll be gentle." Owen only realized after the words were out that his tone was more flirty than he'd intended.

Nancy hung back, holding the kit, letting Owen be the one to put on a pair of nitrile gloves and pretend to evaluate Quill for a concussion. The smell of the gloves reminded him of hospitals, his stomach churning with things he didn't want to think about right then, so he focused back on Quill. Looking into his blue eyes was more than a little disorienting as was leaning close to apply pressure to a nonexistent wound. Quill smelled good. Classic and woodsy, like everything else about him.

"You can press harder than that." Quill's voice wasn't the least bit suggestive, but Owen's face still heated. There were any number of spots he'd like to press harder on Quill, but he forced his touch to be professional, as Quill continued, "Head wounds in particular bleed like the dickens. You get a gusher, no sense in being timid. Same goes for leg wounds, only with one of those be thinking whether a tourniquet is needed."

"Got it." Owen accidentally brushed his fingers against Quill's thick and soft brown hair as he adjusted the pressure. "So we get you onto the field stretcher, wrap you up in the blankets, and one of us relays your condition to the incoming medics."

"Yeah, keeping the victim warm is a big deal in winter injuries. Internal temperature can drop fast, especially if you've got a wait for evacuation. Add in the possibility of shock, and warmth has to be a priority."

"Makes sense." Accepting the blankets from Nancy, he bundled Quill up. "Feels like I should be offering you a story and a pillow." He tried to hide how it good it felt to tuck the blankets around Quill's big, solid body.

"Or a drink." Quill's voice was dry, more uncomfortable than humorous, but even so, awareness rushed though Owen. He totally wouldn't mind getting under the covers with this guy, sharing body heat. And once in his brain, the idea of having drinks with Quill didn't let up. He probably would never see the guy after to-morrow, but that was no reason not to make the most of the time he did have.

He continued to ruminate on how to make that happen as they went through a few other exercises before moving on to the CPR portion with dummies that were brought in for each group. Going first, he relied on past CPR training back in college, going through the familiar motions. Quill was next up, and he surprised Owen by how forceful he was with the dummy, checking the airway with quick, efficient movements before starting a series of chest compressions that rattled the dummy.

Nancy made a startled noise and Quill glanced over at them both where they knelt behind him on the floor.

"Maybe...eh...little less rough?" Owen tried to be helpful without stepping on any ranger boots in the process.

"You ever actually do CPR? In the field?" Quill stared him down, sharp eyes seeming to bore into Owen.

"No," he had to admit. He'd been fortunate in that, maybe even sheltered, and it made his voice more than a little sheepish. "I've been trained since lifeguarding in high school, but luckily, I've never had to actually use it."

"Well, I have, and there's no luck about it, one way or another. If you're in a situation, you have to act. And while you're not out to crack ribs, you've got to exert yourself—if you're not sweaty and exhausted after doing everything you could, then you didn't do enough. Simple as that. I've had CPR work, sometimes fast, sometimes later right when you're about to give up, and I've had it fail too." The shadows in his eyes spoke to experience that Owen was glad he didn't share, and it humbled him, knowing that Quill had probably saved—and lost—many lives over his long career.

"Sorry. I didn't mean to presume. Proceed."

"You try again first." Quill moved out of the way. True to his words, sweat glistened at his temples. And fuck, Owen should *not* find him so hot in the middle of such a somber lecture, shouldn't be wondering about other, more fun ways to get Quill sweaty.

"Okay." Owen scooted forward, arm brushing against Quill as they traded places. *Sizzle.* A surge of energy raced up his shoulder and neck, heading straight for his brain, which should know better than to go getting a crush on a stranger he wasn't likely to see again.

"If the chest isn't actually depressing, you need to go a little harder."

"Like this?" Owen did a few compressions, but Quill's mouth twisted and he shook his head. Leaning over Owen, he placed his hands on top of Owen's and pressed down. Hard. A light he hadn't noticed earlier on the dummy went off. "Oh! It has a sensor."

"Yeah. You want it to trip that sensor every compression." Quill pushed down again, demonstrating, and Owen had to force himself to focus on the whole life-saving skill acquisition thing and not how good Quill's nearness felt, how warm and calloused his big hands were. He wasn't a huge man, but he was beefy in all the right ways, and his big, capable hands were sexy as fuck. "Okay, now you do it. Count it out and focus on making each compression a good one."

Owen followed directions and was surprised at how much strength it took to make it light up each time. Quill hadn't been lying about it being a workout, and

Owen considered himself in the best shape of his life, so it wasn't like he was unused to exertion. Nancy struggled even more than he had, and Quill moved closer to the dummy again.

"You can do this." With his strong, patient tone, he was the kind of man one *believed*, on a deep, cellular level, able to chase out uncertainty. "But hopefully you're not going to be the only person on the scene, and you can do two-person CPR like the instructor talked about if you've got a trained partner. You focus on rescue breaths for five cycles, and I'll do the chest compressions, then we'll switch."

Watching him work with Nancy, Owen was struck again by how competent he was. He wasn't simply hot ranger eye candy, and there was something incredibly sexy about watching him work. As Quill and Nancy finished their five cycles, Hattie came striding over and bent to tap Quill on the shoulder as he sat back on his heels.

"Sorry to interrupt. I just wanted to let you know that I need to take a rain check on dinner. Val's still feeling poorly, and I don't want to leave her."

"That's fine." Quill scrubbed at his short hair, still catching his breath after the CPR. "Family first. I'll find something on my own."

"You're staying over?" Owen couldn't help interrupting, all but bouncing at his good fortune.

"Yeah. It's only a little over an hour drive in when weather's decent, but Hattie and I had plans. Didn't make sense to turn around again early tomorrow."

"Me too. I just arrived in the state yesterday, actually. We should get dinner together." He kept his voice casual, aiming for the same pragmatic tone Quill had used. And because while he was totally an opportunist, he wasn't also rude, he gestured at Nancy. "You could come too."

"Thanks, but I've got plans with a friend," she said softly.

"Ah. Well, you and me then," he said to Quill. "Better than eating alone, right?"

"Excellent idea." Hattie squeezed Quill's shoulder. "I'll feel better staying with Val if I know you've got company."

Quill was silent a long minute, some sort of unspoken conversation happening between him and Hattie. Finally, he sighed. "Guess that would be okay."

Owen would happily work with his underwhelming enthusiasm. Some time alone with Quill? Huge win and great opportunity to find out whether all those sparks of energy he'd been feeling were one-sided. At worst, he didn't have to eat alone in a strange city. At best... Well, at best, there were *other* things he might not have to do alone too, and simply thinking about that made his muscles hum pleasantly. Sure, it might only end up being a shared meal with a reluctant dinner partner, but the chance that it could be something more was one Owen had to take.

Chapter Three

"I'm only doing this because it lets you get on home to Val," Quill grumbled to Hattie as he helped her pack away her materials from the presentations onto a little rolling cart. It wasn't true, of course, and Hattie undoubtedly knew it, in the same way she knew so many of Quill's inner workings, but he needed the illusion of doing her and Owen a favor rather than *wanting* to spend more time with Owen. Wanting was dangerous, an emotion he hadn't felt in years, and he wasn't welcoming it now.

In the rear of the room, a number of attendees still loitered, drinking the last of the coffee and chatting. Owen was among them, talking both to Nancy from their first-aid group and the same older couple he'd sat near at lunch. Not that Quill had kept track of his whereabouts or how his mouth looked when he'd swallowed some soda…

Stop it. He gave himself a mental shake. Getting hung up on this guy wasn't going to do anyone any favors.

"It wouldn't kill you to be social." Hattie patted his arm. "I know group stuff isn't your thing, but one-on-one can be nice. Better than eating alone, like he said.

And he seems like a nice guy. You worked well together in the first-aid class, right?"

"Went fine." Quill wasn't the sort to lie simply to prove a point, and even if he'd been surprised by Owen's take-charge nature, he hadn't hated the experience. Far from it, actually. Usually these trainings were so boring that his eyeballs hurt, but something about Owen kept things interesting, had Quill smiling at more than one point. He'd always appreciated earned confidence in a person, and Owen combined that with an almost infectious good humor. Even when he got things wrong, like with his approach to CPR, he'd been friendly. Seemed like nothing could faze the guy, make him drop his chatty exterior. Touching him had been absolute torture though, but he sure as hell wasn't confessing that to Hattie, who would take that information and run with it.

"And I'll have the question of your winter caretaker sorted out by morning—we're meeting before training to go over some possibilities in the event that your volunteer remains a no-show."

"I trust you." Quill didn't ask to sit in on said meeting. HR type meetings were possibly one of the few things worse than trainings.

"Try and have fun." Hattie gave him another pat as she headed toward the door.

Fun. Problem was that his fun wasn't the same as what others seemed to value—concerts, movies, bars, gatherings, that sort of thing. To him, fun was snow-shoeing through fresh powder at dawn. A perfect sunset over his favorite ridge. Watching the northern lights with a hot drink in hand. His hobbies. Far from noise and drama and chaos.

Because almost all of it was solitary, he didn't have

the highest hopes of having fun with Owen. However, there were plenty of worse things in life to have to tolerate than a meal with a good-looking guy. As Hattie left, he headed over to Owen, who broke away from his group. Sunny smile firmly in place, he greeted Quill with a nod.

"Do you need to change out of your uniform before dinner?"

"Don't want to keep you waiting," Quill hedged, even though he would have changed for dinner with Hattie and Val—no drinking in uniform and he liked blending into a crowd more in regular clothes when he was off duty.

"It's no bother. Are you at the place just down the street?"

"Yeah," Quill reluctantly admitted, already both dreading and thrilling to Owen's response.

"Great. Me too. I'll change into something more casual myself, meet you in the lobby in twenty minutes?" He gave Quill an expectant look.

Resisting the urge to sigh, Quill nodded as he followed Owen out of the room. Who was he to argue with sound logic? "Sounds like a plan."

"Now, where should we go?" Apparently not one to walk in companionable silence, Owen was already digging out his shiny phone with a surprisingly whimsical case featuring cartoon characters before they even cleared the doors to the DNR offices. "Let me see what's close."

Somehow Owen managed to both click around his phone and keep walking without tripping. His…self-sufficiency, Quill guessed one would call it, was both appealing and amusing, making Quill do something he seldom did and involuntarily laugh.

"What?" Owen frowned, looking up from the phone.

"Figure I've been downtown here a time or hundred. You might try asking me, not Yelp, for recommendations."

"Oops." Owen's grin was endearingly contrite. "You're right. Sorry. My bossy side seems to know no limits today."

"Nothing wrong with that," Quill said before he could think better of the words. He didn't mean to sound flirty, because that was a skill set he simply didn't have, but from Owen's wide eyes, that appeared to be how he took it.

"Just saying, I respect resourcefulness. That's all." His lame explanation probably only dug him in deeper.

"Good." Owen's tone was warmer than strictly friendly now. "So, what do you recommend?"

A vision of Owen's mouth popped into his brain again, the exact way his lips pursed when sipping a drink, and the low curl of arousal made it hard to stay focused. His body was more than happy to answer that question for him, but he coughed, forcing himself to push aside the temptation for a flirty reply. He didn't flirt. Period.

"Any allergies? Do you eat meat?" He was never sure with West Coasters, who always seemed to be on whatever the latest fad diet was.

"I eat some meat." Owen shrugged. "Seafood, yes. Chicken, mostly. Not crazy about heavy meats like steak. And I'm always up for ethnic or unusual, local places."

Quill had to discard the classic chain steak place that was his standard when in town, racking his brain for other options as they arrived in front of the hotel, the same budget place favored by all state employees. "I know a place in walking distance with first-class salmon. Not especially ethnic or unique, but it's got the local flavor you're probably after."

"Perfect. See you in a few." Owen gave him a little wave as he headed for the stairs. Giving him a moment, Quill checked his own phone for any message, not wanting the added temptation of knowing which floor Owen was on. When he finally reached his room, he changed quickly, pulling on a polo shirt, jeans, his same boots, and a jacket in deference to the bite in the air. First snow wasn't far off at all.

Owen too had dressed warmly, in a hooded Stanford sweatshirt and faded jeans that made him look both younger and more approachable than the business clothes had.

"You've got winter wear, right?" he asked Owen as he headed back toward the street.

"Of course. Coat. Snow pants. Insulated gloves. I talked to some prior volunteers about what to pack." Owen sounded mildly put out that Quill had questioned his preparedness. "There's a message board with forums for parks volunteers around the country. I got a lot of great info."

"That's good." In Quill's mind, there was no substitute for actual firsthand experience, but he didn't want to further irritate Owen by questioning the value of online opinions.

The place Quill had picked was a few blocks over, a local brew pub known for Alaskan cuisine like elk and seafood, a little touristy for his tastes but Hattie had dragged him there enough times for him to trust the food.

As usual, the sounds of downtown kept distracting Quill—traffic passing them by and other pedestrians to navigate around. Ahead of them, three well-dressed men were having an impassioned discussion about some work matter, the largest of the group with a bombastic voice that carried, sending part of Quill scurrying back three decades and making him glad yet again that his contact with colleagues was minimal.

"Oh, cool sign." Predictably, Owen whipped out his phone to snap a picture of the wood and wrought iron sign as they arrived at the restaurant. The two-story building was otherwise very industrial looking with few windows. The interior was a weird mix of industrial, Alaska kitsch, and wood and iron details that echoed the sign. Luckily, even though it was typically crowded and noisy, there wasn't a wait for a table, and a young server with wavy blond hair led them to the second-story seating area. She stopped in front of a curved booth with a black leather padded back.

Fuck. This was the sort of social dilemma that Quill hated. Did he sit close to the edge, hoping Owen took the hint and sat opposite him? Or did he scoot farther in so they'd have a chance of hearing each other over the din? Would that look too much like a date?

Owen, however, seemed to have no such internal angst, and gave the server a winning smile before sliding in, more toward the middle, giving Quill no choice but to do the same or risk looking even more antisocial than he actually was. The server handed them the mammoth menus, which were at least half drink options. Quill already knew exactly what he was getting, but he opened his simply to have something to do with his eyes other than stare at Owen.

"Do you drink?" Owen asked. "All these local brews are tempting me, but I'm not sure which to try."

Quill with his simple tastes was a piss-poor tour guide for a gourmand, but he dutifully turned to the drinks section. "When I moved here years ago I was still a Bud Light drinker, but Hattie got me onto the local brews. The Solstice IPA is what I get, but if you want something darker, Hattie loves the stout. They've got tasting flights too. But you like unusual, right? Hattie's wife likes their Twig and Berries cocktail."

God, why did places have to use such ridiculous names for ordinary foods? He hoped he wasn't blushing. Perhaps sparked by the men on the sidewalk, his father's voice echoed in his ears, a harsh tease about how easily he'd become flustered. And he'd worked damn hard at leaving all that behind, being a man who could handle darn near anything, even a little innuendo.

"I do like…twigs." Owen's eyes sparkled. "But I'll try the IPA. Back home, I drink a lot of Liberty Ale, so that one looks good to me too. Would you like to split the seafood artichoke dip with me for a starter? That sounds really tasty."

Splitting things felt suspiciously date-like to Quill, but he did it all the time with Hattie and others, so he supposed he shouldn't make a fuss. "Sure."

"You said you drank Bud Light back home? You're not originally from Alaska?"

"I—"

"Ready?" The server came back for their orders before he could answer—Quill getting the same elk burger he got every visit here and Owen ordering the grilled salmon.

After she left, Owen leaned forward. "You were saying?"

"No, I'm not originally from Alaska. Been here twenty years though. But I grew up in Spokane, Washington." More memories crowded his brain, most things he tried not to think about, so he worked hard to keep his voice neutral, distant even.

"How'd you end up in Alaska?"

"Roundabout way. I knew I wanted an outdoor career like being a ranger, either state or national. Went to college in Seattle, majored in Resource Management, did some fieldwork around the northwest in the summers. Then after graduation, I took a summer ranger position at Denali. Wasn't really looking to settle down anywhere, but a job with the state opened up right as I was about to start my hunt again, and I've been based out of the Mat-Su area ever since. It suits me here, I guess."

He left out a whole bunch of essentials, like how he'd been running from so much—his dad's death, JP, family expectations, all of it—when he took the Denali job, and how he'd found himself drawn to staying, to this way of life, to what he'd discovered about himself while here. The years here had chased a lot of that noise away, the not-so-great memories fading, countless moments that proved he was more than he'd thought, letting this place into his veins and psyche over the past two decades until he couldn't imagine being elsewhere.

"I'll say." Owen's assessing look made Quill want to squirm. "Funny how life seems to work like that. Putting us in the right place at the right time. I had no clue what I wanted to do in college. Bounced around a variety of programs my first two years before my parents told me I had to get serious. I ended up friends with a lot of business majors, and next thing I knew I was on the MBA track—there might have also been a cute guy involved though."

"Ah." The back of his neck went hot and prickly despite not being all that surprised. It didn't take particularly strong gaydar to have a clue that all Owen's warm looks and light tones probably indicated a certain level of interest.

"He didn't last through graduation." Owen gave a dismissive wave of his hand. "How about you? Married? Kids?"

"Married to the job." It was the answer he always gave, sidestepping any tricky questions. "No room for anything else."

"Nothing?" Owen's dark eyes sparkled.

"Not really." Quill wasn't lying—he hadn't been celibate since JP, but he also hadn't dated since coming here. There was a bar in Anchorage he went to on occasion, but he sucked at the pickup game and wasn't about to get one of those phone apps, up his game to include cyber-flirting when simply making small talk was often beyond him. It wasn't that he didn't have a sex drive, but sex was…messy. Complicated. And often left him feeling way lonelier than before, so most of the time he made do with his own company, which hadn't failed him yet.

"That's a shame." Owen shook his head, but his easy smile said that Quill being single was hardly unwelcome news.

Their beers and appetizer arrived right then, and Quill was more than relieved at the excuse to change the topic. But sharing the food was even more torture than touching Owen during the first-aid training had been, each accidental brush of their hands when grabbing chips sending electricity crackling to parts that really didn't need any more of a reason to take notice of Owen. It didn't help that Owen made little happy noises while eating, making Quill want all sorts of dangerous things he couldn't have. He had rules. Compartments. Work life and private life, and he'd worked decades keeping them separate. And given how disappointing hookups often went for him, he had no desire to break down those barriers, but Owen had a way of wiggling right past his resolve. Hell, at this rate, he might not survive the entree.

Chapter Four

Quill was exactly the sort of challenge Owen had been craving. Owen still hadn't figured out whether his reticence was a sort of shyness or simply a love of brevity, but he liked the effort of getting Quill talking, getting him to open up. When he did speak, he had a great voice, deep and rich and self-assured. The shyness, if that's what it was, was more subtle—a sort of bashfulness around the eyes that went away the more he talked, only to return when Owen pressed him about things like being single.

Owen took "married to the job" to mean "closeted as hell" but that was okay. It wasn't like he wanted any grand romance with the guy, so he didn't need to deconstruct Quill and figure out whether he was simply a private person or had something deeper going on. Owen liked the guy, a lot more than he did some hookups, but ever since the letdown of his last breakup, he'd been more pragmatic about these things. Closeted or not, they could still have a nice night together if Quill were open to that, and if not, well simply having pleasant conversation was good too.

"You were right. The fish really is good." Owen always enjoyed eating new food and trying new things whether it was appetizers or sports or sex, but the food at the place Quill had picked really was tasty. "And yours is elk? Was it hard getting used to regional food differences when you moved here?"

"I ate game most of my life." Quill shrugged. "So, no. My grandfather was a big hunter. He always made sure we had venison for the freezer and fish in the summer. I had a hunting license long before a driver's license. You'll see when you overwinter, though, it's often humble food, especially when you can't get out. Nothing I wasn't used to from camping and eating simple, but for some it can be a challenge."

"Other than not caring for heavy meats, I can eat almost anything. I grew up with my grandmother making a lot of traditional Vietnamese foods, my mom doing a mix of cuisines, and having many friends from other cultures. I'll be fine."

Quill looked skeptical, but aloud he only said, "Probably. If you've got a favorite candy or something, stock up here in town before you head out. Little trick I learned from Hattie. Makes it easier when it's the same canned soup four nights running if you've got something you like squirreled away for after."

"You and Hattie worked together a lot of years?"

"Fifteen out in the field." Quill's tone grew distant and somber as he studied his half-eaten burger. "Lot of good years. She's one of the finest people I know."

"It's awesome having friends like that. I wouldn't have made it without my crew. And even now it helps, knowing I've got people cheering me on."

"They're cheering you on? No one tried to talk you out of volunteering?"

"Oh, my parents think I'm nuts." Owen laughed away

years of caring too much what they thought and all the work that had gone into reaching this place of relative peace with his own choices. "But even they know how much this means to me. And my friends are all hanging on my social media, following along."

"Support is good." Something in Quill's tone said he hadn't always had that in his own life, and Owen felt a deep pinch in his chest.

"It really is. I never would have made it through the last few years without having people to count on."

"Oh?" Quill tone was curious but not prying, and Owen appreciated that. He took a few more bites of food before answering, trying to decide how much of his story to share.

"I had cancer two years ago," Owen explained at last. "And it's true what they say about having a village making a difference—I had friends who took me to appointments, family who made me food, long-distance contacts who sent funny messages. I'm not sure I would have gotten through without them."

"I'm sorry to hear that." Quill's voice was matter-of-fact, not drama-filled pity. "You in remission now?"

"Yeah. It was testicular cancer, caught early, so high survival rate, but the chemo and associated procedures were still no joke."

This was usually when people got way nosy and personal about which body parts Owen had left and how they functioned, but Quill just nodded. "I lost my grandfather to late-stage prostate cancer. It was…awful. I'm glad they caught yours early."

"Thanks. Anyway, when I was at my sickest, I made a bucket list of sorts—everything I'd always wanted to try and been too chicken to go for. I know it sounds like a bad country song cliché, but it really got me through some dark days, thinking of things I'd do with a second chance."

"Not too silly at all." Quill nodded sharply. "So you quit the whole investment banking world?"

"Yeah. It wasn't that hard a decision really. I'd been fortunate that I had some investments pay off, allowing me to decide to take a few years off to do my bucket list. Eventually, I'll probably need to get a real job again, but I'm lucky that I can take my time deciding on what and where."

"Nice." Quill said it with the sort of absentness of someone who'd never questioned his place in the world, skated through his thirties without a similar existential crisis. Owen both pitied and envied people like that—pity because they missed out on a lot of fun and experimentation, and envy because they didn't have to deal with the uncertainty of being well past college and still not sure what they were doing with their life.

They both turned their attention to their remaining food for a few minutes, but then Quill surprised him by asking, "So, what was on the list? I mean, if that's not too prying... Just curious."

"Curious is fine," Owen assured him. Damn, Quill was seriously adorable when he was less than certain. "In case you haven't figured it out, I'm something of an open book. I like talking."

"I noticed." Quill gave him a wry look.

"Yeah, guilty." Owen laughed. "Anyway, it was a mix of big and small things—things like go to Carnival in Rio, learn to bake bread, have a threesome, ski in Aspen, do New York Pride, go to Space Camp, run a triathlon, and this, of course, winter in Alaska."

Quill coughed. "I'm not going to ask which of those you've accomplished."

"Oh, you can ask." Owen couldn't resist teasing back. "I spent my summer as a volunteer at Space Camp. My inner eight-year-old was in heaven. And as to the rest…" He gave Quill a pointed look. "I've made decent headway on the list."

"Good." The tips of Quill's ears were pink, and Owen had to seriously restrain himself from touching him.

"How about you? Anything on your personal list that you haven't done that you'd like to do before your life is over?"

"Nah." Quill pushed his near-empty plate away. "I'm not the list type or much on travel."

"Really? Nothing?" Owen tried to convey with his eyes that if Quill was holding back on anything sexy on his list that Owen would welcome hearing about it.

"Dessert?" The server arrived to clear their dishes before Quill could answer. "Something to share maybe?"

"None for me. And we're splitting the check." Quill shifted away from Owen, seeming in a hurry to make sure the server didn't assume they were on a date.

"I'm good." Owen liked sweets but the huge portions had been more than enough food.

They each paid their share, then headed outside. The light had started to fade, the midnight sun of the summer long past, the crisp bite to the air making Owen wish he'd grabbed more than his hoodie.

"Cold?" Quill asked as Owen rubbed his arms.

"A little yeah." *Warm me up. Please.*

"I know a shortcut through the alleyways back to the hotel."

"Lead on." Owen followed him as he ducked down

a narrow alley, both of them walking too fast for much conversation.

"Whoa." Quill's arm shot out, holding Owen back as an SUV unexpectedly backed into the alley. Yanking Owen into a dark doorway with him, Quill frowned at the vehicle, which took its sweet time vacating the alley, long enough for Owen to sense Quill's warmth and nearness, more of that classic, intoxicating scent, the harshness of their breathing that much sexier in close quarters. The charged air around them was made worse with every brush of their arms.

"You sure there's *nothing* on your bucket list?" As the SUV finally moved on, Owen turned to block Quill from an easy exit. "Nothing I could help with?"

"Not sure." Quill hissed out a breath. Which was decidedly not a resounding no, so Owen moved closer.

"I'm very…open-minded. And discreet. You could tell me."

"You're something else," Quill whispered, but his tone was more awestruck than censuring.

"So I've been told." Taking a chance, Owen put a hand on his shoulder and was relieved when Quill didn't immediately flinch away or tell him off. "Come on, take a chance. Nothing you're *curious* about?"

"Like what?" Quill's voice was a harsh whisper.

"Hmm." Owen pretended to think as he leaned in close enough to brush his lips against Quill's neck. Quill was taller, but not so much that Owen had to overly stretch. His skin tasted good. Warm. Ever so slightly salty. "This maybe?" He moved to flick Quill's earlobe with his tongue. "Or this? So many delicious possibilities…"

A shudder raced through Quill's larger body, but he still didn't pull away. Didn't speak either, inhaling sharply. Feeling more confident, Owen moved to brush Quill's cheeks on both sides with his lips, deliberately missing his mouth. And when Quill twisted, making a frustrated noise, he was right there to claim victory.

Quill knew the kiss was coming, knew logically that two steps to the left would free him from this temptation, but he might as well have put down two-hundred-year-old fir tree roots for all he could move. Owen might be aggressive—in all the best ways possible—but he'd also given Quill ample time to object or pull away. And Quill hadn't been lying when he'd said he had no bucket list, but right now, finding out what Owen tasted like rocketed up to the top of his previously nonexistent list.

So much so that when their mouths finally met, Quill was the one to gasp first, taken aback by how much he wanted this. Owen took advantage of his gasp to deepen the kiss. He tasted sweet, like he'd popped a mint when Quill hadn't noticed, and he kissed like a guy who knew exactly what he was doing, who wasn't going to wait for Quill to figure himself out or take over. But he also didn't rush like some might, no hurtling ahead, instead exploring slowly, like they weren't in a doorway, blanketed by chilly air. He kissed like they might get to do this again, like learning what Quill liked and responded to was of vital importance. Despite being most definitely in charge, Owen wasn't taking—he had a generous mouth and seemed intent on giving as much pleasure as he could.

And that turned out to be a hell of a lot of pleasure— the slide of warm lips, the rub of an agile tongue, the firm clasp of strong hands, the well-placed nip or suck that had Quill groaning. Seeming emboldened by Quill's noises, Owen pressed him against the door, and Quill happily welcomed the pressure of his body. As surprise faded, Quill met Owen's kisses more readily, giving as good as he got, gratified when Owen made a low moan that was half pain and half pleasure.

"Fuck. You're killing me." Owen didn't give Quill a chance to answer before claiming his mouth again, kissing him like he'd been as long without this as Quill. Of all the things that Quill tried not to miss about having sex on the regular, kissing was on the top of the list. Kisses like these—desperate and hungry and all-consuming.

Somewhere down the alley, an engine revved. Fuck. Quill had lost sight of how exposed they were. Another car could pass by at any time, and while it was dark, that didn't mean the risk of discovery was zero.

"We can't do this here." He panted against Owen's mouth, not wanting to break the contact, but sanity started to return in unwelcome waves that brought with them a healthy dose of regret and shame.

"Right." Owen's grin was visible even in the dim light of the alley. "Race you to my room?"

"We can't." Quill gently pushed Owen back, needing the separation if he was to have any hope of thinking clearly again.

"Oh, we so can." Stepping back farther, Owen held out a hand. "You're single. I'm single. No reason for us to not enjoy ourselves tonight."

"I think I've given you the wrong idea…" Quill scrubbed at his head, trying to shake loose his last remaining brain cells.

"The wrong idea?" Owen shook his head, skepticism clear in his tone. "Kinda hard to get anything other than that you wanted more of that, from your tongue in my mouth, your dick hard against mine, and your sexy noises."

"I don't do this."

"Like ever? Because you're not gonna sell me on that being your first kiss, sorry." Owen's grin was part humor, part frustration.

"I didn't mean it that way." Quill wasn't capable of flat-out lying to Owen, something about him pulling out truths that Quill ordinarily had no problem keeping private. "I mean that I don't hook up with coworkers. Ever."

"I'm not technically a coworker—not on the payroll—and I told you I'm discreet when I need to be." He wasn't lying. The winter volunteers received a place to live and a subsistence payment but weren't classified as employees. "One night. You probably won't ever see me again. Why not have some fun?"

Fuck. Quill wasn't sure he'd ever been this tempted to toss caution to the wind. But he also knew himself, knew that the remaining walk to the hotel would sober him up from this lust-drunk state, and knew that he didn't want to spend tomorrow even more full of regrets. It wasn't so much that he thought Owen would gossip, but he'd worked two decades for his reputation, and he wasn't going to risk that on a few hours of passion. He'd already gone too far as it was.

"I'm not really the fun type." He didn't add that in his experience sex could feel good, could be a release, could temporarily meet a need, but wasn't exactly *fun*. And the sort of emptiness he often got afterward frankly sucked. He didn't need to add that to the regret stew that was sure to follow this lapse of control.

"I could prove otherwise to you." Owen's self-assured words went straight to Quill's already aching dick. And maybe he could, maybe he was the one guy who could show him he'd been wrong about sex and fun. But it didn't matter because Quill wasn't going to find out.

"No, thank you. Sorry." He didn't claim to not be interested since they'd both know he was lying. "Listen, we better head back."

"Suit yourself, but you go on. I'm going to explore downtown here a bit more."

Fuck. The only thing worse than going back to Owen's room was the thought of Owen going back with someone else. A fierce jealousy he hadn't possessed in years raced through him, and he had to remind himself that he was not a rash person. Owen wasn't his, wasn't ever going to be his, and like Owen'd said, they might never see each other again. Quill had no business caring about what Owen did with the remainder of his evening.

"Fine." The word came out a growl because apparently he *did* care. Acutely. And Owen's raised eyebrow said that he had Quill's number.

"See you tomorrow." Owen headed back down the alley, toward the restaurants and bars.

Tomorrow. Fuck. So much for probably never seeing each other again. He still had to make it through tomorrow's training before he could put this whole mess behind himself.

Chapter Five

"You want me to do what?" Quill blinked against the morning sun filtering into the meeting room. He'd slept like crap the previous night, something that was hardly a new problem for him. His stupid brain hadn't wanted to shut off, unable to decide which he regretted more—not giving in to the temptation of going back to Owen's room or letting things get so out of hand to begin with. God, he couldn't ever remember wanting something the way he'd wanted Owen. Maybe…

But no. He'd done the right thing, walking away. Even with his churning head, he'd wolfed down toast and black coffee from the hotel buffet and dutifully hurried to the office for this early meeting with Hattie. But now he had to entertain the very real possibility that he was still dreaming.

"Your caretaker has some sort of family emergency," Hattie explained patiently again. "We talked about all the options. We can't leave the position unfilled—it's simply too much work for one person. Moving Owen Han over from Chugach makes sense. There's a surplus of volunteers there, and you did seem to get along with him yesterday. Giving you someone you can work well with is a priority."

"I don't… I can't…" Fuck. This might be Hattie, but he still wasn't going to confess the ways in which he'd made a fool of himself the night before. And besides, if thoughts of his reputation had kept him from going further with Owen, that same reputation definitely couldn't afford for him to object on the basis of Owen being too big a temptation and risk for his sanity. "There's really no other option?"

"Not a good one. There's no time to relist the position and get someone in and trained before the first snow. Our other volunteers are harder to move—couples and people who specifically requested a given post. Owen applied for placement anywhere in the state, so he was less likely to object than some might. And yesterday he seemed friendly enough toward you. Did something… change?" Hattie's eyes shifted slightly, as if she was trying to give him an out, but they weren't alone in the conference room. Other attendees were filtering in, some in hearing distance, including Hattie's boss, who had apparently already signed off on this change.

Nothing Quill could do other than force himself to shake his head. "No. I just hate putting anyone out. Figure he was looking forward to Chugach."

"I spoke to him this morning. He's fine with the idea. Not put out."

"Ah." Fuck. Well there went Quill's one hope of getting out of this. If Hattie had already spoken to Owen, this was a done deal. But why the hell hadn't Owen objected? He should want nothing to do with Quill. Damn it. What a mess.

"Will that work?" Hattie's head tilted, concern clear in her brown eyes.

"Yeah, I guess so." Really, what choice did he have? He hadn't worked twenty years at this job to suddenly get a reputation as a diva or difficult to work with. At the rear of the room, he spotted Owen helping himself to some hot water for tea. "Anything else I should know?"

"Nope. Just..." Quirking her mouth, Hattie let out a little sigh. "Keep an open mind, maybe? I really do think this will work well for everyone concerned."

"Will do." Quill had no hope of this thing working well for anyone, but he'd already done what he could. No sense in upsetting Hattie, who was simply trying to do her job. He saved his ire, heading to the coffee table where Owen was still fussing with his tea.

No way could Quill stomach a beverage of his own right then. God, but he hated uncomfortable conversations, confrontation, but there was no avoiding this. Not bothering with trying to figure out a greeting, he gave him a hard stare and nodded at the hallway. "A word?"

"Of course." Owen gathered up his tea and followed Quill out to the hall, far friendlier than Quill would have expected given how they'd parted. Maybe he'd gotten better sleep than Quill. And fuck, wondering whether Owen had slept alone was not what Quill wanted to be doing right then. Not that any of this was, but he didn't need jealousy on top of everything else.

"Did you ask for this?" Quill asked when they were clear of the doors. "Ask to be moved?"

Owen's eyes went wide. "No. Not at all. Your friend Hattie called me this morning. I was beyond surprised."

"So why not tell her no?"

"I didn't feel I had any choice." Owen's voice was infuriatingly calm. "It's not like you would have wanted me to tell her that we left things on…not great terms. I thought you'd value my…discretion."

"It's not unappreciated," Quill ground out. Anger, as it turned out, was a good antidote for avoidance. He might not want to be having this conversation, but irritation was good at keeping his voice firm, making him hold his ground. "But, hell, this is a mess. You don't really want to winter with me."

"More like *you* don't want to winter with me." Owen laughed lightly. Damn it. Why did Owen have to be so reasonable? "I'll be fine. Like I told you yesterday, I'm adaptable. And I'm not picky about which state park I'm based out of. This should be fun, regardless."

Fun. There was that damn word again, and this time, Quill couldn't hold his temper back. "If you're looking for fun, you're looking in the wrong place. This is hard work. Grueling even. Long days. Hattie wasn't wrong that it's more than a one-person job, but it's way more than a lark. And if you're thinking I'm up for…anything *extra*, you'd be wrong."

"Hard work and fun aren't mutually exclusive." Owen's dark eyes flashed with more emotion than Quill had seen from him thus far. "I'm prepared to work hard. You're the one who has doubted that from the start. Guess I'll simply have to prove you wrong."

"I didn't mean…" Quill trailed off lamely because he *had* meant that he didn't think Owen could last the winter. Hadn't meant to be rude about it, but he still couldn't deny the opinion. "Look, things don't have to be this awkward. You could ask—"

"Things are only going to be awkward if you let them." More from Mr. Reasonable. "And no, I'm not going to ask for a change. For what it's worth, I'm not planning to spend all winter hitting on you either. I can take a hint, and closet cases might be fun for a night, but it's hardly my regular jam either."

"I'm not… That is…" Fuck. Was that seriously disappointment wiggling its way around Quill's spine, getting into his head? He didn't *want* Owen hitting on him. And what did it matter what Owen thought about him? "I'm a private person."

"Hey, I'm not judging. You do you." Owen's tone was somewhere between understanding and patronizing and made Quill's neck muscles tense. JP had had a similar judgy tone, always unable to understand Quill's aversion to drama. And Quill wasn't without understanding that most people preferred to live a little more loudly than he was capable of. But he still resented the implication that he was some sort of prude.

Prude implied a certain unreasonableness, an insistence on clinging to irrational fears. But Quill knew all too well that his issues weren't arbitrary. Others hadn't walked his path, hadn't endured all the teasing and prodding until the very idea of being open made him break out in a cold sweat. Even so, he'd tried, once upon a time. Let himself be young and foolish. And he'd carry his father's red face and angry words and everything that happened after to his grave. No, he wasn't being irrational. Life wasn't always rainbow T-shirts and jubilant parades. Sometimes openness carried a steep price, and Quill wasn't going to apologize for not wanting to pay that price, not again.

"Professional is best in any event." Quill made himself sound as reasonable as Owen had, like they were negotiating a used car sale, not letting memories of the night before cloud his judgment. The best thing really would be if they could forget the kiss ever happened. If that was even possible with his lips still tingling, remembering how Owen had felt and tasted.

"I can do professional." Owen shifted his tea to his left hand and stuck out the right. "It'll be a good winter. Promise. And you never know. We might actually end up friends."

Ha. It had taken Quill and Hattie *years* to approach true friendship. No way was Quill getting there with Owen in a matter of months, especially not when he'd need to keep his distance to avoid falling into temptation again. Not when merely shaking Owen's hand caused warmth to snake up his spine. Survival, not friendship, had to be his goal here.

Owen meant what he told Quill—he wasn't going to spend all winter hitting on someone who'd made it clear he wasn't interested. Even if Quill's reaction to their kissing and the heat in his eyes this morning, when Owen would have expected nothing but cold and awkward, said he *was* interested. Owen might favor the direct route to getting what he wanted, but he wasn't going to make a pest of himself. A miserable winter for either of them wasn't what he wanted. But all that didn't mean he wasn't a pragmatic optimist—it was likely to be a long seven months, and he liked his chances for getting more kisses at some point, even if he didn't go out of his way to make Quill uncomfortable with repeated invitations. Some things were just inevitable, and anything with as much combustible energy as they'd had the night before was bound to catch fire at some point.

And man, he craved the flames, craved finding out what Quill would be like if he ever lowered his iron self-control completely. The kissing had been so good, so all-consuming that even now, hours later, it was all he could think about. He'd walked around downtown Anchorage last night, had another beer at a bar his review app touted as being inclusive, but simply couldn't get up the enthusiasm for socializing, let alone hooking up with someone else. He wouldn't go so far as to say Quill had ruined him for kissing others with a single make-out session, but it was a close thing. He wouldn't soon be forgetting how Quill had tasted, what he'd sounded like, how he'd let Owen seize control while still being very much an active participant.

But he really needed to stop thinking about Quill's kisses, and focus on the training. On the agenda for the second day was more preparedness education as well as certification tests for the CPR. He needed to pass the tests, not wallow in thoughts of the previous night. Or their testy conversation that morning. Quill was understandably pissed about the change in plans, but really, all Owen could do was try his best to prove him wrong.

As luck would have it, he was back in Quill's group for the CPR test, which had a hands-on portion in addition to a written quiz. Owen's last class had been all in one day, and the way they had split this one up had him worried that he might have forgotten something overnight. Quill, of course, went first and easily passed the demonstration portion. Owen had never been a nervous test taker, but knowing Quill's eyes were on him made it that much harder, that old need to impress driving him to strive for perfection. Somehow he made it through though, getting his certification card.

"Nice work," Quill said on their way back to their seats for the next scheduled session, which was on land-use regulations and conflicts they would need to be aware of. Something in his tone made Owen bristle—like he kept expecting Owen to fail. He didn't mind pleasantly surprising people, but constant negative assumptions got old quickly. He also had a feeling Quill's attitude was going to translate into him not trusting Owen in the field, which was going to suck. And maybe Quill wouldn't trust any volunteer they assigned him, but Owen was determined to prove him wrong, even if he had to do it with gritted teeth.

It turned out that Quill was helping Hattie present the topic, talking about how to resolve disputes between irate residents and day users peacefully. No matter his ire, Owen did like listening to him speak, and was almost sad when they shifted to the final session on emergency maintenance—generators, vehicles, roofs, and other pitfalls to watch for.

Speaking of vehicles, that was next on Owen's list after the training wrapped up. The stipulations for the volunteer position required that he have a personal four-wheel drive car, and rather than deal with the hassle of shipping or driving something up, he'd simply sold the SUV he wasn't particularly attached to in California, and would buy something used but reliable here, looking to sell it again before leaving in early May.

As the training wrapped up, he was finishing an email exchange with a local dealership when Quill came over.

"So…uh…guess I'll see you in a few days?" Quill's uncertainty would be adorable if he weren't also looking like he was heading for a seven-month tour of sewer systems or something equally unpalatable.

"Yup. I've just got to pick up my car, then I'm playing tourist until the fifteenth. Unless you need me sooner?"

"No, no, the fifteenth is fine." Quill swallowed hard before his expression turned more thoughtful. "Car? You need help getting a vehicle? Need me to go with you?"

"I've got it handled." Owen held up his phone. "I'll get a ride to the dealership—they've got a newer used SUV for me to look at. Assuming it checks out, I'll probably be out of there and on the road shortly. I'm headed to Talkeetna and Denali for the weekend."

"You're very…" Quill's head tilted as he paused for a long second. "Self-sufficient."

"I'll take that as a compliment," Owen said, even though he wasn't sure if that's how Quill had meant it. But he saw his hard-won independence as a good thing, too many years of being the coddled younger sibling and too many months of being unable to do even the simplest tasks for himself after chemo giving him a serious aversion to being dependent on others.

"Just don't let it lead you to taking silly risks. I've seen that happen with tourists more than a time or ten."

"I'll be fine. Besides, if I get eaten by a bear in Denali, you'd probably be relieved, right?"

A pained expression crossed Quill's face. "No. Not

relieved. You do seem determined to make keeping you alive until spring a challenge, though."

Quill's concern was both sweet and maddening. "I'm not your responsibility. I'm coming to *help* you, not be another chore."

"Everything up there is my responsibility." Quill's voice was firm. "You included."

"We'll see about—" Owen cut himself off as Hattie came striding over.

"So glad to see you two talking." She did a good job of being oblivious to their simmering tension with her cheerful tone. "Owen, you'll be in my old quarters. I left behind a number of things you'll probably find useful, and don't hesitate to call me with any questions or if you need something."

"Thank you." For some reason, her concern grated far less than Quill's. And he happily took advantage of her presence to extricate himself from further argument with Quill. "See you soon, Quill. I better be going to see about this car."

"Quill knows cars," Hattie offered, and Owen barely suppressed a groan.

"So do I." He wasn't lying—he had been forced to take auto shop as a high school elective when his first three choices were all filled, and he'd bought enough cars over the years to have a good idea what he was looking for. And he really resented the implication that Quill might be better suited to the task of car buying than him, one more in the pile of assumptions Quill kept making about him and what he was capable of. "I've got this."

And as he headed out of the room after a few more

goodbyes, he could only hope that was true. He wanted to impress Quill in the worst way, not be a liability. However, his innate confidence had never failed him before, and he had to believe they could get beyond this somewhat rocky beginning. Even if it meant putting his hot ranger fantasies on the back burner, focusing first on winning Quill's respect. He didn't want to stop and examine why he wanted—needed—that regard so much, but he could already tell that he'd do everything he could to earn it.

Chapter Six

A surprisingly sharp wind bit into Owen's skin as he loaded up his new SUV for the drive to Hatcher Pass, and he hoped it wasn't a sign of the chilly reception awaiting him there. He was back in Anchorage after spending several days driving around—spending time both in the Denali area as well as going south to the Kenai Peninsula. While Hattie had left her quarters mainly furnished for him, he'd still had to round out the suggested supplies he'd need until his next chance to make it into a city. And a few days of spotty cell service had convinced him to indulge in an upgrade to a sat phone. Much as he usually enjoyed shopping, especially for electronics, he'd tried to hurry, wanting to be there at the time he'd told Quill to expect him.

I'll be waiting.

The period made Quill's text seem even more ominous in response to Owen's message about his arrival time. He'd also curtly denied needing anything from a store. Whatever. A few days of exploring had helped Owen's mood, reminded him of why he wanted to do this, and left him more determined to make it work. He ignored Quill's protestations that he didn't need anything, picking up some good-quality chocolates and the Solstice IPA he liked as a peace offering.

Knowing how tightly Quill was wound, he did his best to make good time coming out of Anchorage, but he still wasn't used to the curving mountain roads he encountered after he left the highway. As he'd already found in his travels the past few days, getting behind a line of slow-moving RVs could easily double expected travel times.

Not that he blamed them for creeping along—in addition to the roads being tricky as they gained elevation, the views were spectacular, fading golden scrubby grass and bushes interspersed with proud green fir trees and jagged gray rock stretching up to meet a gentle blue sky, not even a hint of clouds. This area of the state was known as being one of the crown jewels of Alaskan tourism, close enough to Anchorage for easy access but rugged enough for even seasoned outdoor enthusiasts. The Department of Natural Resources labeled the region Mat-Su, short for Matanuska-Susitna Borough, with the regional office in Wasilla, where Quill's boss was based out of.

On either side of the road, snow-covered peaks hugged the narrow pass, and he could easily see how challenging this road would become once winter arrived in earnest, especially once he hit gravel, the last couple of miles to the visitor center being especially bumpy. Once the snow hit, plowing would stop about a mile and half from this section, the only way in and out via skis, snowshoes, or snowmobile.

A small collection of buildings greeted him—historic mining cabins and equipment interspersed with a modern visitor center and public restrooms. Parking in the large lot, he shouldered one of his bags as he made his way toward the buildings. Large signs advised of the various trailheads nearby, and Owen's stomach fluttered happily as his excitement built. He couldn't wait to—

"You're late." A scowling Quill in front of the visitor center put an abrupt end to Owen's daydreaming. In his uniform, Quill seemed even more imposing than Owen had remembered.

"Sorry. Hit unexpected traffic." Owen shifted his weight from foot-to-foot. "I didn't mean to keep you waiting."

"It's okay." Quill's heavy sigh as he reached for Owen's luggage said it really wasn't. "Let me get that."

"No, it's fine. I've got it." Owen snatched the bag back. "Just show me where to put my stuff, and then you can put me to work."

"Figured I'd let you get a lay of the land today so to speak. I'll give you a quick tour to start, and you'll come on patrol with me later too. Tomorrow's soon enough for the maintenance projects we've got waiting for you."

Given Quill's obvious discomfort, the offer of a tour was generous, and he tried to reward Quill with a smile. However, Quill's going-into-surgery grim expression didn't waver as he led Owen into the visitor center and up a flight of stairs. He'd already known from the job listing that both he and Quill had small apartments up here with shared common space, not unlike the dorm Owen had occupied in college. The common room was large and homey with a kitchen at one end, table and chairs in the middle, and then couch, bookshelves, and a large wood-burning stove on the other end.

"Bathroom." Quill pointed to a room beyond the

couch. "Old plumbing is such that it's shared, sorry. We're lucky they managed to rig a shower up here at all."

"It's okay. Shower is good." Not having to traipse downstairs in the middle of the night was good enough for Owen. Unbidden, the image of Quill showering crept into his head—big body filling the small shower stall, water rolling off…

Get a grip, he lectured himself as he tried to return his focus to what Quill was saying.

"And this is your space." Quill opened another door on the other side of the bathroom. Bigger than most of the dorm rooms Owen had occupied, it had a full-size bed on one wall, dresser, bookshelves, desk, and a small counter with hot plate and coffee maker.

"Nice." Owen set his bag on the bed. Calling it an apartment had been overselling the room, but it was comfortable enough and Owen wasn't someone who needed a ton of space—he'd lived with San Francisco rents too much of his life to be picky about that. The whole place was humble and rustic but comfortable, unlike the stilted conversation. He could easily live here for the seven months, but he wasn't as sure about the tension simmering between them. Forget mattresses and hot showers—he needed them to be on good terms more than he needed any creature comforts.

To that end, he opened the bag, removed the beer and chocolate. "I brought you some beer for the fridge. How did you and Hattie usually work meals? I'm happy to cook."

Quill frowned. "I'm usually good with fending for myself. I eat at odd hours anyway. Don't worry about me."

Owen had a feeling Quill was at least partially lying.

He and Hattie were too close not to have shared some meals, but Quill's firmly set mouth seemed ready to shut down any further overtures. And Owen would have argued the point, but there was something uncertain in Quill's eyes that gave him pause.

"That's fine." He'd just have to work on other avenues to friendship, figure out how to make Quill more comfortable. Going back into the common room, he placed the beer in the fridge before turning back to Quill. "So about that tour? Or should I get the rest of my stuff first?"

"We can do both. I'll help with your luggage, then we can take the ATVs out for the tour. Do you know how to drive one?"

"Yup. They had us driving them all over at the resort in Tahoe when I worked there, and I've ridden with friends since then." He enjoyed Quill's look of surprise far more than he should have. Quill was simply going to have to learn that Owen really was up for anything he wanted to throw at him.

Quill was in hell. Owen looked far better than he had any right to, dressed casually in that Stanford sweatshirt that was forever going to make Quill think of dark alleys and hot kisses. He'd paired it with a pair of sporty cargo pants and hiking boots and looked more suited to the job than he had on their first meeting. But still way too attractive for Quill's peace of mind, and way too chatty to boot, all full of stories about the drive and shopping in Anchorage and his travels the past few days. It wasn't that Quill didn't like listening—quite the opposite, actually—but rather that he couldn't seem to get his bearings where Owen was concerned, couldn't seem to get the sort of professional, polite distance that he needed.

Maybe the real problem was that Owen was simply too easy to like. Friendly. Capable. Nice too, bringing the beer. Maybe more than a little overconfident but that seemed to be part of his charm, even though Quill worried that Owen's boundless optimism was going to lead to him taking on too much. Like now, when he circled the ATV with a critical eye, squint saying he was working out something puzzling, but not asking Quill for assistance.

"It's been a few years, but I think I'll manage," Owen said as he accepted a helmet from Quill. Their fingers brushed, and there Quill was, right back to thinking of that kiss.

If each glancing contact was going to have this effect on him, it was going to be a long winter indeed. As per his usual, he fell back on the job to cover any discomfort. "Department regulations require a helmet, even though you'll see tons of riders without one around here. And I keep to a reasonable speed, even when on a callout. Can't help anyone if you're on the side of the trail yourself."

"Got it." Owen's impatient expression was just short of an eye roll. He was probably tired of Quill's reminders, as Quill had used the time carrying up Owen's luggage to issue more warnings amid pointing out the nearest structures and trailheads. Officious wasn't exactly what Quill wanted to be, but he couldn't seem to help it.

"I'm going to lead you on the perimeter of the main visitor's area here in the valley, then head to a few of the more popular spots that I patrol this time of year. Most of your duties have to do with maintenance, not patrol, but you'll want to spend some time in the next few days before the snow hits getting familiar with the terrain, so you're ready if we get a call and I need backup."

"I'll be ready." Owen grinned even as it pained Quill to have to add that last bit. Damn budget cuts. He didn't like knowing Owen was his primary backup, his fellow Mat-Su rangers helpful but all with large territories of their own that made immediate assistance difficult. And not that he expected trouble, but an unarmed newbie was probably more of a liability than a resource with most situations. However, he had his marching orders, which were to use Owen as much as possible. They'd have in-termittent help from other volunteers, but otherwise it was just them and a never-ending to-do list.

"Won't be too much longer, and we'll be switching to the snowmachines. There's already some powder at the upper elevations, and we're likely next."

"I can drive a snowmobile too." Owen gave him an-other ready-for-anything grin even as he fumbled the ATV's ignition and had to try a second time to start it. An older, state-owned vehicle, it was a little tricky to start, but still it wouldn't kill Owen to ask for advice.

"Follow me," he said before climbing on his own machine, not at all sure Owen would listen. True to his word, he started off nice and slow, a gentle sweep of the valley, hitting the parking lots and trailheads that he made a regular part of his patrols.

Stopping at one of the biggest lots with a sweep-ing view of the valley, he pointed to the restrooms. "We've got a company that does latrine maintenance, but you'll still be responsible for keeping the supplies stocked. Anything you notice out of the ordinary, you let me know."

"Like people going at it or something? That's something we ran into a fair amount in Tahoe." Owen's laugh invited Quill to join in, but he couldn't seem to manage more than a tight smile. And he really didn't need an allusion to sex. Bad enough his brain kept going there all on its own.

"It's pretty rustic, so that's not a frequent issue. Figure the smell puts even the kids off."

"Noted." Owen's grin didn't waver. "And trust me, I'm plenty grateful that we've got basic septic or whatever at the visitor's center. I know some of the volunteer positions have accommodations with outhouses."

"Yup. Trust me, you'll be singing its praises in January."

"Have you always lived on-site?" Owen asked, apparently in no hurry to resume the ride. "I know from talking to other volunteers that it really seems to vary—some rangers living at ranger stations, especially in the more remote areas, others with cabins or houses nearby, and some living in towns and commuting into their jurisdictions."

"Yeah." Quill shrugged. "They offered me the apartment when I was a green new ranger, ridiculously low rent that comes out of my check, and it seemed like a great deal at the time." A quiet place after years of noisy houses and dorms had felt perfect at the time. And now, if he sometimes wondered what it would be like to put his own stamp on a place, like what Hattie and Val were doing, he pushed those thoughts aside. Last thing he needed was a bigger space to rattle around with only his own company in. "I've never been one needing a ton of possessions, so it suited me. Never saw fit to leave."

"Cool. I admire that minimalism—I sold a bunch of my crap before leaving the Bay Area, and I felt so much better for it. Who knows, maybe I'll do the whole tiny house thing after I'm done with my list."

The mention of Owen's list was a needed reminder that this was just a temporary lark for him, that he'd be leaving in the spring, and that there was an end date for all this awkwardness. He waved at their ATVs. "Let's go."

"Wait." Voice hushed, Owen's eyes went wide as he moved toward the other side of the road that led to the parking lot, a gentle slope of land currently occupied by a large moose, looking like he was deciding whether to cross or go back.

Quill stood there quietly next to Owen, not wanting to spook the moose but also wanting to drink in more of Owen's enthusiasm as he whipped out his cell phone and snapped a few pictures. His wide grin was utterly infectious. After all this time, Quill was used to the sheep, moose, birds, bears, and arctic squirrels that populated his territory, but watching Owen react with such awe made Quill's shoulders unknot as he smiled despite himself.

It was…well, not a *moment*, because Quill didn't have those. But it was something, a quiet companionship that Quill didn't get very often, and it made his pulse thrum. Eventually the moose headed back the way he'd come, and Owen stuck his phone back in his pocket.

"Thanks for not hurrying me there. He was massive. That was so cool."

"No problem." Quill replaced his helmet and resumed the tour, but with fresh eyes now, trying to see things from Owen's perspective of wonder. It was a gorgeous late afternoon, contrast of the snowy mountains and greenish gold valley awaiting winter, views he'd seen for decades but no less breathtaking, despite how easy it was to lose sight of that in the day-to-day demands of the job.

As they returned to the visitor center area, parking the ATVs back in the equipment shed, next to the snowmachines, a strange restlessness swept through Quill. Things had been easier out there, familiar terrain as opposed to the trickier social landscape of knowing that an evening alone together loomed.

"What time are you officially off duty?" Owen asked.

"It's not like police work—not really shifts or set hours. If I need to be off-site for an extended time like for the training, I get coverage from another ranger, but otherwise, if something goes down at midnight, I'm the guy. In the summer, we go by the visitor center hours, and in winter, the shorter daylight hours condense our work, but I keep my sat phone with me, even at night."

"But like, you could have a beer with dinner, right?" Owen persisted. "I was thinking of cooking some of the food I brought from Anchorage, and you could tell me all about the maintenance work you've got scheduled so that I'm ready to start tomorrow."

It sounded nice. Too nice. And sure, he and Hattie had enjoyed meals together and the occasional beer too, but something about Owen's plan felt too cozy. Too much like a gateway drug to wanting more of Owen's company. And the last thing he needed was to slip up, give in to temptation, and then end up with seven months of awkward interactions and drama he simply couldn't handle.

"Nah," he said as they reached the center's doors, looking away, focusing on the old mining buildings rather than Owen's expectant face. "You go on, make yourself something. I've got locks I want to check on the outbuildings, and I need to let the office know you arrived. That sort of thing." Honestly, it was nothing that couldn't wait, but Owen didn't need to know that. "I'll be a while yet, so don't worry about me."

"Okay." Disappointment was clear in Owen's tone, and regret pierced Quill's resolve, making his hands clench against the urge to reconsider.

But he stayed strong, reminded himself that he was likely poor company anyway, and let Owen head up the stairs alone. Better that they get things started on the right foot—separate meals, separate lives, no messy entanglements. He kept himself busy a good long time, checking all the outbuildings for any signs of intruders. It wasn't uncommon, especially this time of year, for people to want to camp where they shouldn't. But still, Quill made the task take twice as long as it should and then hung out in the downstairs ranger office going over some reports and other paperwork.

When he finally headed upstairs, the common room was as empty and still as he'd hoped, kitchen cleaner than ever with gleaming counters. The smell of chicken and spices lingered, though, and Quill's stomach rumbled, reminding him how long it had been since a slapped-together sandwich for lunch. Before he could make the same for his dinner, however, he spotted a plastic container on the dining table with his name on a sticky note.

Quill—I made extra. Thought I'd save you the trouble of cooking, but if chicken and rice noodles with a mild garlic sauce isn't your thing, just put it in the fridge, and I'll eat it tomorrow. ~Owen.

Fuck. Quill exhaled hard. Flirting he could repel pretty easily. But friendship...man, friendship was proving far harder to turn down. And the only thing more dangerous than his inconvenient attraction to Owen might be liking the guy. Like actually *liking* him. Because attraction led to awkwardness, but liking...

He had to stop and rub his suddenly tense neck, reminding himself that liking led to hurt and other places he refused to go again. Avoidance was probably his best option, but hell if he felt good about it. Damn Owen for being so tempting on so many levels.

Chapter Seven

Owen hated being ignored. Thank God for upbeat play-lists and long battery life as he worked on the various projects on his list. That morning's to-do list—written in Quill's neat if cramped handwriting—called for trash duty. And, as had proved typical over the past few days, the list had appeared on the dining table sometime prior to Owen's wakeup. It didn't matter how early Owen set his alarm. Quill was the master of being up and gone before dawn, leaving a three-quarters full coffee pot and note of instructions. If not for his extensive music collection, Owen'd be going truly stir-crazy with the whole limited-contact-with-humanity thing.

His mood had deteriorated to the point that running into some tourists yesterday while cleaning restrooms had been the highlight of his day, and he'd kept the group talking probably longer than they'd wanted, just so starved for a real conversation. And it wasn't that he never saw Quill, but when he did, their interactions were limited to the blasted list, Quill showing him what needed doing and then disappearing again. And sure, the guy undoubtedly had ranger business, but it was also beyond obvious that he was avoiding Owen, up early, back later, and never lingering when working together on something. He was unfailingly polite, thanking Owen for food and leaving coffee, but distant, and it was driving Owen ten kinds of crazy. It reminded him too much of the long, lonely days of doing chemo—contact with the medical staff, but really desperate for more personal connection.

When he'd signed up for this position, Owen had focused on his long-held fantasies surrounding Alaska—snow, scenery, adventure. And sure the ad said to be prepared for working alone, sometimes for days on end, but he hadn't really dwelled on that part, figuring he'd cope with that challenge same as he did everything. Yet in actuality, his extrovert's soul was struggling, and the snow hadn't even really arrived in earnest. No way was he giving up, but at the rate he was going, he'd be full-on talking to himself by spring.

As it was, he rocked out to his music as he worked, letting the pulsing beat work its magic in his headphones, and adding a shimmy to his step as he emptied parking lot trash cans, placing full bags on a little cart that attached to his ATV. He was almost done with one of the lower parking lots when Quill came roaring up, driving his ATV faster than Owen had seen him. He pulled up even with the trash cans, shaking his head, no doubt scoffing at Owen's silliness, dancing alone outdoors.

"What's up?" he asked as he yanked off his headphones. It had to be serious for Quill to seek him out in the middle of the day, but his grim posture kept Owen from pointing that out.

"We've got a situation." Quill pulled off his helmet. "Two hikers were out on one of the steeper trails. One slipped, fell. Bad knee and wrist injuries, possible concussion. The other hiker came back for help because she wasn't strong enough to transport on her own. I came for you because if a field stretcher is needed, I'm going to need a second person."

"Of course." Owen dusted off his hands. "What's the plan?"

"We can get close with the ATVs, but then we're still looking at around thirty or forty minutes or so to reach the victim. I've radioed that we may need a medevac, but it'll be on us to get her down to a spot where the helicopter can land."

"Got it. I'll follow you back to the center, drop the trash off. Bet we'll need the cart for possible transport, so that can stay on. The trailhead's up there, right?" Adrenaline thrumming, Owen fell easily into crisis mode, taking stock of what would need to happen.

"Yes, but we'll be taking a roundabout way to reach the victim. The trail is steep and narrow, so we'll go wide, then intersect and go the last part by foot. I've got the supplies we'll need already packed up."

"Where's the friend?" Owen found his helmet and straddled his ATV, ready to follow Quill back.

"She came down far enough to get a signal to call for help, then headed back to the victim. Hopefully, she beats us there."

"Here's hoping. At least it's a clear day."

"Wind's no joke though. We need to make good time, as I think weather's on the way. Snow might come overnight even. Surprised we still haven't had our first storm of the season. But that's probably why we've had an increase in hikers this week—trying to get a last trek in before snowshoe and ski season."

Sensing Quill's impatience, Owen nodded and

started his machine. "Makes sense. See you back at the center."

They made short work of the drive back, ditched the trash, checked Owen's fuel level, and added blankets to the cart to make possible transport easier. He followed Quill on a bumpy ride, first on a trail he'd been on before, then cutting through hills, trusting that Quill knew where they were heading. Finally, they intersected with a narrow trail heading up a steep incline.

"This is where we hoof it." Quill stowed his helmet and retrieved a large first-aid kit, collapsible stretcher, and some blankets.

"What can I carry?" Owen held out his arms, giving Quill little choice but to fill them with the blankets. Set, they headed up the trail, Owen watching his step on the unfamiliar terrain, Quill moving more quickly and sure-footedly. Every so often, Quill would swivel his head, taking a wide sweep of the area.

"I've got this, promise." Owen was already itchy with Quill's constant observation.

"Not watching you. Gotta be alert for bears or other wildlife—wrong season for many bears, but you never know. Awareness is essential."

"Ah. Sorry." Humbled, Owen tried to pick up the pace to match Quill's long strides. Trying to defuse the tension, he kept his voice light. "I guess you've seen a lot of bears over the years and not the fun kind."

"There's a fun kind?" Quill's face creased adorably as he failed to get Owen's joke.

"You know, the two-legged, burly variety…"

"Oh." Quill's cheeks darkened. "Yeah. No. Not that…" He coughed and his flusteredness was enough of a distraction that Owen had to be extra careful on a tricky section, readjusting the blankets to keep his balance.

"And the other kind?" He took pity on Quill before he could stammer further.

"Wildlife is so common around here that I've lost track of sightings. Had a close call or two with a mama bear, but mainly being aware is the best defense." Quill spent the next stretch giving bear avoidance tips, and Owen indulged him by asking follow-up questions, letting him retreat to the familiar territory of his warnings.

Much as ruffling Quill was fun, Owen didn't want to flirt his way into one of them tripping. The view of the valley beneath them was breathtaking, but he tried to focus on the job at hand since this wasn't a pleasure hike and Quill had set a pace that didn't allow much reflection on the surroundings.

"Should be close now," Quill said as they finished a series of switchbacks, ground leveling out again at the higher elevation. "Damn lucky they didn't fall on that section with the sharp drop-off. We'd be looking at a much tougher situation. As it is, it's going to be challenging, carrying the victim down. At least they didn't cross the snow line."

"Yeah." Owen was breathing hard, both from the pace and the increase in altitude. He wasn't looking forward to going back down, but first they had to reach the hikers.

"Over here," a woman shouted, and Owen's heart sped up along with his feet. An older woman in thick hiking clothes with a knit hat atop gray hair waved them over to where another woman of similar age lay off the trail, down a short hill. She had a backpack under her head and a space blanket covering her.

"Found you! We're here to help. Tell us about the injuries." Owen scrambled down next to the women, realizing a moment too late that he should probably be letting Quill take the lead since he was the one with far more experience. "Sorry," he murmured to Quill, stepping back so Quill could approach the victim and assess the situation.

"Well, Helen here started to feel dizzy, and then next thing I knew, she was tumbling down. It was all so sudden." Speaking in cultured East Coast tones, the uninjured woman gestured at her companion.

"She was dizzy before she fell?" Quill's eyes narrowed, and he gave Owen a quick, pointed look that confirmed Owen's initial fear that that wasn't a good sign.

"How are you feeling now? Any chest pain? Weakness? History of diabetes or other condition?" Owen's brain raced ahead, considering several awful possibilities.

"In pain." Helen's forehead creased, eyes glassy. "I'm not diabetic. I'm healthy as a horse usually. Norma can vouch for that. I don't know what happened. My head's still swimming."

"I think a medical evacuation is the right call here. I'm going to try to get a signal to let the helicopter personnel know that we've reached you and that we'll rendezvous with them ASAP." Still frowning, Quill stepped away as he pulled out his sat phone.

"I agree." Owen pitched his voice as soothing as he could. "The sooner we can get you looked at, the better. Now tell me about your other injuries."

With Norma's help, Helen pointed out her wrenched knee and rapidly swelling wrist. "I feel so foolish."

"Don't. These things happen." Crouching again, Owen gently squeezed her shoulder. "And I'm no doctor, but it could be worse. I don't think you broke the leg. I've had a knee sprain from a skiing accident before, and it swelled up exactly like that."

"Oh, I don't want knee surgery." Helen's voice was thready and distraught.

"Sure some knee injuries need surgery, but not all. Mine healed with only some rest. And talk about foolish—at least you had the excuse of being dizzy. Mine was that I was talking with a friend, not watching the hill, and before I realized it, I was picking up speed and ended up tangoing with a tree." He kept his tone light, trying to earn a laugh from the women before Quill returned.

"Okay, the helicopter's going to try to meet us at a clearing right beyond where we left the ATVs," Quill reported, coming to kneel next to Owen. "Because of the dizziness, I don't want you attempting much movement, even with our help. We'll carry you down."

"My pack…" Helen fretted as Quill unrolled the field stretcher next to her.

"Don't you worry about that. I've got it." Norma gently removed the backpack from under Helen's head and attempted to shoulder both packs. "We won't leave your camera behind, promise."

Owen didn't like how Norma wobbled under the weight of both bags. "Wait. I'll wear her pack."

He quickly put the backpack on, buckling the chest and waist clips. Helen was apparently a hardy trooper as the pack was a considerable weight, but no way was he letting on that he had growing doubts about their ability to get Helen down. The women needed him confident and upbeat, especially with Quill so dour and task-focused. Forcing an easy smile, he got in position to help Quill transfer her to the stretcher.

"This part may hurt," Quill warned. "On three?"

Owen followed his directions as they positioned Helen on the stretcher, wincing right along with Helen as she groaned. Cool wind whipping around them, they wrapped her in the blankets they'd brought as best they could.

"Tell me about your camera," he said, wanting to distract Helen from her pain.

"It's a Nikon…" She trailed off to breathe deeply, eyes squishing shut.

"Hey, stay with us." Owen worked to keep any panic from his voice. "What kind of Nikon? D-SLR?"

As they started back down the trail, he kept up a steady stream of questions, mainly yes/no ones, but needing the assurance that Helen wasn't drifting into unconsciousness, either from a concussion or from whatever made her dizzy in the first place. *Please don't let it be a stroke.* He wasn't the praying type, but he'd lost two grandparents to stroke, and he took a moment to ask the universe to help Helen get to medical attention as soon as possible. If it was a stroke, time was absolutely of the essence.

"Doing okay, Owen?" Quill called, voice tight as they navigated a switchback. He was taking the lead, undoubtedly shouldering more of the weight, but Owen's shoulders still strained from the stretcher and backpack both. But the greater concern was his feet—every step mattered, and the descent was hell on the calves as he worked to avoid skidding.

"Yeah."

"Owen?" Behind him, Norma said his name carefully, the way a lot of people did when they tried to match Owen's name to his heritage.

"Yeah. I'm Owen and this is Quill. Guess we should have introduced ourselves better." As Owen finished, Helen let out a soft moan, and he resumed his efforts to keep her distracted. "I've got a great story about my name too. Last name is from some Chinese ancestor several generations back in Vietnam. But my first name is where it gets fun. Both sets of my grandparents immigrated to East San Jose in the sixties, and my parents lived in the same general neighborhood but weren't friends. Then their tenth-grade social studies teacher Mr. Owens made them work together on a group project, and by the time they made their presentation, they were already crushing on each other. They got married between high school and college. Everyone thought they were nuts, but they've been together forty-some years now."

"And, Quill?" Helen's voice was decidedly weaker now, and Owen's back prickled, worries over her condition mounting.

"My parents were young too. Too young. Someone gave my mom a baby book, but not the sense to use it." Quill expanded on the answer he'd given Owen when they'd met, and his relative talkativeness told Owen that he too was concerned.

"Why not just use your middle name?" Owen asked. "If you dislike it so much, I mean."

"Not happening. It's even worse. Like I said. My mom's…a bit different."

"Now I want to know," Owen teased even as he had to watch his step on a rocky section.

"Nope. Careful now. Trail's about to narrow." Right as Quill gave the warning, Owen had to dig in with his heels and adjust his stance. His arms and legs burned, but sore muscles were the least of his anxieties. Helen's pale skin and shallow breathing had him on edge.

"Head still swimming?" he asked her.

"Yeah," she managed a weak reply. "Maybe I did hit it on the way down. Not sure. Sleepy."

"Stay awake. You're about to get the sort of scenic helicopter ride most tourists pay good money for." Somehow, Owen managed to keep his voice light. "Now, who back home are you going to tell about your adventure? Kids? Grandkids? I need details."

He kept Helen and Norma both talking, learning that they were lifelong friends from Maine, with widespread extended families, and a penchant for shared adventure travel now that both were retired widows.

"Okay, next section's going to be the trickiest." Quill sounded mildly frustrated, like maybe Owen's chatter was too much for him. He'd simply have to deal. Owen could tell the women needed the distraction even if Quill didn't. The trail went up before swiftly descending again, rocky outcroppings making each step a challenge.

But when the path leveled out again, Owen recognized the view and some tension left his body. "Not much longer now, Helen."

"Good." Her voice was a bare whisper. "Dizzy again… Funny, not even walking."

"We're going to get you help," he promised, even as his stomach churned with fresh worries about a possible stroke. "You'll have a great story for the kids while you rest up. And then you'll be ready for the next adventure."

"That's right," Norma chimed in. "You're going to be okay."

Mercifully, he heard the distant drone of a helicopter.

"Can you go faster?" Quill asked. "With these winds not sure how many chances they'll get to land."

"Yup." Adrenaline surging, he followed Quill's lead, quickening the pace, as they worked to make it to the clearing where the ATVs awaited. His jaw tightened with the memory of what Quill had said at training—that sometimes efforts to save someone failed. Owen refused to have that happen here. His shoulders burned and his legs ached, but he wasn't going to give in to his exhaustion until Helen was safe.

Chapter Eight

Urgency thrummed through Quill. He needed this rescue to be a success in the worst way. No longer a simple leg injury to manage, he was increasingly concerned about a possible head injury or stroke. But even as his worries grew, he had to juggle other concerns—they only had so much daylight left, the wind was continuing to pick up, and a shift in the weather seemed imminent, and he could hear the strain in Owen's and Norma's voices—the pace had taken a toll on their stamina. He was more than a little in awe of how Owen kept his optimistic attitude going for the women, chatting and joking even though his muscles had to be burning as much as Quill's. Hell, Quill was lucky to manage a few well-timed warnings while Owen had conducted a full conversation.

The elusive human skills Quill had always relied on Hattie for seemed to come so naturally to Owen, but even more than his ability to calm the women, Quill was impressed at Owen's overall handling of the situation—not freaking out, watching his step even as he talked, working with Quill to get things done. And sure, he still had that take-charge streak, but Quill couldn't deny they made a good team.

And as they reached the ATVs, Owen did a great job

following Quill's instructions on how to prepare for the helicopter's arrival while Quill handled talking to the dispatcher on his sat phone. Waiting until Owen and the women were situated, he stepped away, relaying his concerns about Helen's dizziness. Because many times in the past the helicopter had been unable to land, Quill was prepared to have to transport via the ATVs and try a second rendezvous point, but he honestly wasn't sure Helen had that kind of time.

"They're going to let a medic down, get her ready for a fast loading for transport," he explained as the helicopter circled closer, noise requiring to him raise his voice.

"Is she going to have to ride in one of those basket things? I've seen that in ski accidents," Norma fretted.

"That's an option. But they're going to try to actually land." He wished he had Owen's gift for soothing tones and was relieved when Owen leaned in, squeezed Helen's shoulder.

"You'll do great," Owen assured her. "Another adventure, right?"

"Exactly. And I'll meet you at the hospital in Anchorage." Norma's friendly face creased with concern, and she too bent over Helen to offer support.

The helicopter dipped low, medic rappelling down with all the speed and grace of a special forces operator. She rushed over, and Quill and the other two moved back so she could assess Helen.

"We're hoping for a lull in the winds," she yelled. "But we're going to need to move fast."

Following her directions, Quill helped her get Helen strapped up, not liking how the medic shook her head after examining Helen's pupils. *Please let the rescue work*. He'd had enough stuff go sideways out here to not truly believe in the power of prayer, not the way Granddad had, but he sent one up nonetheless.

"Okay, we're go for a landing," the medic yelled, and then with the same lightning efficiency that always amazed Quill when he worked with the helicopter crews, the bird touched down and Helen was loaded up in a matter of swift minutes.

"Wow." Owen's eyes were wide as he watched them take off. "That was something."

"Yeah." Quill's throat was scratchy with the force of his desire for Helen to be okay. Forcing himself to stay focused, he turned to Norma. "Let's get you back to your vehicle so you can keep that promise to meet her at the hospital. You going to be okay to drive?"

"Of course. I've driven in fifty years of Maine winters. We're hardy stock, Helen and I." Her tone was confident even as her eyes were weary.

Since Owen had the cart, Quill had Norma ride behind him on his machine, producing a spare helmet as he stowed their other supplies. Even with the wind whipping up and fading light, they made good time back to the trailhead, getting Norma situated in her rental car amid Owen beseeching her to let him know an update on Helen before they drove on to the equipment shed for the ATVs.

"Man, it's almost like the sky waited on us." Owen gestured to the rapidly darkening sky as he pulled his helmet off.

"Yup. Like I said, weather's on the way. It'll probably start as wintery mix but turn to snow overnight. You ready for that?"

"Absolutely." Owen gave him a broad grin that mirrored

some of Quill's own exhaustion. "I've got my skis ready and can't wait to try snowshoes again—that's been a few years. In fact, while I wait to hear an update from Norma, I'm going to welcome the snow with some soup, maybe some cocoa afterward. I don't suppose you want some?"

"Soup?" Quill blinked. A refusal gathered in his mouth, same one he always had for Owen's overtures of food and company, but this time he couldn't quite get it out. Maybe he was tired. Maybe he was more worried about Helen than he wanted to let on, even to himself. Maybe he was simply hungry. But whatever the cause, he found himself asking, "What kind?"

"Really?" Owen's eyes went wide, and his pace back to the center quickened, almost as if he wanted to get cooking before Quill changed his mind. It would have been cute had Quill allowed himself to find anything about Owen cute. "I was thinking this quick chicken and ginger one that my mom does. Not traditional pho— that broth takes all day—but this has noodles in it too, so it's filling. Which we need after all that." He reached the center doors first and unlocked, holding the door for Quill. "That sound good? Or do you want something like a minestrone? I've got a recipe for that one too, if you like more traditional."

Quill had never been a particularly adventurous eater, but he also didn't want to put Owen out. "The one you were planning sounds fine. I liked what you did with noodles the other night."

"You did?" Beaming like Quill had given him a gift, Owen hurried up the stairs.

"Yeah." Quill had left a thank-you note along with his to-do list, but as much as he didn't want to encourage Owen, he wasn't going to lie. "It was tasty. But

I'm not as picky as you might think. It's just habit—I tend to stick to routine, and I've never been one for a lot of complicated cooking. A lot of the time I settle for a sandwich or big bowl of oatmeal, things like that. Having something hot and homemade was a nice treat."

"Well, good." Owen's megawatt smile continued as he started riffling in the kitchen area's cabinets.

"That doesn't mean you need to do it more," Quill was quick to add as he hung up his coat. "Just that it was nice."

"Well, unfortunately for you, I like doing cooking experiments, and I know how precious ingredients are with the store far away and the possibility of being snowed in, so I'm going to keep offering. I brought a lot of my own staples from Anchorage—rice noodles, fish sauce, spices, broth, stuff like that, and I like sharing." Owen's jaw took on a defiant tilt, and Quill foresaw many more plastic containers in his future. Old enough to know when he was beat, Quill let out a sigh and stretched his shoulders.

"Okay, put me to work. What has to be done?"

"You're helping?" Owen's eyes went wide.

"Of course. Not going to sit here and watch you work while I tap my fingers." He had way too many memories of his father doing just that at their small kitchen table, inevitably the start of an argument between his parents, starting with snipping while his mom cooked, progressing to a full-blown shouting match over dinner.

"Hmm…" Head tilting, Owen worked his jaw as if he were trying to decide on the easiest task to give Quill that wouldn't insult him.

"I'm perfectly capable of chopping." Quill bristled at Owen's skepticism.

"Awesome." Smile too bright, Owen handed him a hunk of ginger and an onion. "Usually I'd char the onion and ginger, but that doesn't work the best with this stove. Just dice the onion small and either grate about two inches of ginger or mince it fine, your choice."

No way was Quill going to admit *now* that he'd never dealt with raw ginger and wasn't entirely sure of the difference between mince and dice. Grabbing a cutting board, he took it to the table and started with the onion, struggling with the peel. This was why he didn't often bother with cooking—too many fiddly bits.

"Here. It peels way easier if you take off the ends first." Owen reached around him, grabbing the knife to demonstrate. And Quill supposed that he was imparting more cooking wisdom, but he couldn't focus on Owen's tips with him this close, smelling good—like hard work and that expensive scent of his mingling together in a way that made Quill's brain go straight to sex. Their hands brushed and forget the coming storm outdoors, the air right here in the kitchen positively crackled like the charged sky right before the heavens opened up with a deluge or blizzard.

But if Owen felt it, he was damn good at not letting on, finishing up his little demonstration and flitting away, taking the onion with him back to whatever he was doing at the stove, leaving Quill to take a few steadying breaths before resuming his task. He needed to get a grip—Owen had promised not to hit on him and indeed had stuck to that. It was all on Quill that he couldn't put the attraction behind him.

He tried to force himself to focus on the ginger and

not Owen's scent next, taking his time to get the piece peeled and cut finely, stupid impulse to impress Owen, show him he was plenty able to hold his own in the kitchen. Meanwhile, Owen kept up a steady stream of explanations as to what he was doing until finally Quill had to laugh.

"Do you have aspirations of being on one of those cooking shows?"

"What?" Owen stopped mid-stir, cheeks darkening. "No. Sorry. Bad habit of chattering. My family used to tease me that I didn't know to get dressed without narrating it. Silence doesn't exactly come easily to me, annoying as that probably is."

"I didn't say it was annoying." Now Quill felt bad, his clumsy attempt at a joke having fallen flat. "Just that it reminded me of a TV chef, how you know your stuff and make it nice to listen to."

"Oh, well in that case..." Owen resumed smiling. "If it's *fun*, you can totally pretend you're my assistant on *Cooking with Owen Live*. Bring the carrot over here and I'll demonstrate how we get the rice noodles ready next."

"Not sure cooking's supposed to be fun." His mother had always made cooking seem like the worst chore, complaining and harping at his father until he started escalating things, volume increasing until Quill had to sneak away.

"Sure it is. You should see my mom when we've got a house full of people. She's happiest with a crowd to feed." Owen put the dried rice noodles in a large bowl, adding water. "And she'll get us all in on it, making dumplings or cookies or something like that. My grandmother was like that too, humming to herself as she made the broth for pho."

"That wasn't how it was in my house." Quill's chest pinched, old pain at what had come so easily to others. "More like my mom would smash dishes if she had a big group waiting to eat."

"Really?" Face thoughtful, Owen stirred the soup.

"Yeah." Quill's neck heated, same as it had when he was younger, not wanting others to know how dysfunctional his family could be. "It wasn't always that bad. Some nights my dad worked late, and she'd make breakfast for dinner. She did good pancakes."

"But sometimes it was bad?" Owen's face softened, sympathy clear in his eyes.

"Sometimes," Quill admitted. Even now, after decades of distance, he swore he could hear their raised voices, whatever that night's fight was. He could still smell the inside of the closet in his room where he'd liked to hide until the arguing was done and his mom would come coax him out, sing to him when he was younger, give him a snack when he was older. Quick to anger. Quick to recover, at least back then. "Like I said earlier, she and my dad were young when they had me, and then my sisters followed quickly after. Part of it was them being…less than mature, but part of it was just escalation of the drama that all relationships have over time. Their personalities didn't help any, but all couples have their bickering."

"False." Laughing lightly, Owen poured in a box of broth. "Again, you haven't met my family. My parents are ridiculously happy with each other. I'm sure they've had arguments, but never that I've seen. They totally ruined me for relationships because I kept expecting it to be that easy—find a soul mate, settle into forever, laugh a lot."

"Hah." Quill had to snort. "Soul mates are a myth."

"Maybe." Owen sounded far sadder about that fact than Quill was. "And maybe my parents simply got lucky, but that didn't stop me from wanting it, trying to find a relationship that didn't feel like work. But that's easier said than done, you know?"

"They're all work." Of that, Quill was convinced.

"Said exactly like someone married to the job." Owen rolled his eyes at Quill. "Not that I don't get that impulse. After my last relationship, I'm kind of out on love myself. I wouldn't turn down a soul mate, but I'm done twisting myself into knots and trying too hard to make something out of nothing."

"What happened with your last…person?" Quill was far more curious than he had any right to be.

"Boyfriend. You can say the word. It's not contagious, promise. Anyway, things were going great, and we were talking about moving in together. Then I got the cancer diagnosis." Owen's shrug held a world of regret in it, making Quill's hands clench, already wanting to find this bastard, tell him a thing or two. "He drifted away, not really breaking up until it was obvious he'd checked out, and I called him on it."

"Passive aggressive bullshit. At least there wasn't screaming, but still, that sort of treatment isn't right."

"Oh, there was yelling once I realized what he was doing." Somehow Owen managed a laugh even though Quill didn't see the humor. That was the problem with relationships. Someone *always* ended up loud and disruptive, making relationships far more trouble than they were worth. "Okay, now the soup is almost done, and you can add the rice noodles. Drain them first."

Strangely, Quill kind of liked following Owen's directions. After having to be in charge out in the field, so much riding on his every decision and move, knowing Owen could handle the food let him relax in a way he hadn't anticipated, invisible fist loosening its stranglehold on his chest. And watching Owen move was its own sort of pleasure, the way he almost bounced as he cooked, similar to the dancing he'd been doing earlier. And that had been a sight, one he hadn't been able to appreciate at the time with the urgency of the situation, but now the memory made him smile.

"What?" Owen's forehead crinkled. "Do I have something on my face?"

"Uh…" Geez. Quill apparently couldn't even manage a smile without looking off. "No. Just…hungry," he finished weakly, not wanting to admit how much he was enjoying himself.

"Good. Get two big bowls, and we can serve it. I do chopsticks plus a soup spoon, but you might want a fork for the noodles."

"I can eat with chopsticks." Quill enjoyed Owen's look of surprise more than he should have. "I had a… friend in college. He and his friends loved trying different places. Insisted on teaching his country bumpkin… friend chopsticks."

The memory of JP made his mouth go dry, faint bitter tang that even the years hadn't been able to erase— he'd always made fun of how Quill liked to order the same food over and over while he tried something new every outing.

"A…*friend*?"

Damn it. Of course, Owen had picked up on his unfortunate pause.

"Friend," he said more firmly. He'd already shared enough personal stuff for one evening, more than most coworkers knew about him, that was for sure. And reminding himself about the coworker part of this equation, he took a seat with his bowl of soup at the far end of the table, away from Owen.

"Tell me about Quill in college." Owen pursed his lips to blow on his soup, making Quill's groin tighten and making it tough to concentrate. "I'm picturing you all full of warnings and reminders for your friends, doing a safety lecture before a bar crawl…"

"Nah." Quill studied his soup, knowing his cheeks were undoubtedly dark. "I was more reserved, I guess you could say? Too quiet, really. My friends were all more lively."

"Ah. You were shy." Owen's eyes were sympathetic, but he smiled like he'd had some sort of internal bet with himself that he'd won.

"Maybe a little," Quill allowed.

"There's nothing wrong with being shy," Owen said with the confidence of a guy who'd never had the label hissed at him by an unhappy parent or school bully. *You're too shy, Quill. Stop being such a weakling. You're not a little mouse, boy. You give those boys a piece of your fist.* His father's coaching hadn't made any difference, hadn't been able to give him confidence to stand up for himself. That had taken years, a conscious effort to transform shy into stoic, to leave that kid behind.

"Soup's good." Quill was ready to change the subject. "Not too spicy."

"Yeah, it came out well." Thankfully, Owen finally

settled in with his food, fewer probing questions about Quill's life, and more small talk over food and recipes he might like to try.

The soup was good enough, full-bodied and rich with ginger and garlic, that they each had seconds, and as he took his empty bowl to the sink after, his stomach was pleasantly warm even as the rest of him was reminding him of the long haul down the trail with the stretcher, his arms and legs still burning. He rolled his shoulders, trying to work the kinks out, resorting to rubbing his own neck.

"Feeling it?" Owen asked, coming up behind him. "You must be—you had more of the weight the whole way down, and I know my muscles haven't ached like this in years."

"Yeah," Quill admitted. "Have you checked your phone? Any word on her condition from Norma?"

"Checking now." Still standing way too close, Owen pulled out a different phone than he'd had back in Anchorage—this one a sat phone, a similar model to Quill's own, and more likely to get coverage up here. He held it up to his ear to listen to a message before sharing, "Good news! The doctors do suspect a stroke, but she didn't end up with any broken bones, and Norma says Helen's alert and feisty as the doctors decide on the best course of treatment for her."

Relief evident in his voice, he clapped Quill on the shoulder, a warm pressure Quill felt all the way to his toes.

"That's good." Quill's voice came out far huskier than he'd intended, throat tightening further when Owen didn't drop his hand but instead dug in with his thumb.

"Damn. You *are* tense. How about you let me help?" Using both hands, Owen steered Quill back to the table, applying gentle pressure until Quill sank into his chair. He followed Owen's directions as easily as he had while cooking even as his mind bounced around like a branch in a wood chipper, rational thought starting to flee as Owen started a gentle massage.

"Uh…" He grasped for the last of those logical responses, knowing he needed to do something even as the baser part of him was wallowing in how good Owen's touch felt. "Bad idea. We shouldn't…"

"It's a great idea," Owen countered, not stopping the work of his sorcerer's hands, finding knots in Quill's neck that had been there decades. "And all I'm proposing is a simple, friendly massage, not a hot-and-heavy make-out session. The sort of thing friends do for each other all the time."

Quill wanted to drop-kick the swift rush of disappointment that coursed through him. He refused to let himself want more kissing, especially not if Owen had changed his mind about wanting that too.

"I don't have friends like that," he hedged, traitorous body refusing to pull away.

"Maybe you should start." Owen did a thing with all ten fingertips that had Quill all but humming his approval.

"Us and friendship is a bad… *Hell*. That feels…" He gulped, trying to stay with one train of thought. "Terrible idea."

"Ha." Owen let out a warm chuckle as Quill fought a losing battle against giving in to this wonderfully awful proposition. "Come on, Quill. Let yourself enjoy this. What do you have to lose?"

Everything. He had everything to lose but still couldn't get the gumption to end this conversation and head to his room, far away from massages and cozy companionship, wanting more time with Owen too much. He was so, so screwed.

Chapter Nine

Please say yes. Owen was trying not to go for the hard sell, so he stilled his fingers while he waited for Quill's reply. He had no intention of turning this into an unwelcome pass, not when things were finally easier between them, tension melting away under the shared experience of cooking together. The post-rescue adrenaline didn't hurt either—they'd been through something together now, same as how coming through a big deadline as a team in his old job had bonded people. Quill had been most impressive in his handling of the situation, and Owen did have a certain amount of gratitude toward him, not to mention sympathy for his aching muscles.

Owen wasn't lying. He'd rubbed plenty of friends' shoulders over the years, and while he could undoubtedly do a far better massage with less clothing and a bed or other flat surface, he also knew himself and there was only so much temptation his resolve to not push Quill into something sexual could take. Quill shirtless would lead to using oil, which would lead to slippery, heated skin begging for kisses…

Yeah. Not going there. But a nice friendly back rub to put ignoring each other behind them and establish a more congenial tone going forward seemed like a great idea, not the mistake Quill feared.

Silent for several long moments, Quill finally shuddered, shoulders relaxing into Owen's touch. "You're too damn good at this."

"Is that a 'yes, please keep going'?" Owen couldn't resist teasing.

"It's not a no." Quill groaned like the admission cost him a mortgage payment, so Owen rewarded him with more purposeful movements, rubbing the broad expanse of his upper back, not simply focusing on his neck and upper shoulders. He was far from a pro, but he'd done this enough to be pretty confident in his abilities. Shoulder blades tended to hold a tremendous amount of stress, so as Quill slumped more forward, he worked there, digging in and finding hidden pressure points. Quill's breathing deepened, a sexy little hitch to each inhale, barest hint of a moan on the exhale.

"So…middle name?" Owen grasped at the nearest random topic to distract himself from the blood rushing to his cock over Quill's reactions. His subtle noises were pure sex, and it was only too easy to imagine Quill in bed, truly letting go.

"What?" Quill sounded like he'd pounded back a shot, and it was sexy as hell.

"Your middle name. It can't be *that* bad."

"It is."

"Tell me." Owen traced the column of Quill's strong spine with his thumbs.

"Nope." A quick peek revealed that Quill's eyes had fluttered shut. Since Owen didn't want to ruin his relaxation, he dropped the topic. For now. One more thing about Quill to be curious about, to obsess over until spring. He'd get Quill to fess up at some point, one way or another.

"I bet your arms are sore too." He started rubbing Quill's biceps, intent on working his way toward his meaty forearms and strong hands.

"That part of the back rub deal?" Quill didn't pull away, so Owen kept going, working on spots he knew from experience felt good like the upper arms and mid forearms.

"Sure it is. Repetitive stress injuries were rampant in grad school. I had a flare-up of ulnar nerve pain, and massage helped me a ton. And later I had a boyfriend who was always massaging my hands." He picked up one of Quill's meaty paws to demonstrate, a surprisingly intimate gesture, practically holding hands. Where Quill's sounds had gone right to his groin, this intimacy hit him square in the chest, made him want Quill on a deeper, more personal level. It wasn't so much that his hand was a little larger as much as how it radiated capability, as if this was a guy who could carry considerable weight, and not simply physically burdens.

"Can't say as I've ever tried it." Quill's eyes were still squished shut, his breathing more audible than the faint whisper of his words.

"That's too bad. I mean, I know you and Hattie were isolated up here, but don't you miss touch?"

"Not sure." Quill exhaled hard, chin falling to his chest as his arm lost all traces of resistance. Fuck. He was so hot when he gave himself over to this, let Owen do his thing the way he wanted. That sort of supplication made his brain fizz like champagne, made his head swim to the point that he almost missed Quill's next words. "Been so long… And even then, not like I came from a touchy-feely family."

Something about the longing in Quill's voice spoke to tender parts of himself that Owen didn't often connect with. He couldn't imagine denying himself touch for years on end. Everyone needed human contact, especially people like Quill, who gave so much to others.

"And your…friends?" he asked, tone cautious as he moved back to the other hand. "No touch there either?"

Quill was silent for several breaths before muttering, "Complicated."

"I see." And he did—a guy who was closeted or close enough to it, living in a remote area, was probably low on both friends and opportunities. But it still made his jaw clench, thinking of all Quill was missing out on.

Quill's muscles were undoubtedly loose enough now that Owen could stop, but an almost primal urge to give Quill more touching drove him to return to Quill's neck, fluttering his fingers softer now, relishing the feel of warm skin. Maybe Quill could live without pleasures like this, but Owen sure as hell couldn't.

Mouth dry, his lips ached to join his hands. He could almost hear Quill's surprised gasp, taste his skin, feel the heat of his back if he pressed close…

But he couldn't. He'd promised that this wasn't prelude to a make-out session or a come-on, and he wanted to be a man of his word even more than he wanted to sneak that kiss. Quill's head tipped back, eyes closed, lips offered up like a prize, waiting for Owen's claim. He caught himself right as he started to lean forward, intent on meeting Quill's silent demand. *Not going there.* Reluctantly, he dropped his hands before his rising need led to him doing something irrevocably stupid that might break this lovely spell between them.

"How's that?" he asked, voice rougher and lower than usual.

Quill took a long inhale and exhale before straightening. "Good. Really good. Feels like I could sleep for a year."

"Excellent." The way his blood hummed, Owen doubted he'd be able to sleep himself for hours yet, but he was gratified to be able to get the perpetually on-duty Quill to relax.

"Are you still…uh… I should return the favor. Doubt I'm as good as you, but…"

"I'm good." No way was he sticking to his no-kissing promise if Quill's hands landed on him, expert or not.

"You sure?" Quill's face creased. "It's not fair to you."

The way he was so earnest about being fair told Owen that Quill had some experience with quid pro quo sexual encounters, and reinforced Owen's decision to not let him reciprocate. The last thing he wanted was Quill offering out of guilt. And Owen liked the idea of being able to give him some no-strings-attached touch.

"Don't worry about it. And I'm about to be the unfair one and take the first shower," he said lightly, not wanting to let on that he was near-desperate with the need to go jerk off. God, he needed to get Quill out of his system, get over the hold this man had on him.

"Take all the hot water. I'll shower in the morning." Quill yawned again before giving him a sheepish smile. "Sorry. You stole all my energy. And…um…thank you."

The pink on Quill's cheeks was all the thanks Owen needed. "It was my pleasure. Night."

He headed for his room to grab a towel before the temptation to kiss that adorable smile off Quill's face could win out. He wanted to kiss each corner of Quill's mouth, going slow and deliberate, swallowing his gasps until neither of them could stand it any longer. But he wouldn't. However, he also wasn't made of ice. He wasn't sure how much longer he could keep promising no deliberate passes, not when Quill had this kind of effect on him. Eventually the heat they kept generating was going to boil over, and damn if he couldn't wait for the inevitable collapse of both of their resolves.

Snow greeted Quill in the stillness before dawn, white and pillowy and far more welcome than the regrets that kept stabbing at his conscience. He shouldn't have let Owen touch him last night. Didn't matter how good it felt. Or how much he'd needed it. It wasn't professional and was the exact opposite of keeping his distance. And now he had to move forward knowing how damn amazing Owen's hands could make him feel and knowing he couldn't go there again. It was like he'd always imagined a tropical vacation in January to be—a nice idea, but one always had to come back to reality in the end, so why bother getting all used to the sun and sand when they were but temporary distractions?

Owen was like that—all heat and distraction and promise of pleasure—but temporary. So very temporary. He'd be gone even before Quill got acclimated to his presence, so there was no point getting attached, letting himself start to crave everything Owen could offer. Especially not when it left him this unsettled afterward. He didn't know what to make of Owen not wanting him to reciprocate when he'd been obviously sore too. Didn't he trust Quill to do a good job? Or was it that he didn't want Quill to touch him? Like maybe he'd just been massaging Quill out of some misguided sense of obligation?

Quill hated that particular thought. He'd had enough of expectations with JP and his insistence on things being equal, and all his parents' arguments over fairness and who did what still echoed in his ears. He didn't need Owen holding his nose so to speak just to try to get Quill to be nicer or whatever his end goal had been.

And with that in mind, Quill hesitated over his notepad at the dining table. What was the protocol for this, anyway? Should he even mention last night?

Fuck. This was why he avoided human interaction. Too damn complicated. Finally, light starting to peek over the horizon, he forced himself to stop dithering, listing a few tasks that shouldn't take Owen too long, then added a more personal note at the end.

Snow should be coming down off and on all day. Bet you'll want to get out in it, but stay warm. It's colder than it looks, with low visibility predicted for the worst of it. You did good yesterday. Thanks for everything. Let me know if you hear an update on Helen's condition.

There. Surely "thanks for everything" worked without needing to spell out that he appreciated having his muscles turned warmer and limper than the noodles in their dinner soup. God, he really wasn't sure the last time he'd fallen asleep that easily and slept through to his alarm.

Note done, he crept down to his small office, check-

ing in with the regional headquarters and getting the
full weather report before heading out on his morning
patrol. This time of year, the visitor center opened only
limited hours on days with a high number of expected
visitors like holiday weekends, but that didn't mean that
they didn't get tourist traffic. Some brave souls would
undoubtedly risk the storm for the chance to be among
the first to lay down tracks. His patrol was also to make
sure that no one had been fool enough to try camping
in this. It wasn't uncommon for RVs to try to use the
day lots as makeshift campgrounds or intrepid tourists
to want to sneak in some permit-free tent camping. It
was up to Quill both to enforce the regulations and to
keep the rule-breakers alive.

Enough snow had come down overnight to meet
the minimum seven inches or so that he liked to see
before taking the snowmachine out for its first spin
of the season. He'd dressed with an eye to the newly
freezing temperatures—insulated gloves, boots, snow
pants, thick parka. A loose, flaky powder was continuing to fall at a sleepy rate as he made his rounds.
With the storm expected to continue for at least the
next twenty-four hours, even the main roads wouldn't
be plowed until tomorrow at the earliest, which meant
hunkering down after his patrol to wait it out.

But that might mean running into Owen back at the
apartment, so he took his sweet time putting the snowmachine away, checking its treads and maintenance,
making sure their fuel reserves were looking good,
and generally putting far more energy into organizing
the equipment shed than was needed. The midmorning light, such as it was, arrived gray and without much

warmth to raise the temperatures, bringing with it a howling wind that rattled the walls of the shed.

He was starting to think about hot coffee and balancing a break against the chances of running into Owen when the guy himself appeared in the doorway of the shed. He'd bundled up—new-looking coat and colorful wool hat pulled down over his ears. Gloves were too thin though, and his cheeks were already pink with the cold.

"Hey. Sorry to bother you." Owen gave him a crooked smile. "You got a minute?"

"Yeah." More like Quill had a couple of hours, but he wasn't letting on about that quite yet.

"Something's up with the generator. The lights went out, and it's getting colder in the center. I stoked up the woodstove, but the space heater in my room is off too."

"Okay, let's go take a look." The generator was a heavy-duty continuous-use one, designed to provide unlimited hours of power each year, not a backup model, which were typically limited to a set number of hours. In addition to electricity, the heat it generated was captured and used to help heat the center, so it was no wonder that the center was getting cold without it running. The generator was housed in a small insulated trailer adjacent to the main building, a trailer that immediately seemed half its usual size with Owen there beside him, marveling at the equipment.

"Wow. This is so much more complex than the emergency ones I've seen before."

"Yup. It's older, but it was designed for remote, cold sites. It's seen us through a number of good years. Last year, though, it started to show its age, needed a couple of repair visits. Hopefully it's something I can fix on my own because no way are we getting someone out here in this storm."

"We should probably begin by trying to restart it. I would have done that without bugging you, but wasn't sure how." Somehow Owen managed to be both apologetic and take-charge at the same time.

"Restarting is the right call." He tried to give Owen credit without bristling too much. Quill had twenty winters under his belt, not to mention time with his grandfather at his hunting cabin. He wasn't a repair technician by any means, but he'd coaxed more than one generator back to life. "But first we need to make sure the snow hasn't blocked the exhausts. It's got two main ones, and it's designed to shut off if the snow or something else keeps the air from getting out."

Going outside, he checked each exhaust point, but they were clear.

"Heck." Owen echoed Quill's own frustration, their sighs hanging in front of them in the frosty air. "That would have been the easy answer. Now show me how to restart. Please."

The hastily tacked on *please* wasn't enough to avoid Quill's neck tensing. "I'll show you, but generators can be tricky. Assuming we get it started, you'll want to call for me if it fritzes out again."

Owen nodded, but Quill wasn't sure he believed that he wouldn't attempt a fix on his own first. He talked Owen through a hard reset of the generator—which was more involved than just flipping a single switch like with a computer or appliance. And…

"Nothing." Owen's voice echoed off the metal equipment in the silent room. Not even a few creaky groans or rattles. "Connection points? Tell me what to check."

"I've got it." Quill's irritation, both with Owen and the situation, boiled over into his voice.

"You know, you don't have to go it alone all the time anymore. We're a team." Owen's voice was infuriatingly rational and level.

"I can take care of myself."

"Are we talking about the giant piece of machinery, which undoubtedly does need a second pair of hands, or your back, which also could use a helping hand now and then?" Owen was typically blunt, and Quill should have known they wouldn't manage to make it the whole day without bringing up last night.

"Both," Quill gritted out. Despite the cold, his face heated at the memory of the massage. God, how could he have been so impulsive?

Head tilting, Owen considered him a long moment. "You're embarrassed," he pronounced at last, somehow able as always to see what Quill tried to keep buried, even from himself. "And you shouldn't be. It's no big deal."

That made Quill growl. Because maybe it wasn't to Owen, maybe he had a stable of friends he did back rubs for, but Quill didn't do this, wasn't cut out for this kind of temptation.

"It can be a not-a-big-deal that we don't repeat. Now, if you don't mind, I need to check some things."

"Fine." Owen stepped back against the wall. "You want me to leave you to it? I can go check the woodstove, start a kettle for tea and coffee."

"Sounds good." Even when Quill was being rude and dismissive, Owen was so damn nice. Quill didn't deserve him and his repeated offers of friendship, that was for sure.

And as Owen left the generator room, leaving him alone with his whirring thoughts, Quill already knew that he'd have to apologize at some point soon. If he couldn't get this stupid generator to work, they were in for a long, cold day in way-too-close quarters. Forget electricity—he needed *space*, space from his confusing emotions, space from Owen and all he represented, and space from this growing sense of dread.

Chapter Ten

Owen had been cold before, plenty of times, but there was something about the panic-tinged cold that made his bones ache, feel brittle with the sort of chilliness that underscored how vulnerable their situation was if they couldn't fix the generator. They had dry wood, a woodstove, supplies and sturdy shelters, and pioneers had surely survived on far less, but still his pulse galloped, each new worry like a fresh shot of espresso.

Even though he was a tea drinker, he still knew how to make coffee for Quill using water boiled on top of the woodstove and a French press coffeemaker he found in a cupboard. Probably one Hattie had left behind as Quill seemed more than content with his economy drip coffee, which he made eye-wateringly strong and didn't temper with sugar as far as Owen had seen.

Quill wasn't a caricature of a grizzled old ranger who ate gravel for breakfast. Nor was he an unfeeling guy. Owen had seen flashes of his quieter, tender side. Indeed, Owen was coming to understand that it wasn't that Quill didn't want little luxuries like sweet coffee, but that for whatever reason, he didn't often allow himself to have them.

But everyone needed sweetness, especially those

who tried to tell themselves otherwise, so Owen improvised a mocha for each of them—adding the strong coffee to large mugs with a hot cocoa packet added and some milk he steamed. He'd just finished his creation when Quill's footsteps sounded on the stairs. He'd removed his boots downstairs but still had his coat on, gloves and hat dangling from the pockets as he rubbed his hands together and headed right for the stove.

"Bad news." Quill didn't meet his eyes, but he also didn't mince words. "I've done what I can. I think the problem is a short in the ignition switch. That's why nothing's even trying to come online. I talked to a tech. Reception's terrible so it was a short call, but he can come tomorrow if the roads get plowed or day after as a worst-case scenario."

Words heavy with regret, Quill sank into the couch in front of the woodstove. The way his shoulders slumped inside his coat made Owen's fingers flex with the urge to massage him again.

"It's okay," Owen assured him. "At least it's not January, right? And I know you did your best to get it working. Maybe after you get warmed up, we can go back down, and you can show me what you found, but I doubt I'll have any better luck."

"Probably not." Exhaling hard, Quill scrubbed at his short hair before setting his coat aside. "There's not much to see—no broken parts that I can see. Even so, I shouldn't have chased you away earlier. Sorry. I was rude."

"A little." Owen would let him own his bad mood even as he forgave it. "But it's okay. I made you something hot to drink. It's kind of like a mocha. Might not be coffee-shop quality, but it's got to beat black and lukewarm."

"Thank you. That was…sw—*nice* of you." Quill accepted the mug from him, taking a long sip before he straightened. "It's good. Hot. Man, it's really cold out there now, more so than usual for late October. But you're right. It's not January. We should probably both sleep in here, near the stove, but otherwise we should be okay."

Okay sounded like something of a hopeful overstatement as Quill's distaste for the idea was clear from his furrowed forehead and tight mouth. Well. Tough. He might hate the idea of consigning himself to such close proximity with Owen, but Owen also wasn't stupid enough to try roughing it with his arctic-rated sleeping bag and a cold room simply to avoid more awkwardness with Quill. They were grown men. They could go twenty-four hours both without fighting and without jumping each other.

Not that Owen would turn down that last idea, but he also wasn't going to push Quill. If Quill wanted something, he could damn well ask or at least give a clear sign. And in the meantime, there was no reason they couldn't make the best of a crappy situation. Grabbing his own drink, he took a seat on the other end of the couch, stretching his feet toward the warmth of the stove.

"Kind of like camping out in the living room as kids. It'll be fine. And now I both get to test my sleeping bag out and to cross 'snowed in with no electricity' off the bucket list."

"That seriously on the list?" Quill regarded him with

too-solemn eyes over his steaming mug. "Right up there with tire blowouts and flash floods?"

"I was joking." Owen gave in to the temptation to roll his eyes at Quill. "I mean, obviously I like adventure and excitement, but I'm not looking for bad things to happen. And when they *do* happen, I've always found that a sense of humor helps."

Quill snorted like he wasn't so sure. "Nothing funny about hypothermia."

"Of course not. But life's too short to take yourself too seriously. Trust me. I know. I used to be way more serious myself."

"Sorry." Quill studied his drink. "I do respect all you've survived and that your list helped you find some perspective during chemo. I can't say what I'd do in a similar situation. I didn't mean to make light of it. I'm just pissed at the generator and at myself for not being able to fix it. And I know damn well that a bum generator wasn't on your list, no matter how much you want to joke."

"Well, stop it," Owen said firmly. "And my list isn't so much about finite experiences as it is about a certain mindset. Like I said, I stopped taking everything so seriously. And that's freeing. I lived so many years not doing things I wanted, living someone else's life. I'm done with that, and if it means I have to deal with snow or a broken generator or whatever, that's okay. At least I chose this."

"Yeah. I get that." Quill's voice was more compassionate now, and for a second Owen thought he might reach for him, but then Quill seemed to pull back into himself, hugging the mug closer to his chest. "Did it really feel like someone else's life all along, or maybe it was more like you met a different self during your illness?"

"Hmm." It was an incredibly insightful question, and Owen let himself have a minute to give it the proper consideration. "Maybe some of both. I grew and changed the year I went through treatment, but a part of me knew all along that I was following a path laid down by others."

"How so?" Unlike a lot of people, when Quill asked a follow-up question, he asked it with his whole body, leaning forward, eyes opening wider, breath slowing, like he actually cared about the response, like he was happy to listen and not simply coming up with a witty story of his own for when it was his turn to talk, the way some of Owen's friends would.

"I was the youngest kid, so a lot of my hobbies were simply extensions of things the others were already doing. I never loved soccer, but the other two were already playing… I went to the same extracurricular programs as them, but no one really stopped to ask me what I wanted to do. And I know that sounds kind of whiny. It wasn't a bad childhood, and we were rather privileged. It's not like my parents heaped the pressure on, at least not any more than my friends and cousins experienced. But it was easy to follow my sisters to the same magnet school, aim for my dad's alma mater to make him happy, follow my friends to business school, make everyone proud with the MBA. It was easy, and I won't say it wasn't fun because parts of it really were, but it wasn't *me*."

"What would have been more you?" Quill's eyes seemed to bore into Owen, like they might discover answers he wasn't aware he had.

"I'm still figuring that out," he admitted. When he told people about the bucket list, he usually kept it light, avoided dwelling on the restlessness driving him, the sense that he still hadn't found the person he was meant to be. And sure, he was having a good time, checking items off, but nothing so far had done much to ease that clawing in his gut, the little voice that whispered that there had to be more to life that he simply hadn't found yet. "But I do know that whatever I end up doing after this time off, it's going to be for me, expectations be damned."

"Good for you." Quill's voice was firm. "And nothing wrong with easy. My grandfather died my senior year of high school. All the way through, I'd been planning to go army, get myself the hell out of town as quickly as I could, figure out which rating would keep me outdoors the most, then his chunk of change landed in my lap. I went away to college because it was the surer route to working outdoors without having to dodge bullets. Don't beat yourself up for having some fun and easy years or for not knowing all the answers. Life's not a one-time multiple-choice test."

"Yeah." Owen's throat went tight. Coming from Quill, that was a long speech, and it humbled him, both the vision of the kid Quill must have been and the sincerity of his words. Rare for him, he wasn't sure what else to say, what else he could add that wouldn't be trite.

Almost as if he too needed a break from the heavy turn the conversation had taken, Quill pushed up from the couch, voice a shade too bright. "So, how about it?"

He gestured at the lone window, the one above the sink, which let in what light there was from outside.

"How about what?" Owen could be up for just about

anything that didn't require more soul-baring conversation. Much as he loved to talk, he didn't care for how raw and open he felt after sharing so deeply with Quill.

"You said you couldn't wait to try snowshoeing again. How about now? I should check the outbuildings again before the storm gets worse, make sure there are no trespassers." The resignation in Quill's tone underscored his general attitude to rule-breakers, something Owen was coming to admire about him. Quill wasn't someone who seemed to take a lot of glee in busting people, always coming back to issues of safety and well-being. Like now, Quill was undoubtedly more concerned with would-be campers out in the elements than he was about enforcing the necessary laws. "We can also look at the generator again together. I won't chase you away this time."

It was a clear peace offering and Owen was quick to nod. "Sounds great. Want me to make you some more coffee for your thermos?" Quill's classic green thermos stood upright in the drying rack at the side of the sink. Quill must have really been in a hurry to avoid Owen that morning if he'd left it behind, which was a sobering thought, one that tempered Owen's enthusiasm. "You don't have to take me with you. I could explore on my—"

"Not in this storm." Quill cut him off with a curt shake of the head. "Safety in numbers, and you're still getting your bearings. Besides, I'm looking forward to seeing you fall."

Quill smiled then, the rare almost-boyish grin he kept hidden under the gruff exterior, right along with whatever playful impulses he had. Owen would give a lot to see that side of Quill more.

"Ha. We'll see about that." He matched his joking tone to Quill's, but his pride was determined to not prove Quill right. They bundled up quickly and retrieved snowshoes from the same downstairs room that also stored their skis and other winter gear. Quill insisted that Owen borrow a pair of his gloves which were thicker than Owen's own. There was something intimate about the gesture that made warmth curl low in Owen's belly, almost like Quill had left his fingerprints behind.

Once they headed out, it didn't take more than a minute before Owen stumbled and tilted precariously. Quill grabbed him, put out a steadying hand that felt far too good on Owen's arm.

"Lightly," Quill reminded him. "Idea is to stay on top of the snow, not to trudge through it. It's not gliding like skiing, but you still have to let the snowshoes do the work of keeping your weight up while you get a rhythm going."

"Yeah." Owen tried again, this time with marginally more success, following Quill away from the center to skirt the perimeter of the buildings, pausing every so often for Quill to check locks. Owen was undoubtedly slowing him down and was far less graceful than Quill, who moved like he'd been born to this. Quill didn't complain though or try to hurry him up, and the more they traveled, the more Owen couldn't hold back his joy.

Unlike the panicking chill he'd had back at the apartment, this was the good kind of cold, the kind he loved so much because it made him feel that much more alive and vital. As they crested a hill, he turned, taking in the buildings below them. Breathing deep, he marveled in the view. Blanketed in fresh snow, it looked like a nineteenth century postcard, gray skies giving it a black-and-white-photography vibe with few signs of modern life, wear covered by the mantles of icy white.

"Damn. Wish I'd brought my camera." He'd accidentally left his phone back on the charger next to his bed, not that that would do any good without electricity.

"Yeah." Something in Quill's voice made Owen turn toward him. Closer than he'd thought, Quill's shoulder bumped his, and his quizzical expression gave Owen pause, made him swallow hard. Quill studied him like he was only just now discovering something key about him, like a second head or rogue tail. Then Quill's eyes seemed to zero in on Owen's mouth and his breath caught.

For a long moment, his belief that Quill was about to kiss him built with each inhalation of crisp air, and he braced himself for the perfection of the contact, the bite of the cold air, the warm man next to him, and the limitless potent energy between them.

"Come on," Quill said at last, and Owen leaned in right as Quill moved the fuck away, shaking his head. "Buildings need checking."

Hell. Owen had to take a second to breathe deep, steady himself, before he followed. He grieved the loss of the kiss that never was with an intensity he usually reserved for an investment gone majorly south, feeling its absence down to the arches of his chilled feet. The moment had been right fucking there for the taking. Hell, he'd had actual kisses, lengthy make-out sessions even, affect him less than that one missed opportunity.

Fuck. I am so screwed. Or rather, he was so very

unscrewed, and that was the entire problem. And how in the hell he was supposed to sleep next to Quill that night, he had no clue.

Chapter Eleven

Quill had almost lost his damn mind back there on the ridge, almost kissed Owen, and as they headed back to the center where warmth and a long night ahead waited for them, he honestly didn't know if he could be that strong a second time.

And it wasn't that Owen had looked particularly sexy in his many layers of winter gear. No, it had all been about the joy in his eyes, the way he'd looked out over the place Quill loved with every gnarled fiber of his being. Owen's reverence and awe had hit a deep, powerful chord within him. A resonant bass note of understanding that made his soul, not his lips, not his libido, want a piece of Owen.

Owen might not be sticking around, but he got this place in the way few others did, saw what Quill saw, and that was heady stuff. Enough to make Quill stand too close, wanting...hell, he still wasn't sure exactly what, but he'd pulled back in the nick of time.

As they let themselves back into the entryway of the center, he tried telling himself that he'd saved them both a load of embarrassment. Maybe Owen didn't even want to kiss again. But that was a load of bunk. He'd seen the recognition in Owen's eyes, the quick acceptance of the almost inevitable...

No, pulling back had been all Quill and all about his tenuous hold on his sense of self-preservation.

"We can heat up some cans of soup on the wood-stove," Owen suggested brightly, apparently oblivious to Quill's inner turmoil. Which was good. He didn't need both of them in knots, even if some petty part of himself wouldn't mind not being the only one out here floundering.

"Soup sounds good." Quill stowed his gear but left his coat on until he was upstairs in front of the heater. They'd spent way too long in the generator room, point-less fiddling with the lifeless hunk of metal that had served no purpose other than chilling them further. After stoking the fire, he warmed his hands back and forth while Owen produced a pan and two cans of soup.

"Here." Quill had a can opener on his pocketknife, and he made fast work of the lids. They made a way-too-comfortable team, and it wasn't long before they were back on the couch, big bowls of soup in their laps as they ate in quiet companionship. The soup was to-mato, a classic that never got old for Quill, but this time it was Owen's closeness that warmed him through, not the familiar flavors.

"This is nice," Owen observed. He'd doctored his bowl with various herbs, and the rich smell of oregano assaulted Quill's senses, made the comforting and time-worn new and edgy again. This...thing happening be-tween them was many things, but *nice* wasn't the word Quill would have chosen. Disturbingly cozy perhaps.

But he wasn't going to try to explain that, so he simply nodded. "Yeah. Yours smells good."

He knew by now that food was an easy topic to get Owen going on, and sure enough, he smiled wide as he held up the spoon. "Yeah. The herbs make a big difference in cutting the canned taste. Want to try?"

"Nah." No way was Quill letting Owen feed him, so he shook his head even as his throat tightened, a bizarre want rising in his chest.

After they'd rinsed the bowls and pan, the late-afternoon sun was all but gone. Quill brought out his emergency propane lanterns and lined up the flashlights they might need later before returning to the couch. He told himself that it was because it was the warmest spot in the room, but the real draw was Owen, who'd been busy exploring the shelves that lined the far wall, and was now sprawled on the end of the couch, shuffling a deck of playing cards.

"Do you play?" he asked Quill.

"Yeah," he admitted. Lying to get out of further interaction felt low, and besides, he was already here. Might as well give his hands something to do other than itch to touch Owen. "Fifteen years with Hattie meant a fair number of hands of gin rummy. Played a lot of speed and spades in college, and my grandfather and I used to play blackjack and other games on camping trips."

Those were some of the warmer childhood memories—Grandpa letting him win, no bickering or fighting out at the hunting cabin, big mugs of hot cocoa in front of them. He still missed that old cabin, missed the escape it had represented. And much as his family was complicated now, he missed the way Grandpa had unified all of them, a larger-than-life patriarch holding them together.

"My grandmother is the one who taught me rummy." Owen offered him a winsome smile that rewarded Quill's honesty with more warmth than the roaring fire. "Want to play a few hands?"

"Sure." Quill arranged himself so that he faced Owen and turned up one of the lanterns on the coffee table so that they could see the cards.

"Good. I did way too many solitaire games while in chemo." Not surprisingly, Owen assigned himself dealer first, shuffling with ease and dealing them each their ten-card hand.

"What did your oncologist think of your bucket-list plan?" The question had been on Quill's mind awhile now, a nagging worry about Owen's continued health.

"She loved it. I sent her a postcard from Space Camp this summer, and she hung it in the office." Owen arranged his cards in a fan, mouth twisting as he studied them. "Testicular cancer has a pretty low recurrence rate, even cases like mine where both surgery and chemo were indicated. Obviously regular checkups are key, but I saw her in September, and everything was looking good."

"And you don't have…uh…lingering effects from the treatment?" Quill's neck went hot and itchy as Owen raised an aristocratic eyebrow. Fuck. Too personal a question, but he couldn't call it back before Owen answered.

"Are you asking if I can still get it up? Pretty sure I answered that question for you already…" Owen's eyes sparkled in the firelight, and at the memory of their kiss, Quill's body sparked like a stray ember had hit it. And yeah, no way was he forgetting that Owen had been impressively hard.

"Not that." God, even Quill's ears were warm with embarrassment. "Meant if you had pain… Never mind. It was prying."

"It's okay." Owen reached over and patted Quill's knee. "I was a little snappy there. It's more that I hate it sometimes because as soon as I say what type of cancer it was, a lot of people think it's open season to talk about my balls. And most know enough to know that treatment usually means removing the cancerous one, and I hate that look on their faces."

"What look?"

"The same one you got a second ago when I said *removing*. You winced. All guys do. No one wants to be down a testicle, and everyone gets weirdly sympathetic like I had to turn in my man card or something, like the surgery and not the cancer was the worst thing to happen to me."

"Sorry." Quill resisted the urge to shift in his seat because he was pretty sure that he had cringed exactly like that.

"The truth is that surgery was less a big deal than the lymph node procedure they had to do to stage the cancer and reduce the risk of recurrence, which was far more complex. I was lucky to get one of the few surgeons in the country who's skilled at doing it laparoscopically, and even with avoiding an open operation, the recovery still sucked. And the two cycles of chemo were when I had most of the side effects. But everyone wants to focus on the loss of the testicle—even strangers ask me if I can still come."

"None of their business." Quill studied his cards because he *was* curious about that, didn't know enough about how that worked post-surgery, but he figured he could look it up next time he had internet. It shouldn't be on Owen to educate people.

"Well...not *everyone*'s business." Owen shrugged, voice returning to his usual light tones, but there was also something new there, an edge perhaps, or maybe a challenge. "I didn't get a prosthetic, so I do usually warn a guy before we get intimate, and sometimes I climax dry, but even though I'm a chatty guy, that's not exactly stuff I want to discuss with someone's grandma from Wichita on a random plane flight, you know?"

"Yeah." Quill's voice came out rough because his brain had tripped right past logistics to imagining what Owen's face would look like when he came, how he'd sound, whether he'd maintain his usual talkative take-charge personality the whole way through or whether he'd lose control...

Stop it. Owen was talking about the rudeness of prying people, not giving Quill an opportunity to perv on him.

"Anyway, shall we play? To a hundred?" Owen waved his cards. There was a vulnerability around his eyes that made Quill's stomach flutter. No matter how flippant Owen tried to play it, this cancer stuff clearly affected him, and Quill wished he had some way to reassure him. The urge to pull Owen to him was damn near overwhelming, but more than simply the pile of cards between them held him back.

"Yeah." He passed on taking the upcard, preferring to stand pat, but Owen quickly scooped up the card. He was a quick, decisive player, which Quill had expected, knocking to score points far more frequently than Quill, leaving Quill scrambling to lay off his deadwood unmatched cards by finding homes for them within Owen's melds, the groups of cards he was attempting to score from. Not surprisingly, Owen took the first game easily, but Quill came back on the second when Owen overgambled and Quill undercut his attack, scoring more points even though Owen was the aggressor.

"We should play for something." Even with the loss, Owen was back to his usual cheer. "A bet maybe."

"What did you have in mind?" Quill had played for chores with Hattie and various crazy bets back in college, but somehow he didn't think Owen would be satisfied playing for dish duty.

"Hmm…how about we play for who gets the couch tonight? Unless it pulls out, in which case we can just share."

A strangled cough escaped Quill's throat before he could call it back. "No, no hide-a-bed."

"Darn." Owen winked at him, the flirtiest he'd been since the training in Anchorage. And damn it, Quill liked it. A lot. "I've got a nice arctic rated sleeping bag, so floor won't be awful, but it might be fun to play for it."

"Sure." Quill had every intention of throwing the game so that Owen got the couch. He was the volunteer, after all, and Quill had plenty of experience roughing it. But then Owen dealt the cards, and Quill got a killer hand, and Owen made a crack about Quill's conservative play style, and suddenly his long dormant competitive side came out of storage.

"Now, this is *fun*." Owen grinned at him, even as Quill pulled ahead in points. "You should play like this all the time. Take a few risks. It won't kill you."

Quill snorted. "That's the thing with risks—people never expect them to fail. Better to plan for the worst-case scenario, if you ask me."

"I suppose then you can be pleasantly surprised." Owen shrugged, swimmer's shoulders rippling under his green sweater. "That or you miss out altogether."

Not entirely sure that they were still talking about cards, Quill swallowed against a sudden surge of emotion. He didn't usually care what he missed out on, figuring he'd leave the adrenaline rushes to crazy kids, but something about Owen made him want to leap without looking, just once, if only to see what it felt like to fly before the inevitable crash.

Distracted, he missed his next chance to undercut Owen as the points evened out. Because the points were inching toward one hundred, the next few turns would likely be decisive. And something in Quill wanted to prove Owen wrong, wanted to show him that he wasn't some stick-in-the-mud. So, he knocked before Owen could beat him to it, trying to trust his cards and ignore his gut, which said to wait a turn.

And immediately paid the price, Owen gleefully taking the undercut, collecting his points and calling game. Fuck.

"Best two out of three?" Owen was practically bouncing in his seat, triumph radiating off him in a way that was sexy as fuck.

"Nah. You won fair and square." Quill wouldn't let it be said he was a sore loser. "I've got a camping mat in addition to sleeping bags. I'll be okay."

"I'm not sleepy yet." Owen's mouth quirked, a devious glint in his eyes that made Quill's toes curl in his boots. Despite the fire, the temperature in the building was dropping with the night winds and storm picking up outside, and Quill couldn't help a shiver. Or maybe that was all Owen and his nearness. He was no longer certain about anything.

"We can keep playing," he offered, words doing nothing to cut the charged energy gathering between them. "You want a blanket first though? Don't want you getting chilled."

"I'm good. Fire's doing a way better job than I'd expected. I mean I'm not about to propose we play strip rummy next, but I'm not freezing."

"No one's stripping," Quill said quickly, even as he couldn't get the image of Owen peeling off that fuzzy sweater out of his head.

"Of course not." Owen shook his head, a weariness in his eyes like he hadn't expected any more from Quill. "It wouldn't be *professional*."

Not entirely sure what was coming over him, Quill growled low, not liking how quick Owen was to dismiss him and wanting to push that judgment from his expression. And there it was, that urge again, to leap and understand the adrenaline that everyone else seemed to run on. Words would be nice, but they failed him then, some baser part of him taking over before he could stop it, and then he was leaning in, claiming Owen's mouth in a decisive kiss, swallowing his gasp of surprise.

Cards fluttered to the floor as Owen looped his arms around Quill's shoulders, pulled him closer. Unlike their first kiss, he seemed content to let Quill lead, let Quill plunder his mouth until they were both breathing hard.

"Oh, *hello*." He grinned up at Quill, and this would be the perfect moment to pull away, regain his sanity, but Quill didn't. Couldn't. Was rooted to the damn couch, awkward angle looming over Owen and all.

"Sor—"

"Don't you dare apologize. If I said I *was* cold, would you warm me up?"

"How cold?" Quill, who didn't flirt, was doing a damn good approximation of it, voice still low and husky and the word *no* nowhere near his lips.

"Very." Owen pulled him down for another kiss, and Quill let himself slide that much closer to hell. And if he was going to be damned, if he was going to let go of professionalism for the sake of a kiss and try to fly instead of sticking to safe zones, then it was going to be a good kiss, one that let him taste as much of Owen as he'd been craving.

Slowing down from his initial attack, he took his time, exploring the curve of Owen's full lower lip, tongue detouring to trace his devastating dimples before seeking entry to his mouth. As their tongues tangled together, Owen hooked a leg around Quill's calf, urging him with his hands and legs to fall more completely on top of him.

"Fuck." Quill had to groan as their bodies met, torsos aligning, Owen wiggling about until their groins were rubbing right along with their tongues, a subtle rocking that mimicked the slow dance of their mouths. Quill might have not spent the past twenty years entirely celibate, but it had been so damn long since he'd made out like this, kissed and kissed with no end in sight, no end goal, that he felt like parched August earth, needing Owen like a garden needed rain, soaking up everything he had to give.

At some point, the dynamic shifted, Owen taking over, his tongue fucking its way into Quill's mouth, a deep, dirty rhythm that Quill welcomed with a low moan. Decades separated him from the last time he'd climaxed from nothing more than grinding and kissing, but he could feel it bearing down on him, like an iceberg of need breaking free from his usual icy glacier of self-control.

"Want skin." Owen pulled Quill's uniform shirt loose from his pants, taking his thermal undershirt with it. His hand was cool on Quill's superheated skin, raising goose bumps and making him shiver and not only from the contact.

"Damn. It *is* cold."

"Sorry. We'll just have to keep each other warm. It's practically medicinal at this point, right? Huddling together for warmth is supposed to help avoid hypothermia…"

"I don't think we're in any danger of that." Quill tried for stern and failed miserably, voice still sounding like he'd been pounding back Jack.

"We can pretend." Owen pulled Quill down for another kiss, pausing long enough to add, "And it sure feels like I might die if I don't get more of this."

"Yeah." Quill didn't even bother denying it because that was exactly how his racing pulse felt, urgent and needy, shutting everything else except for Owen's next kiss, which arrived hot and demanding. He lost himself to it, letting Owen carry him along, only vaguely aware of agile fingers working his belt free.

Then Owen's fingers were stroking him through his boxer briefs, and he almost lost it right then. Bracing himself on one arm, he gave Owen more room to work. He didn't waste any time either, shoving Quill's boxers down, freeing his throbbing cock.

"Holy fuck," he breathed against Owen's mouth, barely able to hang on as he started a fast, tight stroke, as sure as if he'd been in charge of Quill's cock for years, knew exactly what he needed. It had been so long since he'd had anyone else's hand on his cock, but even more than the novelty, it was Owen's kiss, his scent and taste, that pushed Quill up against the edge. He wanted to touch Owen too, wanted so much that his brain could scarcely hold the list of needs, but right then all he could do was pant, eyes squishing shut.

"That's it. Like that." Owen broke away from the kiss, stroking Quill's face and neck with his free hand before that hand dipped lower. A single flick against his balls. That was all it took before Quill was coming, not even present enough to grunt out a warning or care where his spunk landed. No, all he could do was shudder over and over as that glacier he'd built up so carefully over years collapsed, all control shattered.

"Oh my God." As the pure, white-hot pleasure faded, cool embarrassment seeped in. "Didn't mean to…"

"I did." Owen's head tipped back, hands releasing Quill to tug at his own zipper. And damn. Quill knew enough to know that he was supposed push aside his lethargy and get Owen off. Especially after the way he'd shot with no warning, getting them both all messy. But if Owen cared, he wasn't showing it, hand a blur on his thick cock, body stiffening. And like on the ridge earlier, Quill was powerless to do anything other than watch the way joy transformed Owen's face, smoothing his angular features, brightening his skin and eyes. When he came, Owen's expression was almost beatific, embracing the pleasure with his whole being in a way Quill wasn't sure he'd seen before.

Owen's sweater was now a total wreck, and his fingers glistened with come, and the sight was so hot that Quill had to restrain the urge to grab Owen's hand and lick it clean, but he'd undoubtedly shocked them both enough for one evening. Surprisingly, he didn't have his usual post-sex slightly queasy, empty feeling, but regret and embarrassment were doing a pretty good job as stand-ins.

"We're a mess." Straightening, he retreated to his end of the couch, trying in vain to right his clothes.

"I know." Owen grinned like this was the best news in the world, shrugging out of his sweater, revealing a T-shirt advertising some tech company. Damn. They hadn't even gotten all the way naked, and Quill still felt stripped bare, secret cupboards of wants and needs wide open for Owen's inspection. "And okay, yeah, it's cold now. I'm going to go collect my sleeping bag and bedding, and then you can warm me up some more, Ranger."

Owen's tease hit him like an icy rain, the reminder that he was undoubtedly one more item on Owen's bucket list. Be snowbound, fuck a ranger…all part of the adventure for him. Sighing as he grabbed a flashlight, Quill headed for his room, changed clothes in the frigid air, and put on layers of flannel and thermal shirts like that could be enough to ward off the temptation for a repeat. Part of him wanted to remain in here, freezing temperatures be damned. Surely hypothermia would be preferable to whatever awkward conversation came next. What the fuck was he supposed to do now? How did he find his footing after losing the whole goddamn trail of noble intentions that he based his life around? He was lost with no rescue in sight and only himself to blame.

Chapter Twelve

Owen knew as soon as Quill emerged from his room that there probably wasn't going to be more making out on the agenda. Regret and self-recrimination practically rolled off him, apparent in the slump of his broad shoulders, the heavier-than-usual tread of his feet, and the defeated huffs of breath. Indeed, Quill gave the couch wide berth, unrolling an inflatable mat and sleeping bags and blankets in front of the stove. He spent a long time not looking at Owen, fiddling with his bedding, and then messing with the fire.

Despite the fire, the room really was starting to get chilly, and since snuggling up for warmth apparently wasn't going to happen, Owen spread out his sleeping bag on the couch and crawled inside, all in less time than it took Quill to continue his show of avoiding Owen.

"You know, instead of fluffing your sleeping bag for the fifth time, you could try talking to me." Owen tried to keep his voice a light tease, but some of his frustration edged its way in.

"Sorry." Quill still didn't glance over at Owen, instead finally lying down, wiggling into his bag. He had on what looked to be thermal underwear underneath flannel pajamas. It was sweet and old-fashioned and with both of them in their sleeping bags, the whole thing could have a fun camping vibe if only Quill didn't seem so determined to make this awkward. "Not much to say, other than that I'm sorry. Not sure what came over me. Got carried away, and it won't happen again."

"I like what came over you. Very much. And I think it totally *should* happen again. I want it. You want it. We're both consenting single adults, and literally no one else needs to know about what we do with our off-time. I'm not planning on outing you, Quill."

A long-term relationship with a closeted guy still wasn't on Owen's to-do list, but he'd happily take a secret fling, especially if it made it easier to get through this winter. And having had a taste of the passion Quill concealed beneath his stoic exterior, he wanted more however he could get it.

Quill was silent a long moment, then huffed out a harsh breath. "I appreciate that. But it still can't happen again. I'm practically your boss—"

"Except for the fact that you're not. You're really not. As far I know, they don't even have you write an evaluation of me at the end of the season. It's a volunteer position. I already turned down the subsistence payment. My supervisor, such as it is, is your friend the volunteer coordinator. You and I work together, sure, but I'd call us associates, not boss and employee at all. With my finance background, I do get ethics implications for such things, but that's not the case here."

"Ethics goes deeper than merely a signing-paychecks thing. I don't want to take advantage of you."

Owen had to laugh at that. "If anyone's taking advantage here, it's me. And I meant it when I said I wasn't going to push, but I'm also not going to lie and pretend I don't want something on the regular with you."

"I…" Quill finally looked his way but still didn't meet Owen's eyes. "I don't do relationships."

"No one's asking you to waltz down an aisle. I'm talking about hooking up because it's convenient, and we both want to."

"I'm not here to be your drive-through *convenient* sex fix." The way Quill's face shuttered told Owen that he'd chosen the exact wrong wording. "Good night."

"Wait. I'm sorry. I didn't mean—"

"Yeah, you kind of did." Quill shook his head, disgust clear in his eyes.

"Well, I'm sorry. I didn't mean that I don't like you. I do." Owen had a feeling he was digging his grave deeper, so he shut up, swallowing back further explanation, and tried a different tactic. "Who was he anyway?"

"Who was who?"

"The guy who turned you so off relationships."

"Who says there was a guy?" Quill's tone was more wary than bluster. But Owen knew he was right. It wasn't so much Quill's insistence that he was married to the job as much as the way he kissed. He kissed like a guy who'd had it before, but under that experience was an undercurrent of hurt and longing. Quill wasn't simply a man ending a long dry spell. No, his hunger had a depth to it. He'd had someone once. Owen was sure of it.

"There was a guy. Your friend in college perhaps?"

"You adding mindreading lessons to that bucket list of yours?"

"So I'm right?" Owen all but crowed, sitting up so he could see Quill better.

"It's not something I talk about." Quill was hedging

rather than outright lying, which Owen found strangely endearing.

"Maybe you should start. My sister's a therapist. She's a big believer in talking helping people let go of stuff. I'm inclined to agree."

"You're inclined to talk anyway," Quill pointed out. "Not all of us need to air our business to make sense of it. It was what it was, and it's been twenty years. I'm not pining."

"Maybe not pining, but there's no expiration date on hurt."

"I'm not hurt." Quill's tone was defiant, but Owen still believed he was lying. Someone had hurt him and hurt him good. And Owen already wanted to drop-kick whoever this college guy had been. "If anything, the experience proved to me that relationships are far too much trouble. Including the short-term, regular-sex kind you seem fond of. Any sort of relationship always brings drama. Not worth it."

"If you really believe that, you haven't had much good sex. Or a good relationship."

Quill scoffed. "All sex is pretty similar when it comes right down to it. It's messy and complicated, and honestly, not that much different from jacking off except for the awkward after."

"We could be having more sex, not an awkward after." Owen resisted the urge to add an eye roll. "And messy is fun. Don't make me come over there and prove it to you. If that truly wasn't better than jacking off, I wasn't trying hard enough. You should let me redeem myself."

Even in the firelight he could see Quill's deep blush. "It was…okay. Better than okay. But that's rare—"

"Which is all the more reason why we should do it more."

"I'm too tired to argue this more." Quill let out a yawn that sounded fake, but Owen knew when a strategic retreat was in order. They weren't going to settle anything that night. Quill was determined to be stubborn, and Owen wasn't going to strong-arm him into a round two. Even if part of him was tempted to use the falling temperatures as an excuse to get Quill to share body heat, the only thing worse than no cuddling would be reluctant snuggling with a guy who couldn't seem to let himself enjoy anything. Which was sad, really, and added to Owen's chill, the idea of how much Quill denied himself, and the unexpected desire to be the one to give him a taste of what he'd been missing.

"It's going to end up being a ten-dollar-part fix, isn't it?" Quill shifted his weight from foot to foot in the chilly generator room, waiting for the repair technician to finish his assessment. Ron was an older, rail-thin man Quill had worked with before, who had a habit of sucking his teeth while he worked. Okay enough guy unless one made the mistake of letting him talk politics, which Quill had learned his lesson about and tried to keep the focus on the still nonfunctional generator.

"Not this time." Ron straightened. "You weren't wrong about there being a short, and it's fixable, but truth is this generator has seen better days."

"Department's not going to replace it any time soon." Of that, Quill was sure. Hell, just getting the repair order invoice through all the necessary bureaucracy would be a challenge.

"Well, then you're gonna have to baby it along this

winter, be careful not to overload it. It's not recycling the heat as well as the newer models either. You might have to deal with being colder than last year. I can get you running again, but I bet this isn't my last visit here this winter."

"Let's hope you're wrong." Quill wasn't looking forward to telling Owen about rationing electricity and the possibility of their quarters being colder. Not that he wanted to talk to Owen period. They'd made stilted conversation that morning, Owen making him coffee and oatmeal along with another "this only has to be awkward if you let it" pronouncement that Quill had only been able to make a noncommittal noise at. But Owen's cheerfulness aside, it was a pointless warning. Things were already uncomfortable, had been the second his heart rate had returned to normal. Every interaction felt clumsier, like he couldn't stop tripping over his words and intentions.

Owen had been so damn rational the night before, laying out a case for them having something of a… what? Fling? Hookup arrangement? Friends with benefits? Quill wasn't sure exactly what to call it other than not happening. He didn't want to be a convenient fuck for Owen, and that even more than ethics had kept him rooted to his sleeping mat. Owen might be able to flit from lover to lover, celebrating the benefits of regular sex, but that wasn't how Quill was wired. The last thing he wanted was to get attached to Owen, come to depend on him, when all he could ever be was temporary. Missing something was worse than never having it at all—Quill knew that better than most.

And weirdly, he hadn't wanted to talk about JP in years, about what he missed, what he'd had, but something about Owen had made it hard not to open up, had had his lips clenching around unspoken words that wanted to spring forth. It was bad enough that his body wanted to yield to Owen's suggestions. He wasn't going to make the mistake of bringing his mind along for the ride as well. He'd woken up in the middle of the night, chilled despite the warmth of the stove, and he'd been unable to help glancing back at the couch. If Owen had asked to huddle for warmth again, he'd been sleepy enough and stupid enough to say yes. But Owen had slumbered on, oblivious to Quill's continued mental gymnastics.

The flip-flopping had continued all morning, and the wait for Ron to make his pronouncement didn't help matters any.

"It'll take me an hour or so to take apart this wiring harness, get it back together." Straightening at last, Ron punctuated his words with a clicking sound.

"Anything I can do to help?"

"Nah. But Hattie always kept the coffee on. Your new boy do the same? I wouldn't turn down a cup to warm up after."

Quill's neck muscles coiled, tension radiating down his spine. Hattie would have been quick with a remark to put Ron back on his heels, and indeed, Owen himself probably would have had the right cutting defense. But part of Quill was thrust back in time, on the school bus, older boys hurling insults, him unable to think of a single comeback, and he had to struggle not to stammer.

"Owen's our new winter volunteer, yet he's not a kid—older than most of the recent grads who take these slots. Great guy." His words kept on tumbling out as he tried and failed to cover his discomfort. Even now, he hated conflict, hated how it made his gut churn and muscles tense as his words turned into soggy cereal, not good for much. "The coffeepot's electric, so no go until you get things running. But Hattie left her French press behind. I'll rustle you up a cup myself."

"Appreciate it. And I'll bet you twenty he doesn't last until Christmas. He's got Left Coast written all over him." Ron shook his head. He'd met Owen when he'd arrived, as Quill and Owen had brought Ron and his equipment in on the snowmachine from the main road. Owen had headed back out to check the state of latrines and trash barrels. That and perhaps he'd sensed that the three of them in the generator room would be a tight fit in more than one sense.

"He'll last." Quill wasn't sure why he was defending Owen so firmly. He'd had plenty of similar doubts himself about Owen's suitability, but something about Ron's tone had him bristling. Maybe standing up for himself was still a sore spot, but he wasn't going to let Ron insult Owen—he'd brave all the discomfort of conflict to keep someone from bullying him.

Unfortunately, Ron didn't seem content to leave it, clucking again. "Gotta get you a wife, Ranger. Girlfriend back in Wasilla. Something. Don't want people thinking—"

Quill let out a warning growl at that. "They won't."

And this was exactly why he kept his personal life private. Homophobic idiots resided all over the country, and he simply wasn't cut out to be a flag bearer. He wasn't going to let Ron get away with any cracks at Owen, but somewhere deep inside Quill was that skinny, shy eleven-year-old who'd borne the brunt of teasing from the older boys and the pointed digs at home when he'd complained. Even his beloved grandfather had told him to man up. He'd come a long way from those years, but he'd never learned to like being the center of attention or gossip. Speculation like Ron's always felt like burrs worming their way under whatever armor he'd built up, heartbeats away from those insults and slurs that had made his younger years such misery.

"Maybe." Ron shrugged. "Just saying. You've gotta be missing Hattie. Damn shame they gave you some… city slicker." Ron's pause said he'd considered several less charitable labels. And it said something else that apparently he'd never picked up on Hattie being a lesbian in years of contact but had clued in to Owen's orientation in fifteen minutes of interaction.

"We'll manage just fine. I'm gonna go check on some things, let you work. I'll check back in a while." He had to get out of the small space before the walls closed in on him and he said something he'd regret later. There weren't a ton of generator repair specialists as experienced as Ron, but hell if Quill wouldn't be happy to see the last of him.

Up in the quarters, he made a quick round of coffee in the French press, putting Ron's cup in an old travel mug he didn't care about getting back. He also took a moment to check his phone messages including two from Hattie, neither of which seemed that urgent, but he didn't want to make her wait. He wanted to be a good friend, but his insides still wobbled with worry that she'd be able to guess what had happened between him and Owen the night before. Seeing as how her gaydar was far better than Ron's, she too had to have figured out about Owen's orientation. And all morning, he'd felt like he must have a neon sign following him, announcing their make-out session. Which was ridiculous, but there he was, still fretting.

Hattie answered her work line with a cheery greeting followed by "I hear you spent a cold night yesterday. The repair guy make it up after the plows?"

"It wasn't too bad," Quill lied, not wanting to open himself up to further questioning. "We managed."

"Good. Owen's working out, then? Keeping up with the workload?"

"He's doing fine." Like with Ron, he found himself vaguely protective of Owen, not wanting to share any of his own doubts. "He did a great job with an injured hiker a few days back. Handled it like a seasoned pro, even."

"That's great news," Hattie enthused. "Speaking of seasoned pro, that's why I was trying to reach you. There's a rumor going around that the Ranger in Charge at Mat-Su is retiring. Everyone I talk to thinks you should apply."

"Me? No way."

"Quill. You've spent twenty years in the same pay grade. No one is more qualified than you to move into management."

"Management means people. I don't do people," he reminded her. "Hiring, firing…that's not me. And you know that. Fieldwork is where I'm at."

"Yeah, but are you happy? Is this really what you want for the rest of your working life?"

Quill stopped for a second, the memory of Owen's face full of wonder out on the ridge yesterday burning bright in his brain. "Yeah. I think I am happy."

He left the second question untouched. What he

wanted was consistency and stability. Any other stray wants didn't matter.

"I worry about you without me there. I bet you go days without talking much to Owen even."

She wasn't wrong, so Quill simply sighed. "Not everyone needs conversation."

"Yes, but everyone needs friends. And even if you don't want to think about the RIC position, maybe it's time you thought about living off-site. No more sharing space with volunteers. You could get to town more often, maybe have—"

"I've got what I need. No need to move." Even if moving off-site would mean no more temptation from Owen, he wasn't even going to consider it. Remembering Ron's warning about a long cold winter, he knew he was being stubborn and setting himself up for succumbing to Owen's charms. Again. But talking about moving seemed a lot like admitting defeat. He wanted to believe he had more self-control than that.

Liar. You just want more time with Owen. The other part of his brain, the baser part that had taken over last night, taunted him. This had nothing to do with the logic of not moving or proving himself or anything else rational. He simply didn't want to give up the frequent contact with Owen.

Not that he was going to explain that to Hattie. Better that she know him as a loner, a guy who needed no one, and not as the guy who looked forward to Owen's easy smiles and little jokes. As his friend, he doubted she'd care much about the possible ethics implications of him getting involved with Owen, and indeed would probably cheer him on. But he didn't want that. Matchmaking was as bad as censure as far as he was concerned.

And Hattie was hardly the only one in the department. Others might take a different view, one more like Ron's narrow-minded way of seeing the world.

It might not cost him his job, but coming out publicly would change the way people saw him, interacted with him, and he was loath to go there. Pointed whispers would follow him the rest of his career. He'd seen it with Hattie. People certainly respected her, but she was also "that lesbian ranger," the one asked to do every diversity presentation and panel. In many ways, she was defined more by her orientation than by her years of service. Quill wasn't ever going to be ready to have all eyes on him like that. And maybe that meant that he still hadn't distanced himself enough from that inner wounded kid, but at this point it was what it was.

And if that knowledge made him sigh a little deeper, made his hands feel heavier after making Hattie tell him about the baby nursery plans, that was simply the price he paid for this life. Which he hadn't been lying about. He did love his job, didn't want to leave it. It was everything he'd needed for years now. Nothing, not even the appearance of one irresistible optimist, was going to change who he was, what he needed, and who he'd always be. There was no sense in getting wistful over a life that simply wasn't meant for him.

Chapter Thirteen

Restless energy was the worst. And restlessness combined with lack of human interaction had Owen's pulse speeding up as the sound of the door registered over his music, even though he knew chances were slim for anything other than a few moments of distraction.

"Bored?" Instead of heading straight to his quarters, Quill paused to stare at Owen the way he might if Owen had taken to juggling the canned goods. Which, come to think of it, wasn't a half-bad idea. Might be a fun skill to learn.

"Yeah." Pulling off his headphones and straightening from the half-crouch he'd been in, Owen didn't bother denying it. Quill had been in his downstairs office the past few hours, and like Owen, he was bundled in several layers, thermal shirt peeking out near the collar of his uniform shirt, and a jacket over those. Owen had a similar three-shirt layer thing happening and had added fingerless gloves. "And cold. Exercise keeps me warmer."

Nasty winds whipped at the building, another storm rolling in, the unusually snowy November keeping both of them indoors for much of what Quill described as the lull between first snow and Thanksgiving weekend, when everyone would come out to play. They'd flock to the trails Owen was painstakingly helping groom, and the increased tourist traffic would undoubtedly keep both him and Quill hopping. He honestly couldn't wait for the influx. But until then he had hours to fill. At least the generator was functional now, but the building was still cold with electricity at a premium. They had to carefully monitor the load, not use as many space heaters and other power hogs.

Owen's room was particularly chilly, hence why he was out in the common room doing his body weight HIIT routine, using the short bursts of exercise followed by active rest to keep him warm and in the shape he needed to be in to handle all the grueling work with the snow. The dig out tomorrow from this latest round wouldn't be fun.

"Don't you exercise?" he asked Quill, who seemed to have one of those infuriating muscular builds that ran on coffee and double-decker sandwiches and lots of hard outdoor work with no need for formal workouts.

"Some." Quill shrugged. "Pushups and sit-ups when I think of it, but nothing complicated like what you were doing. Looked like you were stalking small game under brush."

A rare smile tugged at Quill's mouth, which made Owen grin back. Man, he wished he knew what to do to get that smile more often. Maybe he should do crocodile lunges more often if that was what it took. Quill seemed determined to keep up the avoidance routine. Oh, he was cordial enough, and his note each morning was unfailingly pleasant, but they weren't exactly friends, not the way Owen wanted. Yet. Owen still hadn't given up trying for friendship. And while his hope of a repeat of making out had dimmed somewhat, he wasn't about to toss in the towel there either.

"We should work out together," Owen suggested, already knowing what Quill's answer was likely to be.

"Nah. I'll leave you to it." Quill rubbed his chin. While usually clean-shaven, he had a little bit of scruff going that only made him that much sexier. "We've got to get you a hobby though. You're gonna wear out the floorboards by January if you've already got cabin fever now."

Owen liked the sound of that *we* far more than he should. "Since when do you care if I make it to January?"

"I care." A faint flush stained Quill's cheeks. "I mean, it's a lot of work around here, and you've been a big help. Not sure Hattie could find a replacement on short notice. That's all."

"You like me around. Admit it." Owen kept his voice teasing, but it really would be nice to be wanted for more than simply his muscles and work ethic.

"You're not bad. Good roommate. Could be a lot worse, that's for sure."

"High praise." Owen rolled his eyes at Quill's guarded compliments.

"Sorry." Quill looked down. "You're a good person. Not your fault that things are…complicated."

"Hella awkward you mean?" Owen went ahead and charged after the big moose in the room. "And me getting a hobby is going to fix that?"

"Dunno." Rubbing the base of his neck, Quill kept his gaze averted. "Maybe."

"Well, I don't exactly have one. Even the last six months or so while doing the bucket-list thing, I've kept too busy for hobbies other than the odd game here or there. And before cancer, it was work, work, work, and socializing with not much time for anything else. Unless we're going to count sex or jerking off in creative ways as a hobby..." He threw that out there simply to watch Quill blush further.

And Quill's long, slow blink was more than gratifying. "Uh...no. Not counting... What the heck is creative... Oh, never mind."

"You want examples?" Baiting Quill was an even better distraction than exercise had been.

"As far as I know, there's only so many ways..." Quill shook his head, but his voice had turned huskier than usual.

"Man, how did you reach forty with such a narrow worldview?"

"I'm not narrow-minded." Bristling, Quill's eyes flashed with more ire than Owen would have suspected.

"Didn't say you were. Just meant that you're limited. Sexually. Missing out."

"Just because I don't go all fancy getting off or make it a production doesn't mean I'm a prude or something." Quill's defensiveness had Owen laughing, because seriously the guy was just too cute when he got all flustered.

And flustered and sparring with him was far preferable to being alone in here. "No, but it does mean you could be having more fun than you are. I mean, why else would nature give us such a fun toy? Figuring out different ways to get off is like a rite of passage or something. And when one is between partners, investigating is better than the boredom of right hand, thirty-five well-placed strokes, and some tissues. You can't expect me to believe that in all your winters alone here that you've never experimented. I already figured out that streaming porn is a no-go here. So you've got to do *something.* No toy chest?"

"We should not be discussing this." Quill's voice was more rough than firm, which Owen took as a positive sign. "But not all men are ruled by their cocks. Or feel the need to celebrate something biological."

"Now that's just sad. Sex is a need. Unless you're ace, in which case I'm being a dick and I apologize, but assuming you've got a sex drive, it should be celebrated. Trust me. I went through some miserable weeks post-surgery and while in chemo, and I damn sure make a point of enjoying myself now."

"I'm not asexual." Quill huffed out a breath. "Although it might be easier in some ways if I was. But like J—a friend always said, it's on men to be more than their baser needs. Just because your body likes something doesn't mean that's reason to do it."

"Sure it is." Owen leaned against the back of the couch, studying Quill carefully. The guy simply was too tightly wound, and Owen had a feeling that this *friend* had more than a little to do with it. "If it's not hurting anyone, not illegal, and involves consenting adults, why not roll with it? Savor the fact that you're alive and that you get to feel so damn good, either alone or with someone else. Unless…does it not feel good? Like are you too up in your head about it to have a good time?"

Quill's blush spread to the tops of his ears. "It can feel good. I'm not… That is, I don't have hang-ups."

"It's okay if you do." Owen gentled his tone because he had a feeling Quill was lying, at least a little.

"Are you sure it's your sister who's the therapist?" Quill's eyes flitted between Owen and the door to his room, as if he were torn between escaping and continuing to argue his case.

"I'm not trying to analyze you. More like I'm offering to help. Give you ideas if you want. Ways to make your solo time more fun."

"A class in jerking off?" That got a laugh from Quill at last, deep and rich. "Does that come with hands-on demonstrations or is that extra tuition?"

"You want it to? You want to watch?" Owen tilted his head, taking in Quill's reaction, his swift intake of breath, flared nostrils, and heated eyes saying he liked that idea. A lot. "I mean, with the lack of porn here, it would practically be a public service, giving you a show."

"So noble of you." The turned-on look still hadn't left Quill's face, and when he shifted closer, Owen had to restrain himself from giving a cheer. "Forget focusing on my boring tastes. I think you *like* showing off. Maybe it's not that I'm a prude, but that you're too kinky for your own good."

"Oh yeah? Gonna teach me a lesson?" Owen wasn't usually one for role-play but if Quill needed a certain context, he could be adaptable. And Quill wasn't wrong. He could own having something of an exhibitionist streak. Eyes watching him got him almost as hot as touch.

"Thought you were the one doing the teaching." There it was, Quill's raspy laugh and warm breath close enough to tickle Owen's cheek as good as a victory lap.

"I could. Happily. But…" Owen took a deep breath because it would be too easy to simply fall into sexy play without further thought. "How many days of not speaking am I going to have to pay for the privilege?

I'm not saying I need after cuddles, but you not ignoring me would be a start. And I don't want you beating yourself up either. I'd like to give you a fun little show because I think we could both use that, but not if you're going to tell yourself that I took advantage or whatever."

"I'm sorry." Exhaling hard, Quill rolled his shoulders as if trying to rid himself of a heavy pack. "I've been an asshole since our...since we..."

"Got off gangbusters together?" Owen suggested.

"Yeah. That. I keep trying to be a damn professional where you're concerned. And failing. And that leaves me angry at myself, not you. But you don't deserve to be ignored just because I can't keep my mind where it needs to be."

"Quill." Owen looped his arms around Quill's neck, pulling him so that he was forced to meet Owen's gaze. "Stop fighting yourself. Seriously. If nothing else, you're going to injure something holding back so much. You're allowed to be attracted to me. And you're allowed to have some off-duty fun. So, why not go for it? Have a little fun with me and talk to me afterward. It's not that hard."

"That easy, huh?" Quill's voice was even lower now, face closer.

"That easy," Owen confirmed. Quill's lips were a mere fraction of an inch away, but Owen wasn't going to be the one to close the gap. He needed Quill to get over himself and choose this, choose him. Hell, choose *himself.* Quill deserved this, and Owen desperately needed him to see that.

"Fuck." The war was clear in Quill's eyes as was the moment he gave in, eyes shifting from icy to sapphire pools of desire. And when he claimed Owen's mouth, it was worth all the wait, victory sweeter because this wasn't only about distraction or the chance to show off. It was about what he wanted for Quill, the complex tangle of emotions he'd carried around for days now— hurt and frustration, sure, but also a level of caring he still wasn't sure he liked.

Owen tried to put all that into returning the kiss, trying to let Quill know how much he appreciated his courage, how much he wanted *him*, not simply another orgasm. Quill might have started it, a harsh slide of lips and tongue, but he yielded beautifully, mouth softly parting as Owen took over, demanding everything Quill had to give right then.

Quill tasted good, like coffee and something sweet. Perhaps he'd been sneaking Owen's chocolates. Owen smiled at that thought, chuckling lightly against Quill's lips because this felt so damn right. Felt like everything he'd been craving for days now, but even better than his memories of their last kiss. Less urgent. More like they were sealing some unsaid bargain or like they had more than enough time for all the exploration they both needed. And explore they did, lips and tongues playing with well-placed nips and sucks that ramped them both up without tipping over into some frantic rush.

As they stood there, arms pulling each other closer, Quill's kiss transformed, his quiet capitulation feeling less and less like a victory and more like a beginning. This wasn't merely Quill letting Owen kiss him. Rather, this was Quill deciding to embrace the experience. Maybe not wholeheartedly, not yet, but there was a certain acceptance, a softness maybe, to the way that Quill gave himself over to the kiss. So much so that Owen entirely forgot about his sexy proposition, content to kiss and rub and see what came next, but eventually they both pulled back to breathe, foreheads resting together.

And apparently Quill hadn't forgotten because he panted, "So...when does class start?"

"Class?" It took Owen a moment to catch up, and then he had to laugh at the rare lightness from Quill. "I like it when you joke. You should do it more. The world doesn't have to be so serious."

"Maybe not." Quill was looking down at Owen's groin when he said it, which made Owen snort-laugh again. Quill sex-drunk was almost too cute.

"You want a lesson? Now?"

Quill licked his lips taking a second before he slowly nodded. "Guess I do. God help—"

Cutting him off with a clucking noise, Owen put a finger over his lips. "Nuh-uh. No regrets. Remember?"

"Yeah." Quill nodded more readily this time, but Owen still doubted whether Quill would be able to stick to that, but he was damn well going to try his best to make him silence that inner critic of his. "So...uh... you're the expert here..."

Owen thought fast, trying to choreograph a fun scene on the fly. "My room's too cold. At least we've got the stove in here."

He didn't add that he was a little afraid that Quill might bolt if they moved to a bed too quickly. Besides, it was much easier to let himself tumble backward onto the couch, grin up at Quill's surprised face.

"Pull up a chair," he ordered as he sprawled out on the couch. If Quill wanted a show, Owen was determined to give him a good one. Hell, Owen wanted to give him so much that the intensity of his churning emotions almost scared him, gave him pause as he pulled off his gloves. This wasn't just some random hookup. Not a distraction. No, this was Quill, and Owen wanted to get it right in the worst way. And he might be the so-called sex expert here, but he was far out in uncharted waters, no clear plan forward, only him sinking deeper and deeper.

Chapter Fourteen

Quill didn't give himself much time to think as he dragged one the dining chairs near the stove, placing it with a good view of Owen and the couch. He might never recover from his insanity in giving in to Owen, but if he was going to do this, he wasn't going to do it by tentative half measures. And really, calling it *giving in* wasn't fair. This wasn't a case of Owen pressuring him into sex until Quill broke down. No, he needed to own his decision here. He'd kissed Owen. Again. He'd asked for this. Sure, Owen was willing, but the ultimate choice was on Quill, for better or worse, and he wasn't going to blame Owen.

Instead, he tried to let himself enjoy the spectacle of Owen pulling off his fingerless gloves and arranging himself facing Quill, feet on the floor, legs spread wide, hands resting on his waistline, teasing by framing his package and looping his fingers through his waistband. He wore stretchy athletic pants, probably double layered if he was as cold as he'd claimed, and another Stanford sweatshirt, which he pulled off to reveal a short-sleeved San Francisco Pride T-shirt over a black thermal shirt.

The happy rainbow on Owen's shirt reminded Quill

yet again how fleeting whatever it was they were doing had to be. Owen had a life to get back to, one where he was surrounded by like-minded friends and activities, experiences Quill couldn't give him.

"Sorry. It might be too chilly even with the stove for a full-on strip tease." Owen laughed, and its rich, musical tones washed over Quill, worked into all his empty, doubting places until he was chuckling too.

"We don't need you turning into an ice cube for the sake of sex."

"Oh, I dunno. There's a lot I'm willing to tolerate for the sake of good sex." Owen winked at him. "Now, on to Professor Owen's Jerk It 101 class. The easiest way to change it up is toys, but you claim to not have a toy box, and I didn't travel with mine."

"I've never seen the point in going into a sex shop when I've got two working hands." That and the embarrassment factor, but Quill didn't mention how his hands went clammy at the thought.

"There's this amazing thing called internet shopping now. You can order anything, and it comes in a little plain brown box. It's magical. And hands are fine, but kind of boring. And fingers can't reach everywhere, even if you're super bendy, which I'm not."

"I don't know. You looked pretty flexible earlier," Quill teased, not quite sure who this lighter version of himself was. "And uh…you don't seem like the toy type." Hot as the image was, he had a hard time picturing Owen fucking himself with some colorful toy. "Thought you're more take-charge."

"You mean I seem more toppy?" Fingering his waistband, teasing Quill with a flash of bare skin, Owen grinned like Quill had aced some quiz. "I am. Love to be in charge. But that doesn't mean I'm not capable of switching it up. And prior to the cancer, I liked prostate play on my own a lot." Making a face, he exhaled hard. "But surgery fucked with my nerve endings, and they haven't been the same. Hence not traveling with my toys."

"That sucks," Quill said, because Owen did seem sad about his body's changed reaction. But he couldn't help his brain flitting to JP and the way he'd scoffed at backdoor play in general and fucking specifically. And he reached for an old JP-ism to reassure Owen. "Plenty of people don't fuck, though. It's not the end all and be all of sex."

"Says you." Owen shook his head, laughing again. "Fucking is awesome. And I didn't say it was out of my repertoire entirely, especially topping. I'm not going to let cancer take that from me too. Anyway, back to jerking off."

"Yeah." Able to sense that Owen didn't want to dwell on cancer and what it had done to his body, Quill leaned forward, stopping the pretending that he was disinterested in the proceedings. "Show me what you've got, Teach."

"You've got it. Toys are great and so is playing with different lubes and slick things—oil, lotions, warming lubes, all that. You like it wet?"

"Yeah, but it gets things messy."

"And that's what showers are for." Owen pushed his waistband down, giving a tantalizing glimpse of his sharp hipbones and patch of hair. "Your homework assignment is to test out oil versus lube versus lotion and report back which you like best."

"There's homework?" Heat rushed to Quill's cock,

which loved this idea more than his logical brain, which
had always been a little appalled at the dirtiest of his
private desires. But Owen made it seem like those urges
were normal. Good even. He had a way of talking about
this stuff as if there was nothing Quill could confess
that would shock him, and that was refreshing. Freeing even.

"You know it. I'm gonna demand a full reporting
over breakfast." Owen's head tipped back, exposing
the long column of his throat as he worked his waistband lower, letting his cock spring free. Quill had felt
it before, seen it briefly in the firelight, but this was
his first good look. Thick and meaty, it had an intrigu-
ing curve as it stretched up his belly. About as long as
Quill's own cock, but with a more pronounced oval,
uncut head and thicker base. Quill's mouth watered and
he almost called a stop to this game so that he could go
touch, but Owen continued before he could give in to
the impulse. "So without toys or lube experiments, that
leaves my favorite lesson in this whole course. Edging.
And you're not going to convince me that you've never
played around with that, sorry."

"I'm not unfamiliar with the concept," Quill admitted, voice primmer than he liked. Maybe someday talking sex would get as easy for him as it was for Owen.

"Good." Owen's eyes fluttered shut as he fisted the
base of his cock, giving it a long, leisurely pull before
releasing it to tug up his shirts, revealing more of that
flat stomach, which he stroked. "I like to touch everywhere. Make my cock wait. Same as how when I'm
with a partner, I like to touch them all over, get them
all worked up before I worry about me."

Gulping because his body wouldn't mind that kind

of attention, Quill squeezed his knee to avoid reaching for his own cock. Not yet. He wanted to see what Owen had in mind more than he wanted relief. And Owen had pegged him correctly—he did like watching, something about the novelty and dirtiness of watching another man jerk it turning his crank big time. When one of Owen's hands dipped under his shirts, rubbing his chest, a needy sound escaped Quill's lips.

"Show me."

"Yeah." Owen pushed his shirts higher, showing off...

"You're pierced." Quill could feel his eyes shooting wide, cock now an almost painful throb.

"And you're cute when I surprise you," Owen countered, looking down at the twin flat bars running through his flat, tawny nipples. "Present to myself when I got my MBA. Like I said, I'm into making my solo time more fun. And playing with these definitely counts." Flicking one, Owen moaned low. "Yeah, like that."

"Fuck." Quill released the word on a huff of air.

"You should try it." Offering him a very dirty smile, Owen continued to toy with his nipples, which made his cock leap against his stomach.

"Think I'll leave that to you." Quill had no desire to pierce anything on his body, but damn if he didn't want to play with Owen's little bars, see if he could make him jump even more.

"It's a game. See how long I can go. Probably gives me more stamina." His eyes sparkled with dirty promises that made Quill shift on his chair. "Get your cock out. Give me some motivation here, not that you in your uniform isn't inspiration enough."

The back of Quill's neck heated. Going from watching

to active participant both made his pulse thrum and his insides wobble, natural modesty at war with his cock's need for something more than fabric to strain against. In the end, hands shaking, he complied, copying Owen by undoing his pants enough to shove them to mid-thigh, more out of a need to see what Owen would do next than to show off himself. Once he had his cock out, he gave in to the urge to stroke.

"Nuh-uh." Owen shook his head, mock censure making his eyes narrow. "None of that. Wait until you can't stand it another second."

"Close to that," Quill growled.

"Good." A clear drop of fluid appeared on the tip of Owen's cock as he continued his nipple play, and he swiped his thumb across his tip, gathering it up. Then, like something out of Quill's most pornographic dreams, he sucked the thumb into his mouth, making a show out of swirling his tongue around, noisily getting it damp and shiny.

"Fuck." Even without a hand on it, Quill's cock twitched and throbbed.

"Told you. I like it slick." Owen proceeded to give his other fingers the same treatment. And damn did Quill ever *want*. He'd been blown before, but he had a feeling he'd never had anything quite like Owen and his deliciously filthy try-anything mind.

"Touch your cock." He had a feeling that Owen would ignore the request, operating on his own time-table, not Quill's, but the need to see Owen come kept building up, an urgency he'd never known before.

"In a minute." Owen rubbed his wet fingers over each nipple, and a legit whimper wiggled loose from Quill's chest. Giving Quill an arch smile, Owen gestured toward Quill's cock. "*Now* you can stroke. Slowly. Lightly."

Given that he was across the room, Owen probably wouldn't be able to tell the tightness of Quill's grip, but he still followed orders, barely grazing his cock with loose fingers.

"Oh yeah." Finally, *finally*, Owen brought his hand back to his own cock, stroking like he intended to make it last until New Year's. Each pass of his hand seemed to take an eon, lifetimes for Quill to get lost in watching his face and reactions, drowning in lust but rooted to the spot, powerless to do more than let Owen direct him with little comments. "Slow down... Don't touch the head... Mmm... Rub underneath... Yeah, like that..."

Filthy words, a steady stream of gasps and moans and orders that spoke to some deep need in Quill's chest, made him fall into an almost trancelike state, chilly room fading away, falling night and snow outside ignored, hard chair digging into his thighs inconsequential, everything tunneling down to watching and listening to Owen. His balls ached, but orgasm danced just out of reach, body apparently intent on waiting for Owen's permission.

Each reaction from Owen was sexier than the last—the way his face scrunched up on a faster stroke, the way his biceps and abs strained when he moaned, whole body engaged in the business of pleasure.

"Show me how you get close," Owen demanded. Quill's throat was too dry to remind him that he was supposed to be the teacher, not Quill, and besides his hand was already speeding up. His thighs clenched, tension coiling tighter. *Almost.*

"Stop. Back it off." Owen demonstrated, letting go of his cock to touch his stomach and chest.

"Yeah." Fingers trembling, Quill did the same. He wasn't the begging type, but damn if he didn't have to keep biting back whines and demands. And then Owen flicked his nipple again. A flash of silver, and a low sound Quill didn't recognize came from his mouth. *"Please."*

"Oh fuck yeah." Owen had apparently been waiting for Quill to break like that because his hand returned to his cock, strokes more deliberate now. "Get there."

Quill struggled to comply, every muscle straining from the effort of holding back so long, climax elusive even as he started the sort of purposeful rhythm that usually got him off. "Need…"

"That's it. Whatever you need. Do it." Owen was shameless, rubbing his chest while his other hand worked his cock, sinking lower into the couch, legs spreading wider. "Come on. Show me."

Quill knew his own body well enough to have a clue as to what might tip him over, but his hands hesitated. Having Owen's eyes on him was both a drug, intoxicating and addictive, but also nervy, making him hyperaware and reluctant. But then they locked gazes, and instead of judgment waiting to happen, all he saw was heat and passion and acceptance. Owen truly meant it—whatever Quill wanted was okay. Good even. Not breaking eye contact, he let his left hand skate lower, rubbing his balls.

"Uh-huh. Do that," Owen encouraged, breath coming more ragged now. "Get yourself there."

Right hand speeding up, Quill dragged his fingers

lower to the sensitive skin behind his balls, to that spot right…

"Fuck. Fuck." His rumble echoed through the room, and Owen's moan joined his as Quill's body finally allowed him to tumble over, orgasm smacking into him like a weak roof breaking under a blizzard, all his muscles giving way to slump in the chair.

His eyes opened just in time to see Owen go, hand a blur, whole body shuddering as he came all over his fist. And then Owen managed to make Quill's cock give one last desperate twitch simply by licking his thumb. Fuck. He really was Quill's filthiest fantasies come to life. And too damn bad he wasn't in touching distance before Owen wiped his hand on his discarded shirt because he wanted a taste too, might have been bold enough to grab Owen's hand.

Almost like he was reading Quill's fanciful mind, Owen laughed, a post-orgasm sound Quill wasn't familiar with, but Owen managed to look both self-satisfied and like he was having a whole amusement park's worth of fun.

"Damn, that was…" Owen shook his head. "Something else. And don't look now, but this is the part where we clean up and you don't go getting awkward and we find some food. And we talk."

The *talk* part sounded way too ominous but he'd promised no more ignoring, so he nodded. "Food sounds decent. I've got some salmon from summer in the deep freezer we could do for dinner."

"It's a date." Owen's dimples flashed brighter than a solar flare, and Quill had never been so thoroughly undone in his life.

A *date*. A date with Owen. With talking. Somehow he'd gone from being afraid that Owen wouldn't survive the winter, to absolutely certain that he himself was doomed.

Chapter Fifteen

As it turned out, Quill actually could cook, even if he didn't seem to like it. He had a certain competence handling the frozen salmon steaks that Owen found sexy. The mashed potatoes were from a packet and the peas canned, but Owen wasn't going to complain. The food was hot, and a little garlic for the potatoes and some Italian seasoning for the peas, and Owen managed to disguise some of the blandness. Working together to make food was its own kind of satisfying as was Quill not shutting him out after the otherworldly orgasms.

Oh, Quill was still embarrassed and uncomfortable, as evidenced by his long pauses and tight body language. But he was making an effort, which was something, and Owen would happily take it over him retreating to his room.

"Can we have salmon again for Thanksgiving?" Owen asked as they finished up eating. Turkey wasn't out of the question. They did have access to the grocery store in Wasilla and could also make a trip to Anchorage if the roads held up, but the oven was tiny and with only the two of them, even a breast might be overkill. "I think I can do a pie or something to go with it if you want."

"Thanksgiving?" Quill blinked like Owen had suggested an expedition to Mars. "Haven't done that in years. It's a busy weekend here, and that wasn't one of the holidays Hattie celebrated."

"I know it'll be busy, but I think I can squeeze in a pie." Why Owen was suddenly into being domestic for Quill, he couldn't say. "Got a favorite kind? Like what did your mom make when she was alive that you liked?"

Quill made a sour face. "Never said she was dead—sorry if I gave that impression. My father is though. And any pie that didn't come with a big slice of family drama and fighting was fine by me but damn rare."

"Ah." Owen had stepped in it again, and fresh sympathy for Quill's younger self welled up. "I'm sorry. I didn't mean to bring up painful memories. My family didn't really do Thanksgiving either, although my mom usually did a nod toward the major US holidays. Presents on Christmas, that sort of thing. I wish your home had been more…peaceful. Do you talk to your family much now?"

"Siblings some. Birthdays and such. My middle sister always sends a funny card. But Mom went from kind of eccentric and tolerable to a bitter person after my grandpa and then my dad died. All those TV news channels all day long. Conspiracy theories and political shit." The hurt in Quill's eyes made Owen's arms ache with the need to hold him. It sounded like for all intents and purposes he'd lost both parents, and that sucked. "My siblings and their kids look after her and let me know if money's needed, but we don't see eye to eye, if we ever did."

"She doesn't know, does she?" Owen kept his tone as gentle as possible, but Quill still tensed, getting up abruptly and putting his plate in the sink with a loud clatter.

He figured that was that, but then Quill surprised him by talking. "No point in her getting all agitated. JP—a college friend—he thought them knowing would be cathartic for me, whatever the hell that meant. Much as my grandpa helped my life and gave me a role model to aspire to and the outdoors to escape to, though, I knew his and my dad's opinions on gay people all too well. Whole damn family was always on me to toughen up, stop being so shy, be a man, all that, even when I was getting the shit kicked out of me on the school bus by older boys. Said I wouldn't have such problems if I'd just stand up for myself, stop acting like…"

"I'm sorry. They should have been the ones to stand up for you. You were just a kid."

Quill's eyes were distant as he leaned heavily against the counter. "That's what JP said too. Said even if my dad was going to be an asshole about it, I needed to stop living two separate lives—one back home and one at college. Gave me an ultimatum. So when my dad came to Seattle on business, I figured I'd make JP happy and tell him."

"And?" Owen could already sense that whatever had happened wasn't good.

"We argued. Or rather, he screamed, same as he always did when pissed, only I was twenty-one, not nine, nowhere to hide, and finally I yelled back. First time I ever raised my voice to him. Like my grandpa, he'd always been this larger-than-life guy, the one I wanted to be like most in the world. Wanted to be respected like him, walk with his sort of confidence. All that kid stuff. But I finally said I wasn't going to take his name-calling. He hollered at me some more before he collapsed. Massive heart attack." Quill's voice was flat, as empty as whatever sympathy Owen could offer. His expression was ashen, and Owen felt ill at having made him relive the memory.

"Oh, Quill. God. I'm so sorry." Bringing his plate over to the sink as well, he stood next to Quill, trying to decide if a sympathetic touch would be welcome or not.

"Doctors said he'd been a ticking time bomb of clogged arteries, but I was the only one who knew the truth about what set him off."

"That's a huge burden to bear." Owen couldn't wait any longer, and he squeezed Quill's arm. Not quite the embrace he wanted to offer, but he couldn't not touch Quill then, not when he was so clearly hurting.

"Better to hold the secret than to lose the rest of them. Not that it ended up mattering much in the end. After he died, Mom's attitude got worse, not better, and there's just no point to bringing drama. Not when JP and I still ended up…falling out. Nothing was ever enough for him. And it doesn't make sense, telling her now. Not when I've got my life here, the job, and we're not really part of each other's lives now."

Owen had already picked up on Quill's massive aversion to conflict of any kind. And some of that was likely personality and some learned behavior from all these past wounds, but it still made his chest ache, thinking of him repeatedly hurt by family and this JP guy too.

"I'm so sorry. Fuck. That's awful." He had to touch Quill again, on the shoulder this time, not surprised when Quill didn't move into the touch, but wanting to offer more than words all the same. "And your point of view is understandable, given all that. I'm lucky that my parents suspected I was gay even before I came out, made whatever peace they needed to with it, and have been relatively supportive since. They've defended me to some friends and relatives, and they've met all my exes. They've got my back. For you, it must suck not being able to be your authentic self with your family, even if they are kinda…suboptimal as far as families go."

"It's okay to say dysfunctional. Or crappy. Not gonna insult me." Quill washed the dishes with quick, efficient movements. "And as to authentic self or whatever you want to call it, that's not who I…associate with. Put me in the high country in summer. Watching the northern lights in winter. Catching a big fish. That's me."

Owen's back muscles tightened, both from the knowledge that Quill simply didn't value connection and interpersonal relationships the way Owen did and from wanting—*needing*—to see more of that true self of Quill's, wanting to see him in his element as much as possible.

"Assuming this storm lets up eventually, will you show me the lights?"

It took a moment for Quill to nod sharply, like he had to actually weigh his options, which made the nod that much sweeter, even before Quill spoke. "Yeah. I'll pick a good night for it."

"Thanks." It felt weirdly momentous, like somehow they were agreeing to more than night sky viewing.

"I do get it." Quill dried his hands with a dishtowel before turning to face Owen. "You with your good family and your big network of friends. Being out matters to you. And same deal with holidays and celebrations. You need that sort of thing."

Owen didn't disagree, but Quill sounded so sad that he didn't argue it, instead pulling Quill into a hug. Maybe Quill still didn't need the touch, but Owen sure as hell did.

"Right now what I need is *you*." He didn't promise to never need more, couldn't lie like that even to make Quill smile. But he could hold Quill close, try to chase out a little of his darkness. "You, me, a long winter, and maybe some pie. It'll be nice. Trust me."

Quill inhaled and exhaled, slowly relaxing into Owen's embrace. Not exactly hugging back, but not pulling away or merely enduring either.

"Pumpkin," he said at last. His lips curved, almost a smile, and his eyes were far away. "I like pumpkin pie. Don't want you thinking it was all terrible. Mom could make a nice pumpkin pie, and she always cut me a big slice, even if she was distracted by whatever that year's drama was. There's some pumpkin in with the canned goods, I think. If not, I can pick some up next trip to Wasilla. And there's a small venison roast in the freezer, if that's not too heavy for you."

"I'll try it." Hell, Owen would try woodchuck if it meant Quill meeting him halfway like this. He hugged Quill tighter, wanting more than ever to give Quill some good memories. "It's a plan."

"You should sleep out here tonight if your room is still too cold." Quill gently extricated himself from Owen's embrace. Eyes distant, he seemed to be retreating on multiple levels, which sucked.

"Will you sleep out here too?" Owen tried to keep his voice light, not needy. He didn't need them to jump to room sharing or something simply on the basis of a few hot kisses and pleasant meals, but not being effectively dismissed would be nice.

For a second Quill looked like he was about to shake his head, but then he nodded. "Guess I could. My room isn't much better than yours. I'll take the floor again."

Ah. Not an invitation to snuggle, which was about as much as he'd expected. But still his muscles sagged. One step forward, four back in this dance with Quill.

"How about we play cards before bed?" If he wasn't getting another round of orgasms quite yet, at least he could get some company.

"I can do that." Quill gave him a tight smile.

Later, after a few rounds of cards in front of the stove with idle talk about the coming tourist snow season and him urging Quill to share winter stories, the companionship they'd built while cooking seemed restored, heavy talk forgotten. And as Quill gathered up the cards, bending close, Owen stole a kiss. A little fleeting thing that invited Quill to stay and linger if he wanted, but not demanding anything more than simply that moment. Mouth softening, Quill returned the kiss with a gentleness that made Owen's eyes strangely itchy. But then he straightened, spreading out Owen's bedding for him.

"Sleep well."

"I will." Owen managed to sound pleasant even through gritted teeth. Damn. He didn't understand how a man could be so infuriating and so sweet at the same time. And he really, really didn't understand how he could want him so badly. This wasn't his usual pattern. He didn't go for guys who were challenges, didn't relish the emotional equivalent of thawing an iceberg with a hair dryer. And yet Quill had a way of making Owen

want to try, made it so that he drifted off, not in frustration but to thoughts of how best to melt that solid block
of ice around Quill's heart.

"I need a favor." Quill meant the request about as non-
sexually as one could, but Owen's quick flash of interest and eager grin said that wasn't how he'd heard it.

"Anything." Leaving his oatmeal on the counter,
Owen came to stand next to Quill by the coffee maker,
close enough that their hips brushed and filling Quill's
nostrils with the scent of freshly showered Owen instead
of his morning brew.

"Not that kind of favor." Indeed, he was only asking in person rather than via note because it seemed
politer and because after yet another cold night spent
in the main room, Owen was up earlier than usual.
Even Quill wasn't a big enough jerk to leave Owen a
list when he could just as easily tell him the day's plan
over breakfast.

"Darn." Owen mock pouted, but Quill doubted he
was that surprised. By some unspoken agreement, they'd
kept their…extracurricular entanglement, such as it was,
confined to nighttime hours. A little kissing. A few more
jerk-off sessions. Owen hadn't pressed for more than
that, which frankly surprised Quill as he'd figured Owen
would want to jump quickly to lots of nakedness and
beds and all the things that happened therein. But he
seemed content to take this…arrangement at Quill's
speed, which was nice.

Instead of escalating sex, there was something else
happening, something rooted in hours of late-night
conversations. He still couldn't believe he'd told Owen
about his dad. Not even Hattie knew that story. And

since that night, he'd told Owen more about his childhood and growing up and JP than he'd ever shared with another human. Even the conversations about mundane things had a…weightiness to them. A significance that underscored whatever fun Owen managed to talk him into sexually. But none of those sexy times had happened during the limited daylight hours, for which Quill was grateful. And counting on that day.

"There's a Girl Scout group coming up to snowshoe. They asked for a ranger-led talk. And I could handle it, but I thought maybe you'd like to come with me?" Quill had hatched the plan of involving Owen yesterday when the dread over public speaking started to gather in his gut. And then he'd come in to find Owen singing along with some pop tune while he cleaned and remembered how Owen, like Hattie, was a total people person. Hell, he'd probably love the chance to see a bunch of tweens and adults. And even though it meant admitting his own discomfort, he couldn't deny that having someone more social along would help.

"Need me to make sure you don't overly scare them with avalanche warnings?" Owen grinned at him as he returned to his oatmeal bowl, taking it to the table. "Good cop versus bad cop? I can play that game."

"Something like that. And you've become familiar enough with everything around here that I bet you can handle yourself with a tour about as well as one of our longtime summer volunteers."

"Aww. Thanks for the compliment. And I get you. You're not much on talking to big groups, right?"

"Not the most. It's not that I'm shy—"

"You're reserved. And there's nothing wrong with that. Or being shy. But you're allowed to be a big, strong, stoic ranger who also happens to be the silent type. It's not a character flaw to not feel comfortable with crowds. And I'm happy to help."

"Thanks." Quill wasn't sure he believed him about the rest of it. He had too many voices in his head telling him to get over himself, those childhood remnants of never measuring up, especially when dealing with unfamiliar or uncomfortable situations. Public contact was a part of the job, and he was fine one-on-one or in smaller groups. And maybe relying so many years on Hattie taking point with the big presentations had left him out of practice. Now he was begging favors from Owen, who admittedly did seem eager, but still Quill had those voices saying he should be able to manage.

"Tell me what they want to know about, and I'll brush up on those areas before we meet up with them." Businesslike Owen was back, grabbing the notepad and pen from the center of the table. Hell, he'd probably have a full outline of talking points by the time Quill left for his patrol. "We'll let you talk risks, but I can do the welcome and all that."

And sure enough, Quill headed off with an agenda for the talk in Owen's neat handwriting and a promise to meet up with him in a few hours. Simply having a plan settled Quill down in a way that was both unfamiliar and comforting. Midmorning, he and Owen used their snowmachines to reach the lower parking lot, where they would meet the group and snowshoe with them around some of the easier terrain while they talked.

"Hello! How was the drive?" Owen turned on all his charm for the scout leaders as they unloaded the vans, learning names and history with the sort of ease Quill had expected. Watching him work was a weird sort of pleasure, the way he effortlessly helped kids with their snowshoes and fielded rapid-fire questions. And he was good at directing Quill in subtle ways, involving him in the flurry of activities but not requiring him to be at the center of the action the way Owen was.

"Okay. Now, who here thinks that snow can be dangerous?" Owen finished his presentation on the history and topography of the area, giving Quill the opening they'd discussed to talk about avalanches and other dangers. He stayed involved, repeating softly spoken questions and calling on kids by name, and generally making Quill's job that much easier. Indeed, it was actually an enjoyable few hours, watching the kids explore and Owen in his element around people.

"We make a good team," Owen declared as they stowed the snowmachines back in the equipment shed after saying goodbye to the group and doing a fast patrol.

"We do." Even if he didn't want to give Owen's ego more fodder, he had to admit that they had worked together seamlessly, him filling in the gaps in Owen's knowledge and experience and Owen balancing out his more limited social skills. "I might use you for more presentations. If that's okay?"

"Please do. But…" Owen paused near the door, mischievous grin unfurling on his face. Damn. Those dimples undoubtedly meant he was up to no good, and still Quill took the bait.

"But?"

"I mean if I'm doing you a favor, I think I should get a little something in return."

"Of course. I can help with trash—"

"No, not trash." Eyes sparkling in the rapidly dimming

afternoon light, Owen laughed. "More like I was angling for a kiss. That was hard work today and all."

"That so?" Quill needed to remind him that they needed to be professional, at least when not in their quarters, but somehow what came out was far flirtier. His feet stepped closer to Owen, not waiting for permission from his brain. They were both bundled up in thick winter gear, and it wasn't like Owen was proposing a quickie next to the snowmachines. "Guess one could be arranged."

"Really?" Owen's head tilted like he'd been expecting a fast rebuff. Perversely, that made Quill more determined to prove that he wasn't always so predictable and boring.

"Sure." Quill pulled him close, their parkas bumping together before he dipped his head and claimed Owen's mouth in a soft but thorough kiss. It was usually Owen stealing kisses late at night so this felt strangely new— daylight, outdoors, him initiating. But then Owen took over like he always did, deepening the kiss to own Quill's mouth with his determined tongue, and it was as familiar as his favorite boots, warming him through despite the chilly air.

"Race you upstairs?" Breathing hard, Owen broke away. "I think you need another lesson before dinner."

"Less—*oh*. You want to…before we eat?"

"Uh-huh. And how." Owen grabbed his hand, pulling him through the door.

"You're going to be the death of me," Quill muttered, not nearly as put out as he was acting. "We really do need to get you a hobby other than…you know."

"You can say sex, Quill, and the world won't stop turning. No one here but us and the wind." Owen set a brisk pace back to their building. "And I've been thinking on that. I'm not really the type to take up knitting or poetry or other hobbies like that."

"What did you used to do as a bored kid?" Quill was genuinely curious, pausing to remove his snow-covered boots at the bottom of the stairs. They'd talked a fair bit about Quill's childhood, the unhappy bits and the happier memories of various hunting and camping trips with his grandfather, but Quill didn't have the best sense of Owen as a kid other than as an energetic younger sibling tagging along with the older kids.

"Hmm. Good question. My mom was always trying to get me to read, but books didn't often keep my attention. I loved comics, but my parents didn't think they counted as real reading. Of course, now graphic novels are everywhere, and Mom gets them for the grandkids, but back then they both gave me a hard time about liking comics. I used to make my own, sold them to my friends and stuff before we discovered dating and going out places."

"I can totally see you selling comics to your friends. Always enterprising." Laughing, he followed Owen up the stairs. "And you should try that again if you get super bored. Better that than you starting to talk to trees."

He was joking, but underneath the teasing was the lingering worry that Owen wouldn't finish the winter, that Quill wouldn't be distraction enough to keep him.

"Maybe." Owen kicked the door shut. "But right now, only hobby I care about is getting you out of the rest of this gear."

"Let me stoke the fire, and then, yes." And maybe Quill wouldn't—couldn't—be enough to keep Owen,

but he could darn sure do better at keeping him happy
while he had him. And if that meant letting him make
a fuss over Thanksgiving and making sure he had his
daily quota of orgasms, then Quill was all for it.

Chapter Sixteen

"We've got a problem." Quill came into the equipment shed with Owen's least-favorite sentence. Owen had been gassing up his snowmobile for a check of the public-use areas. Thanksgiving had dawned clear and cold, and he'd more or less invited himself along on Quill's midmorning patrol. They'd had a steady stream of traffic all week, and as the tourist numbers rose so did Owen's spirits. He'd had some great conversations with skiers and snowshoers the past few days, and even if it meant longer hours and more work for him, he'd happily take this level of busy.

But not problems. Problems meant getting to use his critical thinking skills, but they also invariably meant a cranky Quill.

"Generator again?" He braced himself for another frigid night. Stupid thing wasn't doing the best job as it was.

"No, not that. Got a call about an SUV down at the lower lot with a bad flat tire. Screw straight through the tread. I went to check it out, and I'm not sure they'll get a tow truck up here on a holiday weekend. I could use a hand. You said back at the training that you knew cars. Ever seen frozen lug nuts?"

"No, but I'm game. And I've changed tires before. Do they have a jack or should we bring one down?"

"We'll bring ours just in case." Quill grabbed one from a shelf in the shed, stowed it on his snowmobile. "They've got those beefy tires, which makes it more of challenge. Luckily, they say they have a spare. And uh… the family's rather high-strung. Crying kids."

"Ah. Now we get to the *real* reason you came for me." He couldn't help the warmth that spread out from his chest. Quill needed him. And maybe it was only his people skills and tolerance of kids, but Quill had come for him, and that made him unreasonably pleased. "Give me three minutes to run upstairs and grab some candy, and then we can roll."

"Candy?" Quill frowned.

"For the kids. I found a bunch of it when I was organizing one of the stockrooms. Still good. Trust me."

"Okay. I need to collect some hot water as well anyway."

Once they had the supplies they'd need, they headed off on the snowmobiles. They were greeted by a large family with five redheaded kids of varying small sizes—baby to about ten, Owen would guess. Possibly two sets of twins. One worried-looking blonde mom who had a puffy face from crying, and oh hey, pleasant surprise, a second mom or aunt with long dark hair and a calmer demeanor. Owen wasn't going to make assumptions, but he gave them all a broad smile. The oldest kid was out with the women while the others fussed in car seats.

"You came back," the blonde said to Quill. "Thank God. You were right. No luck getting a tow truck up here. And our friends aren't answering. They left before us because we had to change a diaper. We didn't notice the flat until after that. They're probably already back in Anchorage. And—"

"Breathe," Owen told her. "We're here now. We'll get you on the road fast."

"Thank you."

"All part of the job." Quill crouched low, examining the tire. "You ran the heater for a while like I suggested? Hopefully that warmed up the bolts a little."

"Warmed up the kids too," the other woman chimed in. "Sorry they're so fussy. Getting on to both lunch and nap time."

"Do they have allergies?" Owen asked the women, still not sure which one was the mom. "I brought them some lollipops."

"Bless you." The dark-haired woman took the suckers from him and passed them out while he bent next to Quill.

"So what's your plan?" he asked, trying to do better at not taking over and running things.

"Mine?" Quill smiled at him—still a rare event, but less so recently. More smiles and more joking, at unexpected moments too. "Figured you'd have a ten-point plan of attack by now."

"Well, I do have some ideas," Owen admitted.

"Knew it." Quill's look was almost affectionate before turning serious again. "We should get the spare out first, make sure it's properly inflated."

"F—crap. We're going to have unload. It's under the floorboard in the back." The blonde looked on the verge of tears again.

"It's no problem," Owen said before he saw the massive assortment of winter gear, baby supplies, and luggage in

the rear of the SUV. It took a bit of doing for them to unload everything and free the tire. Some other tourists on
skis stopped by to see if they could help, and one family
had snacks they shared with the kids. The cold made everything more of a challenge, and Owen and Quill both
had to keep rotating gloves on and gloves off to com-
plete tasks, but other than that, helping the women was
almost fun.

As he always did, Owen got most of their story as
they worked. They were sisters-in-law, not a couple,
one with a deployed military husband and the other
with an oil-rig-working husband, and they'd come to
the area with friends for the holiday for a little fun in
the snow to take their minds off not having their men
home. They seemed like a lovely family, and Owen
liked being able to save the day for them. His shoulder
blades loosened, some long-held tension falling away as
he felt more needed than he had in a long time. Knowing he was able to do this made him vital and alive, like
sex or a good workout, but the helping part satisfied
some deeper need he hadn't even been aware of having.

Eventually they got the women back on the road, and
he and Quill continued on patrol until the early sunset
chased the tourists away. Quill did pull the whole big,
bad ranger you-can't-camp-here lecture for a group of
older, inadequately dressed teens. Owen's own inner
teen in search of a heartthrob did a swoon at Quill's
stern voice and commanding presence. He was fast
coming to love Quill's contrasts—large, hulking ranger
capable of handling any crisis and shy, almost wounded
man who struggled with opening up and letting go.

Which was why Owen treasured his little jokes and

smiles that much more, stored them away as evidence of Quill's gradual thaw.

"You did good out there. With the kids especially." Quill let him go ahead of him on the stairs back up to their quarters. "But I probably kept you out too late for that pie and roast we planned, didn't I?"

"Wrong." Turning, Owen preened down at Quill before opening the door at the top of the stairs. "I made the pie this morning, right after you headed out. And I put the roast in that slow cooker Hattie left behind. A quick call to my mom helped with the seasonings and cook time."

"You? Needed advice on something?" Quill shook his head as he peeled off his outerwear, another of those rare teasing smiles widening further.

"Well, it was also an excuse to call home," Owen admitted, hanging up his coat and the rest of his gear, leaving him down to two long-sleeved T-shirts and stretchy fleece pants. Something about this week and all the tourist families had had him a little nostalgic for his own.

His mom had advised a ginger-garlic-chili combo that Owen probably could have come up with on his own, but sometimes a guy just wanted to call his mom. However, he also knew that Quill didn't have that, which made his hands itch. He'd like to shake Quill's family for not seeing what a great guy they'd had in their midst. And not surprisingly, he'd spent far too much of the tinny-reception call sharing Quill stories and dodging questions about what he'd be doing after his volunteer stint was done. He honestly wasn't sure, which wasn't going to be the answer his planner-loving family wanted to hear. But he hadn't pulled out his list in weeks, hadn't been able to summon enthusiasm for deciding what came next. He missed the people more than the chaos of city life. Sure, takeout was great and he missed regular internet, but otherwise his stir-crazy cabin fever had markedly decreased the past few weeks.

"It smells good." Quill headed to the kitchen area.

And yeah, Quill was absolutely responsible for Owen's newfound commitment to living in the here and now and not making future plans. Because future meant no Quill, and Owen didn't want to dwell on everything he'd be leaving behind, not when there was still so much he wanted to experience here.

"I'll check the roast, make sure it's done." Owen padded over to the slow cooker, hoping the electricity hadn't crapped out on them again.

"You do that. I'll make a packet of potatoes to go with it."

Owen had been thinking noodles, but he supposed potatoes were more Thanksgiving-y, and he was nothing if not open to compromise, especially when it came to making Quill happy. As Quill put the water on to boil for the potatoes, he paused by the stove, forehead furrowing.

"What?" Owen hoped he hadn't just remembered a chore, because the last thing he wanted was to go back outside.

"Oh, nothing. A memory. Not exactly a bad one either." Quill's voice was thoughtful. "When my grandmother was alive, she always made people at Thanksgiving say what they were thankful for. JP's family did the same thing, just without the arguments and hurt feelings that always seemed to happen at my house."

"We could do that." Maybe a tradition was exactly

what Quill needed to make peace with his past, something he could use going forward.

"Nah. I'm not a speech maker. You know that. More like the memory made me realize that I don't say thank you enough. Not simply for the help with the tire and stuff like that, but for…everything else." Quill's cheeks were shiny pink by the time he finished.

"You don't have to thank me." Heart swelling, Owen suddenly felt inadequate to hold in all the emotions coursing through him. Quill was grateful for *him*. It was humbling, and frankly, Owen wasn't sure he deserved it. "I like doing stuff for you."

"I've noticed." Quill's eyes went hooded and hot. Owen hadn't meant sex stuff, but if Quill's brain had headed straight for his like of jerking Quill off when they made out, he was happy to follow him to the sexy place, relieve them both from the sudden emotional turn the conversation had taken.

"You know…" He waggled his eyebrows at Quill. "If you're really wanting to share gratitude, feel free to show me after dinner."

"Just might do that." Looking away, Quill blushed, it deepening as he added the packet of potatoes to the water.

"Good." Owen gave his shoulder a fast squeeze before taking out the meat, which at least smelled decent. Probably spicier than Quill would have done on his own, but not overpowering.

Quill was a little too worried about the possibility of a late-night callout to drink with dinner, but the roast was good over the potatoes, spices covering the natural gaminess of the meat well.

"So… Thanksgiving with JP's family. How'd that go

over?" Owen figured he was cutting into his chances of getting lucky later by bringing up the college ex, but Quill's mention earlier had him all kinds of curious.

"Probably better than you're imagining." Quill's voice was drier than the potato granules, but at least he didn't leave the table. "His family was rich, large, and didn't care who he fucked around with. I went as a friend, but it wasn't some big drama-filled thing. Not like him visiting mine would have been."

"Ah. Did you like his family?" As he asked, Owen pictured Quill around his own family, eating Owen's mother's cooking, getting overwhelmed at the chaos of the nieces and nephews and extended family. It was a sweet image, even if it was one that wasn't ever meant to be.

"They weren't the issue. I was." Quill speared his last piece of meat with an angry jab. It was a nonanswer, one that made Owen that much more heartbroken for younger Quill.

"I didn't know you at twenty, but I find that hard to believe. You're a great guy."

"Thanks." Quill didn't meet his eyes, but his tone softened. "People want different things. Drift apart. I wasn't what he needed for his big shiny future. That's all."

"He's an ass if he didn't see you as a part of whatever future he had."

"He wanted more for me. Wanted me to take a corporate job with his father's software company or maybe get a master's in environmental engineering. Had all these plans and hopes."

"You would have been miserable." Even Owen could see that. Quill was born to be outside, not behind a desk.

"Likely so. Anyway, it drove a wedge between us. But

I guess it worked out in the end. He's a plastic surgeon now in Seattle. Big practice. Married to the CFO of his dad's company. And I'm here. Where I'm supposed to be." He said the last bit defiantly, like Owen might be scheming to take him from this life, which couldn't be further from the truth. It would be like trying to move a two-hundred-year-old spruce or reposition a river on a whim. Not happening and rather arrogant to assume it could.

"I'd say you dodged a bullet. Anyone that determined to change you isn't healthy. A good partner supports you in your dreams, not shoots them down."

Quill made a noncommittal sound as he reached for the pie Owen had placed in the center of the table. "Pie?"

"Sure." Owen didn't want to torture him with more unhappy memories of a guy who was probably better left forgotten. "I had to roll out the crust with a glass jar, but it smells good at least."

"It's good," Quill reported after taking a generous bite. "You got the spices right. Store-bought pies never seem to add enough seasoning. Mom always had a heavy hand with the cinnamon."

"I'm making a note that we've found the one food that you want more spices in, Ranger Salt-and-Pepper."

"Hey now, nothing wrong with simple." Quill joined in the teasing, but his smile was tinged with wistfulness, which was probably Owen's fault for bringing up the evil ex. So Owen made more of an effort to be amusing as they finished the pie, telling Quill about the long list of ingredients in some of his grandmother's recipes and his sister's disastrous attempts to replicate them.

And it seemed to work, Quill's mood lightening by the time they put the plates in the sink.

They'd fallen into something of a routine with Quill usually washing and Owen drying, hips rubbing, hands brushing, a comforting familiarity that Owen hadn't had with past boyfriends and was going to miss like hell. He'd never thought of himself as domestic—way too much a social butterfly to stay in—but Quill had him reconsidering a lot of things.

"Want the leftover pie for breakfast?" Owen asked Quill as he wrapped the pie plate up in foil.

"I can do that?" Quill sounded like a kid allowed to stay up until midnight for the first time.

"Absolutely. All yours." Owen grinned at him, insides heating when Quill's return smile turned feral as he backed Owen against the counter. He moved slowly, like Owen might seriously have an objection to this turn of events, and Owen could see the kiss coming long before Quill's lips brushed his, sweetest kiss ever because it was entirely Quill's idea, not Owen goading him into getting physical.

Way curious about what Quill had in mind, Owen let him drive the kiss, welcoming his gentle explorations. Quill's stubble tickled as he kissed Owen's jaw and neck, but hell if Owen was going to ruin this with an ill-timed laugh. Quill aggressive and on some sort of mission was a not-to-be-missed experience, and when Quill released him long enough to sink to his knees, Owen hissed in a breath.

"If I'd known pie would have this effect on you, I would have baked weeks ago." The joke kept him from floating away as Quill shoved his pants down his thighs, breath warm even as cool air greeted his already-over-heated skin.

"Not the pie," Quill growled. "You."

As far as romantic declarations went, that was right up there with the sexiest things Owen had heard, more so because it was Quill's deep rumble, Quill on his knees for *him*. Quill's lips skated over Owen's hipbones while his hands palmed Owen's ass. And okay, this was also going to be one of the quickest blow jobs ever because he was already halfway there even before Quill's mouth touched his cock. In their steady diet of making out and jerking off, they hadn't ventured into oral yet, in part because Owen was well aware that Quill had something of a *thing* about reciprocating, and he hadn't wanted to blow Quill if it meant him feeling pressured into doing something he wasn't ready for.

And if Owen was honest, the other part had to do with the uncertainty lurking behind his arousal. Making out and jerking Quill off were good because it kept any weird insecurity about being touched himself at bay. He tried not to let his differences post-surgery bug him, but sometimes, like now when Quill was so close to his scars and such, it was hard not to let a few doubts sneak in. Focusing on Quill's hand as he stroked up Owen's shaft was a good distraction from those doubts though, as was the anticipation of his mouth.

Fuck. Every moment of waiting was worth it when Quill's tongue snaked out to lick his cockhead. Not exactly a tease, more like a warning shot before the real onslaught began as he took Owen's cock deep, no hesitating there. He'd either done this before or had the best imagination on the planet because he moved fluidly, setting a fast, devastatingly deep rhythm. But even more than the wet heat of his mouth, it was his sounds, eager gasps and muffled moans as he went after what he wanted from Owen that had Owen riding the edge in record time. There was absolutely nothing better than getting blown by someone who loved every second of what they were doing, and Quill's pent-up need had Owen panting, eyes squishing shut, trying to hold on long enough to enjoy it.

But then Quill moved, adjusting his grip so that his fingers could tease Owen's ball. Probably more because Quill himself loved attention to his rather than curiosity, but Owen still batted his hand away.

"Not there."

Quill nodded sharply before returning to sucking Owen's cock, and damn, but his shiny, wet mouth had Owen forgetting all momentary awkwardness. Quill had a way of attacking his cock like he needed this more than oxygen, and that was sexy as hell. Owen's thighs and back muscles tensed, right back there in gotta-come-now territory.

"Close," he moaned. "Fuck. Don't stop."

Not that there appeared much chance of that, Quill sucking and licking like his next paycheck depended on him getting Owen off in the next thirty seconds. Using his big hand on Owen's ass, Quill wordlessly urged him to thrust, and that was all the encouragement Owen needed to start meeting Quill's rhythm, sliding in and out of that talented mouth. Quill's needy growl vibrated against Owen's shaft as he urged him faster, and that need, that hunger was what propelled Owen over into orgasm, ass digging into the counter to avoid sinking into Quill as he came down Quill's throat. The sexy sounds of Quill swallowing were enough to coax out a few more spurts, his mind blissfully empty other than the onslaught of pleasure.

But not so far gone that he forgot about Quill, hauling him up as soon as he'd caught his breath, pulling him close and going straight for his fly. Quill's hips jerked as Owen withdrew his cock, rubbing up against Owen's side and belly.

"That what you want? Want to rub on me until you come?" Tugging Quill tight against him as he pushed up his shirts so Quill would have more skin to feel, he encouraged him to move while his mouth sought Quill's for a kiss.

"Uh…" Quill hesitated, lips a fraction from Owen's. "You want… I just…"

"Oh, yeah. I know. I want." If nothing else, he was determined to show Quill that messy sex was the best sex, let him indulge in the urges he could sense simmering beneath Quill's buttoned-up facade. Kissing Quill, tasting himself, was almost enough to get Owen up for a round two, as was the eager way Quill returned the kiss after his initial hesitation.

"Come on me," he whispered against Quill's mouth, meeting Quill's frantic thrusts and stroking his broad back. "Wanna feel you go."

Quill's only response was a low, almost pained moan as his body tensed and shuddered. A second later, warmth splashed between them.

"Fuck. Fuck. Fuck." Collapsing against Owen, Quill rested his forehead against Owen's.

"Good?" Owen rubbed circles on Quill's back. "You do know that this means from now on I'm likely baking a pie a week if it gets me blown like that. Damn. You're amazing."

"Eh. More like rusty."

"If that was you out of practice, I'm really looking forward to you honing your game. Because *damn*." Not liking the thought of Quill doing that with anyone else, Owen was strangely gratified that Quill had chosen him to end whatever dry spell he'd been in prior to their meeting.

"I got you and your shirt both." Quill's eyes were sheepish as he moved away from Owen.

"We're both washable, and that was hot as hell. And admit it, you liked getting me messy."

"Maybe." The tops of Quill's ears darkened right along with his cheeks.

"Uh-huh. How about we both squish into the shower and you can get me messy again before we both get clean?"

"I think you vastly overestimate my powers of recovery." With a nervous chuckle, Quill darted his eyes between Owen and the bathroom door.

"How about you let me prove you wrong?" Righting his clothes enough to move, Owen tugged him toward the hall.

He wasn't ready to end this evening, wasn't ready to let go of this almost magical closeness, wasn't ready to let the real world intrude again. Soon enough reality would close in, and he'd have to face all the worries that hovered—his future, leaving, emotions he'd rather not be having—but right then, all he wanted was more Quill.

Chapter Seventeen

"I'm telling you that scratch wasn't there when we pulled in." The jacked-up yahoo in a red parka with a shiny black truck that cost more than Quill's annual salary continued to stare at the other idiot, the one currently lurking behind Quill, seeming happy to let him be in the middle of this little pissing contest in the lower parking lot.

"And I'm telling you that you're not going to fight on my watch." Quill stared down Mr. Muscles. He might be bigger than Quill, but Quill had no doubt that he could take him if it came to that. "Moving along would be the smart choice. Leave me some contact info for the incident report, and I'll send it on, and you can use it for your insurance if it comes to that."

Quill hated incident reports almost as much as he hated drama and confrontations, and having had both in the same day had him beyond cranky even once the arguing men finally headed out. Funny how it wasn't the men's size or volatility that got to Quill as much as those loud voices. Hell, let them throw a punch. Quill would have them in cuffs on the snowy ground before a second happened. But raised voices arguing? Made his stomach hurt and neck ache and made him in no way fit for company after his patrol.

The short days meant darkness was coming, light already rapidly fading, and underscored his exhaustion from the long holiday weekend. Monday was supposed to have been a respite from the chaos, but instead tourist traffic had remained higher than normal, people seeking one more day of fun and trying to outrun the big snowstorm scheduled for midweek, and he'd had all his usual end-of-the-month paperwork to worry about as well. The last thing he'd needed was this confrontation. He stowed the snowmachine, angry voices still ringing in his ears, revving his adrenaline.

As he entered the visitor center, he was tempted to stay downstairs, hide out in his office. He had the excuse of the need to file the incident report, but that wasn't what had him hesitating. It was late enough that Owen was almost certainly upstairs, and he was more than astute enough to pick up on Quill's bad mood. He'd want to talk, and Quill just wasn't up for conversation right then. But as he peeled off his snow boots and gear and stowed his piece in the safe, a pleasing aroma wafted down the steps—cinnamon and yeasty with an undercurrent of something savory as well. The hastily put-together sandwich he'd had midmorning seemed a lifetime ago, and his stomach won out over his better sense as he climbed upstairs with heavy feet.

The good smells got stronger after he opened the door, but instead of Owen at the stove, he discovered Owen on a stool, attaching lights to the doorframe that led to the little hall.

"What the heck are you doing?" His voice came out harsher than he'd intended, hours of frustration seeping in. But if Owen was offended, he didn't show it, flashing all his dimples and inherent good cheer as he gave him a wave.

"I was cleaning the storeroom as per my to-do list, and I discovered an old box of holiday decorations. Amazingly, even though they're probably ancient, the lights work. I thought it might be festive to put some up." Owen gestured at the room, which, sure enough, had lights over the window, lights along the top edge of the bookcase, and some colorful baubles on the coffee table.

"You celebrate Christmas?" he asked without thinking, totally earning Owen's answering eye roll. He knew that Owen's fairly affluent Californian family wasn't particularly religious.

"Most kids in American public schools talk about presents in December. My parents indulged us in the secular parts of the season, including lights on our house to compete with our Christmas-crazy neighbors. And then those same neighbors would get invited for my mom's big Lunar New Year celebration, where all the kids get little red envelopes of money. As kids, we loved all the holidays. More chances for gifts and sweet food. Besides, even if I'm not the biggest Christmas person, *you* need some holiday spirit."

"You're decorating for me?" Quill frowned, not liking the wobbly thing his gut was doing.

"Well, yeah." Owen offered him a crooked smile as he came down from the stool. "That, and I've always liked the idea of lights in December chasing out the darkness. And this whole dark at four and only five and a half hours of daylight is crazy making. I'm not sure how you're still getting up at six. If anyone needs lights, it's you."

"Habit." After shrugging, Quill gave in to the urge to sink into a kitchen chair, partly because he was that weary and partly because he wasn't sure he deserved Owen's kindness. "The work doesn't go away with the sun. Still got paperwork like incident reports. Speaking of, there was a fight in the lower parking lot today. You let me know if there's any trouble when you do trash tomorrow."

"Let you know?" Owen bristled, shoulders coming up and face hardening. "Why didn't you call for me today? I'm supposed to be your backup, right?"

"It wasn't that big a deal. More law enforcement than rescue or tourist relations. Sort of beyond your job description." Quill could tell from Owen's increasing frown that he was digging himself a deep hole, but he also wasn't sharing the truth, which was that he hadn't wanted Owen near a dangerous situation, hadn't wanted to have to worry about him getting caught in the middle of fisticuffs. He, at least, had been armed and had the statutory authority to detain the men until the closest police could arrive. All Owen had was his charm, which wasn't going to get him as far as he thought in a potentially violent incident.

"Seems like a big enough deal. You came in all exhausted and wrung out. I think you could have used an extra pair of hands. You can't only call on me when you need a cheerful face for the kids." Shaking his head, Owen retrieved a covered dish from the small oven and slid it in front of Quill. "Careful, it's hot."

"You're pissed at me, but you're giving me food?" Quill struggled to keep up with Owen's conversational leaps. In his experience, conflict usually meant shouting or pouting, one person storming off, slammed doors.

Not a warm meal and the other person taking the seat opposite him with a mug of tea, still looking irritated with narrowed eyes but also seeming rather intent on sticking around while Quill ate.

"Well, duh. You have to eat. I made myself a baked potato for lunch while I was experimenting with this cinnamon quick bread thing. It wasn't any trouble to make extra potatoes for you. I had mine plain, but I opened a can of chili to top yours." He gestured at Quill's plate. "And yeah, I'm not happy about you dealing with a dangerous situation and not calling for help, but that doesn't mean I'm going to give you the silent treatment all night. I'm more adult than that. Give me credit."

"Sorry. My experience with arguments...isn't quite so rational."

"I figured." Owen took a sip of tea. "But in a real friendship—and we *are* friends now, no matter what other benefits we've got going on—you get upset with someone, you talk it out, and you move on. I do think you should have called for me because you should trust me more, but it's not a friendship deal breaker."

"Ah." Quill let himself eat some of the potato while he thought about how to proceed. "It's not about trust. But it was a volatile situation, and there was no need for you to get involved."

"Ha. It *is* about trust. You would have called for Hattie. Or maybe even a more seasoned volunteer."

Quill sighed because Owen had a point. He would have radioed for Hattie without much thought. But Hattie wasn't Owen, and he had no idea how to put his jumble of emotions into words.

"Look." Reaching across the table, Owen patted

Quill's hand. "I get that things are complicated. I'm new. We're sleeping together. You prefer to work alone as it is—I get it. But maybe next time you call me. That's all I'm saying."

Quill had a strong feeling that "we'll see" wouldn't fly as a reply, so instead he nodded even as he knew he'd do everything he could to keep Owen out of danger, even if that meant risking his anger again.

"Okay." Seemingly satisfied with Quill's nod, Owen brightened. "So, tell me what went down and how you handled it. That way I know protocol and all that."

"One guy accused the other of scratching his truck. It escalated from there." Not used to having someone other than Hattie to talk shop with, Quill started off slow as he continued to eat, but as Owen asked follow-up questions, he was surprised to find talking easier and some of his stress melting away.

"Do you want to try the quick bread now or maybe later on?" Owen asked as he cleared Quill's plate and his tea mug.

"Later. I'm so full now that I'm sleepy and it's not even six thirty yet. Any more and I'll end up asleep on the couch and not much good to you."

"You won't be much good to anyone this tired." Owen abandoned the dishes in the sink to come tug Quill over to the couch. "You can nap. I'll babysit your phone and wake you if a call comes in."

"I don't nap," Quill protested even as he let himself be pushed onto the couch. It was soft and welcoming, and he couldn't help the groan that escaped as he settled in. "Not sure why you're being so nice to me."

"Because maybe I like you?" Owen laughed before he dropped a fast kiss on Quill's cheek. He loosened

Quill's collar buttons with deft fingers before kneeling to untie his boots. "And you've had a shit day on top of a busy week. I want you to feel better. If only because you less cranky benefits everyone."

"I'll try to be less irritable," Quill promised, helping Owen by kicking off his boots. He expected Owen to join him on the couch or maybe head back to the kitchen area to deal with the dishes, but Owen stayed crouching as he reached for Quill's belt buckle.

"Oh. Hey. You don't have to do that." Staying Owen's hands, his temperature climbed twenty degrees.

"Since when have you known me to ever do something I don't want to do?" Owen's eyes were bright and mischievous, no hint of guilt or obligation there. "I wanna blow you, help you fall asleep. Not because I feel bad that we disagreed but because blowing you is a hell of a lot of fun, and I want that right now."

"How is me falling asleep fun?" Quill's eyes were already heavy, and he wasn't sure whether he could keep them open by sheer force of will if Owen succeeded in his little plan. Ever since Quill's impulsive blow job in the kitchen on Thanksgiving, their sex had ramped up. More touching. More sucking. More rubbing off. But Quill always tried to make sure Owen got his.

"Are you kidding? You all boneless and limp because I sucked your brains out? That's the biggest ego trip there is. Now lean back and let me work." He shoved Quill's legs wide so that he could kneel more directly between them, his breath warm against Quill's fly. "If you're truly feeling guilty, you can owe me one, but sex isn't about turns or fair or whatever. It's about fun. And blowing you to sleep, that's gonna be fun."

Fun. Quill needed to keep that in mind. Sex was fun

for Owen in a way it had never been for Quill. And it
didn't matter how shaky his insides got from Owen's
domestic gestures like the decorations and the food.
Owen was only in this for the fun. The lark. The distraction of hot sex in the darkest month of the year. Quill
needed to remember that, tattoo it on his soul before he
got too attached. He needed to find distance and not
be plotting nice gestures of his own that he could do in
return. But as Owen's warm mouth worked its magic,
colorful lights twinkling above them on the shelves, he
knew he was hopelessly lost for this man and that there
wasn't much he wouldn't do for him.

"Need a hand?"

The sound of Quill's voice startled Owen. He was
shoveling out after the latest snow, a doozy of a storm
that had left Owen with a ton of work to do to maintain
the necessary paths and access points to things like the
restrooms and the trash. Not that he personally wished to
use an outhouse in frigid temperatures, but the facilities
needed to be accessible to those without other options.
He'd had to wait until almost 10 a.m. for adequate light
to work, and he'd have to push to get it all done by the
time darkness fell. Quill had been at a ranger meeting in
Wasilla and then on patrol, but he had a shovel in hand
now and looked ready to work alongside Owen.

"Sure." He wasn't going to turn down either the help
or the unexpected company. "Thanks."

Quill had been strangely helpful ever since their disagreement several days prior about his handling of the
parking lot fight, seeking Owen out during the day more
than he had before, and being more active in their evening doings, suggesting cooking together or a game. It

was nice and cozy and made Owen ache for things he couldn't have. But he'd sure as heck take it, take having companionship as he battled through the melancholy of the short days. Doing nice things for Quill like his baking experiments and the decorating helped as did exercise and him finally taking Quill's advice about hobbies, doing silly little doodles on some paper he'd found while doing the storeroom organizing.

"You want to stay up late tonight?" Quill asked, voice casual, not suggestive, but Owen still took the opportunity to leer at him.

"I'm always up for being up late with you. Or going to bed early. Either one." Bed was a bit optimistic of a euphemism as most of their sex still happened on the couch pre-bedtime with them sleeping apart either in the common room or in their own spaces. Quill still had yet to invite him into Quill's own quarters, and Owen didn't want to ask and come off as either needy or pushy.

"Not sex." Quill both blushed and whispered even though there was no one around, hadn't been most of the day. "It's supposed to be unusually clear and cold tonight with no moon. Perfect for viewing the northern lights if my powers of prediction are worth anything. There's a tourist group coming up, and my boss asked that I meet up with them in the parking lot. I promised you that I'd try to show you the lights and that I'd ask you for backup more. So, I thought you might want to come along?"

"Absolutely." Owen was unreasonably pleased that Quill was asking.

"You'll want to dress even warmer than usual as temperatures are set to drop. You can borrow some of my

better gloves again. And I've got extra thermal socks
if you need those."

"Thank you." Owen bit back a reminder that he could
dress himself because Quill was being sweet, and Owen
had already figured out that lectures and warnings were
part of how Quill showed he cared. Instead, he let Quill
give him more pointers as they worked clearing the
snow, and he in turn talked Quill into an early-evening
make-out session and napping on the couch on the pre-
tense of conserving energy for the late night. Quill
might be good at keeping him alive, but Owen liked to
think he was equally good at making Quill *feel* alive.

Both of them dressed for the frigid night with thermal layers followed by snow pants, parkas, double hats,
and Quill's preferred super-insulated gloves. Taking
the snowmobiles out at night was surreal—relying on
the headlights and trying to trust the trail to the lower
parking lot. He went slower than normal, as did Quill,
but they still arrived in time to meet the tourist group,
which consisted of around a dozen adults and a tour
guide. They were apparently part of a photography-
centered expedition, and Griffin, their guide, had fas-
cinating tips for trying to capture the night sky. Other
people not part of the tour group were also milling
around, word having apparently gotten out that the night
might be ideal for viewing the light show.

They used headlamps with snowshoes and skis to
venture a short distance away from the parking area to
a flat section unobstructed by trees. Quill undoubtedly
only noticed a head count of people, potential risks and
hazards, his focus on giving everyone a safe experience. But Owen was more fascinated by group dynam-
ics, the interplay among various tourists as they made

their way to the viewing spot. There were two couples from Japan, along with some highly fashionable women who managed to make their winter gear look like the latest fad, all brand-new and bright, matching colors. It didn't take long to figure out that one of the guys, with blue hair tucked into a thick knit hat, wasn't actually another group member but some sort of assistant to the guide, or maybe simply along for the ride. But they were rather obviously a couple, affectionate in that sort of longstanding shorthand way.

The pair reminded him of him and Quill, the way the assistant guy was far more social, joking and laughing with the tourists, serving as a sort of buffer for the gruff guide, who seemed more comfortable with his cameras than with the group. Or rather, they *would* remind him of him and Quill if they were a real couple like that, one with both a history and a future. One that had the sort of comfort level with each other where they had zero fucks for the world figuring out that they were with each other. Not that they were engaging in PDA or pet names or anything like that, but assistant guy wasn't shy about dropping things like "our cabin" in sentences either.

Feeling more jealous than he had any right to when he returned to Quill's side, his tone came out a bit snappish. "I don't see much of anything."

The faint glow to the sky was rather underwhelming, nothing like the pictures he'd seen of the northern lights.

"Just wait." Probably picking up on Owen's mood, Quill's response was impatient, like Owen was a kid needing amusing on a long car trip. "It's not on a timetable."

The cold seeped into his bones the longer they stood there, conversations swirling around them, the tourist group reflecting on other stops on their trip, the sort of fun vacation stories that should have made Owen itchy to travel again. If he was smart, he'd already have his summer planned. And if he had any sense of self-preservation left, he'd be craving the chance to explore other places, meet new people, not standing here wishing he was alone with Quill, wishing yet again for impossible things.

"Look!" One of the tourists pointed up at the sky where slowly a curtain of yellow-green light unfolded, undulating across the sky, rippling with tendrils of light traveling across the inky now-purplish backdrop. Those with camera setups rushed to get pictures, but Owen merely stood there, transfixed by beauty far surpassing anything his imagination had conjured up.

"This do for your bucket list?" Quill asked him quietly, a certain satisfaction to his voice, like he alone had procured the spectacle for Owen. It was almost too cute, and he had to fist his hands to keep from touching him.

Some distance ahead, assistant guy grabbed Griffin's hand, laughing and briefly resting his head on the guide's shoulder. Like the rapidly moving lights, they quickly separated, but Owen caught Quill glancing their direction as well. Did he feel that same longing as Owen? Wish for that easiness of being? Or did it make him uncomfortable or maybe even disdainful?

The brightness of the sky was almost blinding, hues shifting as the aurora shifted, a constantly evolving show, wild and unpredictable. Unlike Quill, who was solid and steadfast, rooted to this place and this time, unchanging. He wasn't ever going to be like that other couple, wasn't ever going to be publicly out like that, even casually. And Owen had known that for weeks now, known it prior to their first kiss if he were honest, known that getting involved with a guy who'd made an entire life inside a closet he had no intention of leaving was foolhardy. But he'd stupidly thought he could handle a no-strings fling. Damn Quill for making him want so much more than he was ever going to get.

"Too cold?" Quill asked him. "You should drink some tea as soon as you get back."

"Not cold," Owen lied even though he was chilled through with his realizations. And the worst thing was that it was too late to pull back now. Even knowing all the hurt that awaited him, he still wanted more. More time. More Quill. More magic like the lights, this moment both unspeakably beautiful and not nearly enough either.

Chapter Eighteen

Quill was sticky and messy and should have been profoundly uncomfortable, not laughing. But that's exactly what he was doing, a sound he almost didn't recognize.

"I'm not good at this."

"No one is their first time," Owen soothed.

"Guess the only important thing is that they're edible." Quill studied his handiwork, uneven circles and lumpy stars arranged on a baking sheet. It had been years since he'd attempted this—hazy memories of being in his grandmother's kitchen, her turning out oatmeal raisin cookies, or helping his cinnamon-loving mother make snickerdoodles. She'd liked to bake the nights his dad had worked late, music videos on the TV, house way happier than usual and smelling good.

But neither his mother or grandmother had been industrious enough for fancy rolled cookies. However, Owen had returned from a stock-up trip to Anchorage with an actual rolling pin, more baking supplies, and cookie cutters. Apparently, he'd decided that Quill needed gingerbread. And instead of greeting him with the results of his latest baking experiment, he'd enlisted Quill's help.

"Yup." Owen's cookies were perfect diamonds and

crescent moons. He'd been in a weird mood ever since Quill had taken him to see the northern lights, quieter, a little withdrawn, and more reflective than his usual spontaneous self. Thus, when he'd proposed cookie baking, Quill had decided to indulge him, hoping it got his playful Owen back to normal.

Quill wasn't stupid—he knew that Owen had likely noticed the tour guide and his boyfriend. And Quill wished he had the words to reassure him, knew how to jolly him up with a well-placed joke or comforting word, but that was hardly his strong suit. Further, he couldn't lie to Owen, couldn't say that he was about to change his whole world, the way he'd lived his life for decades now. If Owen needed the sort of easy affection the other couple had shared, he was looking at the wrong guy for it. As much as Owen deserved that sort of real relationship, merely thinking about him with some nameless future boyfriend who would happily hold hands publicly was enough to have Quill slapping down his cookie cutters far harder than he needed to.

"What did that dough do to you?" Owen laughed, mood lighter than it had been in days, which was seriously nice to see. He put the first sheet in the oven and set the timer.

"Sorry." Quill tried to be gentler as he filled his sheet. "Told you, I'm not sure I've done this before."

"First time for everything." Owen's wink promised sexy fun later and made Quill's pulse speed up. If Quill were any good at flirting, he'd make a promise of his own back, confess that he'd been thinking about blowing Owen all day, thinking about how good it felt when he was on his knees, everything falling away other than the two of them, nothing to worry about other than getting

Owen off. "And everyone needs to know how to make cookies. It's like basic life skills. My mom makes incredible cookies including these iced coffee-flavored ones, and almond ones that are out of this world."

"Sounds tasty." Quill finished with his part of the dough and moved to wash his hands.

"Want me to ask her to send us a care package? I bet she would love to do that for you."

"Cookies for me?" Quill blinked, not sure he'd ever gotten a care package before. "Why would she want to do that? She's never met me."

"She's heard enough stories. Trust me. She'd be happy to send some cookies. I'll ask next time I call." Owen dusted off his hands like it was all settled.

"You've...uh...told your mom about me? Us?"

"She's like, what? A thousand miles away?" Owen's tone was the verbal equivalent of an eye roll. "And no, I don't tell her about my sex life. But she likes hearing about things like the northern lights and clearing snow from the roofs, and I'm sorry, but you do crop up in my stories from time to time."

"Oh. Okay." Quill swallowed hard. Owen had promised not to out him at work, but the guy did like to talk, and it wasn't reasonable to expect no one to guess. Of course a social guy like Owen was going to talk to his family and friends. And similarly, he wasn't going to understand why Quill got uncomfortable knowing he was the subject of said conversation.

"Come on. You can't tell me you never mention me at all? Like to your friend Hattie?" Owen's tone was curious, but an undercurrent of hurt there made Quill's neck ache.

"I told her you're doing a great job."

"And that's it?"

"No need to tell her anything else." When Owen's face fell, he scrambled to add, "Wouldn't want to put her in a…weird situation at work. Her knowing more than maybe she should."

"Yeah." Owen sounded far from convinced, but before Quill could further insert his foot into his mouth and ruin what was left of Owen's good mood, his sat phone rang with a number he recognized all too well.

"Hang on," he said to Owen before answering, instinctively moving closer to the window where reception was always a little better. And unfortunately the news wasn't good. Never was, getting a callout after dark.

"I've got to go," he told Owen after he ended the call, already gathering his gear. "There's report of a two-car accident with injuries on the road, just inside our boundary. I'm closer than the rescue crew, which is en route, but I can get there quicker with the snow-machine, triage the situation, and help the crew block the road and get set for medical evacuation if we need a chopper. Don't wait up."

"I'm coming with you." Owen started yanking on his own gear, putting his snow pants right over his sweats.

"No. You've got cookies in the oven, and I'm not sure what we're looking at here. No."

"Quill. You *said* you'd use me for backup." Still buttoning his pants, Owen yanked the cookies out of the oven and shut it off. "And like you just said, someone needs to block the road. I can set out flares and whatnot while you assess. I'm not going to pretend to have your first-aid skills, but I'm not useless either."

Quill seriously didn't have time to argue, but not

knowing whether there were fatalities or gruesome injuries had him wanting to keep Owen far away. However, Owen had a point. He might well need another
pair of hands.

"Okay. You let me handle the injuries though, okay?
And listen to me."

"Not a kid. I can take directions." Owen finished
bundling up and followed Quill down the stairs. On
that point, Quill begged to differ—Owen lived to be
in charge, whether it was baking or snow removal or
in bed. He had his doubts that Owen would stay where
Quill put him.

Taking the snowmachines with the headlights blaz-
ing, they made good time to the road where three cars
awaited them. A badly mangled SUV had tangled with
an equally mashed-up pickup truck, and an undamaged
SUV had stopped to help, an older male driver with a
grim expression waving them over.

"Do the flares," Quill ordered Owen before approaching the scene, first-aid kit in hand.

"You the ranger?" the man asked Quill. His pale
face was somber, eyes panicked. "How soon you think
they'll get an ambulance here? It's bad."

"Help's on the way," Quill assured him, stomach
sinking, already knowing this was going to be one of
those nights that got under his skin, the kind he wore
on his soul. His ears strained, listening for distant sirens, but only coming up with crying coming from the
SUV. Kid. Crap. Racing between the two vehicles, he
did a fast assessment of the situation. Truck had two
male victims, driver who was already gone, damn it all
to hell, and an unconscious passenger who was in bad
shape, but not a lot Quill could do until rescuers arrived.

SUV had an unconscious female driver bleeding profusely from her thigh and an apparently unscathed kid yowling in a car seat in the back.

Quill immediately got to work, made a fast call to let dispatch know that a chopper was absolutely warranted, and then moving to apply pressure to the driver's leg. Meanwhile, the kid kept up a steady cry. And much as Quill hated to admit it, he did need help, and the panicked good Samaritan wasn't going to be it as he was back over by his own vehicle, leaning heavily on his hood.

"Owen!" he shouted, only for him to immediately appear at Quill's side.

"Yeah? What do you need from me?"

"I've got to keep pressure on this wound. Need you to check out the kid in the back. Don't remove him from the car seat—gotta let the EMTs do that in case of neck injury—but assess for injuries I didn't see, and maybe you can calm him down a little?"

"I'm on it." Owen wrenched open the dented rear door and climbed right in next to the car seat, which occupied the middle space. "Hey, buddy, how you doing?"

Somehow simply having someone focused on the crying kid helped Quill to keep his attention on the driver, doing his best to assess vitals and keep her alive until medical help arrived. Meanwhile, in the back, Owen spoke to the kid in soothing tones before raising his voice.

"No injuries that I can see. His name's Gus and he's three. Scared, but I don't think he's in shock."

"Good work." Quill didn't look up from his victim, but he was still impressed.

"Yeah. We're making friends. There are some blankets back here that I'm packing around him. What's up with the people in the truck? Need me to head there next?"

"No." Quill kept his answer curt, matter-of-fact because he needed to, couldn't let emotions swamp him, not after all these years on the job. He knew how to keep his distance. "Driver was gone when we arrived. Passenger's not bleeding that I could see, but also not conscious. I'd like to check vitals again, maybe get some blankets on the passenger, but I can't leave this victim to go back there yet."

"Yeah, I feel you. But I can."

"You don't need—"

"Gus, buddy, I'll be right back. Got a lollipop for you here." There was a rustling sound and then Owen was gone before Quill could even curse at him for not listening.

Quill got the driver's bleeding to slow a little. Still no sound of sirens. Breathing hard, Owen returned, climbing back in next to Gus.

"Thready pulse on the passenger. Shallow respiration. I put blankets all around him, best as I could." Owen sounded like he was holding it together by a single fingernail.

"Okay. You did good. All we can do." Damn it. Quill didn't want to lose both victims from the truck. Where was that crew?

"Gus, how you doing?" Owen shifted his attention to the kid, voice brightening, but Quill knew him well enough to say it was forced. Miraculously, though, he started playing some sort of counting game with him, kept the kid calm, until finally Quill heard sirens.

The EMT team took over, quickly followed by Highway Patrol, which assumed responsibility for working the scene. Quill spoke to the trooper in charge, a tall, capable woman, as he moved aside for the medics to work on the driver.

"I've got the mom's cell phone." Owen came jogging over to Quill and the trooper and handed her the phone. "Gus says his dad's name is Brian. Figured you might need this for finding next of kin for him."

"Smart thinking." The trooper nodded at Owen, respect clear in her dark eyes. "After the medics check him out, I'll transfer the kid and his seat to my vehicle and get to work on locating the dad, see if he can meet us at the hospital. Sorry for the delay. This is the third accident we've worked tonight. Second with a fatality. Been a hell of a night."

"Yeah," Quill and Owen agreed in unison. Owen's shoulders slumped, and the sharp lines in his face looked years older, a weariness about him that belied how light and good he'd been with the kid. Quill yearned to pull him into a tight embrace, tell him again that he did the best he could, tell him that tonight would suck, but that it did get easier with time. He'd been here before and he'd be here again, but this was Owen's first time with a scene like this, and all Quill's muscles tensed with the need to make it okay for him.

The troopers had many questions for them and for the driver who had stopped to help, and it was quite some time after the ambulance left to rendezvous with a helicopter that the scene was finally cleared. Owen stayed the whole time, despite Quill telling him more than once to head back, stubbornly insisting on staying. By the time they were finally able to leave, Quill could barely feel his feet, chilled to his marrow.

"Tea for everyone. Then a hot shower and lots of

blankets," Owen declared as they entered the building, bossy streak making a blessed reappearance right when Quill really needed to not be the one thinking. If Owen had a plan, so much the better because Quill wasn't good for much besides stripping off his gear, stowing his piece, stomping upstairs, and flopping into a kitchen chair. Owen draped one of the blankets from the couch around his shoulders before doing the same for himself, wearing it like a cape as he made tea. "Bourbon in yours? I found a bottle in the cabinet the other week."

"Yeah." Quill didn't often imbibe, but he needed the burn of the liquor even more than any warmth-giving properties. The bourbon was there exactly for nights like this one where Quill had done his best and it still hadn't been enough. Fucking universe and its random acts of cruelty.

After adding a healthy glug of liquor to each of their mugs, Owen shoved a cup at Quill. He also put a plate of cookies from the batch that got baked on the table. "Here you go. Eat something so the alcohol doesn't hit too hard."

"Feels like I should be the one taking care of you," Quill admitted after he'd had a few sips of tea, let the warmth and burn work past the tightness in his throat and chest.

"We can take care of each other," Owen countered, pulling his chair close to Quill's. "That's what we're here for, right?"

A few hours ago, Quill would have argued that being alone was the best way to cope with something like this—find a way to push through and on to the next day either with the aid of some strong drink or just a restless night spent replaying the events until sleep did its thing, softened the edges of the awfulness. But when Owen grabbed his hand, squeezed, and looked at him with such compassion in his eyes, Quill couldn't find it in himself to pull away.

"Yeah," he said, even as he knew that he shouldn't let himself come to need Owen like this, to lean on him. He and Hattie had always tended to retreat to their own corners after a hard shift, and he prided himself on being a strong man. Sure, accidents like this affected him as they would anyone, but he'd always tried to handle those emotions on his own. Harsh memories of his father's comments about men who showed their feelings didn't help any, but lately all those memories, all the family drama, seemed more distant. Less sharp.

And funny how without that mantle of a painful past, his present seemed somehow more hopeful, old wounds and past fears no match for Owen. In fact, they'd been on the verge of another disagreement when Owen had dropped everything to come help. And now here he was, taking care of Quill yet again. Owen simply didn't seem to have it in him to hold a grudge too long. Quill would be a fool to pull away now, even if he knew the next night like this, the inevitable one after Owen left, would hurt that much more. But that moment, all he wanted to do was hold Owen close, take every comfort he offered from Christmas lights to hot toddies to underdone gingerbread to that strong hand of his, holding on when Quill needed it most.

Chapter Nineteen

Owen had reached the point with winter where he was fairly sure he'd never be fully warm again. Ever since that terrible car accident, his bones felt more brittle, like all the hot toddies and showers in the world weren't going to be enough to thaw the ice encasing his limbs.

"Can't believe it's Christmas Eve already." Quill's voice was distracted as he bundled up to go out on his afternoon patrol before the sun set completely.

"Yeah." In the days after the accident, Owen had pushed the holidays and seasonal stuff from his mind. Oh, they probably needed distraction now more than ever, but it was hard to throw himself into cookie baking or decorating knowing that for some the holiday season was already ruined. But that didn't mean he'd forgotten entirely about his desire to make a good memory for Quill. "The mail you brought yesterday had a box from my mom. We can have the cookies with dinner. She sent presents too."

"Presents plural, for you?" Quill blinked.

"There's something for you too. Told you. I talk about you." Which he knew made Quill less than comfortable, but it wasn't like Owen was sharing any private details, hadn't labeled Quill his boyfriend or anything like that. Sure enough, Quill frowned, and Owen had to sigh. "Come on. You're the only other human I see a lot of days. It's mention you or just give her the weather report."

"Yeah. I suppose so." Finishing with his gear, Quill headed toward the stairs, pausing at the door. "I'll be back in time for dinner. I can help. We should do something nice to go with the cookies."

"I'll think up something." Owen tried to convey with his smile that he appreciated Quill making an effort and not getting in a funk over what Owen shared with his mom. And dinner to look forward to had his own spirits lifting too. Somehow, they'd slid from most meals separate to most meals shared, cooking together most nights.

Daydreaming over dinner possibilities got Owen through the next few hours of trail grooming before the rapidly fading light chased him back in. It was cold and clear again. They'd had a great view of the northern lights a few nights back, delighting a fresh group of tourists, but snow was scheduled to roll in again in the next few days, with a real chance that they'd be snowed in for New Year's.

"Salmon pot pie," he announced to Quill when they were both back in the kitchen.

"You just want to use your new rolling pin again." Quill laughed, even though his eyes were somber, the memory of the cookie baking night there too. "But sure, I'll cook some fish. You can talk me through a sauce, and maybe we can sneak a cookie while it bakes?"

"Hungry?" Owen waggled his eyebrows at Quill. He had more than a few ideas for how to kill a half hour or so while the pie baked.

"Maybe." Quill's blush started at his neck and worked

its way up. For once, he was in neither uniform nor heavy outdoor gear, having beat Owen back to their quarters and apparently having showered, judging by his damp hair, thick sweat pants and thermal shirt. "But I wouldn't want your creation to burn."

"Can't have that." Owen made quick work of a simple crust, then they poured in the filling and popped it in the oven. Straightening, he announced, "We need music."

"Music?" Quill looked thoughtful. "Like the kind you dance to when you think I'm not around? Or the seasonal kind?"

"Either. I've got a winter playlist in my saved stuff that's more like snowed-in music, but I think there's a few holiday songs in there too."

"I…I like holiday music." Quill delivered this news with almost comical formality. "That was always my favorite part of the season. The music at church and school. My parents didn't fight at church, and everyone was always quiet when the choir sang. I've got some CDs you might not hate."

"Might not hate? High praise, there." Owen laughed. "And I'm not laughing at *you*. I think it's adorable. I knew somewhere in there was someone who liked seasonal stuff. Yes, get your CDs."

Quill ducked into his room and returned a few moments later with a box of CDs and small portable stereo— the sort of thing Owen hadn't seen in years. And instead of making out, they spent the time the pot pie was in the oven digging through Quill's music collection. It was a little like seeing a time capsule or photo album of Quill's younger self—learning the bands he'd loved in college, the songs he still loved from childhood like the 80s VH1 staples his mom had apparently favored and the classic country of his grandfather, and the music he'd discovered as an adult.

They left an acoustic holiday CD on while they ate, and it was so cozy that by the time he retrieved his mom's package and his own present for Quill everything from his teeth to his toes ached with want. This felt too sweet to not be the start of something magical, the sort of traditions a couple would fall back on year after year.

He had some sort of reverse flashback thing going, a vision of future Quill playing music and eating salmon pot pie for the tenth year in a row simply because they'd done it the once and he "didn't hate it." Owen had to blink hard, keep himself centered in the present, in what was actually possible.

"Here. Let's start with the cookies." He set the package on the table, almost failing to notice that a wrapped present had also appeared next to Quill.

"What's that?"

"I believe you said something about all kids wanting presents in December?" A shy smile tugged at Quill's mouth, making him look younger and more bashful. "Maybe you were extra good this year."

"Oh, I plan to be later, trust me." Owen had to squeeze the joke out past an almost painfully tight throat. Opening a plastic container of iced coffee cookies nestled next to almond cookies, he was immediately transported to his mom's house, the same kitchen he'd grown up in, all the smells and flavors of home. And more than wanting to be there, wanting to be among his family, he wanted to give that to Quill, give him tastes and memories and *home*. That grounding place deep inside that kept a person warm when nothing else worked.

He wanted to be that for Quill in the worst way, and all the longing made time seem to slow down as they sampled the cookies and opened the presents from his mom. She'd sent colorful thermal socks and hand-knit scarves from a craft bazaar for both of them along with a typically breezy note about the crafters she'd met at the fair. There was also local chocolate and tea for Owen, his favorite Bay Area brands.

"She likes color." Quill studied his gifts, but the faint stain to his cheeks and his bright eyes said he was pleased.

"Tuck them in and no one will know other than you." Owen laughed, but damn if that wasn't a metaphor for Quill's whole life.

"Guess that's true." Quill slid his wrapped package toward Owen. "Here. Since we're doing presents."

"The wrapping is super nice." Owen's mother and grandmother had raised him to take note of such things and to open presents slowly, which he did now.

"It's from a gift store near Wasilla. They did the wrapping, not me. But I do hope you like it."

"It's a sketchbook. And pencils." Owen beamed at him as he uncovered a bound sketchbook of nice paper and sets of both drawing pencils and colored pencils.

"Well, you can't keep using up all the copy paper. And like I've said, we need to get you some hobbies. Still a lot of winter left to go." Quill's explanation was practical, just like him, but the undercurrent of affection there made Owen's heart pinch. Winter wasn't nearly long enough, was going much too fast.

"I like it. Maybe I'll make you some comics. And bring on more winter." He kept his voice light in case time was dragging for Quill and he didn't feel the same way about wringing out every drop of joy they could with the time they had left. Maybe part of him was counting down to spring, when he could have his quiet life back. And Owen knew he could just ask Quill, but he didn't want to spoil this lovely mood. "Open yours now. It's not as useful as your present to me, sorry."

After unwrapping the box, Quill lifted out the contents. "It's…a moose?"

"Yeah." Owen had spotted the adorable stuffed moose on his last trip into Anchorage. "Maybe it's silly, but I was thinking both about my first day here and about how you need a friend to lighten up with. You don't always have to be the serious big, bad ranger. He can live on your desk or something."

"I like it. Thank you." Quill's smile was tentative and boyish. Owen had weighed and discarded dozens of other present ideas—cold weather wear was more of a mom present, most books far too impersonal, food too temporary, and anything sexy too presumptuous. "Your first day feels so long ago now. It feels like I've known you far longer than merely months."

"And that's a good thing, right?" Owen couldn't resist pushing a little, earlier doubts crowding in.

"Think so, yeah. The moose is cute and all, but you forgot that I've already got a friend to make me lighten up." His smile morphed into something so tender that Owen's sinuses got embarrassingly tingly, totally undone by something as small as Quill acknowledging them as friends.

"We should dance," he said as the music shifted to a holiday love song, a slow bluesy number. Hiding his face in Quill's shoulder sounded about perfect right then, not wanting him to see all the emotions coursing through Owen. Standing, he didn't give Quill much chance to object, tugging him out of his chair.

"I'm hardly good at this," Quill protested even as his arms came around Owen.

"There's nothing to it. Pretend we're at a school dance. Just stand and sway, Quill. Stand and sway."

"I can do that." Quill's voice was solemn, almost as if he were promising more than simply a dance, and Owen's chest expanded, trying to contain everything he felt for this man. And as they danced there in the kitchen area, holiday lights twinkling around the room, presents and discarded wrapping paper on the table, Owen had that flash-forward sensation again, a deep yearning to be here, not just now but years from now, song transforming from a random tune to their song, the one they came back to over and over. Maybe that would never happen, but Owen let himself fall into the fantasy as the music washed over them. And when Quill's mouth sought his, he totally gave himself over to whatever was coming next, whatever Quill needed and wanted.

Chapter Twenty

The kiss was slow and sweet, and unlike anything Quill had ever had before. With most of their kisses, Owen seized control quickly, but this time, he seemed content to simply sink into Quill, let the moment drive them, let the music sweep them away. Owen tasted sugary and familiar—the taste that Quill couldn't remember not craving. He hadn't been lying earlier when he'd said that he couldn't believe it had been only a few months of friendship. It felt so much longer, as if they'd had decades together, the sort of connection he'd never had before, never even realized he was missing, and the kiss reflected all of that. Even if talking were easier for him, he doubted he could put his emotions into words, so he put it all in the kiss. Gratitude. Longing. Desire. Need.

Eventually the CD ended with a click, leaving them there in the silence, clinging to each other.

"Damn." Owen broke away first, looking up at Quill with shining eyes. "That was…"

"Yeah." Quill tightened his hold on Owen, not ready to let go, not yet.

"Guess that's one way to say Happy Holidays." Owen nuzzled in to Quill's neck. "Merry Christmas, Quill. Tell me I get to unwrap you next."

"Yeah." Quill's voice was gruff, want that he'd had for days now building inside him. "We can do that."

"Excellent." Tugging Quill in the direction of the couch, Owen gave him a dirty smile, one that went straight to Quill's dick.

"Not that." Quill stopped him. Need welled up in him, but it didn't make it any easier to speak.

"Shower?" Owen's head tilted. Damn it. He was always so solicitous of Quill's boundaries, so careful not to push further than Quill was comfortable going, but he also wasn't a mind reader. Quill really was going to have to spell this out.

"Bed." He reversed their linked hands, pulling Owen towards his room. He'd never invited Owen in before, but the last few times he'd slept in here and not in the warmer common room, loneliness and longing had blanketed him, made him toss and turn. He'd never been curious about sleeping next to another person before, only done it a handful of times with JP thanks to roommates and dorm rooms, and indeed he'd been a little apprehensive about sharing his space like that. But slowly, what used to make his back muscles tense had transformed to arousal at the thought of Owen in his bed, Owen all night long, Owen completely naked at long last. Owen making Quill's filthiest fantasies come true.

Anticipation had a happy shiver racing up his spine, but Owen must have read his shudder wrong, pausing to squeeze Quill's hand. "Would my bed be easier? And we don't have to do anything new or different. All the things we already know we love are fine by me."

It was the way Owen said *we* that gave Quill fresh courage. This was Owen. Owen who made sex fun,

Owen who was always up for anything but was not demanding, Owen who genuinely liked it all from sweet to messy and all the dirty destinations in between.

"My room is fine. I want to have sex," he said in a rush.

"Oh?" Owen's eyes went wide but wary. "We've had plenty of sex, so you mean fucking, yeah?"

"Yeah." God, Owen really was going to make him get specific.

"Okay. Okay." Owen nodded, eyes still guarded. "Like I said, sometimes my post-surgery nerve endings don't cooperate, but we can try. I'm game for trying for you."

Fuck. Of course Owen, like most of the damn planet, would assume Quill meant that he'd like to top.

"Not that." Both his cheeks and throat were flaming hot. "Want you to fuck me."

"Oh, *yeah*." Eyes going from wary to hot and feral, Owen's eagerness was exactly what Quill had been hoping for, and he had to grin back when Owen beamed at him. "Way better idea. Merry Christmas to us. You have supplies?"

"Bought some last time I was in town," he mumbled. He'd been thinking about this for weeks now, couldn't get the images out of his brain along with his deep certainty that it would be different with Owen. Better. No feeling terrible after. Every time they had sex was good, and the crushing loneliness he'd often associated with hookups was a distant memory. And this was Owen, who seemed to genuinely love all aspects of sex. He wasn't going to make Quill feel bad for wanting this.

Indeed, Owen had a bounce in his step as he followed Quill into his room. Despite his inherently curious nature, Owen didn't spend a long time looking around Quill's space. Although honestly, there wasn't a ton to see. Double bed on the far wall, thick brown comforters that were more practical than fashionable, stuffed bookshelves lining the walls—reading being his one indulgence—everything else in the room chosen for durability and space-saving design. But he didn't have much time to contemplate the room from Owen's point of view because Owen was back to kissing him intently while he pulled up Quill's shirt.

"If I promise to keep you warm, can we get all the way naked?"

"That would be the point." Quill had to tease him. "Kinda hard to fuck otherwise."

"True, true." Owen had them both undressed and under Quill's covers in short order, fast efficient moments that still managed to ramp Quill up from nothing more than glancing touches and the sight of Owen's clothes on his floor. He didn't get nearly long enough to study Owen's nude body either, the miles of smooth golden skin, those defined arm and chest muscles and swimmer's shoulders and back with a high, tight ass. He'd seen him in the shower a few times as well, but he was never going to get tired of looking at that gorgeous body.

But even without the visual, having all that bare skin pressed against his under the covers was unspeakably hot. Somehow, in his fantasies, they always headed straight to the fucking, but he should have known that Owen would want to take his time, kissing for a long time, keeping to his promise to warm Quill up with long strokes of his broad hands.

Owen kept it playful too, rolling from their sides to Quill on top, erections rubbing together as the kissing got deeper and more urgent. The newness of having Owen in his space melted away, along with the awkwardness of asking for the sex, leaving only hot, intoxicating desire coursing through him. Right when their thrusts started to get more purposeful and Quill was close to begging him to get on with it before he came too soon, Owen flipped them again. He straddled Quill, covers around his shoulders as he sat up enough to trace circles in Quill's chest hair.

"Tell me how you usually like it. What makes it good for you? Fingers okay?" Owen continued to play, hands dancing over Quill's nipples, distracting him from his rising embarrassment from the question, one he wasn't sure he'd ever gotten before, at least not like this. Owen's tone was genuinely curious, eyes kind, not judgmental. And if Quill was going to do this, was going to let himself have this fantasy, he might as well go all in.

"On my stomach. And fingers are good. Been… uh…a while," he mumbled before he turned to dig the condoms and lube out of his nightstand. His brain echoed with JP's trademark sneer, the way he'd always gone on about how anal, particularly in certain positions, was degrading. Shaking his head to free it from those voices, he told his past to fuck off. Owen had already shown him several times over that not everyone was JP with his opinions and idiosyncrasies about sex. And whatever other past experiences he'd had no longer felt relevant either. This was blessedly new, a giving partner, one who seemed to want nothing more than to make Quill feel good.

"Fabulous. Flip." Owen gave him a last tweak of his nipple before rolling off Quill and shoving at his shoulder. "And get comfy. I'm planning to take my time."

He wasn't lying either, starting with rubbing Quill's shoulders, something he'd done any number of times since he'd first given Quill a massage in the kitchen, all those weeks earlier, but it felt different now, more laced with anticipation, more designed to ramp Quill up with little kisses and drags of his short nails. He worked his way lower, rubbing Quill's lower back, all the tension he carried there easing as Owen worked him over, and by the time Owen progressed to massaging his ass, he was in a pleasant, almost sleepy, half-drunk state, one where it was easy to spread his legs, give Owen more room to work.

When Owen bent to pepper his back and ass with kisses, Quill was too relaxed to tense, even though he kind of knew where Owen was heading with this. Hell, if he was truly honest with himself, he'd thought about this while he'd showered before dinner, wondering if he'd get up the courage to invite Owen into his bed. While he hadn't been rimmed before, he'd had a feeling given Owen's love of all things oral that it was in his repertoire and had let himself fantasize about it more than a few times. And Owen didn't disappoint, wiggling backward on the bed, licking and biting at Quill's ass cheeks before settling in to tease his crack. It was wet and hot and—

"Fuck." He moaned low when Owen's tongue connected with his rim for the first time, so much better than any furtive late-night fantasy.

"Yeah. That's it. Let me have my fun," Owen said before resuming his onslaught, licking and teasing, alternating broad swipes of his tongue with pointed little flicks.

And if this was truly fun for Owen, then Quill was

content to let him have it all he wanted, because *damn*. The sensations were almost overwhelming, one on top of the other, nerve endings singing. It was weird too, being this turned on but not on the verge of orgasm either. More like he wanted to wallow in the pleasure, bathe in it, let it go on and on.

And it did, Owen ramping up his attack every time Quill moaned, seemingly rewarding him for not holding in his groans until a steady stream of nonsense was spewing from Quill's mouth.

"Yeah, yeah. Like that. Please."

"Fuck. You're so damn hot when you beg." Owen moved back, and the sound of foil crinkling and lube being opened echoed in the small room. His fingers were cool and slippery against Quill's rim, rubbing and teasing before pressing in. When Quill fingered himself, he always went straight for two fingers, too impatient to go slow and loving the friction and burn of two at once, and somehow Owen seemed to know that, finding the perfect mix of stretching and insistent pressure as he worked his fingers in deeper.

"God." Quill was legitimately gasping for air now, sucking down oxygen as Owen's deft fingers robbed him of the power to do anything other than moan. "Now. Please now."

"Oh yeah." Withdrawing his fingers, he pushed Quill's knees up, kneeling behind him and rubbing his cock up and down Quill's crack, a delicious tease.

"Please." Quill kept his torso low, loving the drag of the sheets against his aching cock.

"Ask me again. Tell me what you want," Owen demanded, voice low and rough.

"Fuck me." The words came so much easier now, especially now that Owen was asking for them, no intent to demean or humiliate, just two incredibly turned-on guys who both wanted this. Needed it even.

"Fuck, yes." Owen pushed in slow, giving Quill lots of time to adjust. The position created a tighter angle than when Quill did himself on his back or side, but he welcomed the pinch and burn, the all-encompassing sensations of being penetrated. Breathing deep, he tried to memorize the feel, so different from fingers, so full. His chest expanded with the breath, oxygen reaching newly created spaces as he let go of years and years of tension, totally gave himself over to this, over to Owen. No more judgments. No more holding back, denying himself something this good.

And *good* was a vast understatement, especially once Owen's broad cock connected with his prostate, angle perfect, pressure exquisite.

"That. That. More." Quill's hips started rocking back on their own, urging Owen deeper and faster.

"So hot. So good." Owen's praise and moans mingled with Quill's own, a symphony of arousal that he never wanted to end. For once in his life, he wasn't chasing orgasm as efficiently as possible, instead simply letting himself ride the ever-cresting wave of good feelings. He'd seen Owen's stamina working out in the snow, and he put all that into fucking, taking his time to reduce Quill to nothing more than a babbling heap of nerve endings, one unerring thrust at a time.

"Quill. God. Can't…" Owen's voice was ragged, at odds with the precise slide of his hips, and listening to him come undone was possibly even sexier than the fucking. His muscles tensed as Owen moaned, that elusive climax suddenly barreling toward him.

"Think I'm gonna..." He couldn't keep his amazement out of his gasp.

"Get there. Please." Owen's thrusts lost some finesse, which only ratcheted up Quill's desire, physical proof that this was affecting Owen as much as him.

"Yeah, yeah." The combo of friction against the sheet and pressure in his ass was almost enough, everything he'd ever thought that fucking could be and so much more than even those fantasies. Like swinging out on a rope swing, closest thing he'd ever had to flying, and part of him didn't want to let go of the rope, wanted a little more time in the air before the drop. But his body had other ideas, especially once Owen shifted his weight, working a hand under Quill's stomach. His fingertips brushed Quill's dick, not enough room to stroke. Simply that limited contact had Quill making a sound he didn't even know he was capable of, a low, keening whimper of pleasure as he came.

"Yes. Oh my God. Yes." Owen thrust hard and fast, moans changing to the gulping sounds Quill always associated with him about to come. Even before Quill's cock and ass had finished pulsing, Owen was collapsing on him, a warm, beautiful weight. "I'll move. Promise. Someday."

"No hurry." Quill's words came out rough, throat rawer than he'd realized. He should be embarrassed, how he'd moaned and carried on, but right then, he couldn't summon any shame. Only person who he cared about was right here, breathing equally hard, and he didn't seem to be in any hurry to berate Quill for his loss of control. In fact, Owen kept dropping little kisses against Quill's shoulders, murmuring muffled words of praise.

Eventually Owen did move, Quill's ass protesting his withdrawal, body missing his warmth as Owen took care of the condom before sprawling next to Quill. He was sticky in multiple places, would probably need to change sheets before sleeping for real, and his ass along with other muscles would be feeling that tomorrow. In short, he was an exhausted mess, and he wasn't sure he'd ever been happier.

"Give me a minute and then I'll help you clean up." Owen yawned. "And I don't have to sleep in here."

"Yeah, you do." Quill reached over and squeezed Owen's arm. "Stay."

God, had he ever meant a single syllable so completely? The request seemed to echo though every emotional place he'd opened up that evening, a new sort of need, one he wasn't sure he'd ever experienced before. An almost spiritual ache. *Stay. I need you to stay.*

Owen needed to stay. Right here, in this bed, possibly forever. Like spring could come and he'd still be here, not quite recovered from the cataclysmic shift that had happened inside his brain that evening. And it wasn't just the sex, which had been world-altering good in and of itself, but also the presents, the dancing, the sheer excess of feelings that had been building all day. All month maybe. He couldn't even say when it had started, only that he was here now, in this place where he couldn't remember ever not feeling this intensely for Quill.

He'd had boyfriends before, including ones he'd deeply liked. But nothing had ever made him ache quite like this. A boyfriend before had been something to work into his life, slot into the space in his existing life he made for socializing, not something to build around, the cornerstone of a life he hadn't even known he'd wanted. He'd always sworn that he wouldn't change for love, that he wasn't about to rearrange himself and who he was for another person. And he'd believed that love, if and when he found it, should come easy, not have to be worked for like grades or a job or a fitness goal. He wasn't here to run a relationship triathlon where the outcome was anything but guaranteed.

Except...

Maybe he was. He'd been goal oriented his whole life, but so much of it had been other people's goals—parents, siblings, friends, society at large. Then he'd transferred that energy to his bucket list, his own goals for the first time, but still nothing had felt as right as lying here next to Quill did. He'd never wanted anything the way he wanted Quill. Hell, he even wanted Quill more than he wanted sleep, not wanting to waste these precious moments.

Despite the late hour, his pulse still galloped, he was wide awake, and his legs moved restlessly against the sheets as he watched Quill stretch and settle.

"Cold?" Quill pulled the pile of blankets more securely around them. They'd showered and put on pajamas in deference to the chilly air earlier, then remade the bed with clean sheets like a couple who had been doing domestic tasks together for decades. He'd half expected Quill to change his mind about sleeping next to each other after the sex coma wore off, but either Quill was still riding the sex high or the evening had affected him as deeply as it had Owen because he certainly seemed like a changed guy, all cuddly and solicitous.

"A little." Like his own, Quill's room was colder than the common space, but mainly Owen wanted the excuse to burrow deeper into Quill's side. And Quill took the hint, gathering him close.

"This is…nice." Quill's voice was muffled by Owen's hair.

"You sound surprised." Owen laughed before kissing the arm Quill had wrapped around his chest and shoulders. "I mean bed sharing isn't for all couples, and you certainly do seem to have high personal space needs, but if you ask me, sleepy cuddles are the best."

"They're not bad." Quill kissed the top of his head. "Can't say as I've ever had this before, so not really any comparison, but I like it with you."

"Never?" Owen resisted the urge to preen. He liked being the first to give Quill this sort of closeness and ease.

"Not really a spend-the-night kind of guy. And JP, he was one of those high-space-needs people, way more so than me. But I was young and he was the first, so I didn't know any different, but he wasn't big on touch."

"How'd you guys meet anyway? You hardly seem like the type to show up at an LGBTQ campus event."

Quill snorted, but for once, he didn't try to sidestep questions about his past. "I wasn't. He was more into that sort of scene and other extracurriculars. We were in the same first-year seminar together. Our group went on a camping trip prior to the start of school, and we were assigned to share a tent. He hated every damn thing about being outdoors, but somehow he decided he liked me."

"You're easy to like."

"You're being nice because you want another round

to make you fall asleep." Quill's laugh was light, nothing like the seriousness he all too often carried around with him. "Anyway, it's ancient history now. I can see now that what we had wasn't exactly healthy. I'm not over here pining for him if that's what you're worried about."

"I'm not," Owen said quickly, even though he kind of had been. He didn't want to have to compete with a memory for a slice of Quill's tightly guarded heart. And hearing Quill admit that the relationship had been flawed had his pulse surging, hope turning out to be more potent than adrenaline.

"Liar." Ducking his head, Quill pressed an open-mouthed kiss on the back of Owen's neck. One of his big hands snaked under Owen's waistband. "And how is it that you're still so awake? My alarm's gonna piss you off if you don't sleep soon."

"You should do something about that." Owen stretched into Quill's explorations.

"Guess I could." Quill faked disinterest, but Owen could feel him hard against his ass.

"You *are* a public servant." Owen laughed as the need to kiss Quill triumphed over how good he felt against his back, and he spun in his arms so that they were front-to-front. And when their mouths met, he found not just hope waiting for him in the kiss, but faith as well. Faith that this wasn't some passing fling, sureness permeating his every cell. He might not know much, might not have a clue as to what came next, but he had faith in his feelings. *Their* feelings, because he had to have faith that Quill felt the same way. And maybe Quill wasn't ever going to say it, but his kiss spoke volumes. The way he clung to Owen, the tenderness of his lips, the reverence in his touch. All of it said that this thing they'd found together was real. Bigger than either of them alone. And Owen was going to do whatever it took to keep it, wasn't going to let this go without a fight.

Chapter Twenty-One

Quill had never been as grateful for the short daylight hours as he was in the days leading up to the new year. Short days meant long nights, meant more time with Owen. More laughing. More cooking. More sex. More sleeping. Hell, had he ever loved sleeping this much? Twice now he'd actually hit the snooze button to get a little more time with Owen in his arms. Working alone in the dark predawn hours had never held less appeal for him. No, his greatest pleasure right now was working side by side with Owen, being able to glance in his direction and get a smile that kept him warmer in the frigid temperatures than even his favorite gloves.

Like right then, Owen's smile and delight were almost blinding as they used their cross-country skis to do a check of all the buildings and some trails that couldn't be done easily on the snowmachines. In a short time, the sun would set by four again, making for an early New Year's Eve for those energetic souls out on the trails. At least, Quill hoped it would be an early night. He had a surprise for Owen, and a callout wasn't part of his plans. However if the weather held, by midmorning tomorrow the area would be clogged again with people looking to make the most of the first day of the year. Which was

why he and Owen needed to check both the safety and
functionality of some of the more popular trails.

Technically, he could have left the work to Owen,
but his paperwork was caught up, patrol done, and the
impulse to spend more time with Owen undeniable.
So here he was laughing right along with Owen as he
pointed out a particularly gorgeous snow-covered vista.
The baby blue sky showed no traces of the storm that
had hit after Christmas, simply another clear, cold day
that perfectly showcased the snowcapped mountains,
craggy tips reaching toward the sun. But that same sun
worried Quill. Avalanche concerns this time of year
never disappeared, especially the ever-present risk of
human-triggered ones. Changing temperatures contributed to increased risks. The higher elevations were the
most concern, with forecasters warning of both slab
and loose avalanches, especially along steeper slopes.

Coming from the other direction, a young family
headed toward them—two adults on skis, trailed by two
elementary-aged kids with a smaller one riding in some
sort of back carrier, so bundled that Quill could barely
make out a face. They were all in blue and red parkas,
and it took him a moment to realize that it wasn't a dad
and a mom, but two men, laughing and joking with the
kids. Quill supposed it could be two uncles, same as
the women with the flat tire had been sisters-in-law, but
something about their ease with each other said they
were likely a couple.

"Afternoon!" Owen waved at the group. "How's the
trail looking back there?"

"Oh, we didn't make it very far." The smaller of the
two men laughed. "Short legs, short attention spans,

you know? But that's what a vacation's for, right? Making our own agenda. You guys with the park service?"

"Yup." Owen continued to beam at the family. "We're just out checking a few of the trails. Where are you guys from? First time to the area?"

"Portland!" The younger of the two kids piped up. "Our dads like snow for Christmas."

"Awesome." Owen gave the kid a high five. "Me too. And we've got plenty of it here."

Owen made a little more small talk with the family, doing that thing of his where he got their whole story in only a few minutes—college friends turned husbands who'd adopted the older two kids a year prior and the youngest a few months back. Eventually the kids got restless and the family continued on, leaving Quill and Owen to go forward down the trail.

Smile dimming, Owen gave the group a last look over his shoulder before following Quill. And when he stayed quiet, Quill didn't need a degree in mind reading to know that like with the tour guide and his boyfriend a few weeks earlier, the two-dad family had given Owen envy issues. Or more accurately, he'd probably compared Quill to what the other couples had and found Quill lacking. Which wasn't surprising, even if it did sting. The surprise he had planned seemed silly now. Whatever he had to offer Owen wasn't going to be enough, wasn't going to compare to what other established couples had, wasn't ever going to be the gift of openness that Owen deserved.

"Nice family." This time, Quill wasn't going to let him stew in silence. Not that he wanted a confrontation or disagreement, but Owen had shown him that sometimes uncomfortable conversation beat foreboding silence.

"Yeah. They were." Owen offered Quill a half smile.

"Kids on your bucket list?" Quill kept his voice casual, gaze ahead on the trail, not on Owen's face.

"For myself?" Short on breath from the skiing, Owen's words came in little huffs. "I'm honestly not sure. I've got nieces and nephews, and I love seeing kids and interacting with them, but I also like sending them home with their parents. I like my freedom—breakfast in my underwear, sex in the living room, last-minute vacations. Parenthood seems like a lot of work. And I'm not saying never, but it's not high on the bucket list, no."

Quill wasn't sure he entirely believed him—he could all too easily visualize Owen with a pack of kids crawling all over him, him laughing up a storm, freedom and workload be damned. But if Owen could pretend, so could Quill. "Ah. Never really thought about it for me."

"Yeah, I know. Married to the job and all. You don't have room for anything else." Owen's tone managed to be both affectionate and resigned.

Quill wanted to correct him, wanted to say that that wasn't accurate, especially not recently when he'd proved to himself that he did have a need for human contact. Friendship. A relationship. And sure, some might quibble and say that it wasn't a relationship if no one knew and it already had an end date, but Quill knew in his soul that this was the most significant interaction he'd had as an adult.

"Got room for you," he said at last, then feeling rather raw and exposed like he'd whipped off his gloves in negative twenty windchill, added quickly, "And Hattie. Friends. That sort of thing."

"Yeah." Owen's eyes were compassionate, but there was a sadness there too that Quill would give a lot to remove.

As they finished the rounds, he tried for distraction, falling back on old habits of pointing out places that looked ripe for avalanches or other dangers. Oh, he tried to find pretty views too, but some of the shine was gone from the day. And when they made it back to their quarters, he'd almost forgotten again that it was New Year's Eve.

"What's this?" Owen made a delighted sound as he finished stripping off his outer layer at the top of the stairs. He finished pulling off his heavy pants and padded over to the table. When Owen had been on trash duty earlier in the day, Quill had crept back upstairs to lay out his surprise—a nicely set table with a bottle of nonalcoholic champagne and two flutes in the center of the table. It was nothing really, and after the heaviness of their earlier conversation, embarrassment heated his face.

"You like holidays," he said lamely.

"I do." Owen's smile was wide and easy, earlier storm clouds in his eyes replaced by his inner sunshine again.

"We can't exactly leave to go out to a fancy restaurant with the amount of tourist traffic we're expecting this weekend, but I thought..." Quill licked his suddenly dry lips. "Thought I'd bring the nice dinner to you. I put salmon out to defrost, and I'll do the rest of dinner while you shower."

"I love it." Owen gave him a fast hug, brushing his lips across Quill's cheek. "Let me duck back downstairs to put some snow in a bucket to chill the champagne."

"It's not the real stuff. New Year's Eve is notorious for late-night emergencies. Sorry."

"It's perfect." Owen gave him another kiss, this one lingering. "And I'm crossing everything that there's no callout because I've got big plans for you at midnight."

"I have to wait until midnight?" Quill mock pouted simply to hear Owen laugh again.

"Dessert then. And midnight later." Owen grinned like a kid proposing ice cream for breakfast. "We'll start a new tradition of toasting in bed."

Tradition. The word left a scuff mark across Quill's brain. Tradition meant doing something year after year. And as someone who liked things a certain way, Quill had a million little traditions—same restaurant most trips to Anchorage, same laundry detergent, same seasoning for the fish, same first-of-the-season hike after the thaw. But almost all his traditions were solo ones. What Owen was referring to in his casual offhand manner were shared traditions. Something unique to them. Something they'd start now and come back to.

Except they wouldn't. Next New Year's wouldn't have a single damn tradition. Quill wouldn't let it, would lose himself in work, same as he always had, would try not to count how many days it had been since Owen. And in the years to follow, Owen would undoubtedly acquire a laundry list of traditions and holidays because he wanted that. Deserved that. All Quill got was this year, this one chance.

So, he'd push all thought of tradition aside. Make Owen the night he deserved because this was Quill's one shot to be that guy for him. Someone else would be the tradition guy, and Quill would be right here on this mountain, same as he'd been decades now, both nothing and everything changed. It was simply how it had to be, and he had no right to shake his fist at the universe and ask for more.

Owen was all too aware that life didn't contain many absolutely perfect moments. But right then, sitting up in Quill's bed, surrounded by a mountain of covers, cool fake champagne in his hand, hot ranger behind him, nineties love songs on Quill's stereo, and clock ticking toward midnight, life was pretty darn amazing.

"We should make a wish." He tapped Quill's glass with his own.

"It's a New Year's drink, not a birthday cake." Quill's laugh was easy, voice still sex-rough. True to his promise of sex as dessert, Owen had spent the past few hours fucking Quill until they were both incoherent messes. In the days since Christmas, they hadn't suddenly leapt into daily fucking or anything like that, but Owen was learning to pick up on Quill's subtle signals when that was what Quill wanted most. And after dinner when Quill had stretched and said, "Guess my room isn't too cold, if you wanted to…ah…" Owen had happily abandoned his blow job in front of the woodstove plans in favor of fucking Quill silly.

He still wasn't sure exactly what he'd done to get so lucky—big, sexy, take-charge ranger who happened to also love getting done. But now he had Quill, and he wasn't going to waste a second.

"Wishes are more fun than resolutions," he countered. After dozing a bit, they'd showered then collected the snacks to eat in bed, laughing like kids at a sleepover, and Owen wanted to keep that lightness going. "Everyone else is all making New Year's diet and healthy habit resolutions. I think it's way more fun to close our eyes and hope for something we want most in the New Year."

"Wishes without a plan are kind of pointless. No sense in hoping for something you're not gonna get, like fourteen hours of sun in January." Of course, Quill had to go and be the practical one. Under his resignation though, there was a certain wistfulness to Quill's words that damn near broke Owen's heart.

"Come on. If you could have one wish, what would be it be? Pretend I'm a wizard or something." Whatever it was, Owen would do everything in his power to make it happen for Quill.

"You are pretty amazing." Quill held Owen tighter. "And the way I see it, I've got what I need."

Owen couldn't help his heavy sigh. It must be nice to not have any restlessness, any doubts about one's place in the world, to not want anything more than what a person already had.

"Everything?" Working hard to not sound like he was fishing, Owen kept his voice light. But dude, would it kill Quill to have at least one Owen-centric wish? It made Owen feel like he was alone on a raft in an unfamiliar ocean, no land in sight. He had a long list of things he wanted, both realistic and not. And Quill insisting on being dour wasn't going to stop Owen from dreaming. If anything, it simply made him that much more determined. Ever since Christmas, he'd had a much clearer idea of what he wanted from life. He wanted Quill, wanted to erase the stupid expiration date on their fling. He might still be a little fuzzy on the details of how to accomplish that, but he wasn't going to give up without a fight. However, there was no denying that it would be easier if Quill would admit that he too yearned for more than a highly temporary secret relationship.

"I'm a simple guy. Give me a year with no fatalities, plenty of fish for the freezer, a generator that doesn't crap out, and less paperwork."

"Those are decent wishes." Owen had to swallow hard. The churning in his gut served him right for being foolish enough to give his heart to a guy with a glacier in place of his.

"And you know, maybe a little more of…earlier. Some more *you* wouldn't hurt." Even without looking, Owen could tell Quill was blushing from the way his voice had gone more hesitant. And okay, that was better than nothing and not total indifference to having Owen around. Maybe it was a start.

"That can be arranged." Leaning back, Owen pressed a kiss to Quill's neck. Maybe he'd simply have to wish enough for both of them, hope and plan and scheme, melt Quill's permafrost emotions one day at a time until Quill had no choice but to add Owen to the short list of things he couldn't live without.

"Hey. It's 11:59." Quill plucked the glass from Owen's hand, set it next to his on the nightstand. "Pretty sure that means you get a kiss. You go ahead and make that wish."

Damn it. This would all be so much easier if Quill wouldn't keep showing that he was capable of infinite tenderness and romanticism. Somewhere in there, buried under all the ice and reservations, was a guy who was everything Owen had ever wanted and who Owen was having an increasingly hard time imagining living without. Thus, when Quill claimed his mouth in a sweet, soft kiss, Owen went right ahead and made his wish, wished hard enough for both of them, losing himself to the kiss just as surely as the rest of him was already lost to Quill.

Chapter Twenty-Two

"So, tell me *everything*. How's it going?"

"Fine. Going well." Owen fumbled the phone, narrowly avoiding it hitting the wooden floor. He'd been about to get geared up to see to the latest round of shoveling that the January storms had necessitated when Hattie, his volunteer coordinator and Quill's friend, had called. They'd handled the pleasantries and the purpose of her call, which was to ensure that he didn't want the subsistence stipend for the second half of his volunteer stint, but she didn't seem in any hurry to end the call.

"Is it going okay sharing space with Quill—Ranger Ramsey?"

"Yep. Just fine." As far as he knew, the only thing Quill had told his friend was that Owen was doing an okay job. And Owen didn't want to seem either disproportionately happy or sad, striving for a middle line that would get him off the phone as quickly as possible. Which was funny because Owen usually enjoyed the phone, especially on the rare occasions when the reception was decent. Quill might fulfill most of his needs for human contact, but Owen hadn't had a total personality transplant—he still enjoyed people and socializing. Except when said socializing ran the risk of outing his never-gonna-admit-it boyfriend, in which case he couldn't get off the phone fast enough. "I don't want to keep you—"

"Well, I want to keep *you*. Until spring at least." She laughed, but there was a note of stress behind it. "We've had three volunteers already not last the season. I'm supposed to be working on summer placements already, not finding emergency replacements for winter. Speaking of, if you wanted me to transfer you back to Chugach, this would be the time to tell me, as they're one of the sites that's down workers."

"I'm fine. Right here." God, had that come out too fast? Too clipped? He hoped not, but no way was he going anywhere before he absolutely had to. But something else she'd said had his wheels churning. "How does it work for the summer volunteers anyway?"

"Same as for the winter positions. We post the openings, then applications come in. We give priority to volunteers with prior experience. More of the summer positions are paid. Not very much money, but there's a variety of openings, all around the state. Why? I had the impression this was more of a one-off for you."

"Oh, you know, my plans aren't set in stone…" Owen hedged as casually as he could.

"In that case, think I could interest you in looking at some openings? I've got one near Fairbanks that would be perfect for you. High public contact. Paying. And there's another near Seward with housing. Since your internet is so spotty, I'm going to both email you and put a packet in the mail to you."

"Sure. I…uh…" He struggled with how to word his next question, trying to find the line between eager and indifferent. "Any around here?"

"Well, we've got some regular summer volunteers returning, but they still haven't authorized funding for another ranger, so we'll likely take on a few extra volunteers and seasonal workers to cover the gaps. I can put those openings in the packet for you as well. And if Ranger Ramsey says you've done a good job, that could bode well for one of the paid positions with more responsibility."

"Ah." No way was he telling her or even insinuating that Quill damn well better say he'd done a good job. And he wouldn't dare imply that Quill shouldn't be a job reference for him. Friends were references all the time. He'd done it dozens of times back in his old job. It got a little dicier using a boyfriend or spouse as a reference, but unbeknownst to Quill, Owen had scoured the volunteer manual recently, trying to make sure that Quill's worries about possible ethical implications were bunk, and there was nothing that said that volunteers and rangers couldn't make friends or that explicitly prohibited romantic contact. Not that the manual really mattered when Quill was intent on absolutely no one finding out.

Hell, Quill still winced when Owen mentioned his mom or a friend from the Bay Area knowing that Quill existed in any capacity. His mother had sent another care package, this one in advance of Lunar New Year, with carefully packed moon cakes in several flavors and a breezy note with greetings for them both, which seemed to make Quill bristle even as he'd tried the food. The guy could go from being sugar-coma sweet, like on New Year's Eve with little surprises, to being prickly as a bear interrupted from its winter nap. But all prickliness aside, this call from Hattie seemed like exactly the sort of sign Owen had been looking for about what he was supposed to do next. More time to figure things out, more time to wear Quill down into believing in a future together. It could be precisely what they both needed.

And later, after he'd ended the call, he found himself with a certain boogie in his step as he finished bundling up to tackle the shoveling. This would be good. Better than good even. Could even be the start of his New Year's Eve wish coming true. The day's agenda called for some roof clearing, and he wasn't at all surprised when Quill showed up post-patrol to help. Oh, he'd never admit that he was worried about Owen up on the roof of one of the outbuildings, but him climbing up, shovel in hand, spoke volumes.

"Not working fast enough for you?" Owen teased, hoping Quill could see in his eyes how happy he actually was at the midday visit.

"Nah. You're fine. Figured we could make quick work of it together, maybe finish in time for you to help me check a few trailheads."

"I can do that. Almost done here." Owen resumed scraping, keeping his tone light as he added, "We make a great team."

"We do." Quill's voice was more resigned than upbeat, and Owen wasn't sure what to make of that.

"Your friend Hattie called me today with exactly that question—wanted to know how we're working together."

"She did what?" Quill's shovel made a nails-on-chalkboard dragging sound as his footing wavered. Fuck. On second thought, a frozen roof might not be the best place for this conversation, but he'd already started it.

"Sorry. Didn't mean to startle you. Be safe. I've got plans that involve all your parts in working order later."

"What about Hattie?" Quill completely ignored Owen's flirt, which while not surprising was still maddening. Damn, stubborn, paranoid ranger.

"You can stop worrying. I told her absolutely nothing other than that we work together okay and that I don't want to be transferred to Chugach."

"Transferred?" Quill blinked, eyes glassy against the cold sky. "They want you to leave?"

"A couple of volunteers have left early. There's an opening, but I told her I was staying put. I didn't tell her *why* though, so stop looking like I sent her photographic evidence and a timestamped play-by-play."

"Sorry. If you want to see other parts of the state, though, I don't want to keep you—"

"For real? Are you that eager to get rid of me?" Owen threw more snow over the edge, watching it rain down. This couldn't be going worse.

"No. Of course not." Quill's face softened. "I want you here until spring. I do. I just don't want to stand in the way of you having more adventures. Maybe a yurt or little cabin are on your list…"

"Fuck my list. You. You're the number one item on my list these days, and you should damn well know that by now. You seriously think I'd just pack up and leave because of a *yurt*?" Owen shook his head. "Or is it that you want me gone so that there's no chance of Hattie or anyone figuring what we've been up to off duty? Hell, would you even miss me, Quill?"

Quill winced, face drawing up tight. And he took a damn long time answering. "Yeah. I'd miss you. Going to miss you like crazy in May as it is. But I told you going into this that I didn't want trouble at work."

Whatever warmth the first part of Quill's admission generated froze in the frigid blast of the second half of his declaration, the part where his voice went all firm and hard.

"I've checked the volunteer handbook and DNR website both. I'm not finding any fraternization rules. This isn't the marines. No one's coming for your badge just because you happen to be dating a volunteer. Hell, from what I've seen, they often place married couples together when they both accept a remote assignment. For all that you're wed to the job, it in no way requires you to be a monk."

"Never said it did. But ethics…"

"Fuck ethics. It's not ethics keeping you quiet, and you know it."

"I don't like being the topic of conversation. A spectacle. All eyes on me and my choices. Gossip. All of that." Quill's breath hung in the cold air, steam making him seem even more pissed. "I don't want my private life up for…dissection. Or it to cost me my reputation."

"You do get that if a state agency—in any state— let a twenty-year employee go because they were gay, it would be national news. Like people would be up in arms."

Quill's increasingly sour expression said that Owen wasn't helping matters. "I'm not cut out to be a poster child of equality. But in any event, I don't think they'd fire me. Still, though, there'd be gossip, all the same. And besides, this is moot. You're gone in another four months or so."

"So if I stayed, it would be a different story?" Owen

carefully took a few steps in Quill's direction so that he could better gauge his reaction. "Hattie mentioned that she's collecting applications for summer jobs. Volunteer and paid positions both. That's why I brought up her call—not to make you all paranoid, but because I think I should apply. And if the only thing that's keeping you from treating this as a real relationship, something worth fighting for, is the expiration date, then let's erase that off the calendar."

Quill didn't nod, didn't smile, didn't do any more than huff and shake his head. "You don't want to keep working here, especially not for free. Your list—"

"Can go fuck itself. Screw my plans. I knew when I started out that eventually I'd need to settle down, figure out a path forward. I can't afford to be a professional traveler the next forty years or something. So, why not here? Why not stay longer? Especially if housing's provided, I can conserve my savings while I decide how I'll earn money in the future."

"Your family's back in California." Quill's affect was maddeningly flat, voice as distant as his eyes. "Your parents would want you to put roots down there."

"First of all, my sisters are spread all over the country. Cousins too. It's a big family, yeah, but we're already flying all over the place for gatherings. And secondly, *you* are here. Unless you've suddenly got a thing for sunshine and overpriced studio apartments, I don't see myself going back to California." His heart hammered as he lay his cards on the table, going all in. "I want to stay. At least through summer, and maybe beyond that if you want me. If you'll give this thing between us a real shot."

"It's not about wanting you." Quill was already

hedging, and Owen's stomach plummeted, heading for the snowdrift beneath them. "But I can't be the guy you need—deserve—long term."

"You mean you don't want to *try*. I'm not asking for you to march into headquarters with a bullhorn. We could start small, like with you not freaking out that people who know only me like my friends know that we're a couple. Then you let Hattie know. She's your best friend, and she already knows you're gay. She's not going to be pissed, and you'll feel better, not hiding. Maybe you stop flinching if I stand too close around strangers or say the wrong thing. Baby steps. That's all I'm asking for. A try."

Stone-faced, Quill tossed more snow over the edge before speaking. "It wouldn't be enough for you. And for all that I love Hattie, she's a gossip—"

"And God forbid someone at work start talking." Owen had heard enough. "Seriously? You're going to let your fear of *gossip* stand in the way of us having a future?"

"You're yelling."

"Damn right. I'm pissed."

"This—" Quill gestured between them with his empty shovel. "Is why I don't do relationships. Drama. Someone *always* gets hurt."

"We're adults. Adults can disagree. And *two* some-ones are both going to get hurt if you don't get over your fear of coming out. Don't try to make this about my tone." Owen was genuinely heated now.

"Watch it."

"Seriously? You can't handle—"

"*Watch your footing.*"

It was possibly the first time he'd heard Quill yell.

For all his firmness, he rarely even raised his voice. Startled, Owen glanced down, but it was too late, he was already skidding, away from Quill. His ass hit the roof, but the slick fabric of his snow pants did little to slow him down, his body continuing to slide right toward the edge.

"Fuck it all, *Owen*." At the last possible second, Quill hauled him back, sending both of them sprawling backward, centimeters from disaster. The roof wasn't especially tall and surely the snow would have braced his fall, but he still breathed heavily, visions of broken limbs dancing in his head. Still clutching Owen, Quill was breathing equally hard as he took a moment before untangling them, pulling Owen to sitting. "Damn. I thought…"

"Sorry. This was probably a bad place to have this conversation—"

"You think?" Quill blinked at him.

"But on the other hand, if we'd been anywhere else, you would have tried to get out of it."

"It's not a conversation we need to be having *today*, and we sure as hell don't need to argue our way into your breaking your fool neck." Throwing their shovels down, Quill gently steered him in the direction of the ladder.

"Okay, okay." Owen could take a hint and he waited until they were both back on solid, frozen ground before continuing. "But like when *would* be a good time to have this conversation? May? When it's already too late to get summer work? After the packet from Hattie arrives? Or maybe I shouldn't have said anything, should have just applied? I mean, there is a chance they won't have work for me."

"Yup." Quill's jaw was hard enough to carve ice sculptures. "No guarantees there."

"You don't sound particularly sad about that. Pushing aside the coming-out argument, Quill, do you *want* me to stay?" Staring Quill down, he tried to see past whatever bluster Quill was about to spew to the truth. And fuck. Quill's eyes were shuttered, no hints there, no lurking remnants of their months of connection, giving Owen utterly no clue about what his reply would be.

Chapter Twenty-Three

"No." Quill was proud that the word didn't waver. But one look at Owen's face, ash gray and stark, pain evident in his sharp inhale, and the rest of Quill trembled. "It's not about what I want. It's about you and your needs and what's best for you. Which isn't an indefinite stay. So, no. No, I don't want you to stay and pin your future on me."

"You won't even let yourself think about us, about a future, about a universe where this works out and we're—"

"Life isn't a fairy tale. We get a couple of good months together. No sense in wanting or dwelling on what can't be."

"What you won't *let* happen, you mean." Owen shook his head as he stomped toward the equipment shed where they'd stow the shovels and ladder. "And I'm honestly not sure what you're more scared of, coming out or turning into your parents. But you're forty-something years old. You should have figured out by now that not every relationship is contentious or toxic—"

"My parents. My siblings. Grandparents weren't a lot better. Thought things might be different with JP, but not all drama is loud. He was controlling. Not always

kind." He didn't like admitting how long it had taken
him to figure that out about what they'd had. "And as it
turned out, I'm no good at relationships. Didn't want to
compromise on city life. And yeah, I didn't want to deal
with coming out, not after how things went down with
my dad. So I came here. And I watched Hattie struggle
through a decade or so of on-again-off-again with Val.
Until finally she had to make a choice."

"Which she did freely because she's an adult, capable of deciding that compromise was worth having a
future and family with Val. And I'm an adult too. And
if I want to compromise on where I live, that's on me."
Owen banged his way into the equipment shed, which
wasn't much warmer than the outdoors, but several degrees hotter than the ball of ice currently sitting in the
middle of Quill's chest. Owen's angry tones and abrupt
movements only made the icy feeling worse. His usual
issues with anger magnified because this was *Owen*,
Owen who seldom lost his head, Owen who was always
happy and optimistic. But not now. "And yeah, JP was
an idiot, and you were both young and probably didn't
handle things the best. God knows I had enough ulti-
matums with guys in my twenties, too."

"Any of them kill someone?" It wasn't a fair question, but the more Owen pushed about coming out, the
more Quill kept picturing his father's beet-red face,
his angry words and accusations, and his lifeless body.
Maybe to others Owen's demands would seem perfectly
reasonable, but they hadn't been there, hadn't seen him
go from tirade to deathly silence. And they hadn't heard
his hurled insults, deep barbs about how this was all
because Quill hadn't been able to stand up for himself

as a kid, blaming Quill's shyness and his apparent lack of macho bravado.

The worst part, the part that Quill always tried not to dwell on, was how his father had shifted from being proud of Quill, complimenting his recent grades and internships, the sort of approval Quill had waited years for, to despising him in a matter of moments. That was the part of coming out he couldn't control and the part that caused the most sick terror in his gut—it forever changed how the other person saw him, for better or for worse. And sure, people were great at giving platitudes like "they'll come around" or "you're better off without them." But they hadn't had to sit in an itchy black suit, listening to all the praise for his father, knowing that he'd never get a second chance.

It would have been so much easier if he hated his parents, if all the bad parts of his childhood had crowded out any love he might have had. But as he'd sat there in the church pew that day, all he'd been able to think about was learning to ride a bike, to fish, hitting his first target, a thousand little memories of the man he'd wanted so desperately and failed so miserably to please.

Back in the present, he had to swallow hard, try to focus on Owen and not the return of old fears.

"I am sorry, so incredibly sorry, about your dad. But that wasn't your fault. And not all coming-out stories are that awful. Not everyone's as dysfunctional as your parents or as rigid as JP. And I beg to differ on you and relationships. You're doing just fine with me and you'd be the best boyfriend I've ever had except for the part where you don't want me around."

"I'm not—"

"My boyfriend. Yeah, I got that part." Owen hung

up both of their shovels, loud clatters ringing through the small shed.

"I do like having you around." Quill didn't want him thinking otherwise, wished he could give him more of the words he both needed and deserved. "And I've never felt like this about anyone else. But…"

"But it's not enough for you." Owen leaned against an air compressor. "What we have, it's not enough for you to consider fighting for it, wanting to keep it."

"I care about you too much to want to keep you here in a little box with me." Quill truly wished it were simply a matter of want, because Lord did he ever want. In the dead of night, holding a sleeping Owen, he wanted with every fiber of his being. But wanting impossible, selfish things, even with soul-deep intensity, didn't make them any more realistic or any more of a good idea. "There's a whole world out there waiting for you, one filled with parties and people and exciting jobs. Even as you say, putting aside the me-coming-out issue, I'm not going to stand in the way of your future, and I'm also not going to sign up for one for myself where you come to resent me and we both have that much more pain when things finally fall apart."

"So because we might some day in the future break up, and because you think you know me better than I know myself, you're going to break up with me now? Stop me from giving us a chance to prove your fears wrong? What if you're wrong? What then? What if this really is the forever sort of thing, and you're tossing it aside out of stupid fears?"

"Break up?" Swallowing hard, Quill could barely croak out the word. "We're breaking up?"

They'd had disagreements before, including over him

coming out, and it hadn't hit Quill until exactly that moment that this one could be it, the end, no Owen glossing things over, no pretending they hadn't disagreed, no losing themselves for a couple more weeks in bed before the issue came up again, and definitely no sliding along to May, postponing all hurt until then. He'd become far too used to Owen's capacity to forgive or at least forget temporarily, the way he never stayed mad that long. Even when Owen had startled him by raising his voice, he hadn't really thought about this being the moment everything unraveled for good.

"Are we? I guess that's kind of your call. If you don't want me applying to stay, I'm not sure what the point is anymore."

The ultimatum hit Quill like falling face-first into a snowbank, cold slap of pain. "Don't do this."

"Why?" Owen's eyes bored into Quill, not pleading as much as demanding that Quill have a good reason, all traces of softness gone.

"Don't take away the next few months from us. Please." Quill was never going to be able to articulate how much he'd been counting on those months, precious weeks and days to save up all the joy he could, stockpiling memories against the coming winter of his life. He might not get that forever Owen spoke so easily of, wasn't sure if anyone got that, and frankly, forever scared him—all the millions of big and little hurts that could happen on the road to forever. But he could have this, this one perfect interlude in his life.

"Don't take away our future," Owen countered, stepping forward to put a hand on Quill's shoulder. "I can't do this, can't fall for you more and more over the next few months, can't know that you're probably falling for me too, but that you're planning on letting me go, for reasons I just don't understand. It's fear, Quill, and you've never struck me as a coward before."

"So that's it?" Long, deadly icicles pierced every soft place on Quill, every hope he'd pinned on the next few months, every secret desire he'd never voice. He wasn't being fair to Owen, but he'd had plans, damn it. Fall? He almost laughed at that. He was so far beyond *falling*. More like he'd already crashed on an alien landscape, one where he was inescapably Owen's. He wasn't ready for this to be over, hadn't even contemplated a universe where he might have to see Owen daily but not have him.

"This isn't some convenient fling for me. You keep thinking that's all I wanted here, but what we've found together, it's so much more than just a hookup. You know that. I know you care. And that's what's truly killing me. You care, but not enough. And now you want me to delay our breakup out of…convenience? Fuck that noise." Owen dropped his hand from Quill's shoulder, one more loss in a rapidly growing pile of hurts. Eyes narrow, mouth a hard line, Owen stalked to the door of the shed. "You want me? You want this? Then you can go all in with me. I see you your four months and I raise you a real relationship, one without an expiration date."

"That's not fair," Quill whispered, even though the objection was likely futile. They'd passed fair a long time ago. And yeah, Owen was changing the rules on him, changing the parameters on what Quill had thought they'd had, but if he was truly doing it to save himself some hurt and not out of spite, could Quill really blame him? At the end of the day, they both wanted impossible things. Only difference was that Quill was a realist while Owen was determined to will his wants into existence, regardless of consequences.

"No, no it's not fair. None of this is fair. To either of us." Owen's eyes were deep pools of pain, hurt that Quill had caused. Fuck. He'd known from the very first kiss that this was a terrible idea, that someone was going to get hurt. And at a certain point, he'd made peace with him being that person, knowing he'd spend the rest of his life missing Owen. But he'd been willing to grieve that loss if it meant having Owen in the here and now. He'd assumed, though, that Owen would march onward, maybe with some fond memories, into his bright future, unburdened by the sort of pain Quill had seen coming for himself.

However, Owen's eyes told a different story, one that firmly starred Quill as the villain who'd hurt them both. And that was the last thing Quill wanted, to know he'd hurt Owen, damaged that beautiful, irrepressible spirit. Feet clumsy and hands shaking, he stepped forward.

"Owen—"

"Don't." Owen held up a hand. "Just don't. Don't make this any worse."

So Quill said nothing, let Owen walk through that door, walk away from Quill and away from his life. He was right. There was nothing Quill could say that wouldn't make this worse, that wouldn't hurt Owen even more. The only thing left to do was what he'd known he'd have to do all along—let Owen fly away, not be the two-hundred-pound weight keeping him tied to a life where he didn't belong.

Owen had no idea how dark and cold the short January days in Alaska could be until he and Quill argued,

and he was forced to return to the way things had been
when he'd first arrived. Avoidance. Awkward interactions. Stilted notes. Long nights in separate freezing
rooms. It had only been a couple of days, and he was
already almost ill from the lack of human contact. As
he made himself a mug of late-afternoon tea in the
kitchen, his stomach lurched, joining the low-grade
throb in his head and the dull ache in his muscles. He
needed a phone call, an excuse to go into town, some
tourists with questions, anything to distract him from
what loneliness was doing to his psyche.

Wait. That wasn't quite accurate. It wasn't being
alone that was wreaking havoc on him. He missed conversation, yes, but this weird flulike constellation of
symptoms was more than that, this marrow-deep yearning for Quill specifically, not humanity in general. He
missed talking to Quill, touching him, cuddling with
him, being in the same room with him. He'd gambled
big, making his ultimatum, pretty darn cocky that
Quill would give in and see both logic and the truth of
what was in their hearts. Quill wasn't a coward—he'd
narrowly avoided both of them tumbling off the roof,
risking his own neck to save Owen's. While less of an
adrenaline junkie than Owen, he'd never shied from cal-
culated risks in other situations either, and Owen had
legit figured that Quill would find him worth having a
little courage for. But apparently Owen had either over-
estimated his own appeal or underestimated the inertia of Quill's life because Quill hadn't given in. Hadn't
budged from his "it's best for you" bullshit lines about
not being what Owen needed.

The few times their paths had crossed, Quill had
looked so haggard, deep lines around his eyes, scruffier-

than-usual jaw, stooped shoulders, and it had taken all Owen's self-restraint to not go to him, wrap him up in a hug, say fuck expiration dates and arguments and do his best to make Quill smile again. But despite his inner peacemaker, he was tired of always being the nice guy, always being the one to compromise. It would be all too easy to fall back into previous routines, let Quill have the security of knowing he was leaving in a few months, let them both have a good time now. Owen had happily been that guy before, but he was done with living for the present only.

It didn't matter how many memories they made now if they couldn't have the future Owen wanted. He wasn't going to trade that vision of what they could have for a few moments of pleasure now, no matter how miserable it made him. Ever since the long, lonely hours of chemo, he'd been searching for something to take away the restlessness clawing at him. Big adventures. Little experiences. Silly destinations. Long-held fantasies. But nothing had really worked until he'd come here, until that feeling was gone for weeks. Nothing had ever felt as right as holding Quill on Christmas had, and he wanted more of that, endless days and years. And yeah, Owen was being absolutist and stubborn about this, but despite his body's strange rebellion, he was determined to stay strong.

As if right on cue though, a huge sneezing fit shook his body, making him slosh tea all over.

"You're sick." He'd been so lost in thought that he hadn't heard Quill on the stairs, hadn't realized it was already dark. Not that it mattered. Quill had kept himself downstairs in his office until late the past few days. Him upstairs pre-dinnertime would have made Owen's

heart thrill with fresh hope except for how severely
Quill was frowning. And how utterly awful he felt. "I
heard you coughing and sneezing from downstairs all
afternoon."

"Sorry. But I'm not sick." Well other than the terrible heartsickness he was coping with right then, but
heartbreak was neither contagious nor deadly. Unfortunately. And he sure as hell wasn't explaining the origin
of his symptoms to Quill.

"You're sick." Quill used his big palm to feel Owen's
forehead and damn if the contact didn't feel amazing,
cool and familiar and soothing.

"Your hands are cold." Giving in to temptation, he
leaned into Quill's touch, a shiver racing through him.
God, he missed him so much. How could he miss a person so much when he was right here?

"And you've got a fever." Quill steered him into
one of the kitchen chairs. Quill's eyes narrowed, jaw
stern, practically daring Owen to disagree. "What can
you take? Should you be calling your oncologist for
advice—like is your immune system still considered
compromised?"

Ah. That explained Quill's sudden appearance. He
was worried. Ranger Worst Case Scenario striking
again. Wasn't about Owen personally. He felt his own
forehead. Damn. Maybe he was actually sick on top of
everything else. Great.

"I'm not about to die on you. It's been long enough
since chemo that I don't think it's an immune system
thing. I seemed to catch every bug the year I had cancer treatment, but I've been pretty healthy the last year
or so. I bet this is just a cold, if that even."

Quill's frown didn't relent as he huffed. "You'll keep

an eye on it overnight, and if you're any worse tomorrow, I'm taking you into the clinic in Wasilla myself. A cold is one thing, but you don't want to mess with the flu or pneumonia. And you'll tell them about the cancer, let them do whatever blood work that requires."

"Gee, Quill. Better watch it or I might get the wrong idea, think you cared."

Eyes flashing bright with pain, Quill flinched. "I care. You're not getting hurt on my watch."

"I'm not one of your school groups. Not your responsibility." Head feeling like it had been replaced by a fifty-pound barbell, he gave in to the urge to rest it on the table.

"I'm making you more tea. And soup." Quill ignored his protest and started bustling around, getting the kettle and putting it back on the stove. "Think you can talk me through that ginger thing you like? If you add some red pepper, that soup might open up your sinuses."

Owen raised his head enough to blink blearily at Quill, trying to make sure he wasn't having some sort of fever delusion. "You don't have to take care of me."

"Someone needs to." After the kettle was on, Quill grabbed a pot and started collecting soup ingredients. They might be back where they started, but Quill was different than he'd been all those months ago. He was more confident in the kitchen now, moving with an ease born of all their shared meals together. It would be so, so easy to slip back into old habits and feelings here. "And your room is too cold. That's probably how you got sick. You're going to sleep out here. I'll move the couch a little closer to the stove in a minute."

"You're lucky I'm too miserable to argue." Owen

rubbed his temples, startling when one of Quill's broad hands came to rest on his neck, a light massage.

"Hey, it's my one chance to be bossy with you." Quill's tone was light, but there was a sadness there too, a wistfulness that came out in his touch too. Even through his snappishness, Owen could tell from his tenderness that more than guilt was driving Quill. He cared, truly cared about Owen on a deep, fundamental level. Even when he shouldn't, even when they should both be moving on, Quill cared. It was enough to make Owen's eyes burn. God, this thing was such a mess.

"Quill—"

"Shh. No big talks, okay? You can go back to being pissed at me once you're well." After releasing Owen's neck, Quill washed his hands and resumed soup prep, putting rice noodles on to soak exactly how Quill had taught him.

"I'm not pissed. I'm sad. Trust me, anger would be so much easier." Admitting to unhappy pining was a level of vulnerability he wouldn't attempt if he wasn't already feeling so lousy.

"I'm sorry." Quill's voice had a depth of pain that Owen hadn't heard before, but there was a resignation there that also said his words weren't the start of a true apology.

Frustrated, Owen groaned as he scrubbed at his eyes.

"I hate that you're hurting. I never wanted that. Never." Quill, usually so precise and exact, splashed broth all over as he stirred the soup.

"If we're both miserable…"

"I've got this vision." Studying the soup, Quill took on a distant, almost dreamlike tone. "A postcard from you, maybe. Or social media post. One of those X-years-cancer-free type posts. And you're on a beach, wildly happy, holding a book of your comics, surrounded by a big party of people who love you. You won't be miserable forever."

"And there's no version of that vision where you slot yourself into the picture?" Owen had to know before a coughing attack claimed the rest of his breath.

"Here." Quill slid a fresh mug of tea in front of him. "Drink. I don't belong in that picture."

"Not even as one of the friends?" Owen took a bracing sip of tea, let it soothe his burning throat. "I think I miss you as a friend most of all. I can live without sex, but I miss *you*. And you're being a friend right now, taking care of me when I'm sick."

"I'm not going to stop caring about you. You're the one who wanted to break up. Not sure that I'm the best at being friends with anyone, but if wanting to know that you're safe, that you're well and happy, is being friends, then yeah, we're friends."

It wasn't much of a victory, not with Quill sounding as dark and ominous as the bottom of the ocean. Not with him feeling like crap. And not with him wanting so much more than friendship. And the worst thing was that he was pretty sure that Quill did too, but was simply never going to let himself admit it. He was going down with the you're-better-off-without-me ship, and there wasn't a fucking thing Owen could do about it.

Chapter Twenty-Four

Taking care of a sick Owen was one of the most bittersweet experiences of Quill's life. And he was lying through his teeth. This wasn't friendship or anything close to it. He'd seen Hattie through any number of winter colds, but had never fussed over her to the degree he did Owen, never made her a nest on the couch, never had this clawing worry about her welfare keeping him up at night, never wanted so badly to hold her or any other person. Only Owen. Only Owen could bring him out of his cave of grief and isolation post-breakup. And only Owen could make him feel simultaneously so fulfilled, like Quill was exactly where the universe needed him to be, and so fucking empty at the same time.

He wasn't an idiot. He got the point Owen was trying to make, that they could have this indefinitely. He could have Owen to care for and worry over and not have a date on a calendar looming over them. And he wished he could believe that would be the right choice for both of them. All this we're-still-friends nonsense would be so much easier if so. Friends didn't feel like a part of their soul might wither and die if they didn't get to hold the other person soon. Friends didn't obsess over every cold symptom, think in worst-case scenarios, and invent reasons to check on the other person. Friends didn't pull the covers up around their napping friend, heart so close to overflowing it was a wonder he wasn't a puddle already. Friends didn't do any of what was going on in Quill's brain, missing every kiss, every touch, every murmured word.

And friends most certainly didn't spy on each other. Which wasn't exactly what Quill was doing Owen's first day back on the job after several days spent on the couch recovering from what had turned out to be a nasty cold. Owen had insisted that he was well enough to resume trash duty and his other responsibilities. Since it was a clear, crisp Saturday with perfect cross-country skiing weather, which brought out the tourists in droves, Quill had been in need of the help, but he also wanted to make sure Owen didn't overdo it. Hence the checking in on him midday, taking a thermos full of hot tea and the snowmachine to the lower parking lot where Owen was working.

But as it turned out, he shouldn't have bothered as he found Owen laughing and joking with a trio of male tourists carrying skis, no trace of his cold in sight. No sign of his melancholy over the breakup either, Owen's face relaxed and easy as he chatted with the group, all of whom appeared around his age or slightly younger. Quill wasn't close enough to hear what was being said, but he knew flirting when he saw it, and the tourist closest to Owen was definitely flirting with him. Lots of little touches on the arm, deliberate eye contact, too-loud laughter at whatever Owen was saying, and leaning in like Owen was the most interesting guy in the world.

A growl escaped Quill's throat. He'd parked beyond Owen's line of sight, over by some scrubby trees and near Owen's own snowmachine. It wasn't as if Owen knew he was there, and if Quill were smart, he'd drive on, pretend he hadn't seen, leave Owen to his socializing. He was a single adult, free to flirt with whomever he wanted. But knowing that didn't help Quill one bit, didn't help this roiling black mood, toxic stew of jealousy and longing. The other two guys had to be a couple or at least intimate friends—arms around each other, lots of casual touching. Owen said something that made the taller of the two pull the other to him, a clear he's-mine signal.

What if... Quill tried to imagine being that guy, the one who was all possessive. Would it really be that hard? Hell, he might not even have to touch him. Owen was indeed a social guy, but Quill didn't doubt that he could be loyal too. There was a universe, one where they were a couple, and Quill could walk over there, stand close enough to glower at Mr. Flirty. Maybe he'd hand Owen his tea, and he would smile, the same way he'd smiled for weeks when Quill had shown up unexpectedly, and he'd make Quill's point that Owen was taken for him without Quill even needing to say a word. If they were a couple. Which they weren't. Which meant that Owen was free to flirt away and that Quill had no right to do a damn thing about it.

Right as Quill was about to leave, Owen turned and their eyes met. Quill schooled his expression to remain neutral, but the prickle running up the back of his spine said he probably wasn't doing that good of a job. Owen said something to the guys before heading across the parking lot toward Quill.

"Let us know if you get off later," the flirty one called after Owen, who didn't reply but did turn and wave.

"What's up?" he asked Quill, still smiling from his conversation with the group, good mood almost palpable and pushing Quill's that much further into the black.

"It's nothing," Quill mumbled, embarrassment making his head itchy under his hat as he fished out the thermos. "Wanted to make sure you weren't relapsing. Brought you some tea. But you seem…well."

"I'm better." Owen's eyes flashed with something Quill couldn't quite name as he took the thermos. Too tender for irritation but too edgy for gratitude either.

"You need some time off tonight?" Quill tried to keep his voice casual. Across the lot, the tourists headed for one of the trailheads, leaving him and Owen the only people amid the assorted vehicles. Returning to work would be the better idea, but somehow he couldn't make himself leave, couldn't stop the question from leaving his lips.

"Why? You got opinions on how I spend my time?" *Yes.* "No."

"Liar." Shaking his head, Owen released a world-weary sigh. "They're tourists from California. I don't know them, but we had a nice chat about favorite Bay Area haunts. They invited me to get a drink with them later."

"That's…good." Quill forced the words out. This was the start of being a friend, not lover, of making sure Owen got the future Quill so firmly believed he deserved. "I know you've been lonely. Jonesing for more of a social scene. Doubt there's anything too pressing keeping you here."

"There could be." Owen's dark eyes sharpened, twin diamond-tipped drill bits boring their way past Quill's every defense. "Tell me not to go. Stop lying to us both."

"I…" The denial was right there, each syllable ready to go. He knew how to be commanding, did it often enough with rowdy teens and rule breakers. He knew the exact pitch and tone to strike to tell Owen to go out with the tourists. But nothing came out.

"I see." Voice hardening, Owen looked away.

"I don't know how to do this," Quill admitted in a rush, words tumbling out with zero permission from his brain. "I don't know how to be your friend. I don't know how to watch you move on. I don't know how to watch guys flirt with you and not want to rip their arms off. I don't know how to be alone with you and not want to kiss you. I don't know how to stop wishing…"

"*Quill.*" Owen reached for him then, and Quill went willingly, too foolish and overwrought to pull back. It wasn't simply jealousy at work here. Something deeper was happening, emotions he hadn't even known he was capable of welling up. How had he ever thought he could let Owen go? Even through his many layers of clothing, Owen's firm grip on his upper arms felt so damn good. Necessary. Grounding. He saw now with stark clarity what Owen had been trying to show him. New words rose up, ones he wasn't going to be able to keep down—

Trill. Trill. Trill. The purposefully obnoxious loud ring tone he'd assigned to emergency services made him jump, pulling away from Owen so that he could answer the call. And what he heard replaced all his hurt and uncertainty with cold, steely reality where the job had to come first, before everything, including Owen and this conversation.

"There's reports of avalanche activity in the back-country," he told Owen in clipped tones. "Ski party involvement. Reports of two skiers missing. Avalanche response team assembling and emergency services on the way, but I've got to go. Got to get my gear and try to reach the area via snowmachine. Probably going to need to ski in the last part."

"I'm coming with you." Owen was already swinging onto his snowmachine.

"Too dangerous. The avalanche forecast center is rating today a considerable risk in the mid to upper elevations. And you're still coming off an illness."

"I've had training. By you. You need all the help you can get. Come on. Isn't it time you start trusting me?"

The question hit on so many levels that Quill's ears rang, and he had to take a breath to steady himself. *Trust.* Trust Owen. Was that really all he needed to do? For all of it. Professionally. Romantically. Emotionally. But there was zero time for that kind of self-reflection. No time for life reevaluation. Every second mattered here, and he needed to not dither. There would be plenty of time later to figure out how to make sense of all those emotions he'd felt moments earlier, the sudden realization that he couldn't live without Owen, that no way could he let him go. Later. He'd find the words later. Find a way forward. But first, he had to do his damn job.

His heart clattered with fear and his gut churned with doubts, no easy answers. However, he couldn't deny Owen's logic. He was another trained adult, and he'd proven himself over and over to be capable in emergencies.

"Let's go." He managed to deliver the order with confidence he didn't feel. This wasn't the time for uncertainty. He had to take charge of the situation, trust that he was doing the right thing letting Owen come even as dread mounted. He had to believe his experience would be enough to see them both through.

Owen hardly saw Quill allowing him to come as a victory. It was practical necessity, and wearing down the most stubborn ranger on the planet to get him to accept help and make him believe in Owen were nice side benefits, but the situation was far too dire for any celebration. Or any reflection on their earlier conversation. Quill's jealousy had been both maddening and reassuring, and Owen had been so damn sure that they were on the cusp of a breakthrough when Quill's phone had gone off. Now, though, that emergency had to take priority. Everything else could wait.

"Test it." Quill handed Owen an avalanche beacon to clip on the inside of his parka. They'd used them before for going up to the mid-elevations where the risks markedly increased, but each part of their rushed prep right then felt weighty, precious seconds ticking away.

Luckily they'd both already been dressed for the weather, which saved them time as they gathered skis and the equipment they might need, including first-aid equipment and airbags, which could be deployed in the event of an avalanche. More rescuers were on the way, but he and Quill would likely be first on the scene.

"It was probably a soft slab avalanche. Report is that after several runs without incident, a skier triggered it coming out of a gully and crossing a convex slope. We'll want to be especially cautious about another human-triggered event, but the risk of natural avalanches is also high, so we'll want to be careful about checking the snowpack. We've got some wind to contend with too."

"I'll be alert," Owen promised as they headed out on

the snowmobiles. "You can trust me to listen this time."
He could admit that he hadn't always done the best job
of that—not on the roof when they'd been arguing nor
in other situations when he'd let his own initiative take
over. But if he wanted Quill to trust him—on multiple
levels—he had to trust Quill too. He wasn't going to
take stupid risks and endanger them both.

Once they were underway, there was no more conversation as the roar of the machines filled the air, and
it took all his concentration to follow Quill through the
uneven terrain. Partway to the site, they were joined by
two other snowmobiles, and judging by Quill's sharp
nod, they were part of the avalanche response team,
an impression that was confirmed when they finally
stopped to switch to skis. Quill greeted the two older
men who'd joined them, and after briefly introducing
them as two seasoned avalanche specialists, he asked
them if they had a situation update.

"One skier triggered their airbag and was located.
Still at the scene. Probable leg injuries. As of last update, there's another skier unaccounted for."

"Damn." Quill's mouth narrowed, and Owen knew
only too well how he'd carry the loss if they couldn't
save the second skier. It was a stark reminder of the
dangers lurking in the backcountry.

Both avalanche response team members were fast
skiers, and Owen put some leg muscle into keeping up.
Even though he'd seemed on the mend that morning,
his damn cold had sapped some of his stamina, and he
had to work to not give in to a coughing fit.

The sun shone brightly overhead, soft blue skies, and
acres upon acres of pristine white snow around them in

gently rolling waves. Ahead of them, a few faint dots glimmered.

"Is that the site?" Owen asked as Quill fished out binoculars.

"Yup. Looks like we've got four or five people on the scene. And I don't like the angle of that slope at all."

"Yup. Poor terrain selection." The older of the two avalanche specialists shook his head. Quill had mentioned that he was a retired EMT and longtime backcountry skier and sledder. "Getting the victims to stable terrain where we can get a chopper in needs to be the priority, as well as keeping everyone else in the party safe."

"We'll want to keep tight count of numbers at all times," the other rescuer added. "More help is good, but it also raises the already high risk of human-triggered avalanche events."

The two of them plus Quill hashed out a plan for search management as they approached the cluster of people. Quill in his element was always a sight to see—the way all his experience and caution served him well and the way others clearly respected his expertise. The man could be so reserved about some things that it was easy to forget sometimes how damn good he was at his job. The three men talked in avalanche lingo that Owen didn't quite follow, but he tried to keep up best he could.

Once they reached the site, the former EMT guy went right to where the first victim lay, leaving Quill and the other man to manage the rescue efforts underway to locate the second skier. They were fast approaching a critical time juncture where the odds of survival were rapidly decreasing by the second. Would-be rescuers fanned out, working close to the surface, probing for any signs of the skier's beacon before digging. Owen stuck close to Quill, following his orders.

"Gotta find likely surface catchment areas," Quill explained as he stepped back, surveying the scene again.

"I've got something!" yelled a female skier down the incline from them, and Owen started toward her, but Quill's arm shot out.

"We need to go down one at a time on the incline here. This isn't stable snow. Have to be very careful as we dig."

Owen nodded. "You first."

Carefully, far slower than Owen would have moved, Quill made his way to where the woman was already digging. Crouching low, he signaled to Owen to wait.

"I've got a boot. Oh my God. I've got a boot!" the woman screamed. Owen instinctively took another step, then remembered his promise to Quill that he'd listen and forced himself to wait while Quill dug furiously.

"I've got him." Quill and the woman uncovered an unmoving human form. Quill bent close, checking for vitals, and Owen's own breath almost froze in his lungs, waiting for Quill's assessments. "Owen! I've got a pulse. Tell the others then check on the ETA of the chopper."

"Got it." Moving away from them, Owen shouted for the others. He was too far though, and no heads swiveled, the wind swallowing his shout. Moving the way Quill had shown him, he made his way farther away from Quill and the victim.

"They found him alive!" Owen called as he got closer. Three heads turned, and immediately people started scrambling toward Quill. Owen still needed to check on the chopper as he'd promised. He had to cross a gully to get to the higher ground where the first victim and the other rescuers were. They'd traversed it once already, and he tried to mimic Quill's caution as he stepped forward.

"Fuck." The first step landed him waist-deep in soft snow, not the hard snowpack he'd expected. Hell. This wasn't good. He needed out of this gully and fast. He heard shouts, but wasn't sure whether they were directed at him or not because he couldn't make out words. No matter. He needed out. He scrambled best he could. Almost. Almost—

Crack.

The sound made his head swivel, right as above him on the gully, snow trembled, and then before he could even fully register what was happening, a wall of snow barreled toward him, coming down the gully. Fuck. He wasn't freed enough, wasn't going to be able to get out of the way.

Training. Training. Training.

He hit the button for his airbag, but he was already moving, swept forward. Had it worked? He couldn't tell, time itself accelerating, distorting his reality. His arms came up, shielding his face, trying to do what Quill had talked about, create an air pocket.

He hit something, pain radiating down his shoulder and arm, but he was still moving, no time to register the hurt.

It's the ride down that kills.

Fuck. His airbag and beacon could work, and this could still be it, the end. Cancer hadn't done it, but a single misstep was going to be his downfall, and the stark terror racing through his body was far worse than anything he'd experienced sitting in his oncologist's office.

He'd gotten a second chance to do…what precisely?

As the snow rained over him, Quill's face flashed in his mind. Had he been so focused on securing a future with Quill that he'd sacrificed the present? Precious days they could have had, lost to argument. And now Quill would never know the true depth of Owen's feelings.

Fucking hell. *Quill.* He was going to blame himself for this forever.

Not your fault. Owen tried to beam the message out into the universe as he finally came to a stop, hands still in front of his face. He was alive, but he couldn't move, not even his pinky finger, and darkness was rapidly closing in on his consciousness. *Quill.* His whole being strained one more time before everything went black.

Chapter Twenty-Five

Quill almost didn't hear the shouts. All his attention was focused on the second victim, a male skier in his twenties, who was unconscious but alive with a thready pulse. Ross, one of the avalanche specialists who'd arrived with them, was helping him get the victim ready to move, and a few others loitered around them. But then one of the onlookers shouted, and Quill's head whipped around in time to see Owen, who appeared caught in a gully, get eaten up by a narrow wave of snow hurtling down the dip. One millisecond Owen was there and the next he was gone, nothing but snow where he'd stood, Owen swept to God knew where.

"*Owen!*" The pointless yell escaped Quill's chest.

"Stay with this one," Ross ordered, already moving toward the gully, others behind him.

The last thing Quill wanted to do was follow the command, every cell in his body straining to rush over there, get to Owen. But there was no chance to argue that he should be the one to go, leaving him with the god-awful choice of abandoning his victim or abandoning Owen, who needed him. Never had he wanted to save someone more. Whole body trembling, he *needed* to be over there, joining the others frantically digging and looking for a signal from Owen's beacon. The shouts back and forth between searchers told him nothing, and equal parts hope and terror clawed at Quill's insides.

"Quill." Willie, the other specialist who had been working on the first victim, arrived next to him. "Chopper's on the way. I'll finish here. Go help." He clapped Quill hard on the shoulder. "Deep breath. We'll find him."

Breathing. Yeah. That would be nice. "Can't lose him."

"I hear you." The compassion and concern in Willie's eyes did absolutely nothing to calm Quill. Sympathy wasn't going to save Owen. And even if they could find him, Quill knew all too well all the damage the slide down could do to a victim. But finding him was the first step. The second skier had been located just outside the thirty-five minute window that usually spelled almost certain demise. That he'd survived was something of a miracle. Every minute that Owen remained buried decreased his chances, and Quill absolutely demanded a second miracle out of the day. He refused to entertain any other possibility.

As he hurried to the searchers, Quill's pulse pounded, making it hard to pay attention to his own footing. He wasn't going to be much help to Owen if he too were caught, but it was hard to make himself follow normal protocol because there was nothing normal about the situation. Owen, his Owen, was missing, and life might never be worth a damn again. But the searchers were looking to him and Ross and Willie to keep order and to keep everyone looking safe too.

He went through the motions, answered questions

from other searchers and used his probe to look for signals from Owen's beacon.

Nothing.

Tried again. Nothing.

And with each probe coming up empty-handed, he prayed for the first time since his father's death.

Anything, he offered the universe. *Anything. Take anything from me, just not him.* But what did he have to bargain with? Nothing in his life made any sense, had any value without Owen in it. All the realizations he'd had earlier kept crashing into him, one frantic thought on top of the next. He *needed* Owen. There was nothing he wouldn't give to have him safe.

"I've got a signal!" Ross shouted. Heart clattering, Quill rushed over and started helping him dig. He'd almost given up hope all over again when his glove hit fabric.

"Here!" he yelled to Ross. "Right here."

Together, they worked to free Owen. His airbag had only partially inflated, which probably kept him from a deeper burial, but it hadn't been enough to keep him from hitting debris on the way down, as evidenced by the bruising around his face.

Ross was the first to check for a pulse, and when he shook his head, Quill released an inhuman noise.

"CPR," Ross said firmly. "You know the drill. You start rescue breaths, and I'll do the chest compressions." Turning slightly, Ross gave instructions to another searcher, but Quill was too focused on getting ready to do the rescue breaths to hear what they were.

"Quill." Ross brought him back to the present motion. "Can you do this?"

"Yeah, yeah." No way was he moving from his spot

next to Owen to let someone else give him breath. Quill could do this, could give him everything he had, every breath left in his own body. Quickly wiping more snow from Owen's face, Quill fell back on his training, the years of doing this.

Check airway. Listen to Ross count cycles. Breathe. Breathe. Breathe.

He lost track of how long they'd been at it, falling into an almost trance until Ross yelled, "Switch."

Fuck. His turn for the chest compressions. He'd been here before, knew how severe hypothermia could require long durations of CPR, had felt this burn in his lungs before, but nothing had prepared him for this, for the feeling that it was his own life slipping away. As they moved, he checked for a pulse.

Please. Please. Please. Something. Anything.

Thrum. Thrum. It was slow, so slow, and barely there, but hope rushed in, stinging his sinuses, making him shake. "I think I've got something."

Ross's fingers brushed his out of the way. "Yeah, I feel that. Let's keep it going. And hear that? Chopper's coming."

It was his turn to count, and somehow Quill managed it, counting off chest compressions while Ross did the rescue breaths.

"Switch," he called, shoulders burning. He reached for Owen's pulse again right as his neck flexed. A weak, barely-there cough escaped Owen's lips.

"That's it. That's it. He's coming around." Ross straightened, motioning to someone. "Let's get a backboard over here. We've got a pulse and respiration."

"Owen." Quill trailed a finger down Owen's cheek, oblivious to everything other than Owen's painfully shallow breaths. "Come back to me. Hang on. Please hang on. I need you."

"Medics are here." Ross tapped Quill on the shoulder. "Gotta let them work, buddy. Come on. We've done all we can."

Quill honestly wasn't sure he could have moved on his own, but he let Ross's firm grip pull him back so that two medics hauling equipment and backboard could move in. He knew the protocol, knew they had to operate as if Owen had a spinal injury until doctors could determine otherwise. But it still hurt, seeing Owen collared and strapped to the board, looking so much smaller and more vulnerable than usual, still not conscious.

"What's his name?" the female medic closest to Owen's face called out.

"Owen. His name's Owen Han." Quill's voice shook.

No rescue had ever affected him like this, no gruesome scene could ever prepare him for how awful this was, having his heart, his future, his very purpose for living, lying there, not responding.

"Owen? Owen, can you hear me? We're getting you help, okay? I need you to stay with us." She had a loud but calming voice. "We're starting oxygen. You're doing awesome. Keep with us."

The medics called out vital signs to each other as they prepared to move Owen, a flurry of activity Quill had seen many times before, but never had it seemed so critical, every movement essential.

"They're taking Owen and the second skier first," Ross reported. "Another transport is coming in for the leg injury victim."

"Good." Quill managed a nod. Most rescue helicopters were only equipped for two victims, so he wasn't surprised that multiple crews had been required. The team working on Owen finished preparing him for transport, moving the backboard onto a specialty sled that was used for mountain rescues like this. Then they were away, medics moving with the sort of speed and expertise Quill had come to expect from their profession. But somehow this was all different, nothing routine about watching Owen go, not knowing if this was the last time Quill would glimpse his face.

"We need to focus on clearing the scene safely. Can't have another avalanche event today." Ross's voice was grim. "Willie's with the leg injury victim now. Let's you and I try to get the crowd dispersed and back to stable snow."

It was something to do. A job. How funny that he'd thought that this was his calling, his one true purpose in life. But in the end, all this was was a uniform. A badge to fall back on. Training to help. Activities he enjoyed. A job. And it had served him well all these years, but it wasn't his *heart*. Wasn't the thing he loved above all else. Wasn't the one thing that made life worth having. A life spent married to the job was no life at all, or at least not the rich potential of a life with love in it.

He wanted to rush after the medics, tell Owen all the things he'd realized earlier before the callout, all those words that had finally been ready to come out, tell him that he got it, that he finally understood, and that he wasn't going to make the same mistake twice. But he couldn't, couldn't risk endangering Owen further by slowing the rescue. No, he'd have to wait. Have to keep up those humble prayers. Have to do his job if only to have something keeping him upright.

Somehow time marched on. Everyone who wasn't essential rescue personnel was dispersed back to safer elevations. Then the leg injury victim was away in the second helicopter, and it was time to ride the snowmachines back. A rescuer friend of Ross's had already taken Ross's machine so that Ross could drive Owen's back down to the parking lot area.

"Do you want to call someone?" Ross asked when they reached the lower parking lot.

"Call?" Who would he call? He didn't have Owen's emergency contact numbers with him—would have to call Hattie for those. And even if he called, what would he say? He'd had to make similar calls before, but none that scraped his soul like this.

"For you," Ross said gently. "Let's get a backup ranger in here to cover for you, so you can head to the hospital, check on him. He's gonna live, Quill. Promise. I've never seen you so spooked. Thought he was just a seasonal volunteer. You guys good friends?"

"Yeah. Yeah, we are." Quill had a feeling that the full truth was evident on his face, but he was far past giving a damn about what Ross or Willie or anyone else thought.

"That's good. He's gonna need a friend there when he comes around." Ross kept his voice the same level of considerate. "You think you're safe to drive? I'll take you on into Anchorage myself if you want."

"I'm safe to drive." Quill wasn't sure he could handle miles and miles of being treated like a grenade missing its pin. Pity, even well-intentioned, was almost making him hurt worse, each glance at Ross a reminder of how hard they had both worked to bring Owen back, each kind word another hint at how bad things were.

Besides, he knew what calls he needed to make next, and as much as he was out of fucks to give for people's opinions, he also didn't need an audience.

Mainly though, he just needed to reach Owen. As quickly as possible. The need to know how he was clawed at Quill, a vicious, hard-charging beast that wasn't going to rest until he saw Owen again with his own two eyes, touched him, made certain that he wasn't ever going to leave Quill again. And whatever it took to get to him, whatever difficulties lay ahead, he'd do it if it meant seeing Owen's smile again.

Quill wasn't quite sure how he made it to the hospital. Despite telling Ross he was fine to drive, he probably should have taken him up on the ride because the drive was largely a blur until he reached the large medical center where the rescuers had taken Owen. He made his way through the maze of signs and buildings from the parking structure to end up at the information desk in the main hospital. A tall, broad-shouldered woman with a round, kind face was working the desk, and mercifully there wasn't a line.

"How can I help you?" she asked, cheerful tone at odds with the seriousness of Quill's mission.

"I'm looking for one of the avalanche victims brought in a few hours ago. Owen Han. What…what can you tell me about where he is?" Quill was proud that his voice didn't waver even as his heart pounded and legs shook. His knees weren't going to be able to hold him if the news was bad. The woman typed on her computer, monitor angled where Quill couldn't peek at what she was seeing.

"Looks like he's in ICU."

"*Alive.*" The word came out on a gasp, relief coursing through him. "How is he? Where's the ICU?"

"He's listed as family only for visitors. And I'm limited in what I can share. Are you family?"

"I'm… We're…" *Coworkers* was so far from accurate that the word wouldn't even form in his mouth, and *friends* wasn't much better. Sure, they'd tried to be friends since Owen got sick, but friends didn't capture any part of how Quill's insides felt scraped raw, every nerve ending on red alert, every cell aching to see Owen again. That wasn't friends, and he'd been so very foolish to ever think he could settle for that from Owen. "He's…"

Fuck. This shouldn't be so hard. The woman's kind face softened further, and she lowered her voice to a bare whisper. "Boyfriend?"

Funny how years of Quill's life, decades of fears and insecurities, all came down to a single sharp nod. How could he possibly deny his connection to Owen, miss out on his chance to see him, be with him? He'd brave any sort of exposure if it meant reaching Owen.

"I've got here that we haven't been able to reach any next of kin. I can probably get you up to the ICU, see if they can give you an update and work with you to find the family. I'm going to page my friend Macy in ICU myself, see what she can do to get you in to see him even briefly."

"Thank you. I appreciate your help. I've got someone working on locating emergency contact numbers." Quill managed a deep, shaky breath. Hardest part done, it was easier to speak now. Hattie hadn't had access to Owen's records when Quill had called, but she was working on getting the information. Ordinarily, she'd be the one to make the calls, but given everything else Quill had told her, she'd agreed that he should be the one to call.

"You were on the avalanche scene?" She gestured at Quill's official parka and uniform before resuming typing. "That must have been difficult."

A quick denial died in Quill's throat. No more lying or minimizing. "Yeah. It was. He's…he's everything to me. I just need to know he's okay."

"I hear you, hon. Let me make a fast call to Macy, see what she knows." Turning away from Quill, she made a brief call talking in hushed tones before returning her attention to Quill. "She's on her way. You just take a seat, and she'll come and take you to him."

"Thank you. Really. Thanks. For everything." Finding the nearest chair, he sank down, head in his hands. Owen might be alive, but he still wasn't going to rest easy until he knew the prognosis.

"You here for Owen Han?" A petite woman with dark hair with red tips walked over to stand in front of him. "I'm Macy. Carol says you're his partner?"

"Yeah." *Partner.* It was such a familiar, comforting term. Far better than *friend*, and more hopeful even than *boyfriend*. *Partner* implied a future, one where they worked everything out. One where Owen was alive and well. *Please let him be okay.* He followed her to a bank of elevators. "What can you tell me?"

"He's alive, and actually in remarkably good shape." She hit the up button for the elevator. "We've got him in the ICU mainly for close monitoring, but he's been conscious and that's a great sign. Lots of tests and such still to come, but he's breathing on his own now."

Once they were off the elevator, she led him down a corridor to a glassed-in room with a lot of machines, all of which seemed to be hooked to Owen as they whirred and buzzed. He lay there, still and pale, eyes closed but chest rising and falling in a beautiful rhythm, each exhale sending shivers down Quill's back. His right arm was heavily bandaged and his hair hopelessly mussed, and Quill had never seen such a beautiful sight.

"I'm going to give you a few minutes," Macy murmured, putting a warm hand on Quill's arm. "He's probably not going to be up to much if any conversation, but he can definitely hear you, and just sitting with him can be good for both of you. Try and be positive. We don't want him too agitated as his body works to heal."

"Okay." Quill would have promised headstands if it meant getting this chance to be with Owen. And the last thing he wanted to do was to hinder Owen's recovery.

Fuck. Wait. He hadn't even thought about the possibility that Owen might not want him here. He'd been so focused on simply getting here, and now that he was here, Macy backing out of the room, doubt hit him like a slap of wet snow. What if him being there made everything worse? What if Owen didn't need him or his concern? What if it was simply too late for them?

Feet rooted to the linoleum, he wasted several precious minutes, just watching Owen breathe and trying to decide what if anything to say. But he hadn't come this far to let fear win, so he made himself take one step and then another. God, Owen looked so fragile in the bed, covered in the warming blankets they used with hypothermia patients. The bruises on his face stood out in stark relief to his pale skin.

"Owen," he whispered, coming up next to the left side of the bed, too scared about jostling some of the cords and wires to touch him as he longed to do. Owen's eyes stayed shut, respirations slow and steady. "Owen, it's me. Quill. I'm here." Felt a little weird, talking to Owen's sleeping body, but simply saying the words grounded Quill. And Owen's closed eyes also gave him courage he might not have had, had he been awake. "Keep fighting. I need you to fight. Need you to be okay. Need to you to come back to me."

Owen's chest shuddered and a machine beeped before settling again. His eyes fluttered before he coughed weakly. "Here. 'M here."

Yes. There were no words for the lightness in Quill's chest at Owen's whispered words. "Shh. They need you to rest. You don't have to talk. I'm here too, and I'm not going anywhere."

Never had he meant a sentence more. He wasn't going anywhere ever again, not without Owen, and he was ready to fight for that, fight for him, fight for *them*. Whatever happened next, Quill was here for Owen, here for them both and the future he now desperately wanted. If the universe was going to be so kind as to give Quill this second chance, no way was he fucking it up.

Chapter Twenty-Six

Owen was warm and itchy. The itchiness teased at the edges of his consciousness until it forced him awake. And warm and awake were good things. Last thing he had any memory of was cold darkness closing in, so warm was excellent, as was awake even if he had to blink against bright lights. And itchy, itchy was awesome because it meant he wasn't dead. He was pretty sure the afterlife didn't include sweating or feeling like ants were marching all over his skin, little armies of creepy crawlies making him groan. Gradually, he became more aware of his body—the throb in his arm, the heaviness in his limbs, pinching sensations in weird places. His surroundings also started to come into focus—windowless hospital room with whirring equipment, hard bed underneath him. A rising sense of being alone made panic skate along his nerves until his eyes spied a figure slumped in a chair.

And then he had to blink a lot more because it certainly looked like Quill over there dozing away. He looked haggard—stubble on his cheeks, deep lines on his face, slumped shoulders—but he was also one of the best things Owen had ever seen because he was *there*.

"Quill?" Owen croaked, voice scratchy thanks to a throat packed with what felt like thick wool sweaters.

Quill instantly startled awake, scrubbing at his face. "You're awake. How do you feel?"

"Like a snowplow hit me. And itchy."

"Itchy is the meds. You were mumbling about it last night too. What do you remember?" Quill's voice was cautious as he leaned forward.

"We were on the mountain, helping the skiers." Owen struggled to remember beyond digging in the snow. "Then everything goes fuzzy. Cold. Dark."

"You were caught in an avalanche. We got you out, but you were...in rough shape." Quill's voice got tight, and he looked away. "You're at the hospital in Anchorage now. I don't know everything because they're limited in what they can tell me, but you had hypothermia, a concussion, and your right arm is broken. It's in some sort of cast, so don't try to move it."

"How...how long have I been here?" Owen's head was still foggy, the kind of grogginess that came with hours and hours of sleep coupled with the haziness he associated with strong painkillers.

"About a day and a half. You've been in and out of it. Spiked a fever for part of it that had everyone worried, but they're pumping you full of antibiotics too. I never should have let you work with the tail end of that cold. Never should have let you up on the mountain either. God, Owen, I am so sorry. So fucking sorry."

"It's not your fault." Owen wasn't sure of much, but he knew that at least. Quill would never purposefully put him in harm's way, would hurt himself before he let harm come to Owen. "I wanted to work. Wanted to help. You can't control the snowpack." His mouth was too dry for all those words, and he had to cough. "I need water."

"Let me see what you're allowed. I'm going to tell the nursing staff that you're awake." Quill disappeared without addressing the first part of what Owen had said. Damn it. Owen was going to have to work hard to get him to not blame himself. Quill returned with a short dark-haired woman in purple scrubs.

"Are we ever glad to see you awake!" She bustled around, checking Owen's various machines and vital signs before mercifully fetching a cup of water with a lid and straw and holding it out to him. "Slow now. Just a few sips."

The water was cool and glorious. No drink had ever tasted so good, and he had to work to not gulp it all down. "Thank you."

"No problem. I'm going to let your doctors know that you're awake. And I'll mention the itchiness again to them. But they're going to be thrilled you're alert. You gave everyone quite the scare." She smiled at him before turning toward Quill. "Are you going to let the parents know?"

"My parents?" Owen groaned, already hating that they knew. "Quill's talking to my parents?"

"Your doctor has too, but we figured we'd let your boyfriend handle most of the updates with them."

"Your parents are scheduled to arrive later today," Quill said quickly, before Owen could close his suddenly slack jaw. And Quill neither protested the boyfriend label nor stammered through his explanation. Hell, he didn't even blush, despite the nurse's obvious misconception.

Boyfriend? Seriously?

"They're coming?"

"Yeah. Your mom is sort of…a force of nature." Giving a crooked grin, Quill shrugged. "Couldn't keep them put in California, especially once you spiked that fever."

"Hell." Owen sagged back against his pillow, already tired again. "Hate worrying them. And you."

"You just focus on resting," the nurse soothed. "Let everyone else handle the logistics. I'm going to go see what your doctor says about more fluids."

And with that, she headed out of the room, leaving him alone with Quill again. The room was more of a glass cubicle, which probably meant ICU. Fuck it all. No wonder his parents were worried enough to come, and Quill clearly guilt-ridden enough to lie.

"I am so sorry," he said to Quill after the door shut.

"You've got nothing to be sorry about." Quill reached over and squeezed his hand before taking the chair again.

"The nurse thinks—"

"Oh. *That.*" Quill's tone was dismissive, like it was some minor irritation, a coffee order gone wrong, and not an outing of epic proportions. "Yeah, they weren't going to let me see you if I wasn't family. I figured… *hoped* you wouldn't mind too much." Another lopsided, decidedly un-Quill-like smile.

"I don't. But…" He sighed, any thrill at Quill publicly recognizing them countered by realities. Also, he was more than a little pissed that if the situation had been reversed, he wouldn't have been able to so easily play that card. "I don't want it getting back to your work. And, God, it had to be so difficult for you."

"Department knows. I had to get coverage to be

able to be here with you. Had to talk to my Ranger in Charge, explain everything. Hattie's up there now. Called in a stack of favors, but it's not like I didn't have the leave."

"Quill. Fuck. This is *not* your fault that I got injured. You didn't have to come out for me. That's some fucked-up guilt right there."

"It's not guilt. And it's not for you." Sighing, Quill leaned back in his chair. "Didn't even have to think that hard about it. Getting to you was all that mattered. Everything else seemed petty. Small. Stupid. Like our arguments. If guilt's driving me, it's guilt over our fight. I let fear win. And then it almost won for real. I almost lost you, lost a chance to tell you…to make things right."

"It *was* a stupid fight." Just thinking about their breakup had Owen more exhausted, head weighing five hundred pounds. The last thing he could remember thinking was that he'd squandered what little time they might have had left, but now that they were here, Quill actually with a ready apology, he was hit with boulders' worth of doubts and a not-small amount of anger. "And it shouldn't take some sort of near-death wakeup call to have you realizing you were being ridiculous. If you didn't want me around then, I'm not sure I want you hanging around now out of pity. Or guilt. Because no matter what you say, I know guilt's part of this. You carry the weight of the world around. Of course you blame yourself. It's what you do."

"It's not…" Quill scrubbed at his short hair, which was far messier than Owen had ever seen it.

"Then what is it?"

"Love." Quill whispered the word so softly that Owen had to strain to hear him above all the assorted noises of the room—machinery, AC, voices in the corridor. "Love, not guilt. I didn't realize… Didn't think…"

"I told you it was more than hooking up." Owen couldn't help being a little bitter even as his heart fluttered. "You didn't want to believe me. Didn't think we were worth it. Thought you knew what was best for me."

"I still think you could do better than me. Or this place. Find something safer, warmer, and someone younger, more fun, exciting. But… I see now that I can't let you go. I saw it when you were talking to those tourists. I was so damn jealous of that guy flirting with you. I wanted to tell you right then, but there was the callout. Fuck. Might be selfish, but I *need* you. And I'm sorry that it took this for me to get the right words out." Quill shook his head. "And now I'm getting you all agitated. Which is the opposite of what your doctors want."

"I'm not agitated," Owen half lied. What he was was exhausted, walls starting to creep in, eyelids getting heavier. But he didn't want to give in to sleep with things still so unresolved with Quill. "And I want to believe we would have worked it out too. But we didn't. And now you're here, all best boyfriend in the universe, making friends with nurses and apparently my parents too, and I'm not sure I know who you are. Not sure *you* know."

"Please don't send me away." Quill's voice wavered. Quill who so seldom asked for anything. Quill who never showed emotion. The fist gripping Owen's chest loosened, replaced by the need to hold Quill. He wasn't quite to forgiveness yet, but he wasn't unsympathetic to this strangely emotional Quill either.

"I'm not. I'm…grateful that you're here. I just want you here for the right reasons."

"I am." Eyes bright, Quill reached for his non-bandaged hand again. Electricity zoomed up Owen's arm, like the first time they'd touched. God, they'd come so far since then. Could this really be real? Could he trust in Quill? Trust in them? He wished he had an easy yes to all the questions swirling around in his head. But all he seemed to have was the strength to squeeze Quill's fingers and yawn.

"Good."

"You need to rest now."

"We're...talking." Owen yawned between words.

"I'll be here when you wake up. And we can talk more. Promise. We're going to work this out."

As sleep started to reclaim him, Owen could only wish that he had Quill's sureness. He wanted to believe that they could have the future he'd wanted so badly just a few days prior, wanted to believe that Quill truly was motivated by love, not guilt. He wasn't going to let Quill mortgage his future, no matter how badly Owen wanted him. Among his piles of thoughts were the glittering remnants of his feelings for Quill. He loved Quill too much to accept anything less than Quill's whole heart, and he wasn't going to let Quill hand it over as a form of penance.

A lifetime ago, Quill had met JP's parents, and even though it had been as a friend, he had still quaked in his cheap boots and flannel shirt in their lavish house. But those butterflies were nothing compared to his nerves at meeting Owen's parents, wanting to make a good impression, wanting to prove to Owen that he could do this, could be the boyfriend—*partner*—he deserved. It didn't help that they'd surprised him, coming in looking far too elegant for their hours of traveling while Quill was dozing. At a certain point, the nursing staff had seemed to simply accept that he wasn't going anywhere and had stopped trying to time his visits, letting him essentially camp out here, keeping watch over Owen, like his presence alone might be enough to keep bad things from happening.

"You must be Quill. Owen's ranger." Owen's mother was small with delicate features and the same Californian accent and intelligent, sparkling dark eyes as Owen, which she used to intently study Quill. It was all he could do not to squirm. He hadn't given a thought to what a mess he must look like until they arrived and now he was intensely aware of every whisker and grubby piece of clothing.

Quill wasn't entirely sure whether he was Owen's anything right then, but he wanted to be, rather desperately, and that had to count for something. "Yeah." He stuck out a hand for her and then Owen's dad, who was slightly shorter than Owen but with a similar confident air.

"Mom?" Owen blinked his way awake.

"Owen." Both parents rushed to the bed, one on each side of him.

"My poor Owen." Owen's mom squeezed his shoulder. "The doctors said you're doing better. But how do you feel? Where does it hurt?"

"Mom. Please." Owen had to be feeling a little better because his voice was back to its usual firmness, and he even managed a small laugh. "You're embarrassing me. Hurts pretty much everywhere, but I'm *fine*. You didn't have to come."

"Of course we did." Owen's father bristled. "You're our son. You were hurt. We're coming."

He made it sound like it was that simple, like their support for Owen was that unwavering, that much of a given, when Quill knew only too well that that wasn't how all families worked. Would his even care if their situations had been reversed? If some strange guy had called them up, he honestly wasn't sure any of them would give more than two fucks for his well-being. But Owen's family had been nothing but gracious, his mom even going so far as to ask Quill how he was holding up at several points in their phone conversations.

The reunion scene was almost too tender for Quill, made him feel about as needed as snow boots in July. "Here. Take my chair." Standing, he gestured to Owen's mother that she should sit. "I'm going to go get some food and coffee. What can I get you guys?"

"Coffee would be lovely. It was a long flight." Owen's mom sank into the chair Quill had vacated. "But I don't meant to chase you off."

"You're not. But the nurses probably don't want a crowd in here. I'll be back with some drinks in a few, let you guys visit."

Taking some deep breaths, he headed toward the cafeteria. He didn't know how to convince Owen that he wasn't experiencing some sort of guilt reaction, and he honestly didn't know what he'd do if he couldn't win Owen back. He'd give anything to go back to that argument on the roof, kick his stupid self, get past his fears and insecurities. Or even that moment in the parking lot, when he'd been so jealous that all his feelings had bubbled up, he wished he could grant them another few minutes before the call had come in. But he couldn't live indefinitely in regrets, could only go forward, hoping like heck that he could give them both a future.

He'd done enough of that already, let self-condemnation over his dad's death keep him from living his best life, let fears of being the center of attention guide him instead of listening to his heart. And right then, his heart said that it wasn't giving up Owen without a fight.

Taking his time to ensure Owen's parents got enough privacy for their visit, he cleaned up a bit in the restroom, then got himself some food before collecting coffee for all of them. When he returned to the room, he wasn't terribly surprised to find the three of them laughing. If anyone could make being in the ICU funny, it was Owen. God, how had Quill even thought for a second that he could live without Owen's ability to find the sunny spot in any situation?

"You're back." Owen had a wide smile for Quill, but whether he was faking it in front of his parents, Quill couldn't tell. He passed out the coffees along with sugar and creamer packets. Somehow, he managed to make small talk, asking Owen's parents about their trip and if they'd found the hotel near the hospital that he'd recommended.

"Good news!" Macy, who was now and forever Quill's favorite nurse for all she'd done for him and Owen, came into the room all smiles. "You're going to be moved to a regular room. This would probably be a great time for your family to get some rest while we get you all settled in the new space."

"When do I get to go home?" Owen struggled to sit up farther in the bed.

"That'll be up to the doctors, but I bet they keep you

a few more days. They'll want to make sure the pneumonia is well under control and that you're able to be independently mobile again. They'll probably need to run more tests too."

"Oh." Sinking back against the pillows, Owen seemed to deflate.

"But soon, I promise." Macy patted his hand before completing her check of his vitals.

After she'd left again, Owen looked over at Quill, eyes serious. "Have you been here at the hospital nonstop? You've got to be exhausted."

"I'm fine," Quill lied even though he'd trade a month of summer for a hot shower and a bed.

"You should all go rest. Seriously. Like the nurse said, they're moving me. I can see you again later. If you're coming back that is. Do you have to get back to work?"

"I'm coming back," Quill said firmly. "Hattie and another ranger are covering for me for a few days."

"Then go rest." Owen made a shooing motion with his left hand, then winced. "Crap. Pulled on the IV. And now I'm tired again too."

"We'll *all* go rest so you can nap too," Owen's mom said before she gave him a kiss on the head. She gave Quill a stern look, and Quill couldn't help thinking about how long it had been since he'd had a parent order him to do anything. Her obvious concern was sort of… nice. Reassuring.

In the end, Quill ended up giving in to Owen's demands and getting himself a room at the same hotel he'd recommended to Owen's parents. After a long, hot shower, he collapsed on the bed for a few hours of fitful sleep where he kept dreaming about trying to outrun walls of snow and other horrors until finally he admitted defeat and headed back to the hospital, at least somewhat cleaner and marginally more rested. And as luck would have it, he beat Owen's parents back to the hospital and found Owen alone in his new hospital room, no roommate in the other bed, TV on low.

"Nice having cable again?" Quill asked as he came into the room.

"Eh. It's a distraction. Not even sure what this movie is, but it feels like I've slept enough for a year."

"You need it. It's what your body needs to heal." Quill motioned at the side chair. "It okay if I sit? If you were just being nice earlier about me coming back, that's fine too. I can—"

"Sit." Owen's voice had more than a trace of his usual bossiness, and that was truly nice to hear, a welcome change from the feverish mumbles of the past few days.

"Okay." Quill dragged the chair close to the bed, unable to resist the chance to touch Owen again, stroking a finger down his forearm, avoiding his IV site. "Would it help if I said again that I'm sorry? Or does that make things worse?"

"I don't know." Owen shrugged, then winced. "Fuck. Right shoulder keeps knotting up."

"Get better, and I'll rub it for you."

"*Quill.*" Owen sighed. "I keep expecting to wake up for real, discover this is all a dream. Or learn that you've been abducted by aliens. I don't need you to have a total personality transplant. Never did. I like you, the real you, just fine. I only wanted you to give us a chance."

"That's what I want now too. A chance. I don't know how to prove to you that this isn't some knee-jerk response or guilt talking, but I want the chance to try. I thought I could be strong, let you go for your sake, let you have the future you deserve, but then I saw you talking to those tourists…" Quill huffed out a breath and held up his hands in defeat because jealousy probably wasn't any better of a reason for figuring his stupid self out than guilt. "And then, yes, there were those horrible hours when I thought I might lose you for good. I need you. For two decades now, I've told anyone who asked that I was married to the job. But then you came along, and you made me see how empty that life was. I'm not sure that I can—or *want*—to go back to my old ways. You make my life better. You make *me* a better person."

It was one of the longest personal speeches Quill had made, and he had to take a breath, looking away from Owen, not sure what he'd do if Owen couldn't give him that chance.

"I'm glad. I am. And you make me happy too. I like who I am around you. A lot. I was always striving and thinking of the next big thing. You make me more… settled. In a good way. But… I can't help but think you're going to come to your senses, remember that you don't want to be publicly in a same-sex relationship. And I don't think I can have that argument again. I want it all, not just the private sliver you're willing to give me. And not just being boyfriends when it gets you what you want, like here at the hospital."

Quill actually had some thoughts about that, but he wasn't quite ready to play every last card. Not with Owen still so justifiably testy and peeved at Quill.

"I'm done being closeted. I mean, I'm still me. Like you said. No personality transplant. Probably not going to wear rainbow go-go shorts to the next department meeting, but I'm also done hiding. You were absolutely right that I was being a coward. I was letting old fears about how badly it went with my father drive me into hiding, keep me from finding connection, something real and lasting and good."

"We *are* pretty good." Owen gave him a tentative smile that Quill felt down to his toes. "And—hell. Why am I yawning again? I should be able to have a simple conversation."

"You've been through a huge ordeal. Maybe we don't have to hash everything out right now. That's not fair to you. You rest. I'll be here."

Owen studied him for several long moments. "You really mean that, don't you?"

"I do." Quill took a chance and touched him again, squeezing his fingers gently, stomach wobbling when Owen squeezed back. "I'm here for you. For us. I'm here for this, and I'm not going anywhere."

"A chance." Owen yawned again, voice going sleepy. "You get a chance."

It wasn't full forgiveness, and Quill wasn't going to hold Owen to something he was murmuring on the way to drifting off again, but his heart still thrilled. A chance. He could take that, work with it, prove to Owen that he was worth the risk. They'd been given a gift from the universe, a veritable miracle, and Quill sure as hell wasn't going to waste it.

Chapter Twenty-Seven

Owen had thought the long Alaskan winter nights had prepared him for cabin fever, but being in the hospital was a new level of stir crazy that he hadn't ever achieved before. It took another two days before Owen finally convinced the doctors that he was ready to go. And it took even more fancy talking to try to convince Quill and his parents that he should be allowed to leave with Quill, go back to his quarters and maybe not return immediately to work, but at least head in that direction.

The last thing he wanted was to return to California with his parents while everything was still up in the air with Quill, a weird tentative and unsettled truce having settled over them where Quill kept up the attentive best-boyfriend-ever routine and Owen tried to relax enough to enjoy it. But there was still a lot of talking that needed to happen, a lot of future to be decided on. Further, it was one thing for Quill to be okay with being a couple when surrounded by supportive nurses and Owen's parents, who made no secret about liking Quill, and another thing to be a couple in the larger, public, ongoing sense.

While waiting for the doctors to sign off on his release, Quill and his parents had been conferring in the hall, a development that made Owen's neck ache and made him snappish when the three of them finally returned to the room.

"You can go with Quill." His mother sounded like a peace accord had been reached, and not like Owen was a grown adult who would do whatever he damn well felt like.

"I don't need permission." He glared at all of them. "I'm fine. I have medications. I've got a cast for my arm. I can rest just fine in my room, and there's still plenty I can do, even with the cast."

"We just care about you." Never one to cow in the face of Owen's bad mood, his mother gave him a hard stare back. "You're not a cat. You don't have endless lives. First, the cancer. Now this. You can't blame us for wanting to make sure you fully recover."

"I know." Owen could never stay peeved at his parents long. "And I appreciate it. I do. It was nice of you guys to come. I love you. I'm just ready to not be babied. And you've got lives to get back to."

"I do want to get back to work. But you're always going to be a huge part of our life." Owen's father had always had a more placid personality than his mother, the perfect foil for her. Quiet where she was talkative, they simply fit. Owen had spent years despairing of ever finding the kind of compatibility and relationship that they had. But then he'd been so sure that he'd found that with Quill. And now...hell. He just wasn't sure. His heart wanted to believe in them and their potential as a couple again. He did. But damn those doubts that kept plaguing him.

"Your parents only want to make sure you're cared for." Quill defending Owen's parents was sweet. If nothing else, Owen had enjoyed seeing them get along, even if they did seem to be conspiring against him. "And you will be. You're not going to overdo it and rush back."

Luckily, Owen was saved from further arguing his case by the arrival of his discharge papers and a flurry of instructions from the nursing staff. Seemingly satisfied that Quill could take care of Owen, his parents agreed to head back to their hotel and keep their early-morning flight back to California.

"I'll update you," Quill promised, again sounding like he'd been replaced by an alien double. And he didn't even flinch when Owen's mom gave him a hug, although his cheeks did turn an adorable shade of pink. Finally, they left, and after a tussle about needing to be wheeled out, Owen was at last free and installed in the passenger seat of Quill's truck.

"Damn. How is it already this late?" He gestured at the dashboard clock. "It'll be dark by the time we're back."

"We're not going straight back." Quill had a sly smile that Owen wasn't sure he'd ever seen before.

"We're not?"

"Nope. I've got plans for you." Putting the truck in gear, Quill headed out of the hospital complex.

"What did my parents talk you into?"

Quill waited until they were on the main road to answer. "They didn't. I mean, I told them my idea so they wouldn't worry, but it was all me." Quill was blushing again, which made it damn hard to stay irritated with him.

"Okay, now I'm curious. Where are we going?" Owen didn't want to put a crimp in whatever Quill had planned, but his energy level was still lower than he'd like. "Not sure I'm up to eating out or something."

"Not going out." The truck appeared headed for downtown. "I got us a place. And before you tell me that you're fine and that you're up to the trek back, this isn't me thinking you need coddling."

"It's not?" Owen wasn't so sure. Certainly sounded like Quill not trusting him to make the trip back.

"It's more me thinking you might like a long, hot bath after all that time in a hospital, and you can't get that back at our quarters. But also... Valentine's Day is coming up. Doubt I'll be able to get it off after taking this time, and you're always so big on holidays..."

"I am." Owen couldn't hold back a smile. However annoying Quill going all overprotective was, Owen couldn't deny the appeal of a Quill who was deliberately trying to be romantic. "And a bath does sound good. Hell, I'd settle for an unsupervised shower at this point. I'm seriously scuzzy."

Quill had produced a pair of sweats for him to wear home, but Owen still wasn't going to turn down the chance to get truly clean.

"Oh, you're not that bad. But let me do this for you. You deserve a little spoiling after all you've been through. And we're heading home in the morning, so you can prove yourself soon enough. Hattie's ready to get back to Val, I'm sure. Part of me still thinks I should have sent you with your parents, but I'm selfish and ready to have you to myself too."

"I wouldn't mind some alone time too," Owen admitted. "That's a big part of why I was agitating so hard for going back with you. I know things are still...weird. But I did mean it about giving you a chance. I think we need some time to ourselves. Time to work out whatever the heck comes next."

"No worrying about the future. Not yet," Quill said sternly as he parked in an underground garage. "Right now, I just want that chance. And for you to focus on relaxing and getting better. I already checked in earlier, so we can go on up."

As it turned out, Quill wasn't kidding about up. The elevator took them up to the twentieth floor, and Quill let them into a suite with amazing views of Cook Inlet that was a step up from the average hotel room with a little sitting area, bedroom with a king bed, a large bathroom with a separate tub and glassed-in shower.

"Okay, I can get more into your idea. This is really nice." Owen gave Quill a smile right before Quill steered him toward the bathroom.

"How about you start with that hot bath? Then I can rub that shoulder and anything else that's sore."

"Anything?" Owen winked at him. He hadn't thought about sex in days, but here, romantic setting, alone with Quill, massage in the offering, his body knew a few stirrings of lust.

"We'll see about that. First, your bath."

"Hmm. I think I'll make it a shower. You're making me impatient to get to the…rubbing. Later, I want to see if we both fit in the tub."

"Ha. Good luck talking me into *that*." Quill laughed. "I'm going to order us some food. What do you want? You need to keep your strength up."

"Order me whatever. Anything beats hospital food." Owen smiled at him again, trying to show Quill that his efforts weren't unappreciated. Even if he was motivated by guilt or the whole near-death thing, Owen couldn't deny that Quill was trying hard to win him back. And Owen's heart was already most of the way there, hadn't forgotten how he felt about Quill. He just had to hope that his brain caught up eventually.

Heading to the shower, he covered his cast with one of the plastic protectors the hospital had provided and then stripped and cranked the water to hot. He'd had a tepid shower at the hospital with a medical assistant helping, but being alone under the steaming shower and soaping up with the herbal-scented bath products felt like a huge luxury. Taking his time, he let the water wash away much of the stress of the past few days, letting go of all the irritations over being hospitalized, and shoving aside all his fears over both the future with Quill and questions about his own mortality.

That last bit was something he was trying hard not to dwell on, how fucking scary it had been waking up in the hospital, knowing he almost died, knowing that but for a miracle he wouldn't get a second chance at *anything*. And maybe that was why he was so determined to get things right with Quill, not settle for good enough or empty promises. He wanted everything, Quill's full heart, for all the right reasons, and the future they both deserved.

Resolved, he dried off before wrapping one of the towels around his waist and returning to the main area of the suite.

"Food or massage first?" Quill gestured at the little table where a plate of fruits and cheeses and sandwiches lay. Nothing that wouldn't keep, and Owen's body was far more interested in discovering what parts still worked.

"Massage." Thinking about Quill's hands on him

while in the shower had sent blood rushing south in a promising sign, and Owen was greedy for that. Quill so earnestly insistent on this now was a nice sort of novelty. He'd massaged Quill a lot in the past few months, but he generally enjoyed turning Quill into jelly where Quill let go of any thought of needing to reciprocate.

"I'm...uh...probably not as good at this as you, but I looked some stuff up on my phone," Quill said as Owen stretched out on the blissfully fluffy bed.

"Research? I'm impressed." Owen wiggled around, getting comfortable, loving the space to spread out after the cramped, hard hospital bed. "And I'm still sore enough that anything is gonna feel good, trust me. Even my legs hurt, and I haven't used them in days."

"Let's start there." Quill knelt next to him on the bed, rubbing Owen's calves and feet. He'd lost his shoes at some point, and between the bare feet and his jeans and a sweatshirt, Owen just wasn't used to this version of Quill. He'd acquired some regular clothes over the past few days, but Owen found himself missing the uniform, for more than simply eye candy. Back at their quarters and on duty, he'd known exactly who Quill was, trusted in that person with the deepest part of his soul. He wanted to feel that way about this Quill, the attentive boyfriend and darling of parents and nurses alike, wanted to not feel like Quill was a balloon he needed to hold on tight to. And more than anything, he wanted this to be *real*.

As if sensing the direction of Owen's thoughts, Quill paused in his attentions to Owen's legs. "Relax. We've got all night, and I'm not going anywhere."

"Maybe I was wrong to give you that ultimatum," Owen mused, his realization from the avalanche crowding back into his brain. "Maybe that ruined everything. We had such a good thing going."

"Hush. You didn't ruin anything." Quill moved to rub Owen's neck, firm strokes against his tense muscles. "And I think we've established that my reaction sucked. It wasn't an unreasonable idea or request. You wanted a future. And I wanted that too, but I let my fears win out. Well, that, and I still worry that I'm not the best for you. But I do know that you're what's best for *me*. I need you, and like I said earlier, I'm being selfish and keeping you. And whatever it takes to do that, I'm going to do it."

"I worry you're going to resent me forcing you to come out," Owen admitted, all those fears finally bubbling to the surface.

"I'm not," Quill said firmly, thumbs digging into Owen's neck. "Listen, when I told the hospital that I was your boyfriend—that wasn't for you. That was for *me*. I needed to get to you, and all of a sudden, every objection I'd ever had to being out seemed ridiculous. Same thing with calling my boss. Any amount of censure for getting involved with a volunteer or departmental gossip is worth it because it means I got to be with you. And that's what I didn't see clearly before. I've got so much to gain by being more open. Sure, it means more eyeballs on me and the risk of people taking things badly, but it gets me not just you but also my best self. What was it you called it a while back? My authentic self? I thought that self was in the mountains, was a patch of dirt or the reflection of a sunset, but now I know that self is the person I get to be around you. So, no, no I'm not going to resent you for giving me this gift of myself, of the best possible version of my life."

It was a long speech by Quill standards, and it warmed every last frozen place in Owen, all his hurting parts, and while it didn't completely erase the pain he'd felt when Quill had refused to consider a future for them, it was more than a start to building up trust that Quill knew what he wanted at long last and that Quill wasn't about to bolt if things got difficult.

"Come here." Owen rolled slightly so that he could tug Quill to him. It was their first kiss since the fight, and it felt like the very first all over again, a tentative feeling out of each other underscored by a powerful hunger. God, he was never going to get over this man, had been foolish to think he might. He'd missed Quill, missed this fiercely, and he put all that hurt and longing and waiting into the kiss.

It started soft, but something in Owen turned demanding, wanting Quill to meet his need, wanting evidence that he wasn't alone in floundering around in emotions far bigger than he was. And Quill responded beautifully, mouth parting on a gasp, taking everything Owen wanted to give him, sucking hard on Owen's questing tongue, clutching his shoulders, big body trembling under Owen's hands.

Owen needed more, needed every damn thing all at once, and his left hand fumbled for Quill's fly. Fucking cast, slowing him down.

"Hey. Hey. I owe you that massage," Quill panted, eyes glassy and mouth swollen, hottest fucking thing Owen had ever seen.

"Later. Need you. Get naked with me."

"Glad to see your bossiness back." Quill laughed as he sat up long enough to pull his shirts off. "I should make you wait."

"I've waited long enough. We both have." Owen couldn't keep the seriousness out his voice. No more waiting. No more fears. No room for doubts. Just this, right here and now. This man, all of him, sweet and confounding both. All of his parts. Owen wanted everything Quill had to give.

"Yeah, we have," Quill said roughly as he wiggled out of his jeans and boxer briefs. His mouth found Owen's again even before he stretched out against him, both of them on their sides. Owen tried to pull him closer, but ended up nearly hitting him with the cast.

"Fuck. I hate this thing. I keep forgetting it's on. I want to touch you."

"I'll take the cast if it means having *you*." Quill laced their left hands together while his right one swept down Owen's torso. "And maybe it's good for your inner control freak to take a break now and then. Let someone else take care of you."

"Hey, I let you massage me."

"For like all of two minutes." Quill's laugh was warm and rich. "We're gonna work on that later. But for right now, how about you let me make us both feel good."

Mouth claiming Owen's in a possessive kiss, Quill drew Owen closer, until their torsos rubbed together and legs tangled. Much as Owen generally liked being in charge, he could admit that this was nice, following the kiss to see what Quill had in mind. Which was apparently unraveling Owen slowly, maddeningly soft slides of lips and tongue, and gentle strokes of his large hand exploring Owen's sides and back until Owen was moaning, desperate for more than the glancing brush of Quill's cock against his own.

"Need something?" Quill's eyes glittered as his hand

worked its way between their bodies to rub Owen's stomach.

"Touch me." Owen strained against Quill, trying to free his left hand, but Quill held fast, only laughing at his struggle.

"I'll get you there. Promise."

"In this century?" Voice perilously close to a whine, Owen trembled, body not sure it liked feeling this out of control.

"Maybe even this decade." Kissing him again, Quill lined up their cocks in his hand, jacking them together at a glacial pace. The pressure of Quill's thick cock against his had him moaning again, especially when Quill did this thing on the upstroke that made their cockheads drag against each other.

"Faster." Owen rocked his hips, trying to urge Quill into a more purposeful rhythm.

"Slowly," Quill countered. "I've missed kissing you like crazy. I want to savor this."

"You just like torturing me."

"That too." Quill laughed wickedly before deepening the kiss, thoroughly plundering Owen's mouth as his hand gradually sped up until they were both groaning, kiss losing finesse.

"Yeah. That." Owen's head fell back, and Quill lavished kisses on his exposed neck. "Come on."

"Ask me," Quill demanded, taking a page straight out of Owen's usual playbook.

"Get me off. Please. Need to come."

"Yeah, you do." Voice gruff, Quill loosened his grip, giving Owen more of a green light to fuck into his fist, driving their cocks together faster. Quill thrust too, their cockheads rubbing together each upstroke, shafts moving against each other urgently now.

"Close." Owen's eyes squished shut as the sensations threatened to overwhelm him.

"Kiss me," Quill commanded, lips already seeking Owen's. It was the kiss that did it, the way Quill seemed to put his whole self into it, holding nothing back, giving Owen his tenderness and sweet demands and all his strength too, every part of him that Owen had missed so desperately. Tension coiled in his muscles, body hurtling toward release.

"Yeah, that's it. Come for me." Quill moved with lightning-fast strokes now, quick licks of pleasure that had Owen trying to make it last even as his body strained, incapable of doing anything other than obeying Quill. And it seemed Quill had been waiting for him to go because he groaned mightily as Owen shot all over his fist, his come mingling with Owen's. Owen was still shuddering when Quill released his cock, bringing his slick fingers to his lips.

"The you of three months ago never would have done that," Owen couldn't resist teasing, voice breathless. "I've corrupted you thoroughly."

"I like it." Quill's smile managed to be both dirty and bashful.

"I know."

"Like you too. Like being this way with you. Free and sexy and silly all at once. I never thought that was even possible."

"Quill…" Words bubbled up in Owen's throat, scary declarations and promises, but what came out was a rush of air. There was so much he wanted to say, so much he wanted from Quill, but part of him held back, not wanting to say too much, ruin this lovely peace between them.

"Shh. Rest now, okay?" Quill kissed the top of his head, pulling the comforter up around them.

"Stay with me." Owen yawned, sleepy despite everything churning in his head.

"Not going anywhere." Quill's voice was solemn and soothing, and Owen tried to trust him, trust that he meant that on a deeper level, trust that they could find a way forward, together.

Chapter Twenty-Eight

"I told you we don't fit." Quill grumbled, feeling more than a little ridiculous wedged into the oversized tub, but then Owen settled his back to Quill's front, and the appeal of bathing together finally made a little sense. Warm, slippery Owen was always a good thing. After finding a dimmer switch for the bathroom, Owen had tossed one of the little bottles of body wash into the water, which made lots of rosemary-scented bubbles. The whole thing felt decadent, like an over-the-top birthday cake he didn't really deserve but sure as hell was going to enjoy.

"I think we fit just fine. Which is what I've been trying to tell you." Owen's plastic-covered cast rested on the tub edge and one of his feet dangled near the faucet. His voice was more contemplative than accusatory. He'd been in a mellow mood since the sex and nap and some food. "You've met my parents now. They're so perfect for each other that it's not funny. My whole life, I wanted that. The one person who made me that happy. And I wanted it to be that easy."

"Easy?" Quill peered down at him. He'd spent enough time with the two of them to reach his own conclusions. "It's not easy for them."

"How do you figure?"

"I mean, maybe they've led a more charmed life than some, sure. But it's like this complicated dance they engage in. Your mom will get all agitated, and then right when she's about to go off, he calms her down. Or he'll get…moody. But she'll joke at the right moment, and he snaps out of it. And they compromise all the time. Your mom wanted to leave to come the moment I called to tell them you were in the hospital, but he calmed her down, got her to do things in a more organized way. He's a tea drinker like you, but he'll have coffee because she does."

"Huh." Owen blinked. "You got all that in two days with them?"

"Hey, I know I'm not the most social like you or your mom, but I'm observant. And I can see how to a kid, they probably seemed like some sitcom ideal couple. But if you think they're not working to avoid arguing, I think you're not seeing the whole picture. Trust me, I've been around enough people who fly off the handle at each other. They've got plenty they could fight about. But they don't. And that's work. I think the trick is that they seem to enjoy the work, which I haven't seen very much."

"Yeah. They do." Owen sounded thoughtful, and he was quiet for a long moment before speaking again. "Maybe that's it then. I wanted someone who made the work seem that easy. Someone who made it worth it. And you do. I gotta admit, in past relationships I was always a little selfish, I guess you could say. Thinking about myself. But doing stuff for you, taking care of you, just feels natural, fulfills me in a way that work and success never did. And it fucking *hurt*, you pushing me away, telling me that you knew better than me what I needed for my future. Especially when I was so sure that I'd found what I'd been looking *years* for."

"I'm sorry." Quill held him a little tighter. Maybe it was the warm water. Maybe it was the fact that they weren't facing each other. But there was something about being here like this that made it easier to have a soul-baring conversation. "I really am. I never wanted to hurt you. But that's not an excuse. I *did* hurt you. Mainly because I just never saw myself that way, as having something someone else might want to have. I think I'd told myself so long that I was shit at relationships and that I didn't need anyone that I started to believe it. I didn't think there was any way that I could be good for you, not like that. Not like you're saying. And I'm still struggling with that. It feels like you could do a lot better than me."

"Quill." Owen squeezed his knee. "You're seriously one of the best people I know. I don't *want* to do better. Don't want anyone else."

"I'm working on believing that. It's hard though. I think deep inside, I was worried about coming to depend on you, needing you so badly, and then having you leave to pursue your next big thing. I'm not saying it was right because it wasn't, but that's a big part of why I pushed you away. I thought I was saving myself some pain. You too. But all it did was hurt both of us. And I'm sorry."

"I get it. I do. I'm scared too. But I'm willing to face those fears if it means a future together. But not if you're going to push me away again. I want to stay, Quill. And I need you to believe me on that."

Quill wasn't ever going to get a better opening than

this for his entire purpose in orchestrating that evening. A tremor ran through his body. "I do. And I'm not sending you away."

"You're not?" Owen sounded more than a little surprised at his ready agreement. "You want me to apply for a summer position?"

"Well, yeah. If that's truly what you want. But I've been thinking. A lot. And I've got an idea for how you can stay." Quill took a giant breath, trying to steady his racing pulse. "We could get married."

"We could *what*?" Owen startled, sloshing water over the side of the tub, and Quill stayed him with a hand on his stomach.

"Just hear me out, okay?"

"Okay." Owen sounded far more skeptical than excited, but it was a start.

"First, it makes a certain amount of sense. If we're married, you can stay with me. It doesn't matter what your job is or if they grant you a summer position. Housing extends to married couples. You could draw your cartoons, go back to finance long-distance, go to school. Whatever you want. And you could still stay. And if you do want a job, a certain priority is put on placing married couples together. So that's the practical part of it."

"Please tell me there's an impractical part of it." Owen didn't sound convinced at all.

"Well, yeah." This was the harder thing. He was good with logic and action, not so much pretty words. He'd already talked more that evening than most weeks regularly. But apparently logic wasn't going to sway Owen. It was time to take the sort of risk he'd spent his whole life avoiding. "There's the I-love-you part. That's the main thing. Maybe I should have said that first."

"Yeah." Owen voice was thready, but Quill pushed on.

"I love you, and we could spend years working up to this, circling back around until the practicalities won out, but the truth of it is that I love you. This week has shown me that the future isn't a given. Not everyone gets decades or years. But whatever we get, whatever time I've got, I want it with you."

"So this *is* a near-death thing? An oh-my-God-we're-mortal realization. Quill, I'm not sure I want to be a knee-jerk reaction—"

"It's not that sort of reaction," Quill protested, stroking Owen's slick arms. "I mean, I can't deny that what happened is a factor. Given me a good kick. But I've taken long enough getting over my stupid self. I don't want to wait on this and lose my—*our*—chance. Because you're right. We fit. We've found something special, and I want to keep it. Keep you."

"But—"

"It's not coming from a place of fear. I've lived so much of my life in fear. I know the difference between reaction and…celebration. This is more about that—being willing to celebrate, acknowledge what we've found, what we've built. Because we did build it. Night by night, meal by meal until we were in love. And maybe it wasn't love at first sight like your parents and maybe it was work to get there, but I want to be that person for you, the one you were looking for. Because that's what you are to me—the missing piece of my life."

Quill's skin felt scrubbed raw and tight, more naked

than he'd ever been, and not simply literally. But Owen stayed silent save for the sound of his breathing, more exaggerated than usual.

"Say something. Please." Quill was going to need out of this tub in another twenty seconds.

"I'm...reeling, I guess. Man, when you uncork, you *uncork*." Owen inhaled sharply again. "I love you too, and maybe I should have been brave enough to say that when I gave you the ultimatum. Maybe that would have made a difference. And you're not wrong about life being short and uncertain..."

"But? If I love you and you love me, is it really that crazy of an idea?" Quill's heart beat harder, thrilling at Owen's words even as his muscles stayed bunched up, whole body on edge, the possibility of rejection still looming large.

"For a guy who didn't even want his best friend to know about us a week ago, yeah, it kind of is. There's no walking married back. That's about as openly gay as it gets."

"I know. And I know it's strange, but I like that part. Over, done, settled, mine forever. Fuck other people. No more hiding out, trying to find the courage. It's like..." He tried to think of the right words, the words that might show Owen how right this was. "It's like swinging out on a rope swing, only we let go together. No back-and-forth for years, no indecision and delay and argument."

"So you'd marry me now to avoid future arguments? I mean, I know conflict isn't your thing, but that's a little extreme."

"Did you miss the part where I said I love you?" Some frustration was seeping into his voice. He had expected some pushback, but maybe not quite this much. "I love you. Screw the practical parts. I love you. I want this, and I'm not afraid to want it anymore, and that's a big deal to me. But what I am afraid of is losing you, of not getting the chance to know what forever feels like."

"Forever feels like you trusting I won't bolt when things get hard, ring or no ring."

"I'm working on that. I am."

"And forever feels like you doing this for you, for us, not just because you think it's what you have to do to make me happy or to keep me."

"I am. This isn't simply about winning you back. It's about securing a future for us. For what it's worth, I wouldn't have talked to your parents if I wasn't serious about wanting this."

"You talked to my parents?" Owen's voice was an adorable squeak. "I'm not sure whether to be horrified or impressed."

"Could we go with impressed?" Quill desperately needed some lightness injected into this conversation, and Owen rewarded him with a shaky laugh.

"You're this confounding mix of traditional and romantic, sweet and reserved. I can't believe you talked to them before *me*."

"Well, I wasn't asking permission or anything like that. But they're super important to you, and you're super important to me, and I wanted them to know that, wanted them to know my intentions. Figured it might make it easier for them to head back, knowing you'd be taken care of."

"You don't have to marry me to take care of me." Owen shook his head, damp hair brushing Quill's neck. "I had this plan of my own, you know? The wear-Quill-down plan. Just stick around long enough, and maybe I'd get an invitation to hang out with you and Hattie and Val or something. Stay enough seasons and maybe you wouldn't wince if I used the *boyfriend* label on the phone."

"You deserve a lot more than that," Quill said sternly. "And when it comes down to it, so do I. We both do. I see that now. I don't want to live in the shadows, don't want to settle anymore for a life without love. You've made me believe that I deserve that in my life."

"You do. You deserve forever and you deserve to be happy—"

Because he could almost sense a but coming, he cut Owen off. "It's okay if you can't answer me right away. I kind of sprung this on you. It's enough if you'll think about it. This isn't an ultimatum. I meant it when I said I wasn't going anywhere."

Owen was silent again, body vibrating against Quill before he moved to flip around in the rapidly cooling water. This time, Quill let him, more than half expecting him to exit the tub. But instead, more water sloshed as Owen straddled his thighs.

"Maybe I don't need to think about it."

"Oh." Trying to read Owen's expression, Quill scarcely dared to hope after all Owen's skepticism and the wringer his emotions had been through. All Quill knew was that he wanted this more than he'd ever wanted anything.

Chapter Twenty-Nine

Owen had to laugh at Quill's stricken expression, the way he'd braced himself against the tub like he was expecting a firing squad to appear.

"Maybe I'm just as crazy as you."

"Yeah?" Quill's voice was cautious, traces of his usual reserved self showing through. Strangely, that comforted Owen. Grounded him. Maybe Quill had stunned him with this proposal, but he was still the same Quill deep down. The same guy Owen loved.

"Because I'm tempted to say yes. And not for the practicalities either. But because you're right. We deserve to be happy, and there's no real point in delaying that happiness until a date on the calendar that other people might find acceptable given how long we've known each other."

"If there's one thing you've taught me, it's fuck other people and their expectations." Quill looked up at him, longing clear in his blue eyes. "Say yes."

"I still don't even know your middle name." Owen pretended to pout, enjoying drawing this out more than he should.

"Huckleberry."

"Seriously?"

"Seriously. And let me tell you what a field day the kids at school had with that one. Told you my mom's a bit nuts. And probably my family is a detractor. Can't offer you awesome in-laws like your folks—"

"It's okay. You're more than just your family."

"That a yes?" Quill's hopeful expression made warmth unfurl in Owen's gut, spreading like maple syrup, sticky sweetness that made it almost impossible to hold out any longer.

"Maybe with a longer engagement. In case you—"

Growling, Quill held him tighter. "I'm not changing my mind. Take all the time you need, but I'm not going to get scared off."

He pulled Owen down for a kiss then, a hungry one that also managed to promise that what Quill had been saying was true. It was sexy and reassuring all at once. Owen loved Quill, all of him, but this Quill, the one who knew what he wanted and who wasn't afraid to go for it, was intoxicating, a drug he hadn't even known he needed.

"Yes," he whispered against Quill's lips. "I'm still worried and scared, but I want to do what you said. Leap. Together."

"If it helps, I'm terrified too." Quill released a tentative laugh. "But I want this. For all the practical and impractical and just plain foolish reasons. I want you."

Owen took a breath, letting the words ricochet off every doubt he'd had the past few days, letting them warm him. Let himself believe Quill, really believe him. And maybe it was okay if some of this was triggered by the whole near-death thing because Owen got it, got what Quill was saying about time being finite. He'd spent the past few years running from that fact, trying to outrun that feeling of mortality, believing that if he simply made the most of his time, that hollow feeling would go away. But what Quill was suggesting was the opposite. Embrace it. Accept. Time was short and uncertain and sometimes cruelly unfair. He'd learned that lesson more than once. So why not go for what he wanted most? Wasn't that the entire purpose of his bucket list? Not to put off for tomorrow the dreams he could accomplish today.

And there was no bigger dream than a future with Quill. So, yes. Yes, he could do this. Rather than try to put all that into words, he kissed Quill again, trying to tell him how much he wanted it too, how glad he was that Quill had had the courage to bring this up. Hell, Quill had apparently even talked to Owen's parents. He'd plotted this whole romantic night for them. He was serious about wanting this, and Owen was going to give himself the gift of believing him.

"We're going to give you hypothermia again." Quill pulled back with a laugh.

"Bed?"

"Bed." Stopping twice for more kisses, they scrambled out of the tub and dried off. Owen peeled off his cast cover before racing Quill to burrow under the covers. Naked bodies touching, wonder zoomed through Owen, making him marvel at the simple miracle of being alive, being here to enjoy this.

"Warm me up," Owen demanded. As Quill pulled him tight, fuzzy chest brushing Owen's, bigger body surrounding Owen's, every fantasy he'd had about Alaska, about big strong rangers and cold nights seemed comical now. He'd gotten so, so much more than he'd bargained for. Everything. He'd gotten everything. No more list. This was all he'd ever need. And as their bodies moved together, mouths finding each other again, he pleaded with the universe for a long forever. He needed time to see this work, needed to see who they both became as love worked its magic on their lives. He both needed it all and needed nothing other than Quill, this moment, this man.

"I hate that the generator crapped out again. We don't want you getting sick again." Quill piled more blankets around Owen on the couch.

"I'm fine. Quit worrying." It was a few days since they'd returned to the quarters, and Owen still wasn't at full strength. He was steadily improving, but Quill still worried, tried to make him stay on the couch with his drawing supplies as much as possible. The generator had malfunctioned in the middle of the night, this time beyond what Quill could fix. Again. Which meant a cold night in front of the woodstove and an impending visit from Ron, the repair guy.

And not that Quill would tell Owen, but he was dreading seeing Ron again, back muscles tense as he took the snowmachine to fetch Ron and his tools from the lower parking lot. Quill had known that once he'd told his boss why he needed time off that word would get around. It just did. Small department, small area, not much other February gossip to distract people. It didn't matter that his boss had been professional, giving Quill a short lecture about how getting involved with a volunteer wasn't the best look, but also not censuring him. Little by little, Quill was working on replacing the awful images of when he'd come out to his dad with more supportive experiences like the nurses at the hospital and Hattie and Owen's parents. Even more or less indifference like his boss's was okay. There had been some rumblings when he'd been at a meeting the day before, but he'd tuned it out.

It was harder, however, to tune out Ron when they were in the small space of the generator room, and Ron was looking at him with obvious derision.

"So. Heard your volunteer got caught up in an avalanche."

"That's right," Quill said evenly, trying not to let the vision of Owen's cold body crowd into his brain.

"You all more than friendly is what I heard. First time you've taken consecutive days of leave in ten years." Ron nodded like he had a source in HR, checking leave requests.

"How's the generator?" Quill asked, letting his irritation make his voice rougher. "Short in the wiring again?"

Ron didn't even glance at the machine, still giving Quill a critical eye. "It's true then? You gay?"

Taunts on the school bus and harsh words from family members echoed in his brain, but his long-standard denial didn't even come to the surface. He'd dealt with almost losing Owen. He could deal with the Rons of the world too. "Yep. That gonna keep you from fixing this generator? Because I'm happy to call your boss, see about getting someone else out here."

"Oh, hold on to your britches. No need to call anyone. I'll fix your damn machine. Stick your dick where you like. I just don't hold with them liberal gays like your California boy, but I ain't gonna leave you cold."

"Good. But you insult Owen again, and we're gonna have some words." It was actually ridiculously easy to find the same stern voice he used with rowdy teens, his shoulders back, spine straight as he glared at Ron. Oh, he was never going to *like* conflict, but staring Ron down, standing up for himself, no longer made his stomach churn or his palms sweat. Could have used this backbone years ago, but he wasn't going to dwell on what he'd lost to fear and inertia. Rather, he wanted to focus on what he'd gained—a future with Owen.

Later, after Ron got the generator humming again and Quill returned him to his truck with another harsh glare for his retreating form, he headed back upstairs. Back to Owen. Back to where he wanted to be. Fuck Ron and people like him who would deny them a chance at happiness. And hell, fuck himself for thinking that happiness wasn't worth it. Because it absolutely was, the sight of Owen sitting up at the table, drinking tea and sketching, warming him way more than the return of the building's heat.

"What are you drawing?" he asked, heading to the coffee maker, which Owen had already plugged in with a fresh pot waiting for him.

"A new comic. Cranky ranger, talking animals."

"Cute volunteer?"

"That too." Owen's cheeks turned uncharacteristically pink. "It's pretty gay. But then most of my comics are. Thinking back, that's probably what clued my parents in, all the crushes and guys holding hands."

"I like it," Quill said firmly. "Go with it. Cranky ranger. Cute guy. Some hand holding. Maybe that's what the world needs."

"It does." Standing, Owen plucked Quill's coffee from his hand and set it on the counter before wrapping his arms around Quill's neck. "I'm going to keep it PG, so maybe no kisses, but you can give me one now. I'm feeling lots better, especially now that the heat is back."

"Are you now?" It was the middle of the afternoon, and he did have work to get to, the job waiting for him. But it could wait another five minutes. The work would still be there after he stole a few precious moments with Owen. And as their lips met, he knew that there was nowhere else he'd rather be. Not even the most spectacular hike on his own could compare to the joy he'd found in being with Owen. He'd probably always be an introvert, always be Owen's slightly cranky ranger, but he'd chosen to let love in, let it transform him and his future both.

"Love you," he murmured, pulling back from the kiss to look at Owen, memorize the glint in his eyes, the wickedness of his smile, the strength of his embrace.

"Me too. And I can't wait until later." The curve of Owen's mouth said he meant bedtime, but Quill's heart expanded. He couldn't wait until later either, until the future they both deserved where they belonged to each other.

Chapter Thirty

Nine months later

"Come on, boy. Come on." Owen stopped to pat his leg. Snowshoeing with a dog in snow booties was a new challenge, one they were both getting used to with Yogi still not sure he liked wearing his coat and boots out in the white stuff. A year-old husky lab mix, he *should* like the snow, and indeed the workers at the shelter in Anchorage had assured them that he'd be a great winter companion, but so far Yogi spent more time sniffing and eating snow than trotting through it. "We need to beat Quill back home."

"Too late." Still in uniform and on snowshoes of his own, Quill came around the side of the cabin to the clearing where Owen had been working with Yogi. The light was already fading, short November days chasing away what remained of the day's earlier sunshine. "Training still not going well?"

"Don't say 'I told you so,'" Owen warned.

"I wouldn't dare, but you *are* the guy who picked the dog based on name alone. I did suggest that he seemed a little...common-sense challenged."

"He'll figure it out." Owen tried to sound optimistic

as he followed Quill back to the cabin since the dog had been his idea, a friend to keep him occupied when Quill worked long hours. Although he still helped Quill where he could, he was taking the season off from formal volunteering to focus on the long-distance art classes he'd enrolled in along with the start of his webzine comic, which had proved to be surprisingly popular.

That and there was still so much to do here at the cabin. After much discussion back and forth, they'd finally decided to move off-site to a little place that could be their own, close enough for Quill to reach any late-night emergencies, but far enough to give some semblance of work/life separation. And it had left the quarters to this season's winter caretaker volunteers, a married couple from Montana who were experienced park volunteers grateful for the extra privacy of having the quarters to themselves.

He and Quill had pooled their savings on this property, a nice chunk of land with a two-bedroom cabin in need of some TLC. They were doing most of the work themselves, both to save money and because Owen found something deeply satisfying about rehabbing the place, turning it into a real home for them. Still, though, the work could get lonely as could long days spent drawing, and he'd started agitating for a dog back in the summer, finally wearing Quill down on one of their visits to Anchorage to see Hattie, Val, and the baby. Being honorary uncles had them making the trek more often, especially since the three of them had traveled to California for their wedding in May to support Quill.

"What has you smiling?" Quill asked as they stepped into the mudroom at the back of the cabin to peel off their winter gear, Yogi having decided to bound up after them after all.

"Thinking how much I love this place."

"You should." Quill laughed. "Anyone who spends that many hours on a backsplash for the kitchen better love the results."

"I do. And I was remembering our wedding. Too bad we didn't have this guy yet." He bent to remove Yogi's booties and coat and dry him off. "He could have been the flower dog."

"He would have eaten the flowers. And liked it." Quill shook his head.

"Hush. He's a good boy."

"Good *expensive* boy who ate a hammer, a level, and a piece of flooring last week alone. But hey, you ever talk me into another wedding, he can come."

"You liked it enough to do it again?" Straightening, Owen studied Quill carefully.

"Like *you* enough to do it again." Quill headed for the half-done kitchen, and Owen followed, Yogi at his heels. On the fridge were pictures from the wedding—Quill looking vaguely unsettled in a suit, holding the baby next to Hattie, Owen with his siblings crowded around him, Owen's parents beaming at Quill, him and Quill having a private moment on the deck of the vacation house they'd rented in Lake Tahoe. Wanting to do something between a big wedding and an elopement, they'd decided to get married where Owen's family could come along with a few select friends on a big weekend getaway that was more family reunion than traditional wedding. Quill's family was conspicuously absent, but that was okay. Owen would simply be family enough for him, try to fill the gaps with as many good memories as he could, and it helped that his parents adored Quill, with his mom sending frequent packages their way.

"Dinner smells good. Another recipe from your mom?" Quill asked hopefully.

"Yeah. Ginger garlic chicken thighs. She says hi by the way and that they can't wait to see the guest bedroom at Christmas."

"Better get cracking on that then." Quill laughed, apparently unruffled at the news of an incoming parental invasion. "Might help to have a guest bed. They'd probably appreciate a floor in there too."

"I'm working on it," Owen protested. "I got sidetracked today with a great idea for a new comic panel and then dinner…"

"I'm teasing." Quill tugged him close enough to drop a kiss on his head. "I'll help Tuesday when things are slower after the weekend tourist rush. And you do know that you don't *have* to do any of it, right? Dinner's nice and the home repairs are great, but it's also just fine if you concentrate on your classes and art."

"I want to do things for you. For us," Owen assured him. "I like this. A lot."

He wouldn't say he was a househusband exactly, but close enough, and he found the role suited him in ways he'd never expected. Making sure that Quill was well taken care of to do his job fulfilled something deep inside Owen, an inner caretaker he hadn't even known existed prior to Quill. And maybe it was because Quill did such a good job taking care of him right back, and not just the obvious stuff like tinkering with the generator and making sure they had wood, but the little stuff like showing Owen his favorite summer hikes and bringing him treats back when he had to go into town and letting Owen have the warm side of the bed.

"Is the dinner ready?" Quill asked, eyes locked on Owen's mouth.

"It could keep." Owen shooed Yogi toward his bed in the living room. "What did you have in mind?"

"Uh…" Quill blushed. For all that he'd loosened up, especially in bed and when it came to being around other people, he could still be charmingly shy about certain things. Not waiting for him to continue, Owen started in on his uniform shirt buttons.

"Do I get to guess?" He nipped at Quill's neck. "Because I've got a table you'd look exceptionally hot draped over…"

The sudden flash of heat in Quill's eyes said he was on the right track, and Owen laughed as he continued to undress Quill, utterly in love with this man.

"What did I do to get so lucky?" Quill asked on a gasp as Owen sank to his knees to undo his belt and fly.

"Took a chance." Owen looked him square in the eyes, trying to tell him without words how grateful he was that Quill had wanted to take this leap with him, that Quill had been willing to take the risk and face his own fears in order for them to have this future.

"I'd do it again," Quill said gruffly. "You're worth all the chances."

"We both are." Owen licked Quill's exposed stomach, loving how that made him tremble. He'd taken a chance too, decided to trust in Quill and trust in love, and it had paid off in a level of happiness he still had a hard time wrapping his mind around.

"Uh-huh." Quill's head tipped back as Owen got serious about teasing him with his tongue. "Love you."

"Love you too." They both said it all the time. Maybe even too much, if such a thing were possible, but Owen was never ever going to get tired of hearing the words. They each knew how precious life was, how things could change in an instant, and if they weren't going to miss a chance to say the words, then that was a good thing. The best thing. They had each other and they had love and because of that, they had a future worth having, whatever it brought.

* * * * *

Reviews are an invaluable tool when it comes to spreading the word about great reads. Please consider leaving an honest review for this or any of Carina Press's other titles that you've read on your favorite retailer or review site.

To find out more about Annabeth Albert's upcoming releases, contests, and free bonus reads, please sign up for her newsletter here: eepurl.com/Nb9yv.

Author Note

As with all my Alaska-set books, my research was rather extensive. Curious readers will be interested to know that yes, the Alaska state parks system really does have winter caretaker volunteers at various remote locations throughout the state, who get accommodations and subsistence payment in exchange for volunteer work through the winter. And yes, the Hatcher Pass area is one of the areas that takes volunteers. I tried to stay true to what my research revealed about the location and the work of the volunteers and state rangers. Accommodations vary considerably from place to place throughout the state. However, as I have not personally volunteered to overwinter there, liberties were undoubtedly taken, and all inaccuracies are mine. No resemblance to actual Department of Natural Resources employees or volunteers is intended; all characters are 100 percent fictional. The job of a ranger is indeed part law enforcement and part steward, and I tried to balance the many competing parts of the job for Quill with the understanding that the job often varies from place to place, season to season, and ranger to ranger.

Likewise, I tried to stay true to the nature of winter injuries and dangers. Avalanches are a huge, ever-present risk in the backcountry, and each year, people do indeed die from avalanches. Being prepared for winter risks and the winter weather is critical, and I tried to reflect that to the best of my abilities.

Also, like a great number of American states and local municipalities, Alaska doesn't have a statute protecting people from discrimination on the basis of sexual orientation, so Quill's fears were not without justification. I very much support the work of citizens and organizations working to change this around the country.

Finally, eagle-eyed readers will spot the brief cameos from Griffin and River from *Arctic Sun* and Bryce and Clark from *Waiting for Clark*. If you're curious about these stories, check out their books, and if you're wanting to know what a particular couple is up to now, be sure and sign up for my newsletter as I do updates on fan-favorite characters from time to time.

Acknowledgments

So many people had a hand in bringing this series to life, and I owe all of them a great debt. This series truly was a labor of love and many years in the making, and I am so grateful to all who helped me make this dream a reality. First, a giant thank-you to my readers for taking a chance on this series and coming on this journey with me. I can't thank you enough for your support and enthusiasm over the years. Bringing you the stories of my heart is one of my greatest joys. My dear friend Wendy Qualls originally gave me the plot bunny for this one many moons ago and also helped with plotting, and I hope she enjoys Quill and Owen's journey as much as I did. Thank you to my agent, Deidre Knight, for believing in this series, and to my team at Carina Press for giving it a home. My editor, Deb Nemeth, has now shepherded me through over a dozen books. I would not be the writer I am today without her, and I know in my heart that I'm a better writer now than when we started, thanks in large part to her gentle guidance. My publicist, Judith of A Novel Take PR, goes above and beyond with every release, and I am so very grateful to her. My entire Carina Press team does an amazing job, and I am so very lucky to have all of you on board.

A special thank-you to the tireless art department and publicity team and to the amazing narrators who bring my books to life for the audio market.

All of my beta readers are so appreciated. Crystal Lacy in particular read on a very tight schedule and had invaluable feedback. Erin McLellan and Karen Kiely were beyond generous answering questions about Alaska and supporting this series. I am so appreciative of the many books and online resources available about Alaska and about the life of park rangers. And yes, LGBTQ ranger couples exist, and I am so very grateful to those who have shared their stories via various mediums. Go, trailblazers, go! My core support group of friends keep me writing and helped me tremendously through a difficult drafting process. A huge appreciation to the various writer groups that I am a part of; I'm privileged to know you all and to get to share this journey with you. And thank you to the writers who so generously read early ARCs for other books in this series—your support is absolutely appreciated from the bottom of my heart. My real-life family and friends put up with a lot during the drafting of this book, and I'm so thankful for their patience and understanding. (And a big shout-out to the wonderful delivery people out there making lives easier for people via online shopping, groceries, and takeout!) I know I'm missing people who undoubtedly deserve appreciation; know that I truly appreciate every person in my life and those who help me do what I love. And no one does that more than readers. Thank you so very much for the gift of your readership and your support via social media, reviews, notes, shares, likes, and other means. You keep me going!

About the Author

Annabeth Albert grew up sneaking romance novels under the bed covers. Now, she devours all subgenres of romance out in the open—no flashlights required! When she's not adding to her keeper shelf, she's a multi-published Pacific Northwest romance writer. The #FrozenHearts series joins her critically acclaimed and fan-favorite LGBTQ romance #OutOfUniform, #Gaymers, #PortlandHeat and #PerfectHarmony series. To find out what she's working on next and other fun extras, check out her website: annabethalbert.com or connect with Annabeth on Twitter, Facebook, Instagram, and Spotify! Also, be sure to sign up for her newsletter for free ficlets, bonus reads, and contests. The fan group, Annabeth's Angels, on Facebook is also a great place for bonus content and exclusive contests.

Emotionally complex, sexy, and funny stories are her favorites both to read and to write. Annabeth loves finding happy endings for a variety of pairings and particularly loves uncovering unique main characters. In her personal life, she works a rewarding day job and wrangles two active children.

Newsletter: eepurl.com/Nb9yv

Fan group: Facebook.com/groups/annabethsangels

Want more winter-themed reads?
Out now from Carina Press and Annabeth Albert:

One hard-nosed military police officer. One overly enthusiastic elf. One poorly timed snowstorm. Is it a recipe for disaster? Or a once-in-a-lifetime opportunity for holiday romance?

Read on for a preview of
Better Not Pout,
a stand-alone winter romance.

Chapter One

The Santa suit didn't fit. It itched. And it tugged against Nick's skin as he drove out of Fort End, heading southeast toward the small town of Mineral Spirits. On the rare occasions he ventured off base into what he still thought of as the wilds of upstate New York, he got on the interstate and went straight to Watertown. He did his shopping or went out to eat and never bothered with these narrow state highways and back roads leading to tiny villages and hamlets, most of which seemed to have Mills or Crossing in their name and were pretty interchangeable as far as he was concerned.

Mineral Spirits was slightly bigger than most of the towns, notable for the covered bridge that his older F-150 creaked over on the way into a downtown that seemed fresh out of the 1950s—red-and gray-brick buildings with signs announcing homey businesses such as Nancy's Diner and Pete's Pet Store. And apparently the village was also known for a borderline freaky obsession with the holidays—even now, a week before Thanksgiving, he spied Christmas decorations on more than one storefront and cutouts of turkeys and pilgrims on a few others.

His stupid GPS kept going out—something about

the hills around here made cell service spotty—but the Helping Hand Resource Center was easy enough to find, right off Main Street as Commander Grace had told him. The low white building was decorated with giant colorful handprints on the sides and a large cheerful sign that proclaimed its name and All Are Welcome. He parked in the far corner of the lot, backing into the space, as was his habit.

A bitter wind greeted him, but he didn't bother with his jacket. The damn suit was hot enough, the way it clung to his back, plush red fabric anything but breathable. He remembered to grab the beard and wig, but no way was he putting those on until the last minute. He opened the door to the center only to be greeted by an honest-to-God green-clad elf.

"Nick?" The elf grinned at him like they'd been introduced already. And okay, he wasn't a literal elf, just a small young man with curly blond hair in an elf outfit he seemed perfectly comfortable in—green-and-white-striped tights, hat with a bell, curving slippers, and all.

"Sergeant Major Nowicki, yes." It had been years since he'd been just plain Nick for someone outside of his own head, and he wasn't about to start with this overly friendly *elf.*

"Yes, Miriam told us to expect you. I can't tell you how much we appreciate you filling in for Wallace."

Nick couldn't remember ever hearing Commander Grace referred to by her first name. He knew it, of course, but she was his commanding officer first and foremost, even if she had made efforts over the last few months to make sure he felt welcome at Fort End. And when she asked him for this favor, he'd felt unable to say no, mainly because she was kind and generous and wasn't one to abuse her position and ask for special treatment.

"Of course. Everyone at the base is hoping for a full recovery from Mr. Grace." The commander's husband was an elementary school teacher in Mineral Spirits, and they'd made their home here rather than on base as Nick did.

And apparently, every year they'd been stationed at Fort End, Mr. Grace had played Santa for this charity. The job entailed letting the local paper get photos of him in unusual locations around town so it could run a contest where readers tried to guess "Where's Santa now?" And then he'd appear at a couple of different town events over the course of the season as part of a campaign to raise money for the charity's holiday efforts. The Graces loved this season and this tiny town.

But Mr. Grace had suffered a heart attack two days ago and had been life-flighted all the way into Syracuse for open-heart surgery. Commander Grace had called him from I-81, worried not about making it to the hospital, but about whether there would be a Santa for this year's fundraiser. And he, fool that he was, had said he'd handle finding a replacement. Except everyone he talked to was already committed to something this weekend and, somehow, he'd ended up being the one in the suit.

A suit that was far too small, smelled vaguely of mothballs, and had probably seen better decades. But he was here to do his duty.

"I'm supposed to see Mr. MacNally," he told the elf, who was still looking up at him expectantly.

"That would be me. Call me Teddy though. Everyone does." Another broad grin. And, of course, Mr. Casual was a Teddy. Despite his small stature and baby face, he had to be at least twenty-five since he was the director of this charity. Far too old and in-charge to be a *Teddy*.

"Who's the one taking the pictures?" He was eager to get this show on the road.

"That would be my cousin, Rhonda." He beckoned over a younger woman with similar curly blond hair. "She works for the paper. She's got several locations scouted out already. I thought you might like to start with a little tour of our facilities? Get you up to speed on what we stand for, maybe get you more in the spirit of things."

That wasn't possible as Nick didn't have an ounce of holiday spirit left, if he'd ever had any to begin with. But he wasn't out to be rude, so he nodded. "You've got me for the day."

"Excellent." Another megawatt smile, this one worthy of a dental ad, all perfectly gleaming white teeth and wide, full lips. He really shouldn't be noticing MacNally's mouth, full or otherwise. He wasn't here to get sidetracked by pouty perfection.

One more month, he reminded himself. One more month at Fort End, which ironically really was the end for him. End of the line, the army's refusal to let him re-up bringing a twenty-eight year career to a halt at the nation's most remote, northernmost outpost, a place that often felt like the end of the earth, far removed from his desert deployments and years stationed in Hawaii, California, and other warm states. He still wasn't exactly happy about the army's decision to go all-in on a reduction in forces, but he had a pretty sweet plan B waiting for him if he could just make it through this last month. One month and he'd be in Florida, on a boat, no Santa suit in sight, no obligations or distractions…

Why that vision kept making his chest hurt, he didn't know. It might be the Army's call, but he'd worked nearly three decades to earn the military retirement coming to him. By this time in January, he'd have his own place on the ocean and a partnership with his old Army buddy, who did boat day trips for tourists and made himself a nice little living.

And there would be no snow in sight. Ten months here had been more than enough for him. Even the summer had been unbearable, all muggy and humid with mosquitoes everywhere, and only two really good months before fall hit. And now the weather people were calling for a big storm this weekend. Not even Thanksgiving, and they were already talking snow days. No, Florida would be far preferable to any more time at Fort End.

"So we're a multipurpose resource center here to serve primarily the low-income folks of the village and surrounding towns." MacNally had an unusually energetic speaking voice, all full of bright inflection and exclamation points where a simple pause might do. "We have a food pantry, clothing closet, heating and electric bill assistance, Holiday Giving Tree for kids, and offer a variety of workshops and classes ranging from parenting topics to food preservation to budgeting."

MacNally took him through the large, airy lobby with older couches that managed to look both well loved and inviting. Like the exterior of the building, the room was colorful with a children's play area and library tucked into the far corner. From there, he followed Mac-Nally down a hallway as he pointed out the clothing closet full of warm coats looking for homes, the offices where caseworkers met one-on-one with families, and a meeting room for workshops. Nick tried to make approving noises as MacNally prattled on and on about the work of the resource center. He was relieved when they finally reached the food pantry that took up the rear of the building.

He was trying to listen to MacNally talk about balanced meals and perishable items when he spotted a slight teenage boy struggling under the weight of a huge case of canned goods. The case tottered precariously, and acting without thinking, Nick lunged to save it from landing on the kid's feet.

Riiiiipppp. An awful, foreboding sound happened at the exact instant he steadied the case. He immediately felt a draft on his ass where there had previously been scratchy material. The teen started laughing before scurrying away under the force of Nick's glare.

"Oh dear." MacNally's mouth opened and shut as if his bottomless supply of good cheer didn't have an answer for this turn of events. He wasn't even subtle in how he twisted around, checking out Nick's backside to verify that yes, indeed, the borrowed suit had split. "I guess you are a great deal…*larger* than Wallace, aren't you? But no worries, Santa, I've got you covered." Laughing, he dragged Nick into an office off the food pantry, yelling over his shoulder, "Rhonda, we're going to need your assistance."

"I don't think—" Nick really didn't need even more of an audience for his humiliation.

"It's no bother." MacNally patted him on the arm. "Do you have spare pants in your car?"

"No." He suppressed a groan. On his way he'd

dropped his uniforms off at the cleaner's, so he didn't have a spare in the truck as he sometimes did.

"Hmm. No way are you fitting into anything of mine." MacNally sighed dramatically. "Rhonda, can you check the clothing closet for men's XL or XXL anything? Sweats would be perfect."

"Sure thing."

"Now, I know I've got some red thread here…" Mac-Nally started rustling around a cluttered desk. The small office was busy—desk laden with framed pictures, walls covered with inspirational posters, open box of holiday decorations in the corner, stack of kids' hand-print turkeys on the visitor's chair. "And a needle. We don't want to have to staple you shut."

"You are *not* coming anywhere near me with a stapler." Nick put all his years of MP experience into his voice. As a military police officer, he took no guff, and he wasn't about to start with this…*elf.*

But MacNally just laughed. "We'll hope it doesn't come to that." He leaned in close enough that Nick could smell some sort of fruity aftershave. "But I'll be honest, I had to alter my costume to get it to fit, and I totally used a stapler on the shoes."

"Were your feet in them at the time?" he demanded.

"Of course not." MacNally's laugh reminded Nick of the fresh-picked peaches he'd loved when he'd been stationed in Georgia—warm and fresh and far too tempting. "And you're not going to be in the pants either."

Right as he delivered that alarming bit of news, Rhonda returned, hands empty. "Sorry. I couldn't find anything that might fit." Her eyes flashed with appreciation. She didn't make a secret of checking him out, gaze roving over his frame to the point that he felt his skin heat. "It's mainly kids' clothes right now, and Saint Nick here is definitely not in the juniors' sizes."

"Sergeant Major Nowicki," he corrected, even though it felt somewhat like spitting into the wind with these two. "And perhaps we should just reschedule. I can go back to base, change, and then go see if I can find a costume shop in Watertown that might have something more suitable."

"Costume shop there closed after Halloween—the owner retired, and a new one hasn't popped up yet," MacNally said breezily. "And no need for that. Here's thread and a needle. We'll just step out, you'll pass me the pants, and I'll have you done up in a jiffy."

Jiffy? Who used words like that anymore? Nick was forty-six, and he was pretty sure he'd never done anything in a jiffy.

"Fine." He waited until MacNally and Rhonda had left the room to shed the pants. Even with his black boots on, they'd still been a bit short in the leg and the gaping hole in the seat wasn't helping anything. He set the boots aside along with the wig and beard and shucked off the pants, feeling ridiculously exposed in just a Santa coat and his black boxer briefs, which—because it was laundry day—were the ones that probably should have been retired a few years back. *Like me.*

He passed the pants out the door, and then paced the small space, not wanting to sit in MacNally's chair in his underwear and not wanting to move the kid drawings from the other chair.

"Can I get you some coffee?" Rhonda's voice filtered through the door.

"No, I'm good," he said, even though he wasn't. But coffee would mean opening that door again, and he wasn't doing that more times than necessary. He'd held formations, had platoon sergeants under him, trained hundreds of enlisted men and women, and advised a string of commanders as he worked his way up to sergeant major. And in all his years of service, this ranked right up there for most humiliating moment.

"Okay, I think I've got it." MacNally rapped on the door. "I'm no seamstress, but I've put buttons back on coats and closed up rips on donations before."

Nick opened the door just wide enough to stick his arm out for the pants. MacNally laughed, more of that summer warmth hitting Nick square in the center of his chest.

"You *are* a shy one, aren't you?"

No, I just don't want you seeing my worn drawers. But of course he wasn't saying that, so he simply grunted and took the pants. If possible, they were even tighter now, and they were going to be a devil to get off, but they were better than letting the chilly air continue to batter his bare legs.

"They fit." He opened the door, pulling his shoulders back, straightening his spine, just like he might for an inspection. "Let's go get your pictures."

"Sure. Just let me see—" MacNally craned his neck to see Nick's backside, seeming like he might get in there and inspect his stitches next. Nick quickly moved so that his back was to the poster-covered wall. "Okay, okay. But I'm bringing the needle and thread just in case."

"Where do you want the first picture? My GPS keeps going in and out, so I might need directions, but I'll meet you at the site." Nick was more than ready to get this show on the road.

"Don't be silly." MacNally waved his hand. "I'm parked right out back. My Forester can easily hold all three of us. Rhonda and I already mapped everything out. I'll drive."

No way in hell was MacNally driving him anywhere, but Nick still searched for some manners. "I don't want to trouble you—"

"It's no bother at all. I cleaned out the car this morning and everything." MacNally grinned up at him.

Fuck. Nick did not want a ride—or anything else, those kissable lips included—from MacNally. However, he was also a realist and wasn't going to waste time arguing or risk stomping all over the other two's feelings.

"Come on." Rhonda led the way through the food pantry.

This is simply another mission, Nick told himself. He'd been on patrols in roasting-hot desert temperatures, conducted murder investigations, dealt with bomb threats and more disorderly conduct than he could even remember. Surely, he could get through one day in this blasted suit with the too-perky elf for company and then be on his way back to base, back to his holiday-free orderly life with its countdown to his retirement.

Don't miss
Better Not Pout *by Annabeth Albert,*
available wherever
Carina Press ebooks are sold.

www.CarinaPress.com

Also available from Annabeth Albert and Carina Press,
Rough Terrain, *an Out of Uniform novel.*

The camping trip from hell may be the first stop on the road to happily-ever-after.

Navy SEAL Renzo Bianchi has a soft spot for Canaan Finley, and not only because the man makes a mean smoothie. He's the first guy to get Renzo's motor revving in a long time. But when he agrees to Canaan's insane charade—one all-access fake boyfriend, coming right up—he never expects more than a fling.

Creating a hot Italian SEAL boyfriend to save face seemed like a good idea…until his friends called Canaan's bluff. Now he's setting off into the woods with the very man who inspired his deception, and Canaan is not the outdoorsy type. The sparks are already flying when a flash flood separates them from their group, leaving Renzo and Canaan very much trapped…very much alone in the wilderness.

Working together to come up with a plan for survival is sexier than either of them expects. But back in the real world, being a couple is bringing its own set of hazards…

Don't miss the Out of Uniform series by Annabeth Albert! Order your copy of Off Base, At Attention, On Point, Wheels Up, Squared Away *and* Tight Quarters *today!*

We hope you enjoyed reading

ARCTIC *heat*

by

ANNABETH ALBERT

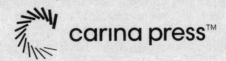
carina press™

Connect with us for info on our new releases,
access to exclusive offers and much more!

Visit CarinaPress.com

Other ways to keep in touch:

Facebook.com/CarinaPress

Twitter.com/CarinaPress

CarinaPress.com/Newsletter

New books available every month.

Everything's bigger in Alaska.

Big scenery. Big danger. Big emotions.

Gorgeous, sweeping vistas and deep,
complicated feelings pair with life-and-death
situations in Annabeth Albert's Frozen Hearts trilogy,
pitting men against nature.

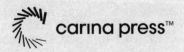
carina press™

Introducing the Carina Press Romance Promise!

The Carina Press team all have one thing in common: we are romance readers with a longtime love of the genre. And we know what readers are looking for in a romance: a guarantee of a happily-ever-after (HEA) or happy-for-now (HFN). With that in mind, we're initiating the **Carina Press Romance Promise**. When you see a book tagged with these words in our cover copy/book description, we're making you, the reader, a very important promise:

This book contains a romance central to the plot and ends in an HEA or HFN.

Simple, right? But so important, we know!

Look for the Carina Press Romance Promise and one-click with confidence that we understand what's at the heart of the romance genre!

Look for this line in Carina Press book descriptions:

One-click with confidence. This title is part of the **Carina Press Romance Promise**: *all the romance you're looking for with an HEA/HFN. It's a promise!*

Find out more at **CarinaPress.com/RomancePromise**.

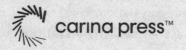
carina press™

Get the latest on Carina Press
by joining our eNewsletter!

Don't miss out, sign up today!
CarinaPress.com/Newsletter

Sign up and get Carina Press offers and coupons
delivered straight to your inbox!

Plus, as an eNewsletter subscriber, you'll get the inside
scoop on everything Carina Press and be the first to
know about our newest releases!

Visit CarinaPress.com

Other ways to keep in touch:

Facebook.com/CarinaPress

Twitter.com/CarinaPress

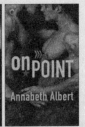

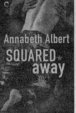
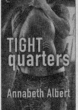

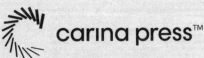